Beer
and
Skittles

Beer
and
Skittles

• A LITTLE MAINE MURDER •

B.J. MORISON

THORNDIKE PRESS • THORNDIKE MAINE

Library of Congress Cataloging-in-Publication Data

Morrison, B.J. (Betty Jane), 1924—
  Beer and skittles.

  I. Title.
PS3563.087167B4   1985   813'.54   85-17238
ISBN   0-89621-094-4

Cover design by Armen Kojoyian.

Cover photograph by Tim Loeb.

Book design by Abby Trudeau.

Map by Kelly Russell Gordon.

This diversion is dedicated to
The Entertainers, those people
of varying arts who are compelled
to use their talents not to instruct,
or convert, or shock, but to disperse,
if only for fleeting moments, the
universal Dark Night of the Soul.

Acknowledgements

"Life ain't all beer and skittles, and more's the pity," as George du Maurier wrote in *Trilby*. It is certainly a comprehensive truth, and a number of writers have expressed the thought, in slightly different ways, although Thomas Hughes, in *Tom Brown's Schooldays*, put it in almost the same way: "Life isn't all beer and skittles."

Recognizing that a writer's life can be the ultimate proof of the expression, some helpful people have assisted the author with her facts. To them, grateful thanks is due: Loy Andrews, Christopher Brigham, M.D., Michael and Robert Gilfillan, Chief Craig Hall, B.H.P.D., Walter Norwood, Henry Ryan, M.D., Pat Toman, Chris Vincenty, Robert Williams, M.D., Dorothy Lee Worcester, Kai Young.

The excerpt from Emily Phillips Reynolds' *Down Memory Lane* is quoted by kind permission of her daughter, Mildred C. Gilley.

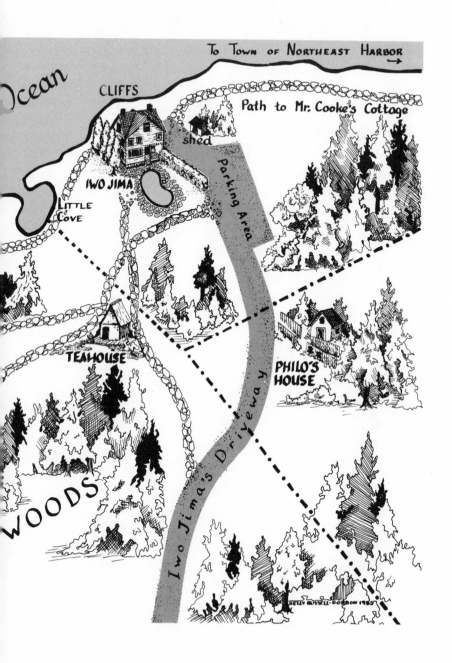

Foreword to My Best Friend and Second Severest Critic:

Dearest Alaraby,

You wanted me to put you in this fantasy. One of your reasons, I know, is that you, as a character, could keep my "fine, fine fictional creation" (as a kindly reviewer once termed Elizabeth Lamb) in line, since you regard her as "that darned little Know-It-All who's always so perfect."

But, Alaraby, although my modest works of manners and murder are set in real places, you have by now realized that everything else is pure invention — the characters, their dwellings, their pets, and so on. Even, usually, the things they say are invented — but not always, for, as Mr. Loeb, my First Severest Critic, has (grudgingly) said: "You do have an uncanny knack of capturing dialogue, B.J."

So, dear, I can't insert such an intrinsically real person as you into a story where almost everything else is Make Believe. No one in this book is based on any person who lives or has ever lived — and you know your mother lies only when it is courteous to do so, and not merely expedient. And, perhaps, someone other than you will someday take Elizabeth Lamb down a peg or two.

But maybe in the next, Alaraby, where she meets — but you already know the plot. Hold fast, and you may yet appear in print, although I think it will be as a creator of fascinating science-fantasy and not as a puppet of mine.

Love,

B.J.M.

Bar Harbor, 1985

The Characters in the Order in Which They Appear

ELIZABETH LAMB WORTHINGTON — *an observant eleven-year-old.*

CYNTHIA HACKLEY DICKCYN — *an uninhibited woman.*

BIX BAXTER — *a saxophone player in a jazz quartet.*

MRS. AUSTIN (CATHERINE) HACKLEY — *mother of Cynthia; a brewer of organic beers.*

PHILIP DICKCYN — *Cynthia's son, a Harvard student.*

PHILO GAYNOR — *a Native, a neighbour, and a mean one.*

GLORIA GAYNOR — *his wife.*

GENERAL LEMUEL OTIS ALISON, U.S.M.C. (RET.) — *after several glorious wars, now a writer of history and of rhymes.*

COLLEEN O'CASSIDY — *his secretary.*

LUDWIG VONN — *a houseman.*

HOHENZOLLERN — *his German Shepherd dog.*

PERSIS HALSTEAD — *Elizabeth Lamb's cousin.*

CECIL (DUSTY) RHODES — *a trombone player in the same jazz group as Bix.*

TATE (CHUBBY) COOKE — *a bachelor neighbour of General Alison's.*

ELISE FAVEN — *a long-time Northeast Harbor rusticator.*

RUSSELL STARK — *a fifteen-year-old Bar Harbor Native; a friend of Elizabeth Lamb's.*

LIEUT. ALFRED (BUZZIE) HIGGINS — *a State Detective, met once before by Elizabeth Lamb.*

MERRILL SARGENT — *another investigator.*

Also assorted relatives, doctors, policemen, party guests, messengers, and incidental innocents.

• Contents •

• Chapter 1 •

Bishop's Pawn

MOUNT DESERT ISLAND is a fairly large island, as islands go, just slightly removed from the coast of northeastern Maine. In many, many respects, it is an unique place, and one of its unusual features is its geography. The Atlantic coastline, from Cape Ann to Mexico, is composed of beaches or marshes or rocks, but Mount Desert, due to good planning by Someone millions of years ago, possesses granite mountains in addition to these. The mountains intrigue the many vacationers who visit the island, for in no other resort have they encountered hilly terrain so near the sea.

On its eastern shore, Mount Desert has, besides mountains, one of the most renowned name-places in the world, the town of Bar Harbor. Only a few miles away, the village of Northeast Harbor graces the island's coast at a point to the south and west of Bar Harbor. Although the distance between the two resorts is slight, the difference between them is as Night is to Day, with, as any Northeast Harbor summer person will tell you, Bar Harbor playing the role of the less enlightened Period. "Oh, Bar Harbor? Dreadful place. We almost never go over there," has been said, in almost unvarying form,

17

by many a Northeast Harbor "Rusticator" — the term used for years to describe M.D.I.'s summer residents.

Although some social historians say that the personages of the Northeast Harbor summer colony first went there, in the ending decades of the last century, as a protest against the showy millionaires of the Bar Harbor summer colony, it is doubtful that any such deliberate action was intended. They simply wanted a healthful and relatively inexpensive place for their families to vacation; Northeast Harbor is today still a family-oriented resort.

Bar Harbor, having lost most of its millionaires to death and taxes, and to fire — the Great Fire of 1947 destroyed many of its large estates — is now, in the summers, something of a *mélange* of tourists, summer residents (a few of whom are still very wealthy), year-round residents who formerly came to the island only in the summers, and, of course, its large population of Natives. (No matter how much prestige the M.D.I. summer people command in their winter habitats, they have for so long been awed by these resourceful islanders that they think of them with a capital "N.")

Bar Harbor has motels, heavily patronized by the tourists; Northeast Harbor, strictly speaking, has none. Bar Harbor has a number of inns and guest houses; Northeast Harbor, but a few. Bar Harbor has many restaurants — too many, say some of the citizens; at this writing, Northeast has only one eating place that might be so termed, although there is a Native café that serves good, inexpensive breakfasts and sandwiches. Bar Harbor has a movie theatre, a huge Art Deco showplace built in the early thirties; Northeast Harbor once had a small, pleasant movie house that burned down — although it is probably a slander to say that the large, unpredictable, and part-Maine-Native lady who runs the former had anything to do with setting a match to the latter. Northeast Harbor, though, possesses an ancient establishment, the Neighborhood House, which has for years, among other offerings, each August presented a program of distinguished chamber music concerts; Bar Harbor has nothing quite such.

And Northeast Harbor still has its many summer families, who may not, to their regret, find "rusticating" there as inexpensive, even comparatively, as their great-grandfathers did, but who certainly find the town to be as healthful now as ever. Too, Northeast provides a place for awed tourists from all over the island to visit, to walk down its brief Main Street in the mornings and observe thin, erect, large-straw-hatted dowagers, often accompanied by their dogs, patronizing the fish shop, the apothecary, the stationery shop, the venerable Pine Tree Market — and maintaining a pleasant but dignified reserve while so doing. Their daughters, on similar errands, may stop and shriek (a well-bred shriek) something like, "Barbara! Darling! I haven't seen you for two days! We did so miss you at Trissy's" — or Prissy's — or Cissy's — "party last night!" And their granddaughters, tanned, blonde, and perfectly attired in faded shorts and shirts that exhibit the proper labels, will ride by on their bicycles on the way to or from the tennis courts or swimming club, their faces composed and aloof. The tourists admiringly relish it all, ignorant of the day in 1870 when it all started so simply, when the first summer boarder was put up at a Native home and heralded, unaware (unlike most heralding angels), the advent of the Bishops.

Although it is true that bishops, as well as other churchmen, played a large part in Northeast Harbor's rusticating history — (during one long-past and memorable summer, *seven* bishops were in residence, including the Archbishop of Canterbury), — in the Very Beginning, there was but one bishop. And, Behold, he was His Grace of Albany, William Croswell Doane. His summer dwelling, built in 1881, was a cottage he punningly titled *Magnum Donum*, since he was a big (magnum) man of great girth. There may be a second pun underlying the first: some have stated that the comfortable cottage enjoyed by His Grace was provided by an admiring parishioner, and if so, surely such a gift could be considered a "big, votive offering, to the gods." Bishop Doane, who has been termed the magnet that attracted many cultured families to Northeast Harbor, practiced the simple life during his summers there. He rowed in his six-oared barge, the other oars being pulled by Mr. Nathan Fenelly, his gardener-caretaker, and by more-or-less willing guests and grandchildren. And he picnicked, and he walked, and he talked — these two latter activities were wide-spread on early M.D.I., but perhaps most extensively performed by the "plain-living and high-thinking" Northeast Harbor summer families who admired the bishop.

Moreover, he supped informally at seven in the evening, regarding a later "dinner" as a corrupting city influence, and one that was held to in the fleshpots of the Bar Harbor summer colony. The Northeast Harbor hostesses followed his lead (at times with some irritation), putting their dinner potage into cups instead of soup plates and issuing their evening invitations for "supper." Bishop Doane was obviously a strong-minded person, and one so conscious of his status that when registering at a hotel with his wife, described by those who knew her as "a fidgety little lady," he signed: "William, Albany, and Mrs. Doane." (It is no wonder that Mrs. Doane was fidgety, after years of expecting a visit from hotel detectives.)

An early evening meal was still the custom in Northeast Harbor in the middle of this century, according to a lady who summered there then. "Everything was very low-key," she says. "We all got dressed up, slightly dressed up, that is, in simple, unobtrusive little silk dresses with matching cardigans, from Mrs. Franklin's, on the Main Line, and went to cocktails at six. Wherever we were, we saw the same people we'd seen the night before, and, after cocktails, we all went back to our cottages for dinner. Except for the Jordan Pond House," — where, until fairly recently, one had to bring one's own bottle — "there was simply no place to dine out. We never thought of going to Bar Harbor.

"And, in those days, Bar Harbor was still dressy. Today," — she at present lives year-round in Bar Harbor — "I often go out to dinner in good-looking trousers, while in Northeast, this generation gets all gussied-up. There is, now, an awful lot of Ultrasuede and cashmere around, and those bright Pulitzer prints. This new money," she concludes sadly, "is different."

That many of the simple, unobtrusive dresses came from a shop on the west-of-Philadelphia Main Line (so called, of course, because it was on the railroad's main line to Chicago) is not surprising, as the summer residents of Northeast Harbor have been for some time mainly — no pun intended — from the Philadelphia area. Northeast Harbor is now facetiously referred to by some as "Philadelphia-on-the-Rocks."

Besides Bishop Doane, two other gentlemen are given credit for having established Northeast Harbor as a summer resort. They were the renowned Charles W. Eliot, President of Harvard, and the renowned landscape architect, Joseph H. Curtis. The latter built, on the eastern side of the harbour, the beautiful Asticou Terraces, which stretch up a hill to his cottage, *Thuya Lodge*, and its gardens. He established a trust that still funds the lovely gardens, which are open now to the public — a generous and greatly-appreciated gesture.

President Eliot, being both a Unitarian and a Bostonian, was by nature a patron of the simple life. It is said that his favourite recreation was a walking picnic — the picnic consisting of a single sandwich carried in the walker's pocket. And he and his cohorts walked in simple tweeds, whereas his friend Bishop Doane stuck to his proper bishopric attire of buttoned gaiters, apron, and shovel hat.

While climbing Sargent Mountain one day, the bishop and his group encountered a small Native boy, who regarded His Grace's lower limbs with sympathy and asked, "Won't your ma let you put on longs?" There was an encounter of a different kind on the same mountain, met by another churchman, Dr. William R. Huntington, Rector of New York City's Grace Episcopal Church and a Northeast Harbor summer resident. Dr. Huntington was so moved by the feeling of sanctity that came to him on the summit of Sargent that he composed a prayer there. It is in the Episcopalian Book of Common Prayer as the Collect for August 6th, The Feast of the Transfiguration.

President Eliot and Bishop Doane, a story goes, first tried to purchase land for their cottages in the region of Southwest Harbor, the village to the west of Northeast Harbor, across the Great Harbor of Mount Desert. (It sits at the western entrance to Somes Sound, the only fiord in America and an arm of the sea that attempts to divide Mount Desert Island into halves.) But they, allegedly, were refused because the owner of the land, recognizing that Eliot was a Unitarian and Doane a High Church Anglican, decided: "We don't need any atheists and papists in Southwest Harbor."

So one can decide, from all the evidence, that the summer colony of Northeast Harbor started simply. And frugally, as well. It was said of the early island summer colonies that: "To summer in Bar Harbor, you need money; to summer in Northeast Harbor, brains but no money; to summer in Southwest Harbor, neither." An obvious calumny on Southwest Harbor, but that's the way of wit: it often gets out of hand.

Although frugal, the summer residents were generous to Northeast Harbor: the library, the old and new town halls, the Neighborhood (community) House, the Episcopal Church of St. Mary's, the golf course (now enjoyed by Natives as well as Rusticators), and more, were gifts to the town. Other benefits, such as the pure, piped water supply, were proposed and aided by them, and all this largesse must have been appreciated by the townspeople. A summer resident says, "The Natives knew what side their bread was buttered on. They were smart enough to say 'Yassuh' when necessary, but they respected us for what we were and what we did, and they loved us."

When this statement was put to a Native, now in her seventies, she replied, "Respected, yes. They did things for the town. For instance, as a child I greatly enjoyed the vaudeville show the younger ones put on every summer in the Neighborhood House; they worked really hard on it. But 'loved'? I don't think so."

Undoubtedly, it would be difficult to "love" affluent visitors to one's home town, a town often, formerly, run to please them. Mrs. Emily Phillips Reynolds, a lady who died but recently at ninety-four, wrote with amusement in her charming *Down Memory Lane,* of a privilege denied her when she was twelve, even though it was a privilege for which she proposed to pay. There was "a Miss Coburn, a coloured lady," who had a beauty shop above one of the stores on Main Street, where for one dollar she washed and arranged ladies' hair "in the latest fashion." Emily saved her money and presented herself to Miss Coburn only to be informed: "I don't do Natives."

It was Mrs. Reynolds' father, the owner of the Asticou Inn, who insisted his young grandchildren remember to "Keep out of the face and eyes of the Rusticators!", a prohibition that was probably given to children all over the village. (Those children grew up expecting to step aside into the gutter when a Rusticator passed, since *they* would never yield.)

Getting one's hair done in Northeast Harbor has been a problem for other than little Native girls. A lady who a few years ago occupied a summer camp (a "camp" on Mount Desert is more simple than a "cottage," which can contain twenty or more rooms) on the rustic "backside" of the island, once called a now-departed Northeast Harbor hairdresser for an appointment. His assistant inquired if she were in the Red Book, a listing of summer cottagers. The lady, who through marriage was entitled to be listed in the Boston Social Register, asked what the Red Book was. There was a pause. The lady, who had gained more from her autocratic Bostonian in-laws than an entry in the Social Register, gracefully and firmly covered the pause by announcing that she understood there was a good French hairdresser in Bar Harbor and that she would take her undistinguished self over to him. End of conversation.

Despite generous efforts for the town, frugality was the order of the early days. And sometimes frugality went too far. The story is told of a Northeast Harbor summer lady who gave a lavish party during which a Native tradesman who was owed a large sum by the hostess sat on the curb outside her cottage for the entire length of the festivities. When guests asked him why, the answer was that he was sitting there "hoping to get paid my money." And his vigil "paid off," so to speak, after some remonstrances by the debtor that bringing up the subject of money at *any* time was in the worst possible taste. Many summer cottagers have revealed that, despite all the talking done each summer, it was "bad form" to discuss finances. This is surely a Philadelphia *tabu*, since Bostonians are all too ready to speak of money — if only to declare, despite outward appearances, that they haven't got much of it.

The outstanding building style of the summer cottages was that termed "shingle-and-stick", and the cottages were built so well that most have survived, unless torn down. Brown or grey are the usual colours, but there is a notable lilac-hued example, said to have been built by a grateful Rockefeller for his doctor. One cottage, though, possessed a large piazza on which, one memorable day, a gala tea-party was being held. The piazza suddenly collapsed, but the party went on, amongst the sticks, if not the shingles. Perhaps it continued because to have called an end to the *fête* would have wasted all that food?

23

One of the buildings that enhanced the town, until it was taken down in the 1960's, was the Kimball House, originally a small, pleasant inn, but later enlarged and made more grand, and that was inspired, it has been told, by "an exclusive Philadelphia group." (A Kimball granddaughter has said, though, that she doubts Mr. Kimball, a large property owner with many business interests, was so "inspired.") It was famous for its Monday evening dances, to which the elite flocked. Allegedly, a young man who later attained what many consider the highest office in the land attended one season with a variety of "most undesirable companions" and was given a severe "talking-to" by the lady manager, who was sympathetic to his political aspirations. The "talking-to" covered, it is said, not only his companions but his conduct, which was often too loud and demanding.

On one occasion, so the story goes, a brother of that young man and some of his crew left the yacht on which they had cruised to Northeast Harbor, and attempted to dine at the Kimball House. Their sailing clothes were not considered proper attire, and they were refused admittance. According to report, a scene then ensued to which "no one, of course, paid any attention, although it was said to have been very difficult to eat and talk in the din."

Besides upholding standards of proper dress, eating chicken fricassee every Sunday, putting an OUT sign in the Indian basket on the porch when one was out (and sometimes when one wasn't), rowing, picnicking, walking and talking, the summer colony started the golf, tennis and swimming clubs. (A swimming club in a town by the sea? Maine water, in the summer, can be as cold as 45 degrees and seldom goes above 55. Many Natives of M.D.I., being sensible people, have never learned to swim; and although today there is a swimming pool at the Bar Harbor YMCA, it is largely patronized by the island young, and so there are still elders who restrict themselves to the land.)

Two of the three clubs figured largely in the "simple but structured" life of the cottage youths, (who went to church on Sundays before they were allowed to go swimming.) On week-days, there was tennis at 10:00, then to the swim club by noon; then they were "on the water" by 2:00. Presumably they were at some point fed lunch, probably at the swim club, or possibly their bikes, their usual form of transportation, took them back to those shingled cottages for their noon-day sustenance.

"On the water" meant that they were sailing in their cat boats (in the very early days, the favoured craft), or their North Haven dinghies (which came later, and are now almost extinct), or their Bullseyes or their Luders or their Internationals, or whatever the privileged young of today sail. The Northeast Harbor Fleet was formed in 1923, and the uninitiated who refer to the "yacht club" are told politely, "We call it 'The Fleet.'" This is a distinction, says a knowledgeable yachtsman, practiced only in Northeast Harbor, of all the seas and of all the yacht clubs he has ever known.

Northeast Harbor is today this country's largest yachting center east of Marblehead, Massachusetts, and on any given day in August the millions of dollars represented by the tonnage of the yachts in the harbour would astound Bishop Doane, possessor of that ancient six-oared rowing barge, could he but view the scene. (As undoubtedly he can; are not bishops given a front-row seat in Heaven, and is not Heaven, on a perfect August sailing day, surely gently moved from where it is suspended half-way between Philadelphia and Boston to a point down-East, above Northeast Harbor, Maine?)

The Bishop might observe, amongst all the graceful sailing sloops, yawls and ketches, a number of smaller and more humble craft, including even motorboats. For, so purists say, even the most scarred and venerable "stink-pot" can properly be termed a yacht if it is used only for pleasure. For a number of years, a miniature tug-boat (not used, of course, for the purpose for which its larger fellows are built) gladdened the harbour view.

Sometimes a "party-boat" — not so termed because it is built for celebrations, but in reference to one of the definitions of "party" as meaning "a group of people" — is in evidence. These are usually large three- or four-masted schooners, joined in their home ports by vacationers desiring a sea-faring diversion, and crewed up (or down) the beautiful Maine coastline by the landlubbers, who are delighted to pay for the privilege of working on the boat, enjoying clean air and tasty food, and visiting the little Maine harbours. The yachtsmen, both local and visiting, are valued by the Natives, and so are the party boat crews. "We only got ten weeks to make our money" is the tenor of the thoughts of many a Native Son of many a Maine resort, and the Natives of Philadelphia-on-the-Rocks are no exceptions.

So now Northeast Harbor is famous, not for walking-and-talking, but for sailing; although walking and climbing, with teas at the enduring Jordan Pond House after the exercise (and seldom is tea there indulged in by Northeast Harbor Rusticators without it), are still popular. And, a number of decades ago, a club was formed in Northeast for the edification of ladies who were accustomed to distinguished conversation in their winter home-places. It was limited to those summer residents who owned property. (An exception was made in the case of one lady because of her wit and charm, which are still with her in her nineties, since she has always preferred to rent her summer domiciles.) It was felt that ladies were as entitled to good talk as their husbands enjoyed at the Philadelphia-inspired Pot and Kettle Club, founded in the late 1800's and (regrettably) located near Bar Harbor.

The talk of the ladies' club was undoubtedly, in the early days, distinguished and erudite. A Northeast Harbor summer resident has described a latter-day meeting of the club, to which she was invited one season, to be "looked over," as she says. At first, she was dazzled by the honour, knowing the "Conversation Club" — which is not its name — to be very selective, maintained primarily by Philadelphians (she is from Boston), and made up of many mother-daughter combinations (her mother, who first visited Northeast Harbor in the early days of this century and there met her future husband is, regrettably, long-dead.)

The lady was first somewhat daunted by hearing that the dues, even for a one month temporary membership, amounted to sixty dollars, since at her club in Boston she pays "only a little more than half that, and, over the winter, we get five delicious *served* luncheons, with an entertaining skit performed at each." Then, "I had to fork over" (Proper Bostonian ladies indulge in explicit slang) "five dollars each time for the boat" (the club meets on an outer island) "*and* then walk *three* miles to the clubhouse." She felt five dollars a meeting, coming on top of the sixty-dollar dues, "a bit much" — summer Northeast Harborites know the value of money. The six-mile-round walk also annoyed her, since she had hurt her foot the previous winter while boating down the Nile — Proper Bostonian ladies, whatever their ages, Get Around.

Well, she made it to the first meeting, carrying the lunch she had been instructed to bring. Hers consisted of an egg-salad sandwich on two heels of bread — "eggs, mayonnaise, and some ends of a loaf were *all* I had in the house." (Although a collateral descendant of President Eliot, she did not carry the sandwich in her pocket.) She found: 1) "that just about *all* the women were Philadelphians, and *many* were mothers-and-daughters, just as I'd heard;" 2) that 25 out of the 30 women present had brought egg-salad sandwiches — "eggs were all *they* had in the house." And the talk, to her astonishment, consisted of exchanges of recipes, although one member enlivened the exchange by producing a newly-acquired bird caller, "and making it go 'tweet-tweet,' and they all *raved* over it!"

She skipped the next two meetings, but appeared at the final one, for which the club provided the luncheon — determined, probably, to get something for her sixty dollars. "It was a *divine* clam chowder, made by the nice woman who is caretaker of the clubhouse, and I *gorged* myself. Then I found that stuffed capons, and an *enormous* salad and then dessert were to follow, and there I was, as stuffed as the capons!"

1950 has been declared by another lady to be "the last good year in Northeast Harbor. In the '40's, my set played, and in the '50's, we came out, and then we married — married boys we'd met in Northeast Harbor, of course. Frankly, people took cottages in July and August so that their children could meet the right people of their ages. The coming-out parties ended in the '50's.

"And now a lot of the old money is gone — divided up among the children, of course. Their boys and girls work at summer jobs, and can't play all through the lovely days, as we did. Or they get tutored, or go to summer camp; oh, they still come up and sail and race, but it's just not the same. And there are scandals now, very discreet and hushed-up, of course; but, my dear B.J., I could tell you —"

So there you have Northeast Harbor, Maine, as a summer institution: an unique place, founded on the virtues of Family Life, and consolidating simplicity, frugality, civic responsibility, love of nature, and respect for the Creator of nature into the familial atmosphere. Perhaps the anonymous writer of a volume of reminiscences about old Northeast Harbor puts it best: "We can only say that no more interesting and agreeable colony exists in the length and breadth of the land."

And to present-day Northeast Harbor, we say: "Pax. You may have long ago entered into play as a bishop's pawn, but the Game became yours, and, whatever has been, or can be, said about you — you play by the Rules. Would that all players, on all Boards, might do the same."

• CHAPTER 2 •

The Fog Comes

MY DEAR, I just don't see the point of it. An unnecessary expense, and you know by now how we cold-roast Bostonians feel about unnecessary expense. Heh-heh."

"General, the place is bloody gloomy. It wouldn't cost you your last dollar to put some white tiles on the floor, maybe on the walls, too."

Tenderly: " 'General,' my dear? Why not 'Lem'?"

"Not after just a three-months' acquaintance. Told you my mum wouldn't like it. Naow, looky —"

"Your mother is in Sydney. How would she know?"

"She's in Adeline."

"Adeline? You must mean Adelaide. Heh-heh. But you told me Sydney."

Firmly: "She's on the move a lot. Has a studio in both towns. Anyway, wherever she is, she wouldn't permit it. I had a right proper upbringing. And she had to do it all herself, mind. My dad skinned off before I was born."

"Colleen, my dear, dear Colleen, aren't you being a touch hypocritical? You don't address me as 'General' when —"

Loudly: "We were talking about the downstairs bathroom. Every lady who goes in there expects to see spiders in the w.c. And so she would, 'cept it's too dark and dismal to see anything. Needs a new screen for the window and a better light and some nice white tiles, that's all. *Your* bathroom's tiled. Why be so bloody penurious about a bit of poshing up, where it'll show, besides?"

With vigour: "Penurious! I've *never* been that! Didn't I buy you that amethyst necklace you wanted? Come over here and let me adjust it a bit. Heh-heh."

"It's fine. No need. Naow, the bloke I talked to could tile the bathroom next week. You said we'd stay another month, till the indexing's done, and I hope to God you have a few more parties and them a bit livelier than the ones I've had to put up with. Maybe we'd even get some guests who were under seventy, at least, and —"

Interrupting: "You said 'put up with.' Never end a sentence with a preposition. You are not so long out of Radcliffe, my dear; don't you remember that? Not once, in my history of The Corps, have I done so."

"They taught me that some Pommy aide, or secretary, or something, of good old Winnie's made a correction on a speech because Winnie'd done it, and Winnie wrote on the copy, 'This is an impertinence up with which I will not put.' Proper put-down, that, I call it; no pun intended.

"Didn't they teach you that at Harvard? Guess not; you were there a bit before Winnie became the P.M., weren't you, General?" A malicious laugh.

"Not so very long before. Now, Colleen, you had better leave directly after lunch to collect little Persis. Our cocktail bash starts at five and, as hostess, you should be back here in good time. Guests in Northeast Harbor, I've noticed over the years, tend to arrive promptly."

"That's not very posh, is it?"

"It shows good breeding to be on time, my dear. I suppose the Philadelphia people may be late, but Bostonians are always prompt and —"

"Can't wait for a shot at a free drink, I guess, those cold-roast ones, anyway. That's one good thing about us Aussies: we don't expect people to eat up every left-over scrap at the next meal."

"— *and* those two musicians Catherine Hackley is lodging are sure to be here at five, if not before. Never saw anyone put away liquor the way that trombone player does. The chamber music group has charming, well-bred lady musicians; can't understand why the jazz quartet the town ends the season with never has them. They wouldn't drink as much as the jazz men do and some of us older people would attend their performances and show our appreciation."

"Bet you would. At least the *sax* bloke talks; the trombonist won't say a civil word. Just stares, like that monster dog of that cook of yours. That beast gives me the willies, she does."

"Hush, my dear. Yes, Ludwig?"

A colourless, quiet voice: "The rum swizzles, sir. General, the caterer called to say that he cannot arrive until four-thirty. The luncheon party where he is now engaged will be later in concluding than he thought."

"Well, well, no matter, Ludwig. Paul is always competent to a fault, and you'll have everything in readiness for him, the liquor and glasses and plates, and all that sort of thing. We Marines know a thing or two about preparedness, hey?"

"Yes, sir. General, shall I serve you and Miss O'Cassidy and little Miss Worthington lunch out here on the terrace? It would expedite the party preparations."

"Of course; of course. Ah — Ludwig, would you keep Hohenzollern in the woodshed while the guests are here? She — ah — well, I mean to say — some of the ladies have been unnerved by her before." After a pause, "She stares," and then a nervous "Heh-heh," followed.

Another pause. The person listening to the conversation concluded that Ludwig was thoughtfully regarding Colleen O'Cassidy and General Alison apprehensively regarding Ludwig. Then, quietly: "Ho is a bit unnerving, sir, to ladies unused to being regarded thoughtfully. Of course, sir."

The speaker left the scene as noiselessly as he had entered it. A pitcher and a glass clinked together.

"I can't stand that bloke, him and his everlasting rubber-soled shoes. I don't see why you need him around, not to mention that damned dog. You said that every summer before this one, you'd had a woman from the village over to clean a bit and get supper ready."

"My dear, he arrived with a strong letter of recommendation from General Stanley the very day my housekeeper decided she'd visit her daughter and new grandchild in Alaska. He's had a spot of trouble, I gather, and just needs a quiet summer to get on his feet. Not only is he a great help, but I couldn't refuse to take on a former Marine, not when the fellow who got me the commission to do the history of The Corps practically begged me to."

"Former Marine! More like a former Nazi, I say. And you just ended with a preposition. Naow, about the bathroom —"

"It's *not* a bathroom, my dear. In my prime, ladies who used such facilities called them powder rooms — and my prime was not so very long ago, as you have ample evidence —"

"*I* use it, too, and I don't fool around with any muck like powder, so far's I'm concerned, it's a *bathroom*, 'cept you can't bathe in it." A sigh, and then, gloomily: "*And* that's why I can't bathe as often as I'd like, 'cause every time I go up to the guest bathroom, that darned kid's there."

"You may use mine. Urged you to."

"No, thanks. Sharing a bathroom could lead to sharing other things. I like to sleep alone."

"Really, Colleen, I hope I have always behaved toward you as a gentleman would, especially —"

"Yah, Alice said you were a proper gent. Else I wouldn't have taken over for her. Indexing's not my line. Too many things to keep track of. Straight secretarial work's what I've done, most jobs."

Enthusiastically: "And you did it very well, my dear, I am sure. As you do everything very well. Heh-heh."

With pride: "Been doing it since I was sixteen. Made plenty Down Home to help Mum out, and saved enough to get me to the States and into Radcliffe, too. Kept right on with it while I was there — that's where I met Alice, on a job of work we were doing this spring, just 'fore I graduated."

Sentimentally: "What a brave girl you are! And so young to

have had to work so hard."

"Yah. Wal, naow, the tile man said — why're you looking so far-away, like?"

Quietly and thoughtfully: "I was just wondering why Alice didn't come back this summer. We got along very well last year, and she assured me she'd return, to help finish up the last of the History and to take on the indexing."

"She got the offer of a better screw, that's why. Thought she told you."

"WHAT did you say? A better WHAT?"

A merry, infectious laugh, and a cajoling tone that made the listener below realize why her cousin, General Lemuel Otis Alison, endured the bumptious manners and the near-rudeness of his assistant: "Lem, sweet, you've been Down Under. You've heard Strine. Alice got the offer of higher pay at another job. Pour me more of that delicious rum, there's a dear."

"Come and sit a bit nearer. I won't bite. And I can't think about the powder room until after the party. I'll decide tonight, my dear. You look very pretty when you dispute with me."

There was movement on the terrace. Elizabeth Lamb Worthington was sitting on the ground perhaps six feet below it, leaning against the fieldstone wall that formed one side of its support. She held a book which she had been desultorily reading, in preparation for her return to school in a few weeks. Then came the sounds of a brief but energetic scuffle and, "None of that, General!"

"Not till after tea-time," announced General Alison's assistant, in her strident Antipodean tones, which were all she ever used to Elizabeth Lamb and to Ludwig, since she evidently considered that "buttering 'em up" would produce nothing of value from a child and a laconic houseman.

"You military types," Miss O'Cassidy went on, "won't drink till the sun's over the yard-arm, whatever the hell the yard-arm is. Wal, there's things more exhausting, not to say more socially unacceptable, than a touch of drink."

Elizabeth Lamb Worthington wrinkled her delicate nose in disgust, put down her book, stood up and stretched her arms above her head and then bent down and touched her sneakered toes. She was a slim child, eleven years old the previous June. Her features were fine and regular and given even more distinction by her enormously large, deep green eyes. Her straight, heavy hair of a silver-gilt colour hung to her shoulders and was held back from her still childishly-round forehead by a wide tortoise-shell headband that matched her dark, thick eyebrows and lashes. Her grandmother predicted that she would be a great beauty; Elizabeth Lamb, as her family called her, considered the prediction, without any complacency, to be reasonably accurate and unbiased.

She exerted herself to move the fifteen or twenty yards to the end of the cliff on which General Alison's summer dwelling was situated. She surveyed the lovely scene before her without much appreciation, since for the last two weeks it had been an exceedingly familiar one to her.

Ever since her mother had left to answer a peremptory summons to the Peruvian mine Elizabeth Lamb's father was operating, she had gone to the cliff's edge to escape the sight and sound of the well-bred but determined efforts of the General to (as her mother had put it once, when they had taken a walk to avoid a particularly blatant assault of his over the tea-table) "cavort unbecomingly" with Miss O'Cassidy. Now that Jane Worthington was beyond range of diverting her daughter's attention from the amorous campaign, the calming view of the Western Way was Elizabeth Lamb's usual retreat; but familiarity . . .

She sat down on a rock in front of the windbreak of arborvitae trees that shielded the terrace, and now muffled the voices from it. She looked out, through a slight haze of fog, at the beautiful Western Way, the passage between islands that led mariners approaching from the west into Northeast Harbor.

"It's what they call a sea turn," she said aloud, observing that the fog was coming in from the sea over the sun. She thought of the poetry she had been reading. "The fog comes —" she murmured; "now, what's next — in, on —" She gave up, with a yawn, and turned her attention back to the seascape.

To her right, around a point of land covered with tall spruce and therefore invisible from General Alison's cottage, which, naturally, he had named *Iwo Jima*, was the town of Northeast Harbor, Maine. The very excellent harbour of that august (or August — since it reached its height of popularity in that month) establishment, contained at that moment, she knew, a goodly number of dozens of sail and motor yachts, now about to be fog-bound.

Among them would be a five-masted schooner, a party boat she had seen arriving via the Eastern Way the evening before. She yawned again and speculated on how its crew of paying vacationers would occupy themselves in Northeast Harbor on a foggy afternoon. "Probably walk up and down Main Street and shop, and stare at the Natives," she thought, "and at the summer residents who didn't do their marketing this morning. And get stared back at."

To her left was a small cove that could be entered from the water only by a narrow inlet between towering rocks, and then only when the tide was high enough to permit passage of a shallow-keeled craft over the rocks on the cove's bottom. Inside the cove was a sand beach, about sixty feet wide, which was a source of both pride and annoyance to General Alison and to his neighbour, Mrs. Austin Hackley. It was reached by a steep iron ladder fastened to the cliff just at the point where the Alison and Hackley properties met, above the very center of the beach.

The beach, despite the distinction of being one of the very few sand beaches on Mount Desert Island, whose shorefront consists mainly of jagged rocks studded with uncomfortably sharp barnacles, was a problem to both households, notwithstanding the pleasure the more hardy took in using it to enter the chilly Maine water. The opening in the rocks was sometimes spotted by the occupants of passing boats, who entered with loud shouts and departed without their picnic debris. Fires were often started, for hot-dog or marshmallow toasting, and Mrs. Hackley lived in constant fear of conflagration, as well as in fear of most other things.

General Alison, at the beginning of the summer, had proposed, with his usual martial *esprit*, that he mount a small old cannon, recently acquired, on the cliff, with a sign informing trespassers that they would be fired upon. "Might even let it off, once or twice, hey?" he had suggested to Mrs. Hackley. "Wouldn't hurt 'em much,

Catherine, just sting a bit where it counts. Heh-heh."

This had produced frantic flutterings in Mrs. Hackley, a nervous old lady who anticipated, besides fires, lawsuits, and the death by accident of her adored grandson, Philip, many other mischances. (Among them, of late, was the apprehension that the police would someday come and find the large stock of marijuana she was certain that Philip's dashing and widowed mother had secreted somewhere about the premises — without, of course, the knowledge of Philip, whom his doting grandmother knew to be a biddable and upright boy, too intelligent to break the law in small matters, as boys of his age often took great pleasure in doing.)

Her moans, wails, and little notes of protestation about the cannon, which were pushed under varying doors and windows of General Alison's cottage, persisted for some time. Finally, Philip and his mother had persuaded the General to let them post a large "No Trespassing" sign on the beach, and to put in writing to poor Catherine Hackley his sacred promise that the cannon would remain on his terrace and never, never be pointed at an intruder, unless that person were, unmistakably trespassing solely on *Iwo Jima* land, far removed from the beach. At Philip's timid suggestion that the statement be notarized, the General had expressed so loudly his intention of adding the verses of the Marine Hymn to the document that Philip had taken it and fled back to *Nihon*, his grandmother's cottage, and peace had reigned.

Peace had reigned, it should be added, only in the matter of the cannon, and its reign was now abetted by the lateness of the season in there being fewer possible targets interloping on private property. The matter of the jazz musicians, two in number this summer, to whom Catherine Hackley rented her little Japanese teahouse, still troubled the waters — or rather, the air. The teahouse was on the edge of her land, well removed from her residence, but it was only a few yards from General Alison's cottage, it having been in existence many years before Mrs. Hackley had sold a part of her property to the General.

He would not, of course, have built *Iwo Jima* so close to the Hackley boundary had he any idea that in her later years Mrs. Hackley would become a jazz *aficionádo*, or that Northeast Harbor would have had, since 1968, visiting jazz quartets at the end of each summer. Certainly he had never entertained the idea that Catherine Hackley, persuaded by her daughter, who liked men of all types — young or old, fair or dark, fat or thin, musical or tone-deaf — would have harboured any of its members in her teahouse.

The General was maddened by the musicians' incessant practising. Sometimes it went on from early morning, when The Flag was being raised at *Iwo Jima* (at which time they often broke into *La Marseillaise*, which especially enraged him, since he had no very high opinion of the French) to, again, early morning, say 2:00 a.m., when they were fond of bringing forth *Good Night, Irene*, performed in a swing beat that caused roars worthy of a drill sergeant to resound from the General's bedroom.

In between, his ears were assaulted by *Georgia On My Mind*, a favourite of the saxophone player; *Bill Bailey*, a favourite of the trombonist, and endless other pieces from their repertoire. General Alison had found, though, that when he invited the two over for a drink (which always turned into the widely plural) and praised their playing, their practising lessened in volume, if not in duration, for a few days. With Marine canniness, he invited them often.

And he was grateful that last summer's drummer and piano player had found lodging elsewhere, since they had often played the Marine Hymn to a jazz beat. Not that the same four musicians returned each summer; the quartet varied in personnel if not in volume of play. This year a new saxophone player had appeared who appealed greatly to Cynthia Dickcyn, Mrs. Hackley's somewhat-cherished daughter. She was, so Colleen O'Cassidy had stated, having a "thing" with him.

The General had asked if Miss O'Cassidy meant "fling," but his slang was then cruelly described as being so out-of-date as to bring on "the sandy blight," whatever that is, so he said no more about the affair. He did, of course, think (but did not dare mention) that Cynthia, who was in her early forties, was a "bit long in the tooth" to be having a fling — or even a thing — with a saxophone player, and especially one who must be ten years or more her junior. If he had mentioned his views, it would have been quite in Miss O'Cassidy's nature to inform him loudly that *he* was old enough to be *her* father, and the General did not, of late, care to dwell on the sum of his years.

He had, though, this very morning dwelt pleasantly upon the sum of the days before Elizabeth Lamb Worthington, his young cousin (a cousin so-many-times-removed that it would have taken the most perspicacious genealogist much thought to determine the exact relationship, the kind of intellectual exercise that Bostonians termed Proper take genteel pleasure in performing over their 4:30 p.m. tea-tables), would be (not cousinly, but physically) removed from *Iwo Jima* and leave him most pleasurably alone with Miss O'Cassidy.

The days now numbered only ten, and that Persis Halstead, Elizabeth Lamb's first cousin and dear friend, would be joining his household for those ten days did not diminish his anticipation. He quite correctly believed that the eleven-year-old cousins would enter-tain each other and leave him more time to correct the galley proofs and pursue the indexing of his Marine History — and to pursue the outspoken but enticing O'Cassidy.

Whether his pursuit had as yet resulted in capture, Elizabeth Lamb wondered at times, although she really did not much care as to whether the first carnal exploration of Miss O'Cassidy's somewhat bulbous charms was behind the General or as yet an alluring (and well-padded) phantom before him. Elizabeth Lamb had lived long in Europe, where carnal pleasures are taken more for granted than they are in supposedly staid (or repressed, or hypocritical) New England.

She was as bored by her schoolmate's excited discussions on the subject that they, with discreet Dedham, Massachusetts giggles, referred to as Essee-ex (which subject seemed to enthrall them lately, although their discussions were carried on without any solid knowl-edge with which to bolster their varying opinions) as she was by the eight weeks she had this summer spent in Philadelphia-on-the-Rocks.

Now she yawned again and closed her eyes, leaned back against a tree and attempted to practise Transcendental Meditation, something she knew almost as little about as her friends at school knew about their favourite subject. A slight splashing of oars against water roused her. She got up and slowly walked the hundred feet or so to the edge of the cliff that overlooked the little cove.

As she walked, she coughed as loudly as she could and kicked rocks with noisy abandon. Earlier in the summer, she had discovered a young man and woman rolling about in the shallow water by the beach performing what her schoolmates' Essee-ex manuals (obtained by doing arduous chores for older siblings) described as Foreplay. The couple had, upon seeing her, looked much distressed and rapidly moved toward their rowboat to vacate the cove, with what clothing they wore still in disarray.

When she reported the incident to her mother, Jane Worthington had merely murmured "from here to eternity" and advised her to forget the occurrence. Elizabeth Lamb, interpreting her mother's words to mean that Essee-ex would be forever with us, world without end, amen, had almost done so. Her inherent good breeding, though, still reminded her not to approach the cove quietly when she chose to swim there instead of in the General's pool.

Today there was but one lone young man on the beach, barefoot and clad in white bathing trunks above which he wore, against the fog, a heavy red pullover sweater. He had heard her approach, for he looked expectantly upward as he seated himself on the edge of the prow of his small fiberglass skiff, pulled up on the sand. Seeing her, he smiled most pleasantly and pushed back into an oilskin pouch he carried what appeared to be a package of cigarette papers.

"Hello, there," he said. "What are you up to?"

He was a prepossessing young man, and the sight and sound of him was most welcome after the last two weeks of confinement with the grating O'Cassidy, her cousin, and his acquaintances, most of whom were as testy and as dictatorial as he. She began to smile in return and to prepare to obtain, with her usual interest in everyone she met, his life history to date and his further aspirations. Then she thought of both family loyalty and the obligations of a house-guest. She checked the smile, pursed her lips and frowned. The youth laughed good-humoredly at her rapid change of expression.

"The question is," Elizabeth Lamb answered severely, "what are *you* up to? Don't you see that sign? This beach is private property and you shouldn't even be here, much less thinking of smoking pot."

"Hey, now," said the intruder. "You're pretty hip, aren't you? A kid as smart as you should know that people can go anywhere on a beach, as long as they stay below the high-water mark, which is about where I am. All us Mainers know that. But you're a summer kid — from Philadelphia, I'll bet."

"I am *not* from Philadelphia," replied Elizabeth Lamb, stung. "If you'd ever been to Philadelphia, you'd know that I don't talk like them. *I* enunciate, and all those Main Liners talk with their jaws clenched — Philadelphia Lockjaw, it's called.

"You don't sound like a Native, either. *And* you'd better get off this beach. My cousin, General Alison, shoots trespassers. You're not below the high-tide line anyway, or not much."

"This is General Alison's beach?" the young man questioned.

"Well, in all fairness," Elizabeth Lamb admitted, "I'd have to say it's only half his beach. You happen to be on Mrs. Hackley's half, but she'll chase you off, too."

"Ayah," said the young man, "whoever she is, guess she would. Wal, I'll shove off right soon. Jest come in here to rest a mite; rowed all the way around Bear Island. Don't tell on me, now, will you? I got to be back to the Harbor by two o'clock, to go to work. Like to git off by myself and think a bit before I start my shift. Some of them summer people are real hard on a waiter; act like they was God's Oldest Son, they do."

"*Now* you sound like a Native. My daddy says they turn it off and on, to suit their advantage."

The young man laughed. He rubbed his curly dark hair and regarded her thoughtfully. "Yeah, I guess we Natives do turn it on and off. If your cousin, General Alison, whom I think I know, sort of, brings you to the restaurant where I work, I'll slip you a Mickey Mouse Martini on the house, for being so smart."

"We *never* go out for dinner, or even lunch, because it costs so much," said Elizabeth Lamb, "but thank you. Now you'd better get going, really."

"Will in just a minute," was the answer, accompanied by another pleasant smile. "Thanks for not telling on me. Hope we meet again."

Elizabeth Lamb walked away. She started back toward *Iwo Jima*, heard louder scuffling noises from the terrace, and stopped in disgust. "More slap-and-tickle," she murmured. She looked at her watch. It was still almost a half-hour till lunch time.

She decided to pay a call on Mrs. Hackley, and perhaps be offered some of her delicious root beer, which would be a rare treat since Mrs. Hackley got very high prices for her product and was seldom moved to offer any to visitors. She sold her brew to exclusive stores all the way from Mount Desert Island to, it was said, Boston. At the end of her M.D.I. summers she carefully packed up what remained and transported it to her winter home in Florida rather than give it away to her neighbours, General Alison had regretfully reported.

"Proper old skin-flint," Colleen O'Cassidy had termed her. Mrs. Hackley, assisted by her grandson in all her efforts, also brewed a ginger beer that Colleen had declared to be "a bit of all right," better than that made by her grandmother back in Sydney, but since it commanded even a higher price than the root beer, Colleen's first taste had remained her last.

Elizabeth Lamb followed the winding path that led through the woods to Mrs. Hackley's *Nihon*, which was on the shore but much further to the east than the little cove. The late Austin Hackley had been an ardent and convivial sailor, obliging almost anyone who asked for a sail. *Nihon* had been built on a high promontory just above where the shore water was the deepest, so that Mr. Hackley might bring his motor-sailer up beside *Nihon*'s float at any tide, and board or disembark his guests without the arduous row involved with moored craft.

His boat was gone, since neither his widow nor their daughter, Cynthia Dickcyn, nor Cynthia's son Philip, was fond of sailing. Philip owned a small punt for rowing about, something he had done little of this summer because of an injury to his arm sustained at Harvard. Through the trees Elizabeth Lamb could see that his punt lay on the float, along with her cousin's tender for his sloop, *Semper Fi*, which was on a mooring nearby. The General's use of her float was a privilege for which Mrs. Hackley did not fail to charge a substantial seasonal fee, fond as she was of "dear Lem" and hard as she tried, according to the outspoken Miss O'Cassidy, to "get him into her pants."

Miss O'Cassidy would then add, whenever she spoke of Mrs.

Hackley's real or supposed *penchant* for the General, "There's no fool like an old fool." The General never failed to chuckle appreciatively and somewhat proudly whenever this happened. The observant Elizabeth Lamb, though, had noticed a hard look in Miss O'Cassidy's protuberant pale blue eyes at these times, and thought perhaps her cousin did not grasp that the shaft might be double-pointed.

The path meandered through pine and spruce, curving every so often at strategic points so that a perceptive walker could view, in a small clearing in the woods, one of Mrs. Hackley's charming "prospects." Actually, Mrs. Hackley, a lover of all things Japanese, used a term in that language, *utsukushii*, to describe these effects, but her Anglo-Saxon neighbours could not — or, in the case of General Alison, most certainly would not — twist their tongues more than necessary, except, of course, in their frequent and impressive use of French phrases. The little views, therefore, were raved over as "prospects," as the ladies of the island's various Garden Clubs, who came each year to see them, had dubbed them.

Sometimes the prospect was of a particularly handsome and rare variety of azalea or rhododendren; sometimes of a small gilded Buddha complacently enthroned on a platform of mossy rock. Often a little stone statue of an animal peered out from tall ferns. Mrs. Hackley, born and raised in Japan of English parents, had, after a few years in the United States returned to the land of her birth as the wife of a U.S. ambassador to Nippon, or Nihon, as the Japanese variously term their country. As a young girl, she had adopted the beliefs of Shinto — the "Way of the Gods," and was sure that all animals, trees, rivers, and waterfalls contained the spirits of gods.

That, following the Second World War (which, Mrs. Hackley firmly believed, the U.S. had provoked Japan to enter), the followers of Shinto are taught that the gods are in the mind of the believer, did not influence her at all. Her small feet, usually clad in the sandals called *zori*, into which, for warmth in Maine, she inserted the divided socks called *tabi*, followed the Old Way of the Gods as confidently as Elizabeth Lamb now followed the path leading to *Nihon*.

Mrs. Hackley's little Japanese spaniel came bounding along from the direction of the cottage. He stopped warily, then, assured that

Elizabeth Lamb was not accompanied by her cousin, who had often jabbed a robust Marine foot in his direction, (in association with a most unfairly non-pertinent allusion to Bataan) leaped happily upon her. Barking, he ran off into the woods, then stopped and waited.

"What's in there, Chin-Chin?" she asked, following. Chin-Chin ran on, in the stylish manner of his breed, and then stopped again. Now she could hear the *Nihon* waterfall, which fell gracefully from high rocks into three charming pools in the forest. The lowest was much larger than the two above it, since it was also fed by an underground spring. The delicious pure water of the lowest pool had assisted Mrs. Hackley, some twenty years before, in beginning the manufacture of her unsurpassed and completely natural root and ginger beers.

What her daughter called "The Health Nut Fad" of the '60's had made her very prosperous; indeed, in the last four years her business acumen had resulted in tuition at Harvard for Philip and a white Mercedes for Cynthia. It also resulted in sounder sleep for Mrs. Hackley, who had found at the time of her husband's death, just after their grandson was born, that she was a much less affluent widow than she would have wished.

Now Elizabeth Lamb, above the delicate splashing of the waterfall, could hear two disputing voices. She recognized them as belonging to Cynthia Dickcyn and to one of Mrs. Hackley's lodgers, Bix Baxter, the sax player.

"Shut up!" Cynthia shrieked. "You're nothing but a damned, lying little opportunist! You're using me!" Her screams were accompanied by loud sounds of churning water, explained, as Elizabeth Lamb came up to the two, by Cynthia's being submerged to the neck in the lowest pool and forcefully flailing her arms to keep afloat. She seemed to be completely clothed. Her luxuriant hair, which was of a singularly unnatural and vibrant auburn colour, was hanging in wet strands over her face. She blew them aside and spoke courteously to Elizabeth Lamb, a favourite of hers.

"Hello, lovey," she said calmly. "Be sure that cursed dog doesn't get in with me. Mother would have fourteen fits if dog hair got into her damned concoctions." She then shouted at Bix: "Get the hell out of here, you little worm. Let me drown. You wouldn't care!"

"Hello, Elizabeth Lamb," Bix said gently. He addressed Cynthia expressionlessly, in the calm voice he used with everyone, but most especially with the excitable Mrs. Dickcyn: "Cynnie, sweet, please get out. You're completely wrong. I *do* care for you, and for nobody else, and I care deeply." He then smiled serenely upon both Elizabeth Lamb and Mrs. Dickcyn and extended a helping hand towards the latter.

"You *don't* care!" Cynthia yelled. "Go away! I'm freezing to death and you're glad! Now you can go back and chase that buck-toothed little bitch in the village!"

"Why don't you get out, Mrs. Dickcyn?" Elizabeth Lamb asked. "You'll just get pneumonia and you know your mother will be very upset."

Cynthia considered this. "If I do, it's all her fault for making me come up to this damned island summer after summer and *forcing* me — yes, forcing me — to consort with little creeps like this one. So it'll serve her right!"

"Cynnie," Bix said quietly, "your make-up's running all over. You're quite a sight. I love you, darling, but you really look very strange. Please get out."

Cynthia put up a wet and deliberate hand to rub her brilliant lavender lipstick across her tanned face. She then began to splash her way toward the edge of the pool. Bix knelt to help her struggle out. "You're a wretch. I don't know why I care for you at all," he said, smiling.

Cynthia laughed huskily and violently embraced him. Chin-Chin lay down to watch the performance. "Essee-ex," said Elizabeth Lamb to herself, walking away. "It's everywhere, and it makes people behave so strangely. I expect to see Mrs. Hackley kissing the gardener, or something."

Catherine Hackley was not kissing the gardener. When Elizabeth Lamb reached the graveled courtyard where the woods path ended, Mrs. Hackley was making an animated speech to her grandson, though in her usual faltering voice. The tiny, frail woman, whose naturally pale blonde hair was pinned up high on her head, was obliged to tilt her completely unlined and still-pretty face upward as she faced him. One small hand was clutching the neck of the printed blue-and-white long cotton kimono she wore in the morning. The other she waved agitatedly at Philip.

Philip's handsome, ordinarily pale countenance, resistant to the sunshine of Palm Beach where he and his mother lived nine months a year, and also to the weaker Maine rays (even abetted by wind), was flushed with anger. "Though," Elizabeth Lamb thought, "he's usually so meek and quiet that he's probably turned red because he's going to cry." She had sometimes seen tears appear in Philip's light blue eyes when his mother made one of her frequent satiric remarks to him.

"Philip," his grandmother quavered to her peroration, "how could you be so careless? How *could* you? What *can* we do?"

"Cat, dear," Philip answered softly as Elizabeth Lamb, with her usual curiosity, advanced closer to hear, "it was simply bad luck. I can't account for it. Things do happen. I put the packet in my back trouser pocket, as always, and buttoned the pocket. It was still there when Philo and I finished changing the flat; I checked.

"It must have fallen out in the restaurant washroom, or maybe some jerk picked my pocket. Philo wanted to stop for a hamburger and I wanted to wash. We were filthy, from changing the tire." He passed his hand across his sweating forehead as he spoke, and his usually sleek blonde hair became almost comically disarranged.

"You're *not* supposed to stop anywhere," Mrs. Hackley said sadly. "You both know that. What are we to do about the next order, that has to go out in just a little over two weeks? It's the largest order of the summer, and the last, and we must be prepared for it. You know how long the brewing process takes and, really, I wanted to begin this afternoon. We *must* be ready by tonight, or at the very latest, by early tomorrow. You *know* how badly we need what you lost."

Philip rubbed his eyes. "I just don't know what to do, Cat. I guess — we haven't got any in reserve?" he asked pitifully.

His grandmother regarded him more kindly, with some part of the look of love and tolerance — a look seldom directed at his raffish mother — which was his usual portion from her. "Before I get any more upset," she said, "are you sure what the wholesaler gave you was correct? It's a long way back to

Augusta, but worth it, in this situation."

"Of course it was," Philip answered. "He knows what we need for *Sakana*. He gave us back the empties, and I counted them; and I looked, as I always do, at the packet."

The man standing beside a huge and dilapidated truck parked on Mrs. Hackley's white gravel (and dripping quantities of oil thereon, as Elizabeth Lamb noticed) now spoke.

"Gorry, Mis Hackley," he said hoarsely, "it ain't Phil's fault, or mine, neither. We got the beer to 'Gusta in good time, like always, and we got the yeast and we brung the empties back, like always, and I saw that Agnostino feller give Phil a check for the beer he sold for you, like always. What you in sech a bate about? I'll run over to the village, or to Ellswuth, and git you some more yeast. Maybe not as good as Agnostino gits special from Boston for you, but it'll do, wun't it? As fer the stuff we lost, leave 'er lay where Jesus flung 'er, is what I say."

Philip and his grandmother seemed unaware that Elizabeth Lamb was there. If they had noticed her, they had been too involved to acknowledge her presence. They both turned to regard the speaker with distaste. So did Elizabeth Lamb, who had found him to be one of the very, very few M.D.I. Natives who were in all dealings tricky and dishonest. He possessed the wit that all the Natives showed, but his constant guile and complete untrustworthiness prevented anyone who knew him from appreciating it.

He was extremely tall and thin, with no chin to speak of, but, below where it should have been, Nature had given him an enormous Adam's-apple, probably to compensate for her error with the chin. One of his numerous relatives, a lobsterman to whom General Alison gave his patronage because his prices were lower than the fish-market's, had told Elizabeth Lamb that Philo's Adam's-apple waggled from side to side when he was lying, and moved up and down when he wasn't. Elizabeth Lamb had replied that it always moved from side to side, and the answer was: "Ayup."

Philo also possessed small black eyes, which shifted frequently, and long greasy black hair, on which a dirty duck-billed khaki cap always rested. This he now lifted, but only to scratch his head, as he grinned amiably at his hostile audience.

"Good morning, Mrs. Hackley," Elizabeth Lamb said loudly. "Hello, Philip. Hello, Philo. Is something the matter?"

Mrs. Hackley and Philip nodded briefly in her direction and then regarded Philo with exasperation as well as dislike. "You can't get even a good *substitute* nearer than Bangor, and probably not there, Philo, and you know it," Philip said; and then, turning to his grandmother, "Cat, we'll simply have to make other arrangements for the shipment. You'll think of something. You always do."

"Sometimes you really are as much of a fool as your mother, Philip," she answered. "You seem deliberately obtuse." Now Philip most surely looked as if he were going to cry. Elizabeth Lamb spoke hastily to divert him.

"There's a young man on your beach, Mrs. Hackley," she said. "I told him to go away, but he might still be there. Maybe Philip should go down and chase him off?"

Philip made no move to leave. He looked as ready to weep as before. "Oh, dear," Mrs. Hackley quavered, "it's not the *time*. Why are they *bothering* us so? Lem . . . Lem . . . hasn't seen him, has he? That *dreadful* cannon —"

"Cat," Philip said quietly, " 'the time' that they bother us is right up to Labor Day, and you know it. He'll go away. Forget him, dearest. General Alison promised not to shoot anybody, unless they're on his land."

A silence ensued. Philo moved aside so that the crookedly-painted legend on his truck, "Let Gaynor the Mainer do it for you," came into view. "I got to git going," he said. "You kin set my pay for this week's trucking down aginst what I borreyed from you, mam. See you next week, Phil, if not 'fore. We got a Portland delivery, too, don't we?"

Mrs. Hackley had been thinking, her small face twisted into an expression of deep concentration. She spoke remarkably firmly. "No, Philo," she said, "I want you to take Philip to Bangor right now. He mustn't drive yet; his arm should really still be in a sling. I've been figuring out — deliveries, and we *must* begin tonight."

"Take thirty dollars, Philip, dear, and try both those breweries where we got yeast before, that time we ran out. If you call," she ended shrewdly, "they'll say they can't oblige us, because they don't want to bother, but if you just appear, one of them is bound to sell you some."

"Oh, Cat, dear," Philip began, "I'm so tired —"

"Do I run *Sakana Beverages*, or do you, Philip? Did I bring you up to respect The Elders? I built up this business before you were old enough to help me, and I am not ready for *inkyo*."

"I kin go by myself," Philo began, but all three of his listeners' expressions eloquently stated their belief that to send Philo Gaynor to Bangor with thirty dollars was akin to, as the Russian proverb has it, "sending the dog to the butcher for meat." He grinned with understanding and spat tobacco juice into the gravel at his feet.

"Cat, Muz can drive me, if you feel it's so urgent, but I still say —" Philip began again.

"NO," his grandmother answered. "Cynthia has been drinking, I fear. I don't want any harm, any further harm, to come to you. Please understand that."

"Mrs. Dickcyn is in the woods with Bix, sopping wet," informed Elizabeth Lamb. "I don't think she'd be willing . . . I mean able . . . to go."

"Sopping wet?" Philip asked. "Why?"

"She was in the bottom pool of the waterfall —"

"*Not* the lowest pool; oh, not the lowest pool, Elizabeth Lamb?" Mrs. Hackley cried. "That must be kept absolutely pure and unsullied. *Sakana*'s reputation depends upon that water."

"Cat, dear," Philip said gently, "even if Muz were in one of the others, they flow down into the lowest, don't they? Why don't we worry about more —"

"Why was Mis Dickcyn in the pool, Lizzie?" asked Philo.

"I think she jumped in because of an argument she and Bix were having," Elizabeth Lamb, who hated to be called Lizzie, answered stiffly. Philo began to laugh. "Damdest thing she ever done," he said. "Did she have her clothes on this —"

"You will be quiet and respectful, Philo," Mrs. Hackley ordered, with a touch of anger in her faltering voice. "Remember that I pay

48

you well for delivering my beers and have helped you every time you've had trouble with the law."

"Now," she turned to her grandson, "are you absolutely *certain* you searched everywhere for the packet? You know how much we need it; that yeast is far better than any we can buy in Bangor. Did you report it missing and offer a reward?"

Philo sniggered. Even Philip and Elizabeth Lamb smiled. "Cat," Philip said gently, "do you think that anyone is going to turn it in for a reward? Really, that's not very likely."

"Yeah," Philo agreed, adding to himself, but audible to Elizabeth Lamb, "Any old bird thinks brewers' yeast is wuth a reward's got to hev more than a couple lights out in the attic."

"Have you got money, Philip?" asked Mrs. Hackley. "Here" — ignoring his nod, she delved into her *obi*, the sash of her kimono — "take this, for gas. And don't rush. Philo, drive slowly and you, Philip, be alert. I don't want to lose anything more."

Philip flushed. "Cat, the one time —"

"Go, and go right now; *massu gu*," his grandmother interrupted, in a faltering but still determined tone. "Dear Lem's party is at five, remember. If you don't get back until after that, go directly there."

Philo, Philip and the truck departed, with another squirt of tobacco juice, a sigh of resignation, and a loud gnashing of gears, respectively. Mrs. Hackley, shaking her head sadly, started toward her house. She remembered Elizabeth Lamb, and turned.

"Would you like some root beer, dear?" she asked, not too hospitably. Elizabeth Lamb fervently assured her that *Sakana* root beer, at the moment, was what she most desired in all the world. They headed for the large, cement-walled building across the courtyard, which was attached to the garage but at an angle to it.

"Why does Philip call you 'Cat' and Mrs. Dickcyn 'Muz'?" Elizabeth Lamb asked. "I always wondered."

Pride supplanted the worry on Mrs. Hackley's face. "It was the first thing the dear child could say," she answered. "He was trying to pronounce 'Catherine', of course. His mother was hardly ever about when he was little. He never did say 'Mama' and Cynthia informed him when he was older that she would prefer to be called 'Muz' so that her maternity was not too obvious and with it her age. My daughter is very vain," she ended with a sigh.

"What did he call his father?"

"His father died before he was born," Mrs. Hackley answered briefly. She produced a mammoth brass key from her *obi* and deftly inserted it into the huge and heavy iron lock.

"Do you always lock it?" Elizabeth Lamb asked with interest, since none of her relatives who summered on Mount Desert Island bothered to secure their doors, even at night.

Mrs. Hackley turned to her, smiling faintly. "With Philo living practically on my doorstep?" she asked gently. "Doesn't he appropriate things from dear Lem's household?"

"Not this summer, with Ludwig's dog always around. But before Hohenzollern came, Cousin Lem said he could never be sure when he went to the woodshed for a hammer, or something, that it would be there. And he had to hide the liquor in the stove. Once his housekeeper forgot and turned the oven on, and the bottles exploded and ruined his stove. And once Philo sneaked an extension cord through a window and ran it down the driveway behind bushes to his house and Cousin Lem couldn't understand why his electric bill was so high that summer, till he tripped over the cord one day!"

"I think that Philo's greatest *coup*," Mrs. Hackley responded, turning the large key with ease in the well-oiled lock and motioning her guest to enter, "was stealing those twenty pews from that church in Nova Scotia and trucking them all the way to Boston. He wasn't found out until someone who summered in Nova Scotia saw them at the restaurant Philo sold them to." She sighed. "It cost me a great deal to get him out of that predicament."

"Do you want me to take off my shoes?" Elizabeth Lamb asked, remembering the rule at *Nihon*. "And why do you keep helping Philo? I think he's nasty."

Mrs. Hackley shook her head regarding the shoes. "But please wash your hands here, as I am doing. Water purifies all, you know, and everything that surrounds *Sakana* must be absolutely pure. Use this dishwashing detergent; we don't have any soap in here. It is a dreadful enemy of a good brew, of whatever kind of beer."

50

She looked around vaguely, as if she had forgotten why they had come. "Oh," she quavered, "that's right: beer, the root beer for you. What did you just ask, dear?"

"Why you keep helping Philo," said Elizabeth Lamb patiently. She was used to Catherine Hackley's forgetfulness.

"Oh, yes. Well, it's out of habit, I suppose. My husband bought our land from his father, who was a very good man and quite unhappy about the way his son turned out. Austin promised to look after Philo, and I honour his promise."

Elizabeth Lamb observed the brewery with her usual curiosity. She had never been invited into the *sanctum sanctorum* of *Sakana*. The room was much larger than it appeared from the outside. It was cool, despite the fluorescent ceiling lights, which Mrs. Hackley had turned on, since the room had but a few very small windows high up on the walls.

Four enormous porcelain vats occupied the center of the room. One of them was covered, and a plastic hose protruded from a hole in its wooden lid and bubbled gently into a small tub of water.

"Are you cooking some root beer?" she asked. "Why are those windows so tiny? And *look* at all those bottles! There must be thousands."

"Some ginger beer is brewing now," her hostess answered, "but not enough for our next order. I really had to send Philip to Bangor, the poor darling. The windows are small so that the temperature in here stays at an even 55 degrees, and, also, strong sunlight is very harmful to beers. And yes, there are at least thirty thousand bottles here."

She went to a large rack at one end of the room and began to turn over some filled bottles that were stacked in it. "Oh, dear," she said. "These are ready to be decanted. We empty them out to remove the sediment, and put the beer in new bottles. It's bitter, you see, from the yeast, and then we save the sediment and combine it with fresh yeast for the next batch.

"Philip should be here doing it, this very minute. Despite the training of my youth, my arms sometimes tire very easily. Why, why must I —" She put her hands to her mouth.

"Oh, no!" she cried. "I completely forgot to have Philo unload the cases of empty bottles they brought back. If they drive fast, some may be broken, and they are precious, precious!" She clasped her small hands together in what Elizabeth Lamb thought was needless anguish.

"But you have so many," she pointed out.

"Yes, dear, but they are irreplaceable. They're unique, you know. Philo's father had a big old shed filled to the brim with them, which inspired me to start making root and ginger beer, years ago, from recipes of his grandmother's that he gave me.

"It's so fortunate that we have these bottles, with porcelain plugs attached permanently by heavy wires. They help to retain the quality of *Sakana*, and we don't have the bother of caps. If Philo could get his hands on them, he would sell them to bottle collectors. That's why I send Philip with him on my deliveries."

"But if they're so valuable," Elizabeth Lamb questioned, "why do your customers return the empty bottles?"

"Because," Mrs. Hackley said proudly, "we charge a three-dollar deposit on each one! I insisted, even though everyone said I'd never get away with it. But we do. People who appreciate *Sakana* are quite willing to pay. A few *are* kept, of course, but enough come back so that we'll have plenty for years and years — for my lifetime, at least. I consider them lucky — look."

She picked up a green and a brown bottle and pointed to the fish that appeared in relief below the orange and black label that read *Sakana Beverages, Northeast Harbor, Maine.* "Fish have always been lucky for me, so I named my product after the Japanese word for them — *sakana*. Old Mr. Gaynor got the bottles from a place in Machias that made cod liver oil back in the early 1800's. The factory had been out of business for years. He was a collector, like Philo — except he paid for what he found. Heaven knows what he would have done with all of these if not for my inspiration." She looked beatifically upward, as if communing with one of her gods, if Shinto gods occupy fluorescently-lighted ceilings.

"Oh," said Elizabeth Lamb, who was becoming maddened by the sight of so much root beer, root beer everywhere, and not a drop to drink. "I thought *sakana* meant 'de luxe,' maybe, or perhaps just 'expensive.' But isn't that fish a cod? Do they have codfish in Japan?"

Mrs. Hackley waved her small hand in a gesture that was both regal and dismissive. "Yes, but it doesn't matter *what* kind of fish it is. Though," she added wistfully, "a carp would have pleased me more."

"I guess I'd better be getting back to lunch," Elizabeth Lamb hinted. Mrs. Hackley nodded vague agreement, but made no move as to in-house distribution of her product. Elizabeth Lamb lingered by the door.

"Why is this building built on an angle?" she asked. "Cousin Lem said it would have cost less if you'd put it flush against one of the garage walls."

"Lem is a *very* poetic soul," Mrs. Hackley replied. Elizabeth Lamb looked doubtful. "But," Mrs. Hackley went on, "he doesn't understand the traditional rules of *hogaku*. Wealth flows from the southeast to the northwest, and there must be a strong room to collect it, with the door on the exact southeast, like this one. *Sakana* is the source of most of our wealth now, so I built this new brewery following *hogaku*."

She looked pleased with herself. Elizabeth Lamb looked both determinedly thirsty and as if she had collected all the information regarding the way Mrs. Hackley's mind worked that she could ever assimilate.

"Well —" she began. Mrs. Hackley regarded her. "Isn't it almost your lunch time? Here," handing her two green bottles, "do take these back for you and Lem. *Konichiwa,* Elizabeth Lamb."

"Good-afternoon," Elizabeth Lamb replied in kind. "Ah, could I please have a ginger beer, too, for his secretary? She loves it so." She then reflected that any bread scattered upon the waters of Colleen O'Cassidy would only return stale, but smiled engagingly at her hostess anyway.

Mrs. Hackley gave her a brown bottle with some reluctance and a slight frown, and ushered her out the door. Elizabeth Lamb could not think of the special word for "thank you" so she replied with the general, *"Domo,"* adding, *"Konichiwa."*

Mrs. Hackley nodded approvingly at the use of Japanese, which she, of course, thought the most beautiful language in the world. "I'll see you at lovely *Iwo Jima* tonight," she said. "So kind of dear Lem to

have a party. It makes everything so much — happier; just perfect."
She locked the door carefully and pattered over to her cottage,
murmuring vaguely to herself.

Elizabeth Lamb departed slowly, reminded not only that she was
unlikely ever again to get so much of *Sakana*'s provender, but that
Mrs. Hackley was quite capable of charging her three dollars for a
broken bottle. Therefore, she eschewed the winding path back to *Iwo
Jima*, not only because Cynthia Dickcyn and her friend might be, as
Jane Worthington would say, "cavorting" somewhere along it, but
because the Hackley driveway went smoothly to the main road,
Peabody Drive. Just before she reached the road, she cut through the
woods, which were less thick there, to her cousin's driveway.

She walked slowly along it, bracing herself for what she might find
on Philo's property, through which, to reach the land sold him some
years ago by Mrs. Hackley, General Alison had been required to
purchase a right-of-way. Philo's house was set back from the road, but
was almost on the driveway, though partly concealed by a series of
high wooden fences, on which, in all seasons, skins of deer and of
smaller animals were tacked. General Alison roared frequently at Philo
to dry the skins, all trophies of Philo's extensive poaching ability, on
the sides that did not face the driveway. "My guests think I'm running
some damned butcher's shop," he forcefully announced, at least once a
week.

Philo always nodded agreeably and promised, his Adam's-apple moving
sideways, to remove the skins. This summer he had a new activity, that
of hauling away trash from some of the summer cottages. Relics
he considered too valuable to consign to the dump — or the sanitary
landfill, as such monuments are now designated — not only were
cluttered along the driveway's edge but were gradually imposing
themselves up toward *Iwo Jima*'s parking area. New additions today
were a refrigerator boasting a chipped coat of brilliant red paint and an
old gas stove. A fat young woman was standing admiringly before
them. Elizabeth Lamb averted her eyes from the pathetic collection on
the fences and looked, without enthusiasm, at her.

"Hey there, Lizzie," said the young woman. "Look what Philo's
gone and brung me. Elegant, ain't they?"

"Hello, Gloria," Elizabeth Lamb answered politely. "He'd better get that stuff out of there before this afternoon or General Alison's going to be awfully upset. We're having a party, and the guests need space to park their cars."

"Philo's independent as a hawg on ice," Gloria announced. "He'll git them out in his good time. Nobody ever tells Philo what to do and nobody never crosses his bow twice, neither."

"Well," said Elizabeth Lamb, "those things aren't even on your land. They're on ours."

Gloria laughed tolerantly and snapped her chewing gum. "*Thank you*," she said sarcastically, and departed toward her home, where the sound of screaming children now reached a crescendo loud enough for even her notice. "*Arigato*; that's what 'thank you' is," Elizabeth Lamb murmured to herself. "I never forget anything for very long." She skirted General Alison's cottage and appeared on the terrace with her booty.

The fog was hanging heavily over the terrace, but the air was warm. Miss O'Cassidy, however, had chosen to drape her charms in a blanket and was shivering ostentatiously. She looked with disgust at the large tray of food, dishes and cutlery Ludwig was placing on a table and wondered aloud why the hell she had to freeze to death to make things more convenient for the help. Then she looked at Elizabeth Lamb.

"Well, well," she said, "here's the sex kitten, back with goodies. How'd you manage that, Marilyn?"

General Alison possessed but a hazy idea of what "sex kitten" meant. He held only a slightly clearer notion of the qualities which had made the late Miss Monroe renowned, although he was somewhat aware that those qualities had been noticed by no less a personage than his former Commander-in-Chief; however, regarding that notice, he had once observed that "something of the sort was only what you'd expect. I mean to say, the feller was clever and he *was* from Boston — I'll give him that — but, still and all, you wouldn't want to invite him to your club and *talk* to him!"

Still and all, his family feeling was strong enough for him to observe the note of derision in his secretary's tone, and so he spoke in his young cousin's defence. "I think this child has," he said mildly, reaching to smooth Elizabeth Lamb's gilt hair, "a most patrician look. Often remarked upon it. Somewhat resembles that Kelly girl from Philadelphia — awfully nice, I heard, though she *was* an actress."

"How are things at *Nihon*, dear?"

Before Elizabeth Lamb answered, she opened her large green eyes and favoured Colleen O'Cassidy with a slightly insolent stare. She regarded a round-faced young woman of somewhat porcine aspect. Miss O'Cassidy's face was red and shiny, her pale eyes bulging, her short, broad nose peeling from sunburn and her dark blonde hair not overly-clean. Her mouth was full and sensually curved, with bright orange lipstick applied more or less accurately within and without its outlines. Elizabeth Lamb put the bottle of ginger beer beside her and turned to her cousin.

General Alison looked at her expectantly, with a smile on his thin, aristocratic lips that was somehow trusting and child-like and belied his years, which were thirty-five or so more than Miss O'Cassidy's. (Though perhaps not as many, Elizabeth Lamb thought, as the lady tried to convey.) He was lean and brown, his blue eyes clear and his sparse dun-coloured hair trimmed in a gentleman's haircut — no clippers had ever touched his neck. He was dressed in his usual morning garb of short-sleeved blue denim shirt above khaki British army shorts, obtained thriftily from Bar Harbor's Army and Navy surplus store. Below them, his still-firm tanned legs evinced a sinewy shapeliness that put to shame his secretary's stubby, plump, white ones. Elizabeth Lamb was often reminded by those legs of her grandmother's dictum: Never trust a woman whose legs are shorter than her torso.

Like Othello — a gentleman the General would not have recognized unless The Moor had appeared to him on a battlefield as a valued fellow-officer — Lemuel Otis Alison was "horribly stuffed with epithets of war," but despite them he often expressed a calm and happy manner, one common to assured Bostonian gentlemen of good family.

"They're sort of upset," she answered. "Philip lost some special yeast and Mrs. Hackley sent him and Philo to Bangor to get more."

"Can't that spoiled kid be trusted out alone?" Colleen inquired.

"You know, my dear, that he broke his arm falling down an elevator shaft at Harvard," General Alison answered. "Did one of my rhymes about it. You remember:

> Philip fell down the elevator
> And wasn't found till six months later.
> His tutors all made laughing mention
> Of how *spoiled* boys attract attention.

Heh-heh. Though," he added thoughtfully, "don't know where he found an elevator shaft to fall down. I can't remember any elevators at Harvard. Lived on the fifth floor at Eliot House and wished for one many times."

"Maybe that was before they were invented," Colleen said rudely. "I don't get that dumb verse. He must have been found right off, the way he'd cry and scream." She took up a fork and pushed the food on her plate about, grimacing.

"*And,*" Elizabeth Lamb went on, to dispel the hurt look on the General's face, "Mrs. Dickcyn jumped into the pool, the big one, and by the time Bix got her out, she looked about frozen. That spring water's awfully cold."

She served herself and eagerly attacked her lunch. "I do love French-toast-and-bacon, Ludwig," she said. "You make it so well."

"German toast, Elizabeth Lamb," Ludwig replied. "That's what it was originally called. During the First World War, its name was changed; just as sauerkraut became Liberty Cabbage and, in England, they changed the name of German Shepherd dogs to Alsatians. And the Battenburgs, of course, became the Mountbattens."

Elizabeth Lamb enjoyed this sort of trivial knowledge, as Ludwig well knew, as he also knew that her ceaseless curiosity and very good manners annoyed the General's secretary. He smiled remotely at Elizabeth Lamb, the only person in Northeast Harbor in whom he had shown any sign of interest or of liking, and went to the kitchen for coffee, accompanied by his German Shepherd, Hohenzollern, who followed him everywhere.

"I think this stuff's rotten," Colleen announced, "whatever it's called. I even hate it for breakfast. Why can't we have a decent lunch, even if Ludwig does have a party to get going?

"And I told you that man was a Nazi. Fancy knowing all that."

Elizabeth Lamb desisted from informing her that many people besides present and former Nazis knew a great many things; in fact, considering what had happened to the German Nazis, the rest of the world had undoubtedly known much more than they. She poured her root beer into the glass Ludwig provided, noticed that Colleen had not been so served, tasted, and sighed with pleasure.

"Do you eat steak-and-eggs for breakfast at home, Colleen?" she inquired. Miss O'Cassidy demanded to know what the hell she was talking about.

General Alison had been slowly masticating, the while his forehead furrowed with deep thought. "Got it!" he shouted so loudly that his two seated listeners started in their chairs. Ludwig and Hohenzollern remained in their usual poised and impassive stances.

"Listen!" said General Alison. He cleared his throat and began:

> "When Cynnie jumped into the pool,
> She found the water much too cool.
> Now she's frozen in the sewer
> And Bix has got a snatch that's newer.

Heh-heh."

"Language, language," Colleen reproved him. "Not in front of kiddie. And what's the point of *that* one? Elizabeth Lamb just said Bix got her out."

She snickered. "Like to have seen him doing it. She must weigh one or two stones more than he does, not to mention being a head taller."

General Alison sighed, an unappreciated artist. Ludwig left for the kitchen again, with no sign of commendation of his employer's talents. Elizabeth Lamb made a mental note to consult an Essee-ex manual as soon as she got back to school, though, as she remembered, they were remiss in short, explicit words, favouring poly-syllabled scientific terms.

Not completely understanding, she still spoke politely. "That's awfully good, Cousin Lem. I'll tell it to Persis when she gets here. When are you going for her, Miss O'Cassidy? I still wish you'd let me come with you. I haven't been over to The Bungalow all summer, with Grandmother and everybody in Europe, and I'd like to see it just once, this year."

"Driving with one kid's bad enough; I told you that," Colleen replied. "Anyway, your grandmother's caretaker called a while ago and said they'd meet me half-way, in Somesville. He's going on to Bangor, to take your grandmother to the airport."

"But Grandmother's been up here a whole week, and I haven't seen her," Elizabeth Lamb protested. "I haven't seen her since they all went to Europe in June."

"T.t.," Colleen answered briefly. General Alison frowned. Miss O'Cassidy grinned and tossed her blanket on the flagstones, grimaced once more at her lunch and left on her errand to Somesville.

General Alison was consoling. "You and Persis will be in Boston in exactly ten days, and you can see Elizabeth then, and for the rest of the winter." He smiled and added softly, "Only ten days."

Hohenzollern sat, thoughtfully regarding Elizabeth Lamb, as Ludwig began to straighten up the terrace furniture. "Wouldn't you like to take Ho for a walk?" he asked. Elizabeth Lamb had had enough of walking for a while. She was looking for more exciting things to ward off the post-hearty-luncheon yawns she felt were imminent.

"There was a man on the beach again, Cousin Lem," she said. "Do you want to shoot the cannon off? I'll help."

Ludwig appeared both interested and willing to assist. It was obvious that General Alison was tempted, but he shook his head firmly and departed for his study and the galley proofs of his Marine History. With Miss O'Cassidy gone, he did not try so hard to conceal the limp with which he had been afflicted by one of his frequent attacks of gout.

Elizabeth Lamb retrieved her discarded poetry book and then wandered about the cottage, observing the actions of the caterer, who had arrived earlier than expected. Ludwig began to vacuum, his gestures indicating that he would appreciate her not getting in the way.

She made for the sliding glass doors that opened on the swimming pool, the same type of doors that, at the opposite end of the large room, led to the terrace. She was feeling sleepy, and thought it would be pleasant to lie on one of the comfortable chaises that occupied the flagstones around the pool. A blue-and-white kimono flicked in the corner of her vision just before she reached the doors. Under one door there was a missive.

"I hope," she reflected, picking it up, "it's not about that darned cannon again. Maybe it's just one of her poems."

It was. Mrs. Hackley had for years, so General Alison said, pushed little notes under the doors or through the opened windows of *Iwo Jima* at any time of the day or night the mood came upon her, and most especially on nights when the moon was full.

Sometimes it was something she had clipped from a periodical, sometimes a quotation she had copied for his edification, more frequently a poem she had written in the style of *haiku* or *tanka*. All of them provided Miss O'Cassidy with much merriment, although she announced often that she "had to hand it to the old girl; she'll never give up trying to get you, General."

Today's communication was a *haiku* and better, Elizabeth Lamb thought, than most of them. It read:

> Fog comes to our isle
> The sea is still and waiting
> The light disappears.

She placed it on General Alison's desk in his study, the door to which was now open, but her cousin was not in evidence. He suddenly appeared on the gallery fifteen feet above her, which served as a hallway for the upstairs rooms — his bedroom and bathroom, the guest bedroom and another bathroom — that were built above the rooms on the east side of the cottage. The west side was taken up by the enormous living room, whose ceiling reached some forty feet into the air. The General had designed it with huge skylights, to admit the sight of tall spruce and pine and Maine sky — and to admit on occasion, to his chagrin, much Maine rainwater.

Now he bellowed to Ludwig that he had no clean socks, anywhere, dammit. Ludwig impassively shut off his machine and nimbly ascended the open circular stairway. The General often announced that enclosed flights of stairs took up too much space, that all Marines had good heads for heights, and that anyone who didn't could stay on the first floor — dammit. Elizabeth Lamb followed Ludwig, passed through the cloud of bay rum her cousin's person had dispersed in the gallery, and went to the guest room.

She lay quietly on her bed for a while, noticing that Ludwig had, of course, perfectly made up the other bed for Persis. Since the approach of her teen-age years had somehow miraculously caused Elizabeth Lamb to become neat and orderly, he had needed to do very little else to make the room ready for her cousin. She closed her eyes and dozed.

She woke suddenly. Down in the kitchen something had dropped. She heard a murmur of voices from there, and ice tinkling in glasses. Then the door was closed. It was after four o'clock.

Elizabeth Lamb went to the guest bathroom and washed perfunctorily, then changed her T-shirt and shorts for a Liberty-print cotton frock, thin white cotton socks, and black patent-leather Mary Jane slippers. That was how General Alison thought little girls should dress on social occasions, and Elizabeth Lamb was always happy to comply with surface conventions. As her grandmother said, doing so "made life simpler."

She went carefully down the staircase; the Mary Janes were new and the soles were stiff and slippery. Ludwig and the caterer were still relaxing behind the closed kitchen door. She heard a car departing and looked through the doors past the pool end of the room. A small, chubby figure, with curly brown hair, attired in a print dress similar to hers, white socks and black Mary Janes, stood there, smiling and waving.

"Persis!" Elizabeth Lamb shouted. There was a long and affectionate reunion, with many things excitedly discussed by the two cousins, who were very good friends as well as schoolmates. "Why are you so late?" Elizabeth Lamb asked finally. "Miss O'Cassidy left a couple of hours ago to get you. And why did she leave you and drive off?"

"Buster's car broke down, just as Grandmother and I and all our luggage got to Somesville. Grandmother asked the secretary to take her to Bangor, so she wouldn't miss her plane. Miss O'Cassidy wasn't very pleased, but you know how Grandmother always gets her own way.

"Elizabeth Lamb," Persis asked hesitatingly, "this secretary — is she what Grandmother calls 'not quite out of the top drawer'? She says 'mike' for 'make' and 'tike' for 'take' and 'haow' for 'how'. And she said" — Persis' voice dropped — " 'Damn It To Hell' a lot, but not till we left Grandmother off. And she drove really fast, through a couple of red lights just as if they weren't there. I was scared."

Elizabeth Lamb laughed. "Daddy says that all Australians sound as if they're not quite out of the top drawer, even the richest and best-educated. It's just their accent. This one is really not nice at all, though. You'll see. But don't worry: we're two against one now."

Persis giggled with relief. She looked to Elizabeth Lamb for guidance in most things.

"But where is she now? Why did she just leave you?" Elizabeth Lamb asked again.

"Where's Colleen?" General Alison asked in turn, entering from the terrace at the far end of the room from where the cousins were sitting somewhat stiffly so as not to wrinkle their dresses. "Glad to see you, Persis." He stamped muddy feet on the rug that Ludwig had cleaned. "Ludwig," he shouted, "better put your dog in the wood-shed. It's almost five."

Persis kissed her Cousin Lem affectionately and explained: "The lady said she had to go to the village for something, damn and blast."

"Yes, yes; I see," Lem answered the factual Persis. "Well, you two young ladies will have to be my hostesses when the guests arrive. I'll be right back, after I get some dry shoes. Took a short walk to put some ginger in my leg muscles. Standing about at a party is awfully tiring. Don't know *why* it's against protocol to sit down at a cocktail party, but it is. Stupid, I think."

"Yes, me too," Persis earnestly agreed. "And when Grandmother and I were at The Bungalow this week, we took long walks every day, after she finished work at her kiln. She says old legs need a lot of movement so they don't stiffen up."

General Alison cast a slightly annoyed glance at the cherubic and literal Persis as he limped up the circular stairway. Elizabeth Lamb smiled. The cousins smoothed up their socks, shook out their skirts and sat primly, awaiting the guests from Philadelphia-on-the-Rocks.

• Chapter 3 •

On-The-Rocks

T HE SHIP'S CLOCK in the study struck two bells. The General descended the stairs in another, stronger cloud of bay rum, and bellowed for Ludwig. "Give me a double Scotch-and-water, would you, please?" he said. "Hello, Paul. Good to see you. Are we going to get any customers this afternoon, hey? It's just gone five now."

Paul, a pleasant, be-spectacled young man, was pushing out the little portable bar and placing it between the kitchen and the terrace door. He quickly made the drink. "No ice, I believe, General Alison," he murmured.

"Glad you remember! There's no sense in cooling down good stuff so you can't taste it," the General answered. "Glad you don't say 'rocks' instead of 'ice,' too. Damn-fool expression."

"Oh," said Paul, "I do to most people, General. I give them what they expect," he added with a smile. "That's the secret of catering: one must cater."

Lem guffawed loudly. Ludwig, whose part in the afternoon's proceedings was evidently to heat up, chill down, and serve the comestibles provided by the caterer, the delicious odour of which, emanating from the kitchen, was maddening Elizabeth Lamb and Persis, moved into the living room and stood to attention.

"Can't understand it," General Alison said. "Nobody's here. Where're those jazz fellers?" He sank wearily into a corner of a large and comfortable sofa and swallowed at least half of his drink. "Ah-h-h, now that's the stuff to give the troops. Look," he observed, "here's the trombone player. Told you so," he said quietly to Persis, who was puzzled.

A tall, muscular, serious-looking young man came in through the terrace doors and immediately made a sharp right to the bar. He was provided with an enormous glass of bourbon-on-the-rocks, which he tasted as he turned to his host. Before speaking, he produced a large red bandanna from the pocket of his grey flannel slacks and passed it over his wet blonde hair.

"Afternoon," he said, and then went to the skittles table across the large room. Persis followed him. "Cousin Lem!" she said. "I didn't know you had a skittles table! Grandmother and Mummy and I learned to play skittles in the hotel in Scotland this summer. It took a sixpence to get it going, but American tourists used dimes. You could use dimes, Cousin Lem.

"They have these in a lot of places in Scotland and England," she informed Elizabeth Lamb, who had expertly played skittles in many a hotel bar in England and Bermuda. "I'll teach you all about it."

She went over to the tall young man, who was reaching into the box of dimes kept conveniently near the table. "I'm Persis Halstead," she announced. "I'm Elizabeth Lamb's first cousin and I'm exactly one week younger than she is. I love skittles and I'm pretty good. Could I play with you?"

The young man dropped a dime into the coin slot, the ivory balls clattered down, and he picked up a cue. He nodded to Persis who then, having permission, happily chose another. "I'm Dusty," he said, and followed with the second complete sentence Elizabeth Lamb had ever heard him utter. " 'Life,' as the saying goes," he solemnly informed Persis, " 'is not all beer and skittles.' "

He placed the red ball on the spot above the D on the felted table, put one of the white balls on the D, and made a perfect shot, stroking the white ball with his cue so that it cleanly struck the red one, which ricocheted from the board at the back of the table and disappeared into the 200 hole, without knocking over the skittle — a wooden peg with arms that guarded the hole.

"Oh, my; you're *very* good," Persis observed. "The red ball counts double, so you've got 400 already. I bet you'll never knock over a skittle, either, and I'll never get to play." She reverently regarded Dusty, who continued his game silently and expertly.

"But you're not drinking beer," she said. "That's whiskey you have. So why did you say that about beer?"

"It's just a saying, Persis," Lem informed her. "It means life is not all pleasure." He signaled to Paul for another Scotch.

"Who's coming to this party?" Elizabeth Lamb asked him. "Who else besides Dusty, I mean?"

"A lot of old trouts, the secretary said," Persis responded for him, her eyes still on Dusty's masterful play. "What did she mean?"

"Heh-heh," came from the General. "Persis, you must not repeat everything so literally. Colleen uses a lot of slang, both Australian and American, which you may not understand. She means old ladies, but young ones, and old and young gentlemen are coming, too. Hope they get here soon," he added to himself, as Dusty headed for the bar again, "or the booze won't last.

"Your Aunt Isabella's invited," he informed Persis and Elizabeth Lamb, without much pleasure. "She cornered me in the Pine Tree Market last week. Wish she'd confine herself to Bar Harbor. She fits in better with that crowd over there.

"Ludwig," he cautioned, "don't light the fire unless you put the screen across it. Some of the old tr — ah, the older people may get chilly, so you might have to start it, but you know what Chubby Cooke is like."

"That's the man who lives next door, on the harbour side," Elizabeth Lamb informed Persis, who had still not got a turn at the skittles table. "Why is he so afraid of fire, Cousin Lem?"

Her cousin sighed. "It seems to be my fate to be surrounded by peculiar people wherever I go," he answered, adding quickly, "except when I was in The Corps, of course. Chub's house on Nahant burned

66

down once, and he's got this fixation that his cottage here, or any place around him, is going to do the same.

"Appeared in a frenzy one day, just before you and your mother came to stay, because he saw a little smoke. Ludwig was burning a few dry leaves. Chub made him stop. Carried on like an idiot. He's as bad as Catherine Hackley about fire, although she has more reason to be, of course. Did one of my rhymes about Chubby. Want to hear it?"

Elizabeth Lamb shook her head in violent refusal, since she saw, over her cousin's shoulder, Mr. Cooke advancing across the terrace. Lem ignored her, and declaimed:

> "When Chubby came to quench the fire,
> It blazed into a funeral pyre.
> Cried thrifty Lem, 'Here's money found!
> Smoked chub for sale, ten cents a pound!'

Lots of pounds on Chub, too. Heh-heh."

"You mean he was cooked and you sold him?" cried a horrified Persis.

"No I wasn't, young lady," said Mr. Cooke, who had been standing in the doorway listening to the poetic account of his demise. "Here I am, in the flesh, and not so much flesh as Lem likes to state. You must be the new little cousin who's come to visit." His smile as he shook Persis' hand was jolly, and it became more so as Paul handed him a large martini-on-the-rocks.

He cast a quick glance at the dark fireplace, beside the skittles table, and, reassured, went on: "Lem's not so witty as he thinks. A legend in his own mind, is what I call him. Must say that the one he did about the poor Dickcyn feller was rather good, though."

He then patted Elizabeth Lamb's shoulder and said she looked very nice. Tate Cooke was a rotund, white-haired man of about General Alison's years who somewhat resembled an elderly Cupid. He patted and spoke so to every female, of every age and type, since he was an ardent admirer of women, although his pursuit of them was less determined than his host's. No one could understand why he had never caught one; caught one for keeps, that is, (nor she *him* as his cynical single friends, including General Alison, had often declared.)

"Where's everybody, Lem?" he asked. "Shouldn't you have a little music, to liven things up?" General Alison, on hearing this, looked apprehensively at the oblivious Dusty. Mr. Cooke also looked at him. "Hello, young man," he called to Dusty, still on his break, as a player's turn at skittles is called. Dusty kept his eye on his ball and nodded a greeting.

"Where's Colleen?" Mr. Cooke went on. "She'd find the radio. Don't see it; guess you hid it, or maybe burned it? Ha!"

"Party's sort of dull, Lem. Give us the one about the Dickcyn boy, before his devoted widow gets here. They're coming over from *Nihon*, aren't they? Come on, let's hear it."

"Philip doesn't have a widow," said Elizabeth Lamb, thinking she was beginning to sound like Persis.

"No, no," answered Mr. Cooke. "I mean Philip's father, Schofield Dickcyn. Don't you know the story?"

Elizabeth Lamb shook her head, her mouth being occupied with several little hot *hors-d'oeuvres* Ludwig had slipped to her, in defiance of General Alison's frequently and loudly stated opinion that children should attend social gatherings because it taught 'em civil behaviour, but that they certainly should not expect to get anything to eat or drink. At least not, as he would add more leniently after having consumed a goodly amount of *l'eau de vie* himself, until all their elders had been served.

"Oh, please do tell it," said Persis, replacing her cue and coming over to them. She was beginning to understand that Dusty's skill was so great that his break might continue all through the party — if the party ever got started — with only slight pauses for him to refresh himself at the bar, as he had, by now, twice done.

Mr. Cooke took a handful of black olives from the tray Ludwig offered, and sat down at the opposite end of Lem's sofa. "Love these things," he said, chewing rapidly. "They don't have to be cooked, either."

"The story," Elizabeth Lamb reminded him, afraid that Chubby Cooke might get waylaid and embark on one of his discussions of how food was not only safer eaten raw, but better for you.

Mr. Cooke sipped his martini reflectively. He cleared his throat, sighed reminiscently, and began:

"You little girls have got to understand that Cynthia Hackley was a bit wild in her youth." He paused and sipped again.

Elizabeth Lamb nodded agreement, realizing that Cynthia Hackley Dickcyn was more than a bit wild now, and remembering the saying her grandmother was fond of quoting: "Age doesn't change you; it only makes you more so." Persis was bewildered, not knowing who Cynthia Hackley was, or had been.

"Very wild," Mr. Cooke went on. "Got up on tables in nightclubs and danced, I heard. All that sort of thing. Never been in a nightclub, myself. Doubt there's a nightclub in Boston, after that one burned down, years ago." He ruminated. "Well, her parents were a bit worried about whom she might marry. Among other things," he added.

"Or not marry," Persis said helpfully. "Everybody doesn't marry, anymore."

"Well," Mr. Cooke responded, "this was twenty years or more ago, remember. There was more marrying then, and less of — other things. The Hackleys knew people who knew the Dickcyn Players. Ever heard of them?"

Both little girls shook their heads.

"But they were famous, weren't they, Lem? Sort of like the Barrymores, because they were two brothers and a sister. Ever hear of the Barrymores, young ladies?"

Both little girls shook their heads.

"What *do* they teach you, nowadays!" Mr. Cooke exclaimed, rhetorically.

"Algebra, and Jane Austen, and about worms and frogs and verbs and infinitives, and we pick up some sex educa —" Persis began earnestly, before Elizabeth Lamb stepped lightly on her left Mary Jane.

"Well," the *raconteur* went on, speaking very slowly and clearly and loudly, as Italian and French waiters are often addressed in English by Anglo-American travelers in Europe, "I've said these Dickcyns were two brothers and a sister. They had a large troupe that played nothing but Shakespeare, in England, and over here, and anywhere they went. They were all three married, and the wives and husband were in the troupe too, along with the son of one of the brothers. That was Schofield, and he grew up with the troupe."

"Only Shakespeare?" Elizabeth Lamb asked. "That's all they did?"

"Only Shakespeare. You *have* heard of Shakespeare?" Mr. Cooke asked, with some apprehension. The little girls nodded reassuringly.

"Just as Martyn Green's troupe played only Gilbert and Sullivan," Lem informed them. The little girls looked puzzled.

"Well," Mr. Cooke quickly went on, "the Hackleys, for some reason, thought this boy would be just the ticket for Cynthia. Don't know why, except he happened to have been born in Japan, when the Dickcyn Players were there, and besides that, he was sort of what you might call malleable."

"A wimp," Persis said.

"Er — yes. Probably. The wedding was set and the Dickcyns were furious. Schofield had begun to play Puck when he was only ten, and got much praise for his performance. When he was in his teens, he'd played junior parts, and done them very well. They were grooming him for Romeo, and the betting was he'd play a greater Romeo than anyone except Olivier ever had — or was it Gielgud, Lem?"

"Don't remember — one or the other; doesn't matter. The Queen knighted both of 'em, and she knows what she's about. England has Marines, you know, so she's got to have *some* sense."

"Er — yes. Well, the Dickcyns couldn't see that marrying Cynthia would be any help to Schofield's career, quite the reverse; and, in any case, Cynthia's parents were pressuring him to give up acting." Mr. Cooke signaled for another martini and gazed reflectively into it.

Lem took up the tale. "The wedding was here — over at the Hackleys', that is. The Dickcyns wouldn't come, simply refused. Maybe," he said bitterly, "it was because they were devout R.C.s and that idiot Catherine insisted on a Shinto ceremony. It was held in the teahouse.

"All this land belonged to them, then, and they had a huge barbecue pit built right there" — he gestured out toward his pool. "Everybody in the wedding party wore those damned silk kimonos.

The men had short ones, over that stupid divided skirt they wear. There was a lot of drinking after the ceremony — *sake* as well as champagne and don't-know-what-all.

"Or so I heard. I wasn't here. I was still on active duty and didn't even know them."

"Well," said Mr. Cooke, "I was here. Everybody was pretty well ploughed, especially that poor boy. The pit had an iron grill over it; it was like a giant *hibachi*, really, and that damfool Austin Hackley was roasting pigs and lambs and chickens — well, to make a long story short —"

"Or shorter," said Persis.

"Er — yes. Well, the Dickcyn boy sat down, or fell down, on this red-hot grill. The damned silk clothing caught fire in a flash, and he was stupid enough, or drunk enough, to run. That Gaynor feller's father was the caretaker, and he had the sense to catch young Dickcyn and to put his shirt around him and roll him on the ground. But it was too late. The boy died in the hospital."

"What!" Elizabeth Lamb exclaimed. "That's terrible!"

"But," Persis asked thoughtfully, "if he died right after the wedding, how come this boy Philip was born? Elizabeth Lamb, it takes nine months after —"

Elizabeth Lamb sighed. "Maybe they Did It before; maybe not," she whispered.

"But if 'maybe not', then this Philip is somebody else's —"

"Hush, will you, Persis! Maybe that's why they wanted her to get —"

"Well," General Alison said in a booming voice, dismissing the persistant Persis with a wave of his hand, "the whole thing was Catherine Hackley's fault. *And* it was very bad luck for *me*, because when she sold me this land, she would do it only on the condition that I put a swimming pool right on the site of the disaster. 'Water purifies all,' she's always saying."

"I *know*," Elizabeth Lamb replied.

"Damned pool," said Lem, gazing moodily out at it. "Costs me a fortune, keeping it free of leaves and sterilizing it and all that sort of thing. Glad I have Ludwig this year; I used to do it myself or pay outrageous amounts to one of those robber barons who call themselves caretakers.

"One thing I will not do is heat it, no matter what Colleen says. The ocean is what Marines swim in, and *it's* not heated." Always fair, he then murmured, "Maybe in the Pacific it is." He thought. "Where *is* Colleen, anyway?"

"But what's the rhyme?" Elizabeth Lamb asked, to divert him.

"A good one," the General grinned, "one of my best. Here goes:

> The members of the Dickcyn clan
> Deserted Schofield, to a man,
> But Cynnie's whole rapacious kin
> Descended in a hungry din,
> And when the *pâté* ran too low,
> They toasted up and sliced poor Scho.
> He'd played at Puck with all his heart;
> Still, Barbecue's a *meatier* part!"

"Oh, surely they didn't —" Persis said.

"No, they didn't!" Elizabeth Lamb was impatient. "Persis, after all these years, don't you realize that Cousin Lem's verses are like those old Victorian *Ruthless Rhymes for Heartless Homes*? They all have horrible endings, but they're supposed to be funny." She glanced at Lem and quickly added: "They're just terribly funny."

"Hi," said a cheerful voice. Bix Baxter had arrived. He was impeccably dressed, in casual Northeast Harbor fashion, and smiling as usual. "Awfully nice of you to have me, General," he said politely. His black hair was as wet as Dusty's had been: the observant Elizabeth Lamb deduced that the undependable shower Mrs. Hackley had installed in the teahouse was, for once, working.

Bix obtained a large gin-and-tonic and greeted everyone happily. "You look as if you'd make a good sax player," he said when presented to Persis. "Elizabeth Lamb doesn't want to learn, so I'll teach you."

Persis was enchanted. She followed Bix to the skittles table where he persuaded Dusty to cease his break and let Persis and him play.

"Well," said the General, in what was for him a low tone, "he's here, so where's Cynthia?"

72

"Maybe she did get a cold," Elizabeth Lamb answered. "She said if she did, it would be all her mother's fault. Maybe she's pretending to be sick to annoy Mrs. Hackley."

The General was now on his third large drink. "Catherine Hackley is a fool; always said so, ever since I met her. But the devil of it is that that daughter of hers and the grandson, too, blame her for everything." He brightened. "Just one more rhyme, Elizabeth Lamb? You'll like it."

"Yes, Cousin Lem," she answered politely, although she knew the one that was coming, from many recitals. She would have preferred to be playing skittles with Bix, since Persis had lost her break and wandered over to them. Elizabeth Lamb smiled with great earnestness at the General.

"Heh-heh," he said. "Well —

> Phil raped by a boy from Exeter.
> Poor Cynnie screamed; we said to her,
> 'Let swoons and screaching cease and halt —
> We'll say it was all Catherine's fault!' "

"He *did*?" Persis was awed. "But how could he? I mean, I thought you could only rape —"

"PERSIS, STOP IT," Elizabeth Lamb almost shouted. Bix and Dusty looked over, startled, and then went on with their game.

"But Elizabeth Lamb, is this Philip — you know, is he a —?"

"No, he's *not*, I'm sure; he's just quiet and shy, a very nice boy," Elizabeth Lamb answered firmly. Her choice of words was purposely discreet, for coming in from the terrace was Philip's mother, her flaming hair clashing outrageously with a low-cut, clinging lavender silk dress, a bit *outré* by Northeast Harbor standards. Around her neck was a long loop of dark red stones that were probably garnets.

She looked both fashionable and, somehow, very attractive, whereas a less flamboyant woman would have looked merely peculiar. She had once informed Elizabeth Lamb that the secret of dressing was to appear as if you didn't *care*, which was a very different thing than appearing as if you didn't *know*.

"Philip's not back yet?" Cynthia inquired. "Oh, thanks, Paul, a Bloody is just what I want." She favoured Paul with a dazzling smile and then turned back to her host. "He's going to be very tired and fussy and it will be *all* Mother's fault" — Mr. Cooke, General Alison and Elizabeth Lamb smiled — "for sending him on an unnecessary errand. *Sakana* wouldn't be ruined if they missed one shipment."

"Where's Catherine?" General Alison asked her.

"You know she won't enter from the terrace, Lem, even though it would save the poor dear from trudging all around your cottage," Cynthia answered, downing her drink and summoning Paul with a gentle wave of her hand. "The terrace has a northeast door, and on a dwelling, you know, that's *kimon*: a 'devil gate.' Here she is."

Catherine Hackley came in quietly by the doors from the pool. She looked around vaguely, smiling. "But, Cousin Lem," Elizabeth Lamb whispered to him, "the terrace faces the southeast; Mrs. Hackley knows directions over at her place. What's the matter with them?"

"Quiet," Lem hissed at her. "Told you the mother's slightly round the bend and like mother, like daughter. Not a word; don't try to tell either of 'em anything, ever. They know directions well enough, when it suits them."

He rushed to put Mrs. Hackley into a chair, noticing with relief that in consideration of his often-expressed detestation of Nipponese garb she wore a conservative black silk dress, an impressive quantity of pearl jewelry, and black slippers similar to Elizabeth Lamb's and Persis'.

"What'll you have, Catherine?" The General was solicitous. "Expecting a whole bunch of guests, so give me your order now. You look a bit fagged out."

"Oh," Mrs. Hackley quavered, "I really think I'd like some sherry. Cynthia, please don't shake your head like that. I'm very tired. It wouldn't hurt just this once, dear."

Cynthia regarded her dubiously. "Mother, you know what the doctor said about liquor, now that you must take insulin twice a day."

"But very, *very* dry sherry? Just a half-glass?" Mrs. Hackley was plaintive.

"You are certainly aware," her daughter said sternly, "that it should

74

be plain tonic water, with a bit of lime. You know your regimen, and if something happens, it will be all your fault!"

Mrs. Hackley looked ready to weep, an appearance that Elizabeth Lamb had noticed she could and did summon up frequently.

"Oh, well; what the hell!" said her daughter. "Paul, perhaps a small glass of that *fino* sherry for my mother. And *no* more than that."

Mrs. Hackley nibbled on a plain cracker and sipped her sherry, looking anxiously from one door to another. Philip did not appear, but almost at once a number of guests arrived, in a steady succession. Paul and Ludwig sprang into action. General Alison was obliged to abandon all thoughts of his sofa's comfort and moved about amiably, being a hearty host and only once muttering in a too-audible tone that he didn't know who the hell half these people were. Persis and Elizabeth Lamb smiled at everyone and, when the General's eye was upon them, even curtsied.

A thin, erect woman, with short glossy black hair that showed very little grey and was arranged in the Marcel styling of the '20's came over to Mrs. Hackley. "Well, Catherine," she pronounced, "you aren't looking very well. Too little exercise?"

"Oh, Elise, dear," Catherine Hackley faltered, "I'm afraid my years are catching up to me."

"Nonsense," Elise responded briskly. "I walked from the Asticou to Jordan Pond for tea this afternoon, and then back. A total of about eighteen miles, I'd say, and I feel the better for it. And I've got almost twenty years on you, my dear!"

Elizabeth Lamb was astounded. She knew Mrs. Hackley to be about the age of General Alison, who had just turned sixty-one. She closely scrutinized the lady called Elise. Carrying yet another Bloody Mary, and coming over to check on her mother's consumption of sherry, Cynthia Dickcyn noticed her interest and said quietly: "It's true, though. She's famous for her marvelous looks as well as her walking prowess. Climbed Katahdin with a friend five years ago. The friend was younger, of course, only seventy!"

She turned to Persis. "I'm Cynthia Dickcyn," she said. "I gather you're Lem's other little cousin. And I've noticed, in spite of this being my fourth Bloody, that you've got damned good manners, like my friend Elizabeth Lamb."

"How do you do," Persis responded, producing a curtsey to bolster the opinion of her just expressed. "I like your name. It's got two cyns in it."

Cynthia laughed heartily. "There are fewer sins in my name than on my conscience," she announced, spying a lone man and heading over to him.

She was intercepted by a girl in her late teens, who had shepherded the man into the party. The girl was wearing the usual Northeast Harbor expression of haughty aloofness, as well as the usual Northeast Harbor printed cotton cocktail dress. Her (inevitably) blonde hair was held back from her forehead by the (inevitable) tortoise-shell headband. Elizabeth Lamb had been introduced to her and thought she was called Muffy, or Buffy, or Miffy, or Biffy (as was also inevitable.)

"Oh, Mrs. Dickcyn, how nice to see you again," the girl said. "I'm Missy Larrabee. Isn't this just the most heavenly party! This is our house guest, Courtney Walker. Mummy's tied up with an unexpected caller so she sent us to do the polite bit."

Mr. Walker, a short, fat, overly-tailored man with popping eyes and unrealistically black hair and mustache bowed over Cynthia's hand and was then led away. Cynthia was amused.

"Walker's a good name for him," she confided to Elizabeth Lamb, none too quietly, "because that's just what he is: her mummy's 'walker.' "

"What's that?" Elizabeth Lamb asked. "You mean he's hired to walk with her mother?"

"It's a British term, I think. Women of a certain age who have money often have one or two available to dance attendance. They're often gay and they're certainly spongers," Cynthia explained, not lowering her voice and not needing to because General Alison's "do" was now reaching an alcohol-inspired volume of happy intensity.

"They come as house guests," she went on, "for anything from a week-end to a year. They have to be presentable — house-broken, as a friend of mine describes it. They act as escorts. You *know* — do what men who used to be called gigolos did. They say the Royal Family has a list of them who can be called on to take Princess Margaret around and see that she doesn't drink too much or disgrace the Royals' image. Such as it is," she ended, wandering off.

Beginning to be worn out with the education she was receiving, Elizabeth Lamb found Ludwig and obtained sustenance for herself and Persis. "You don't look exactly right, Ludwig," she observed. "Oh, Persis, this is Ludwig Vonn, who works here."

Ludwig followed his greeting to Persis with a loud sneeze. "I'm getting a terrible head cold, Elizabeth Lamb," he confided. "I'm probably spreading innumerable germs this very moment that will soon blanket all of Northeast Harbor." With that thought, he looked slightly more cheerful as he went about his duties.

"Of course I know he works here, Elizabeth Lamb. I'm not stupid. But is his name von?" asked Persis, pronouncing it correctly as "fon." " 'Von' what?"

"That's all there is to it, just Vonn, with a 'v'." Elizabeth Lamb looked at their cousin, in animated conversation with a tall, loud lady of commanding appearance who had added impressive elbow-length white gloves to the town's prescribed cocktail attire. Lem was about to be seized from behind by a shapely woman who had recently arrived and, with her escort, gone straight to Paul's largesse.

"Darling, darling Lem!" shrieked the woman, kissing him as passionately as she addressed him. "Here's your favorite cousin come to add family distinction to your lovely party. And I've brought my dear friend-and-partner, Perkie; you remember Perkie. I see Cousin Cordelia and her Teddie are here, but one can hardly count *them* as lively family assets, can one? And there's Cousin Emily, still gathering her dreary quotations, one supposes, and never, but never, writing anything the teeniest bit original. But *I'm* here!"

Cordelia and Ted, an uninspired-looking couple, retreated further into their corner upon hearing this, and glowered at the company, although Cordelia signalled Ludwig yet again to provide Teddie with more food. The attractive, sprightly woman referred to as Cousin Emily paused in her literary conversation, fixed her derider with a clear-eyed regard, and inquired of her, in the pure Bostonian accent so truly described as being "half-Harvard and half-hick," if *she* were ever going to say something original, let alone *write* something? "If, dear

77

Isabella," Cousin Emily finished her off, "Miss Winsor's was ever able to teach you to write — or read?"

The commanding lady with gloves, acknowledging that the derisive newcomer had vocal ability of greater volume than she, backed away to find her husband. She bumped into a woman and immediately screamed, "Darling, you're here! And Jupiter is in Scorpio, you lucky, lucky thing!" She seized the lucky thing, who looked dazed at the greeting, and ushered her to the bar, collecting somebody's husband along the way.

"Hello, Isabella," the General finally addressed his new guest, without much enthusiasm. "Glad you could come over. And Mr. — Ah, too."

"Mr. Walker, I'll bet; another Mr. Walker," deduced Cynthia, heading for the bartender, or a man without a woman, whichever she might find first. Her utterance may not have been understood but her manner was noticed by Isabella, who always managed to find an insult where one was intended.

"Oh!" Isabella was suddenly joyous. "Here's another handsome, handsome man, and with all sorts of good-for-one meaties and veggies! Do tell me your name! I am the Grafin von Lichtenfeld."

Ludwig served his enthusiastic customer and her escort, bowed his head briefly while clicking his heels together, and muttered only a courteous, "*Madame.*" He then took himself and his wares to a far corner of the room, with one quick glance over his shoulder to see if the Grafin were in pursuit.

"Here, darling Lem," said Isabella, spilling a good part of her martini upon his madras necktie as she clung to him and presented a prettily-wrapped box, "is a prezzie for you. Your cousin never forgets a birthday, you know, except hers, of course. Not that I'm counting, sweetest, but you must be in your seventh decade by now, yes?"

"No!" said Lem furiously. Perkie, looking embarrassed, left to speak knowledgeably about jazz to Dusty. Dusty nodded frequent agreement but said nothing, of course, as he cast restive glances over his admirer's shoulder at the assembly.

Colleen O'Cassidy appeared suddenly beside her employer, looking hot and angry and loudly demanding that he secure her some dinkum gin. "Boodles, right? Wherever you've hidden it. And none of that sodding stuff made in Maine. What's this about a birthday?"

Lem gestured to Paul and Miss O'Cassidy's needs, at least as to imbibition, were promptly fulfilled. As she drank, she looked appraisingly at Isabella, who looked appraisingly back.

"Where *were* you, Colleen?" the General asked. "I was beginning to be a bit worried. This is my cousin Isabella, my dear. Isabella, Colleen, my secretary."

"Had to go to the village, that's all," Miss O'Cassidy answered, ignoring the introduction. "Cheers, everybody."

"*My* favourite toast," said Isabella, "is: 'Here's champagne to my real friends and real pain to my sham friends.' Sham is so easy to detect, you know." She dimpled charmingly.

"But," the General persisted, "why in the world go to the village just before guests were due? You were gone very long, Colleen."

"Lem," said Miss O'Cassidy, still ignoring Isabella, "there's things us girls need suddenly, at certain times. You know? And we can't always find the right ticket, all at once. So give over, there's a dear."

"At certain times?" Isabella murmured. "But, surely, at your age, you're past all that?"

Lem blushed. Miss O'Cassidy glared. Isabella smiled sweetly at her and announced to the General that her present was something he would simply adore. "It will," she explained, "save your poor precious leg, in which the gout is worsening all the time, isn't it, sweetest? They say gout *does* appear with age, and, of course, any tension due to disharmony in the household only increases it."

Miss O'Cassidy, defeated for the time, turned away to speak (more or less) civilly to the husband of the white gloves. White Gloves, whom someone had mentioned as being Amalfi, the contralto, left him to it and entered into conversation with a short, fat, elderly woman with dyed red curls. The woman confided to her in a carrying voice that she thought she must be at the wrong party, since she had merely followed some cars in because her dearest doggie was becoming restless, the precious, *and* she had never met that man in her life. "Though," she added, loudly enough to attract the outraged notice of her host, "the used-appliance business must be a profitable one, since this is certainly a lavish do; wouldn't you say so, my dear?"

Elizabeth Lamb turned from her efforts at explanation to a man who was peevishly asking of anyone who would listen to him, *why* Lem Alison was called "General" when he was retired. "Not quite the thing, that," the man kept saying, despite her assurance that her cousin preferred "Mister" but was unable to convince his admirers to relinquish use of his service title. She greeted a young blonde couple who were hovering in the doorway announcing shrilly that they were late because they had got confused and found themselves on the ledges behind Great Cranberry, thinking, so heavy was the fog in the Western Way, that they were approaching Seawall. They demanded of everyone near them if they hadn't been just too ridiculous? And weren't they just too awful not to have changed before coming to this divine party that — ah — er — that this sweet man was throwing? They requested "great, big g-and-t's" of Paul and looked pleased with themselves, despite their being both ridiculous and awful.

Their listeners nodded agreement, although the new arrivals' sailing garb of red Breton pants and Irish sweaters caused no raised eyebrows, and then went back to a discussion of their own individual golf game (if they were male) or golf as that-stupid-woman-who-thought-she-played-a-professional-game performed it (if they were female). The latter group agreed that the woman would play better if she did not drink so heavily. They then demanded of Paul, or of their escorts, double refills of what they had been drinking, and not too many rocks, please.

Isabella was demonstrating her gift to Lem, Dusty, and Bix. "See!" she said. "One merely inserts the plug of the television set into it, then puts *its* plug into the wall outlet, so; presses this dear little thingie one can keep in a pocket, and then turns the set off and on without having to get up on one's poor old leggies! I've brought two units for the darling; one is for his bedroom because I can imagine how bored *and* exhausted he must be there, nowadays."

Lem expressed gratification, ignoring the reference to leggies and boredom, and Dusty began to play with the contraption. Soon the furor of a loud television being turned rapidly on and off added formidably to the general din.

80

Philip Dickcyn arrived and went directly to his grandmother, whose look of love at seeing him was most touching to Persis, a more sentimental child than her cousin. "Oh, dearest," Mrs. Hackley cried, "you've been gone so long! How *could* it take you six hours to go to Bangor and back? It's almost six-thirty and I've been *so* anxious! Did you get the yeast?"

Philip replied bitterly that it was *all* her fault; that if she had not sent him with Philo in that blasted truck with no usable spare, he'd have returned long since. He tossed her a large package wrapped in silver foil, brandished abraded, greasy hands reproachfully, and disappeared into the downstairs lavatory, or powder room, as his host insisted on calling it. The package exuded upon Mrs. Hackley's black silk lap some tiny, yellowish-tan grains, at which she smiled fondly, though more fondly at the disappearing back of her grandson.

He returned, after some resounding kicks and furious rattling noises that caused heads to turn uneasily. He proclaimed that he was exhausted, both from his trip and from becoming trapped in that Black-Hole-of-Calcutta-with-a-broken-doorlatch. Miss O'Cassidy looked triumphantly at her employer and asked him in a resounding voice, "*Naow* will you listen to me about that disgusting w.c.?" Philip regarded everyone with dislike and announced that he was going home.

His grandmother became so pathetically distraught, on hearing this, that he was persuaded to sit beside her and hold her hand, while with the other he grasped a large mug of beer the observant Elizabeth Lamb had quietly instructed the convivial Bix to fetch. Persis and Elizabeth Lamb roamed separately about, listening to various conversations and smiling ardently at everyone and beginning to be rather tired of the whole thing.

They met at the bar, where Paul offered them ginger-ale-on-the-rocks with the choice of an olive or a cherry in it. "How about a Kir?" Elizabeth Lamb asked. "Do you know how to make one?"

Paul smiled politely. "A Kir with soda water or with white wine, Miss Worthington?" he asked gently.

"With white wine," Persis answered eagerly. "Mine with soda, please," her cousin responded, adding to Persis: *"One* of us has got to keep her head, while we're in Northeast Harbor."

"Oh, Elizabeth Lamb," Persis giggled, "I drank lots of white wine in Europe this summer. And why do we have to keep our heads — you said yourself that nothing ever happens here."

The party went on. People wandered out to the terrace or went to sit beside the pool, or took short walks in the woods, as the company had done since it arrived. The exercise motivated many returns to the invigorating bar. Mr. de Amalfi earnestly announced that one could certainly tell this was a Bostonian Northeast Harbor cocktail party and not a Philadelphian one, because there was so much good talk. Mr. Walker looked dubious, but affably agreed.

Philip got loose from his grandmother, after consuming several reviving mugs of beer, and happily joined Dusty, who, having read the instructions that came with Isabella's present, was inserting the cords of various lamps into the plugs and causing them to go on and off. Loud applause greeted each effort.

With her usual perception, Isabella had attached herself to Bix, after a somewhat challenging glance at Cynthia. Cynthia drank and thought quietly for a while and then gracefully ascended the staircase, presumably to visit the upstairs bathroom. On her return, as she was halfway down the steps, she paused. Elizabeth Lamb saw her grasp her necklace and pull hard. Garnets tumbled through the air. All the men, Bix in the lead, scrambled to retrieve them, and Persis dutifully crawled after the ones that had disappeared under furniture. Cynthia, smiling appreciatively, made big eyes at all the gentlemen as she stood regally above them.

"Just like Mrs. Jack Gardiner!" exclaimed the energetic old lady whose name, Elizabeth Lamb had ascertained, was Mrs. Elise Faven. "She yanked apart a string of priceless pearls to get attention at a party. I have to hand it to your gal; she's clever," she admiringly assured Mrs. Hackley, by whose chair she had been standing recounting a long story.

Bix was now by Cynthia's side, counting her garnets for her. There appeared to be one missing. Cynthia asked Teddie if he would look for it, please, as she could tell he had very sharp eyes. Teddie took affront and Cordelia took him out, assuring Lem that Teddie had enjoyed himself immensely. Philip came back to his grandmother and began to discuss his psychiatrist with Mrs. Faven.

"The only thing is," he ended plaintively, "I always feel I must say something to entertain her. Cat is paying a fortune to find out *why* I fell down an elevator shaft, and I feel I must *entertain* the woman! And once, when she asked me how my grandfather died, I was trying to answer 'angina' and I came out with 'vag —' "

Mrs. Faven held up a commanding finger and sent him to obtain a double vodka for her, and advised him to have one himself. "Needs bucking up, that boy, Catherine," she observed. "Does he take any exercise, other than falling down elevator shafts?"

Mrs. Hackley took, not exercise, but umbrage, although she exercised herself to the extent of turning her head away and asking Elizabeth Lamb to get her a small piece of cheese on a plain biscuit. "And another sherry, dear," she requested, "if my daughter isn't looking."

Elizabeth Lamb smiled politely at both ladies and took Persis' hand and led her to the bar. Philip was leaning on it, earnestly explaining to Paul that he knew there must be *something* wrong with him, since when his psychiatrist asked him what his grandfather died of, he had answered. . . . Elizabeth Lamb looked to see if she were being watched by Mrs. Hackley, then quickly ushered Persis out to the terrace. They sank into chairs behind some bushes and breathed deeply of the fresh evening air. A number of guests were departing, with jovial thanks to their host, the ladies assuring him that he was perfectly sweet.

"I think all those people in there are slightly round the bend," Elizabeth Lamb told Persis, "though maybe the ones who had sense enough to leave early are slightly less so. What a zoo, as Daddy would say!" Persis, who had consumed two Kirs, agreed, blinking and swaying a bit from side to side.

"Let's take a walk," she said, "and maybe they'll all be gone by the time we get back. I think I'd like to go to bed early. Entertaining is *very* exhausting."

They slipped off the terrace. Dusk had not yet fallen, and the fog had lifted. "I've only been here once or twice, with Mummy and

Daddy and Gus," Persis said, "and then I had to sit out here by the pool and be polite.

"I've never even seen the cove. Could we go there tomorrow? I really don't much like pools."

They walked to the edge of the cliff. The sky above the Western Way was a beautiful deep pink. "It will be red by sunset," Elizabeth Lamb said. "That means a good day tomorrow. Come over here, Persis, and I'll show you the beach. It's just a little way along the cliff. Open your mouth and breathe in and out. You shouldn't have had two Kirs."

Dutifully, Persis breathed ardently, as instructed. Elizabeth Lamb followed her along the path, kicking rocks noisily from custom. Persis stopped suddenly. She began to breathe in quick little gasps.

"Oh, Persis," her cousin said wearily, "you have *got* to watch your drinking habits. Sit down."

"No; it's not that. Come here, Elizabeth Lamb. There's a man down there on the beach, sleeping or something. He looks — funny."

Below them, moved slightly back and forth in the shallow water by the receding tide, were two objects. One was a small boat, the other a man, face down. He was barefoot and had black curly hair. He was wearing white swimming shorts and a dark red sweater.

"Look at his head," Persis said. "It's turned way over to one side. There's something wrong with him. And he's got to be swallowing water, if he's alive."

"Yes," Elizabeth Lamb said, grimly. "Take off your shoes and socks. We have to go down and see. I'll go first."

They splashed barefoot through the water. Elizabeth Lamb gently touched the man's hand. It was stiff, and very cold. "Help me turn him over," she said.

It was, of course, the trespasser she had seen before lunch. His eyes were open and they held a look of faint surprise. His head, as they turned him, had remained to one side.

"He's dead. And he's younger than I thought he was; at least, he looks younger now. Help me pull him out of the water. There.

"Stop that, Persis! If you throw up, I'll never speak to you again. We've got to tell Cousin Lem. We must go up that ladder, and it's worse going up than coming down. Take in air slowly, through your mouth, and don't look below. I'm right behind you."

Their wet hands and feet were slippery on the iron ladder. At the top, Elizabeth Lamb cast one last look at the pathetic figure on the sand and then caught hold of Persis' dress and pulled her away.

As they ran, stumbling over pine cones and sticks and rocks, she said unsteadily, "He's awfully young to be dead. And if we hadn't come, the tide would have taken him out and banged him back and forth on the rocks beside the opening and — and . . . 'On the rocks.' Oh, Persis, I will never be able to stand hearing anybody say that, ever again!"

• CHAPTER 4 •

Wake, and Remember,
and Understand

BREATHLESS AND SWEATING, Persis and Elizabeth Lamb arrived on the terrace. The General was in the doorway, happily speeding more guests on their way. He ignored Elizabeth Lamb's tug at his sleeve. Chubby Cooke stood beaming beside Lem, glass in hand. As Elizabeth Lamb turned to him, he abstractedly patted her head. The children pushed past the two and entered the cottage in a rush, only to stand indecisively once they were in.

Few guests remained, compared to a half-hour before. Mrs. Hackley and Mrs. Faven were in animated conversation. Bix, Cynthia, Dusty, and Philip were playing a loud skittles foursome, watched by Colleen and Perkie.

Isabella emerged from the powder room, after some violent manipulations of its doorknob and a few lady-like screams that had been pitched to carry a hundred feet or more. "Really, Lem," she called, "even if one could get out without damaging one's wrists and elbows, one could lose oneself forever in there. Have you ever thought of putting more than a 25-watt bulb in that dungeon?" Colleen looked both annoyed and pleased and opened her mouth to speak.

"Cousin Lem," Elizabeth Lamb said loudly, "there's a dead boy on the beach. Do you hear me, Cousin Lem?" Persis abruptly sat down on the floor.

Stumbling over Persis, and cursing under his breath because of it, the General came in, followed by Mr. Cooke. "Heh-heh," he said. "That's not funny, Elizabeth Lamb."

"I'm not trying to be funny. It's the boy I told you about after lunch. He's still there, and he's dead."

The General looked at her as he might have gazed at a lowly Marine boot who had dared to lift his eyes and regard him. "Dead on the beach? I don't know why anybody would want to die on a beach, unless there was a war on. And why the hell on *my* beach?"

"I don't know. He said he thought he might have met you, though. Maybe that's why?"

The General was too furious to answer. Ludwig came quickly in from the kitchen, followed by the caterer, packed and ready to depart. "Shall I go see, General?" he asked quietly.

"Better be two," Mr. Cooke advised. "I've read about things like this. In all those mystery books every time there's a beach, there's a body on it." He picked up a stout walking-stick from a stand by the door and marched after Ludwig, waving the stick and muttering, "Just in case —" Bix ran to join them, saying, "Three's better than two."

"Cousin Lem," Elizabeth Lamb said wearily, "the boy is there and he's dead. You should call the police." She sank to the floor beside Persis.

The General's tanned, spare face was white around the nostrils. "Make me a Scotch, would you, Paul? And then you'd better clear out. No sense your getting mixed up in this, if it's true."

"General," Paul said seriously, as he produced the drink, "I'll stay, if I can be any help. I have no dinner engagement tonight. I'll just call my mother, so she won't worry."

The General drank quickly. "No, no," he replied, his voice steadier. "We're all right. Nothing you could do. You had barely got here when Elizabeth Lamb told me about someone on the beach, and you were with Ludwig till the guests arrived, isn't that right? And then you were busier than hell, so what could you tell the police? Better make a quick and honourable retreat while I phone them." He went to his study.

"But General," Paul called after him, "I wasn't with Ludwig all the time. He had to go out once or twice to get —" The study door was kicked shut. Paul shrugged and left, with an uneasy smile at the company.

"Come, Perkie," Isabella said shrilly, "we are going now. I have no intention of being subjected to questions and questions about some derelict body on a beach. I've been through things like this twice before; that wretched child has a perfect talent for disaster."

She swept out, followed apologetically by her friend. "You never found a body before, Elizabeth Lamb," Persis earnestly assured her cousin. "Aunt Isabella can be so mean, sometimes." She helped Elizabeth Lamb to her feet, urged her gently into a chair, and turned to Miss O'Cassidy. "I'll make her some tea," she said, "if you'll show me where things are. She's had a shock and hot tea with sugar is very good for that. We learned it in First-Aid Class."

Colleen had been staring thoughtfully after Isabella. "Doesn't like coppers much, now does she?" she mused. "Oh, well, can't say I blame her." She started for the kitchen. "Good-oh," she said to Persis. "Tea it is. I'll make some for everybody. Best thing for us."

"Oh," Mrs. Hackley had finally found her voice, "someone is dead on Lem's beach? I *knew* it would come to this! Elizabeth Lamb, why did you tell him anyone was there? Now the police will come and ask questions about — everything." She looked accusingly at her daughter. "Cynthia, I've warned you —"

"Cat, dear," Philip interrupted quietly, "I'm sure it was an accident. Just relax. And don't tell them things they're not here to find out." He began to speak quietly to his mother, who raised her eyebrows and listened patronizingly. The rest of the company sat silent and glum, for what seemed a long time.

The General returned, carrying the study telephone. He plugged it into a wall jack by the skittles table and sank into a chair beside it. "Well, they're coming," he said. "If they want to make calls, I'd like to know what they say." He turned angrily to Mrs. Hackley: "I heard you, Catherine. Dammit, I didn't do anything! Now, don't you go on and on to them about the cannon, and all that sort of thing. 'No names; no pack-drill,' as the Brits say. Just relax."

Elizabeth Lamb was beginning to feel better. "Mrs. Hackley, the man was on *your* part of the beach when I saw him first. Cousin Lem didn't do a thing, I'm sure. He promised."

"Oh, my!" Mrs. Hackley was daunted. "Well, no need to mention that, or everything else we know, as Lem and Philip so wisely advise. Just relax, dear," she added with a half-smile, the only sign of humour Elizabeth Lamb had ever seen in her.

Two uniformed policemen joined them suddenly. Colleen, carrying the tea tray, took a step backward into the kitchen. "Good evening, General; where's the body you found?" one asked abruptly.

"I'll show them the way," Elizabeth Lamb volunteered. "No," the General said firmly, "you stay out of this. Chub" — Mr. Cooke had appeared behind the officers — "would you go back down there with these men?"

Mr. Cooke was red and breathing hard, still clutching his stick. He groaned as he bent to place the little girls' shoes and socks on the floor, then turned on his heel, beckoning the policemen to follow.

Colleen, somehow recognizing authority, placed the tea things before Mrs. Faven. Philo Gaynor, carrying a rifle, knocked on a pane of the open door. "Anybody to home?" he asked with some redundance.

"What d'you want?" demanded Lem, who was fortifying himself with another Scotch. "For God's sake, are you planning to shoot somebody? That's all we need."

"Told you," said Philo, "I'd git anybody who interfered with my stuff. Somebody knocked over a handsome ice-box I brung home for Gloria, stove it all to hell. One of them flatlanders you had here drinkin', I s'pose. Now I seen the pigs' car come in. What's up? A man's got to know, to defend hisself."

"Get the hell out of here," the General roared. "Nothing that concerns you is up. Go clear away that mess in my parking area!"

"Excuse me," Cynthia put in, "but, Elise, you must not give Mother sugar in her tea. Here are the tablets she uses."

"Do you suppose," said Mrs. Faven, ignoring both the new arrival and her host, "the young man was running on the beach and hurt himself? Running is *so* dangerous, as this deluded generation will realize, if it should live to reach my age. Their hip sockets will be quite degenerated, not to mention the bones in their heels. Now, walking —"

"Why, Elise," Cynthia asked impatiently, "should anyone try to run on so small a beach? Milk in mine, please."

"Somebody got hurt on the beach?" Philo inquired, shifting his wad of tobacco in preparation for a long conversation. He was nipped in the bud by Mr. Cooke, re-appearing again, with Ludwig and Bix and one of the policemen behind him. "Is that my rifle?" he demanded of Philo. "Dammit, I told you to stay off my place."

Philo looked apprehensively at the policeman, whom Ludwig was ushering to the phone in the kitchen. "No, it ain't," he answered, beginning to look put-upon. "This here's my own .32 Winchester. Why sh'd it be yours? Guess I'll leave, seein' as how I'm not welcome. You could be jest a dite more pleasant to a hard-workin' man." He backed out, but lingered near the terrace door.

"Why was Philo talking about pigs?" Mrs. Hackley quavered. "No one keeps pigs here." Mrs. Faven informed her in a loud tone that the police were so termed by criminals. Philo disappeared.

"It had better *not* be my gun," said Mr. Cooke, thirstily drinking the tea Mrs. Faven handed him. "Well, as he said," she answered, "why should it be? If he stole yours, he surely would not be walking around with it. The man is shrewd, I've always noticed."

"Left my Winchester out in my rock garden," Mr. Cooke answered. "Took a few shots at some of these damned gulls just before I came over here. Dropping mussels on it as though it was going out of style. They're the ruination of a garden. As to what they do to my roses, the messy mongrels, I cannot begin —"

"Mr. Cooke, it's against the law to shoot seagulls," Persis informed him, too loudly for his comfort.

"Well," rumbled Mr. Cooke, eyeing the oblivious man in the kitchen, "let's not talk about it just now, hey? But" — lower — "my roses take prizes, and not ten of those scrawny, bug-ridden scavengers are worth one rose.

"Well, sir," he said, turning to the policeman who now joined them, "what's going on?"

The policeman considered. "There's the body of a young man on your beach," he said to the General, "and —"

"My God!" came from Mr. Cooke. "We *know* there's a body on the beach. I saw it. What —"

"Not *my* beach," said Lem loudly. He jerked a thumb towards Mrs. Hackley. "Hers, too, and I want to —"

"Lem, dear." Mrs. Hackley was plaintive. "We shouldn't interrupt the gentleman — with things he doesn't really need to know," she ended pointedly.

"Go on, Buster," Mrs. Faven directed quietly.

"— *and*," the policeman continued, now addressing Mrs. Faven, to whom he gave a brief but polite nod of recognition, "the death appears to be of a suspicious nature." He held up an authoritative hand as the General opened his mouth.

"So I told the chief, and he called the District Attorney and the Medical Examiner in Bar Harbor, and they're coming over. Chief says he'd like for you all to stay here till they show up. Don't know how long that'll be. You can always get a D.A. right off but them Medical Examiners are the last to arrive, most every time."

"So we sit here all night?" Lem asked angrily. "Don't know why we fight the Reds; we might as well be in Russia."

"General," Bix said quietly, "what else have we got to do? Dusty and I have no performance tonight, and the rest of you surely —"

"You two could always go over and do some of your damned practicing," snarled the General.

Bix smiled politely, as usual. Dusty was moved to utter another whole sentence. "Do you mind if I have a drink?" he asked, with a civil hesitation before he went to the kitchen.

"Somebody else might show up sooner," the policeman offered. "The chief also called the State Police in Orono; they're in charge of homicides down here —"

"Homicides?" Mr. Cooke asked sharply. "How do you know it was murder? And what's that other feller doing?"

"He's staying beside the body, sir, like one of us is supposed to. And it seems like the boy was killed, either by accident or on purpose, so it's no doubt homicide. I didn't say 'twas murder."

"Isn't suicide considered a homicide, too?" Elizabeth Lamb asked, with interest.

The officer regarded her with respect. "But it don't look like he could have broke his own neck, not on purpose, so —" He quickly closed his mouth.

"Then he died of a broken neck?" Philip asked shrewdly.

"That's for the M.E. to say," the policeman answered. "Alls else I can tell you is that Orono said one of their detectives is down here. Lives over on the backside of the island and had a couple of days off. They told him to head right over."

"What!" said Lem. "How many more of you are due?"

Two men appeared on the terrace, one carrying a black leather bag. The officer turned, with some relief, and led them toward the path to the beach.

Colleen, sighing loudly, collected the tea apparatus and joined Dusty in the kitchen, as did Cynthia. Mrs. Hackley suddenly put her hand to her breast and leaned heavily back in her chair, her face drained of colour. "Catherine," said Mrs. Faven, jumping spryly up, "I'm calling your doctor. He can be here in five minutes."

"Do it. Quickly!" said Philip. "It's her heart again. Are the ampules in your bag, Cat?"

"No, no," Mrs. Hackley said weakly. "It's not my heart; I don't need them. Just the smelling salts, dear. I only feel a little faint, that's all."

Philip rubbed his grandmother's hands as Elizabeth Lamb held the small bottle under Mrs. Hackley's delicate nose. The sharp scent of ammonia mixed with lavender reminded Elizabeth Lamb of *her* grandmother who had carried smelling salts since she was a young girl, and who sometimes produced them when her granddaughters were tired or upset. She smiled at Mrs. Hackley, who smiled back, almost her normal self again. Persis, awakened from a half-sleep on the sofa, smiled too.

"I think I'll just go wash my face and hands in cold water," Mrs.

Hackley said, rising quite steadily. "Not in there!" Colleen called firmly, advancing with a large pink gin as Mrs. Hackley walked slowly toward the powder room. "That place would make you take another turn. Here, naow, I'll help you to the one upstairs." She set down her glass.

"No, no," Mrs. Hackley said with a slight shudder. "I can't go up that staircase, dear. I have no head for heights. This one will be fine."

Philip regarded the closed washroom door anxiously, while the rest of the company rose and stretched, and called out their drink orders to Ludwig. He had been in his bedroom, off the kitchen, for some time, and now appeared among them immaculate as ever, his fair *en brosse* hair recently brushed and his white jacket and black trousers exchanged for the starched khaki shirt and pants the General preferred him to wear on all but the most formal occasions.

He asked Elizabeth Lamb if she would like some *café au lait,* her favourite beverage. His very light blue eyes were kind and concerned, and she assured him she would, although she had very little appetite for anything. "Strange," she thought, "I never noticed how light Ludwig's eyes were. Where did I read that most murderers have pale blue eyes?" With a shiver, she suppressed her thoughts and went to help Mrs. Hackley open the washroom door, which was vibrating from her feeble kicks and rattling of the latch.

Philip was there before her. "Really," he said, "General Alison should get this fixed. Are you all right, Cat, dear?"

"I'm fine," Mrs. Hackley quavered, "but, oh, Lem, that really is a dreadful, dreadful room. If you had a wife" — her eyes twinkled faintly — "she'd make you brighten it up. I'm going to bring over a scroll or two, for those drab walls. And you must get a new screen for the window; that old one is all holes. And as for the light in there —"

"Eggsactly!" said Colleen, with fervour. She took a gulp of her gin and turned on the General. "I've been telling him," she announced to Mrs. Hackley, "and telling AND telling —"

Lem marched to them and began heatedly to dispute their suggestions. Everyone except Bix and Ludwig and Elizabeth Lamb were so engrossed in the entertainment that a tall, thin young man standing in the terrace doorway went unnoticed. Bix and Ludwig went quietly over to him. "Yes?" said Ludwig.

"Lieutenant Alfred Higgins, State Police," said the man, displaying a leather wallet. "You're —"

"I'm Bix Baxter; I live here. I'll show you where they are," Bix said softly. "This way."

Both Ludwig and Elizabeth Lamb went to the terrace and looked thoughtfully after them. "Did he say his name was Higgins, Ludwig?" she asked. "I think I met him once."

Now Ludwig looked thoughtfully at her. A fat, elderly man carrying a black bag rounded the corner of the house. "Are you from the police?" Ludwig asked.

"Why the hell should I be? I'm Mrs. Hackley's doctor. Where is she? Quick, man!"

Ludwig's attempt to answer was submerged in a series of loud sneezes. "She's right in there," Elizabeth Lamb directed, "but she seems better."

She and Ludwig followed the doctor in, Ludwig blowing his nose into an immaculate white handkerchief. "Your cold is so much worse," she said. "I think the doctor should look at *you*, not Mrs. Hackley. Have you got aspirin?" "I don't think so," Ludwig answered thickly, through the handkerchief.

She waited in the kitchen while he rummaged around in the little lavatory in a corner of his bedroom. "No, I don't," he called. "Could you find me some, Elizabeth Lamb?" As she went up to the General's bathroom, Mrs. Hackley was spiritedly expostulating with her doctor.

"My dear Cyrus," she said, "I am perfectly well. A slight attack of giddiness; you know I often have them. There was no reason at all to inconvenience you."

"Now, now, Catherine," said the old man. "Your friend was upset. Let's just have a look at you." He glanced around.

"Want to use my room, doctor?" Colleen inquired. "It's down here, right beside the General's study." She made as if to help Mrs. Hackley to rise. Bix returned, and went discreetly into the kitchen, where Dusty joined him.

"No!" Mrs. Hackley said sharply. "Just check me over quickly, dear Cyrus, if you must, and then get back to your dinner. It will be dark soon and I know how you hate driving after dusk."

The doctor put his stethoscope to Mrs. Hackley's black silk chest, nodding portentously. He placed his blood pressure cuff around her arm and used his stethoscope again. He delicately separated her lids and looked into her eyes. "Well, Catherine," he said, "your heart is as steady as — usual. Have you been taking your insulin and sticking to your diet — and no alcohol, hey?"

Mrs. Hackley nodded vigourously. Cynthia came nearer. "Doctor Phillips," she began. "*Iie*, Cynthia," Mrs. Hackley said quickly, and followed with a firm, rapid, unintelligible speech. Bix, who was hovering in the kitchen doorway, raised his eyebrows and smiled. Cynthia walked over to him, sighing.

"But, Cyrus," Mrs. Hackley went on, now speaking English, "I did forget to have my shot this morning. Philip often gives it to me, but I had to send him to Augusta — and — and I just forgot to take it."

The doctor shook his head and delved into his bag again. "Then we'd just better have one now," he said. "But here?" Mrs. Hackley quavered. "Dear" — to Colleen — "*could* we use your room?"

"Nonsense, Catherine," said Dr. Phillips, "we can do it in your arm this time; sooner, the better. Let's see; you're taking the NPH stuff now, aren't you?" He put back into his bag the colourless bottle he had been rolling between his palms, and selected another. He went through the exacting procedure of sterilizing the bottle top and the patient's arm, and then measured a dosage of insulin. Some of the company averted their eyes. Mrs. Hackley showed no reaction at all at the plunge of the needle and the disappearance of the cloudy liquid into her arm, but Persis, who had remained nearby, gasped. "Oh, my," she said, "you're brave! I hate shots."

"I am quite used to them, by now," Mrs. Hackley smiled. "They don't really hurt, dear. Oh," to Elizabeth Lamb, who had come down, with Lem's aspirin, "I don't really need that, Elizabeth Lamb. But thank you."

The medical crisis over, Mrs. Faven, who had been standing protectively behind her friend and, for some reason, fanning her with a cocktail napkin, sat down beside her and eyed her severely. "*I*," she announced, "think it a great mistake to call a professional person by

95

his first name, and worse to allow him to call you by yours. My husband was quite a stickler for professional behaviour; why, whenever he visited a new doctor who asked him something like, 'And what can I do for you, Curtis?', my husband looked straight at him. Then he would rise slowly and examine all the diplomas on the office wall, then sit down and say something like, 'Well, it's this way, Tom —' And those Toms — or Dicks — or Harrys called him 'Mr. Faven' when next they spoke!"

Dr. Phillips, packing up his bag, looked hurt. Lem and Chubby Cooke emerged from refuge in the study. "Heh-heh," Lem said, and then quickly asked the doctor, "Have a drink? Got some awfully good brandy. And how about a cigar? Friend of mine based at Guantanamo sends me some real ones. Only good thing to come out of Cuba nowadays."

The doctor was placated. Elizabeth Lamb provided Ludwig, whose eyes were now streaming as he opened the brandy bottle, with the aspirin. Mrs. Faven went to the phone in the living room. "I was to dine with a friend," she explained. "I must tell her I won't be able to make it." Just as she reached the instrument it rang, and at the same moment the television blared into sight and sound. "Good heavens!" Mrs. Faven exclaimed. "It's still plugged into that outfit the guest brought," Dusty explained, turning off the set. "The directions say that any sound of a certain frequency near the plugs will activate it."

Mrs. Faven answered the phone and then made her own call while the gentlemen drank brandy and happily puffed on the only good thing to come out of Cuba nowadays. Persis and Elizabeth Lamb were given their hot drink in the kitchen. Cynthia and her son went out to the terrace, and engaged themselves in conversation. Lem and Chubby Cooke explained as much as they knew of the situation to the doctor.

Colleen seated herself beside Mrs. Hackley, who began to give her advice about her complexion. "You have such fair skin, dear," she said. "You should take care of it, and guard against sunburn. Don't you use any cosmetic but lipstick?" Colleen assured her that she did not muck about with anything but a good face cream, and that most Aussies felt as she did about poisoning your system with cosmetics, all of which had dangerous lead in them.

"Oh, but a bit of powder, dear?" Mrs. Hackley quavered. "I have some fine, pure rice powder I get from Japan; let me bring you over some when I bring the scrolls, and a vase, perhaps, to brighten up that dreadful room." Colleen declared she could bring anything she liked, and maybe some deluded old tr — old person would make use of it, but she certainly wouldn't. "A bit of Helena Rubenstein cream's what does me," she asserted.

"Oh," said Mrs. Hackley, "do they have things like that in Australia?" Colleen promptly took offense and went into a long story of how, when Mme. Rubenstein was a young girl, she had been an immigrant to Australia from middle Europe, where her relatives were pharmacists, and that the creams she provided the Australian women from secret family formulas were what made them known as the world's most beautiful. "So that Rubenstein stuff is gum-nut Aussie," she concluded. Mrs. Hackley was impressed, as Elizabeth Lamb, sipping her coffee in the kitchen doorway, noticed, and regarded her informant with a lively interest.

Colleen began to speak quietly and earnestly, with many smiles, to Mrs. Hackley, who no longer seemed impressed. She regarded Miss O'Cassidy with trepidation as well as distaste, murmured that she had very little money and her trustees supervised her expenditures, and rose to visit the powder room again. "Probably telling her that she and Cynthia should switch to something expensive to improve their looks, which aren't gum-nut," thought Elizabeth Lamb, with amusement, observing that Mrs. Hackley had remembered to leave the powder room door open a crack.

Cynthia and her son came in, looking annoyed with each other. Mrs. Faven finished her long explanation to her friend and left the phone, announcing that the incoming call had been from the Medical Examiner's wife, who wanted to let him know that another doctor had taken over for him in Bar Harbor, and that he was now off-call for the evening. "She says to tell him to hurry back, so that they can make the late movie," Mrs. Faven said. "I know her, a sweet girl; her husband is my doctor. I didn't recognize him when he went by so fast."

The doctor entered, following the policeman. "Good evening, Dr.

Bailey," Mrs. Faven greeted him. "All finished, Buster? May we go now?"

Buster was at the kitchen phone. "I'm going to call to have the body removed, now that the doctor's finished, Mrs. Faven. The D.A. just left. But the detective would like to ask you all a few questions before he goes."

"Where the hell is he?" the General demanded. "I don't see any detective."

The policeman was speaking to the funeral home. The doctor, a tired-looking young man, sank into a chair. "He's still down on the beach," he answered. "He photographed the body, and the scene, while it still was light enough and he's just sitting there now, writing in his notebook. He should be up soon.

"I'd like to use your phone next, General," he went on, "to see if there are any calls for me; certainly hope not."

"He's taking enough time to write *War and Peace*," the General irascibly observed. "Heh-heh. He'd better get here soon. I've got more to do than answer questions about some poor devil I never heard of."

Leaving, the policeman turned and spoke with some sarcasm. "How'd you know you never heard of him? We don't even know who he is, and you didn't see the body, did you now?"

The General stamped away for another drink. "You don't need to call, Dr. Bailey. Dear Julia says you're off-duty for this evening," Mrs. Faven informed him, not completely truthfully. "You sit right there and tell us about that poor young man. You've got to satisfy the curiosity of your oldest patient, you know."

"Yes, Chris," said Dr. Phillips. "The General's got some excellent brandy, so just relax a bit and let us in on what you know. That's an order. I'm your senior officer, so to speak. Got quite a few years on you."

The young doctor frowned, but a sip of the brandy Ludwig handed him caused a lightening of his countenance. "Well —" he began slowly; "I suppose I *could* tell what I know, which isn't much. There was no identification on the body. We don't know who the boy was, as the officer said, nor where he might have come from."

"Nor what he was doing dying on my beach?" the General roared.

The doctor looked as if he were both regretting the General's hospitality and as if he were too exhausted to leave it. "I wonder why they didn't call you in, Cy?" he asked. "You're an M.E., too. I've had a terrible day and only four hours sleep last night."

"The chief knew I was at a meeting in Portland all day," the old doctor answered, "and that I'm too ancient a party to traipse around beaches in the dark. Nice to live in a small town — finally. Glad I left Philadelphia and took up practice here."

" 'On the whole,' " Dusty muttered, in a creditable imitation of the voice of the immortal W. C. Fields, " 'right now, I'd rather be in Philadelphia.' " He was heard by only Elizabeth Lamb, since the literal Persis spoke simultaneously with him: "It's only just getting dark *now*, doctor."

"How long was the body on the beach?" Mrs. Faven asked. "Do tell us! You know we'll be discreet."

Dr. Bailey accepted another brandy. "Well," he began, "rigor mortis is a tricky thing."

"I thought it fairly complete four to six hours after death?" Bix questioned. "It takes six to ten hours for full rigor, doesn't it? How advanced is it?" Everyone looked at him. "I — used to be a medical student," he explained, with his usual pleasant smile.

"You always hear that, but that criterion of six to ten hours is based on room temperature, where most homicides occur," Dr. Phillips informed him. "Saw a lot of 'em in Philadelphia. But what about the fellow on the beach, Chris? It was quite cool down there, wasn't it?"

"Well, I'd say that the rigor is such that death occurred around four or five hours before I saw him, and I got here just a little after seven. He might have been mur — might have died sometime near two or three this afternoon. Can't put it much closer because of the damned water; he was most likely partially in it while the tide was in, and cool water inhibits the onset of rigor, you know. So death *might* have been earlier, or even as *late* as five-thirty or thereabouts, if he'd been — moved just before I got here. That ocean water has thrown me right off."

"But not before one?" Mr. Cooke asked. "I was in plain sight of my housekeeper from noon till I came over here, just after five."

"I saw the boy alive around twelve-thirty," Elizabeth Lamb offered.

"What — what did the poor young man die of?" murmured Mrs. Hackley, who had joined the interrogating party.

"His neck's broken; that's for sure," the doctor answered, "but I can't say definitely that was the cause of death. The body will go to Bangor for an autopsy; they'll be here to get it any minute."

"If he just had a heart attack and died, while he was climbing the ladder, maybe, would the autopsy show that?" Bix asked. "Perhaps he did, and the fall broke his neck."

"It would be hard to decide," the doctor answered thoughtfully, "though the chances are that such a young and apparently healthy person wouldn't have suffered heart failure. He doesn't appear to have had a head blow, either, before death, but there are some bruises on his face and neck; possibly from a fall, though. Could have fallen from the top of the cliff, somehow, and broken his neck. We'll just have to wait for the autopsy, and the X-rays, and all the rest of it." He began to rise.

"Do you know, Dr. Bailey," Mrs. Faven said chattily, firmly pushing him back into the chair, "I was reading, once, that when one is doing *very* violent exercise, rigor is already starting in the body. Could that be true? And if the young man had been running for a long time, or jumping, just before he died, then rigor would advance sooner. He could have died a lot later than you think — only an hour before you saw him, perhaps. Or so I read."

"Elise," said Cynthia, "I wish you would get over this idea you have that this person was running and leaping on the damned beach. It would be most unlikely. God," she finished, "I wish I had some pot, if we're going to sit here all night."

"Cynthia!" exclaimed her mother, looking anxiously at the two doctors.

"For God's sake, Mother," Cynthia said. "I have a prescription for it — did you think I get it from pushers? Dr. Noyes in Palm Beach wants me to use it, for my incipient glaucoma, you know," she finished blandly. "Stop worrying about nothing."

"You do have a prescription?" Mrs. Hackley joyfully asked. "Oh, my dear, I've been so worried. As long as you have just the amount called for, I'm sure it will be all right." The doctors looked at each other, with smiles and lifted brows.

Cynthia laughed heartily. "Well, I wouldn't quite say that all I have is —" "Oh!" cried Mrs. Hackley, looking about to weep. "Mother, stop *dwelling* on it," her daughter requested.

"This is getting as long as a snake's liver," Colleen muttered. "Where the hell is that detective?"

The mention of the detective got Dr. Bailey to his feet. "Thank you for the brandy, General," he said. "I'd better be getting back to Bar Harbor. Goodnight, everyone."

"Wait, Chris," Dr. Phillips said, reluctantly setting down his brandy snifter. "I've got to leave, too. Want to ask you a question or two, though.

"Now, Catherine, you be a good girl; Philip, be sure she behaves. Good-night."

Ludwig, obviously in discomfort and snuffling loudly, began to make sandwiches in the ensuing silence. Persis turned on the television. Colleen left for her room. Elizabeth Lamb went out to the terrace.

She sat in the darkness, observing the last faint glow of red in the western sky, and thought of the dead boy. "It's as though we just had his wake," she said aloud, softly, "maybe all the wake he'll ever have. What was it I was reading this morning, in that poetry book? 'Wake, and remember, and understand.'

"But he'll never wake. And I guess we'll never understand. I wonder, though, if there is something I should remember?"

• CHAPTER 5 •

... *What Is The Question*

T HE VOICE from the edge of the terrace was slow and quiet. "Well, if it isn't Elizabeth Lamb. And all grown up, too. Now, what are you doing over here, leaving the backside all on its lonesome?"

"Buzzie!" Elizabeth exclaimed, running to him. "It is you! I'm so glad!"

Lieutenant Alfred Higgins was much changed from when she had first met him when he was but a part-time deputy sheriff in Seal Cove. He was not so thin, nor did his eyes blink nervously. He had abandoned his crooked, wire-rimmed spectacles for a pair with heavy, dark frames, from behind which his pale eyes regarded her steadily. His tweed jacket was well-cut, and his polished tan brogues obviously expensive. He put his photographic apparatus on a terrace chair and smiled at her.

"Yep," he said. "You're looking at a graduate of the Maine Criminal Justice Academy. Been a detective for a time now — might know as much about crime some day as you do. I heard what you did over to Bar Harbor this summer; chief there doesn't spread it around, out of deference to the lady, but he's a friend of mine."

Elizabeth Lamb did not like to remember the part of the summer she had spent in Bar Harbor. "They're waiting inside for you, Buzzie."

"I'd like to talk to you private sometime; maybe tomorrow, when I'll be coming back. It's not often I find an expert witness right on the scene, so to speak," Buzzie answered.

His entrance into *Iwo Jima* provoked, first, relief and then apprehension. "About time!" Lem announced. "I'm General Lemuel Otis Alison, young man, and these are my friends. What d'you want to know?"

"This is Lieutenant Higgins, Cousin Lem," Elizabeth Lamb said, reprovingly. "Perhaps you've seen him when you've been over to Grandmother's camp. He lives near there.

"And couldn't we all sit down? Buzzie would like to talk to you a minute."

"Better be a minute," the General responded, as most of the company grouped themselves around Buzzie. Ludwig, appearing pale and unwell, leaned heavily against the kitchen doorjamb. Philip stood behind his grandmother's chair, with his hands lightly on her shoulders. "And what's this 'Buzzie'?" asked the General. "Are you acquainted with the feller?"

"We're old friends," the Lieutenant said easily. "Hello there, Persis. I met these young ladies three years ago, when that Mrs. Parker, who had the cottage next to Mrs. Worthington's, was killed."

He took out a pen and opened his notebook. "This is just an informal inquiry, seeing as how the dead boy was found on this property, and possibly some of you might have known him, or known why he was here. Of course, the whole thing could be accident; not just his death, but that he happened to die here, not knowing any of you at all."

"Trespassers are always invading *our*" — with a glance at the General — "beach," Mrs. Hackley said quite firmly. "I'm not surprised that one finally died there."

Buzzie seemed a bit amazed at her assumption that trespassers sooner or later die on property they are violating, but quietly obtained her name and then listed the names of the others present, along with the brief descriptions of them he received.

"Now," he said, "they're using a motor launch to remove the body. It seemed simpler, and the hearse is waiting across the harbour. We don't know who the deceased was. Does this description ring a bell with any of you? 'About six feet tall, weight around one-sixty, age probably in early twenties, black eyes, black curly hair, dark skin. No scars or other distinguishing features, no jewelry, wore heavy, dark red pullover sweater and white cotton bathing trunks, carried only an oilskin bag containing nothing but some residue of what is probably marijuana.' " He glanced around questioningly.

"Was the feller a black?" the General asked.

"Why, no." Buzzie was apologetic. "Guess I should've listed 'Caucausian.' "

"Because if he were black, he could be the son of a friend of mine; known him since Guadalcanal — the father, not the son, of course," the General answered as Colleen muttered, "Oh, God. Here we go with more ancient history."

"Sounds just like David," the General went on, "except he's too smart to use marijuana, but he could have been up here and decided to look me up. But since it wasn't he, and I don't know who the devil it was and it seems nobody else here does, either, are we done, hey?"

"Well, General," Buzzie said politely, "I'd just like you all to tolerate a few more questions. They'd help us place where everyone was when death occurred, or so I hope."

"For God's sake!" Mr. Cooke was exasperated. "Why us? Anybody might have rowed into that cove and killed the boy. Or even swum in! When you find out who he was, you'll find out who his enemies were. Simple as that." He beamed complacently at his listeners.

"There were a lot of people around here this afternoon," Colleen offered, in, for her, a diffident manner. "We were having a party, and the guests wandered in and out of the house. Maybe one was some kind of a habitual killer; some of 'em certainly were strange enough."

"A party," Buzzie said glumly. "Of course, there *would* have been a party." He looked reproachfully at Elizabeth Lamb. "Why do all your relatives have so many parties?"

"Because they're up here on vacation, Buzzie. But why don't we tell where we were, and get it over? After I saw him on the beach, around twelve-thirty —"

"What!" Buzzie exclaimed. "You saw him when he was alive?"

"Well, of course. I told him to go away and he said he was just resting from his row. He said he had to go to work as a waiter in an hour or so."

"What else did he say? Did he mention anybody by name? Or any place?"

Elizabeth Lamb thought. "He said he was a Native, but I think he was teasing me." She looked sideways at her cousin and spoke reluctantly: "And he said he might have met Cousin Lem, but he didn't seem sure, Buzzie. Not sure at all. And that's all he said."

"My God!" said the General. "Talk about a serpent's tooth!"

"This lady your daughter?" Buzzie asked him quickly, nodding at Miss O'Cassidy. "I didn't understand if 'twas Miss, or Missus, O'Cassidy. Would either one of you have a list of the party guests?"

Colleen sniggered. The General's face turned an interesting shade of puce. "Miss O'Cassidy is my secretary," he said stiffly. "We know, of course, who was invited, don't we, my dear" — Colleen nodded, suppressing her mirth — "but that wouldn't be of much use, since there were, also, a bunch of damned free-loaders. Those Philadelphia people think they can drag along anybody they please.

"Colleen, the party list is in my study. Would you get it? Give him something to chew on, besides us. And, Ludwig, Mrs. Hackley is shivering; please light the fire."

Philip also left the group and walked quickly toward the powder room. He seemed to consider, and altered course for the stairway. His grandmother watched his ascent anxiously.

Buzzie folded the paper Colleen handed him and put it in his pocket. "The party began at what time?" he asked.

"Now, Ludwig, please make everyone some coffee," the General interrupted. "And let's get this damned thing over. Everybody speak up, in turn. I'll go first.

"The blasted affair," he turned to Buzzie, "began at, say, five. And everyone except those present had gone by — oh, probably, seven.

Anyone at all could have skinned down to the beach and bashed the boy over the head. I was right here the whole time, and had been since we lunched, around one. That's all I know. Now you, Colleen."

"Wait just a minute, please," Buzzie requested. "Why do you say 'bashed over the head,' General?"

"Figure of speech, for God's sake? Now, are you through with me?"

"And you state you were inside the cottage the whole time?"

"Said so, didn't I? I 'said' it; I didn't 'state' it. I'm not on trial yet, sir. Heh-heh."

Persis demurred. "Oh, no, Cousin Lem. When Miss O'Cassidy left me here, you were out walking. Don't you remember that your shoes were wet, and you changed them?"

"*Another* serpent's tooth," Lem muttered, and then said loudly: "I was walking in the woods, for maybe ten minutes. I did not go near the beach. I did not see anyone at all during my walk. And I am not going to say another word unless my lawyer is present."

"Now, now, General." Buzzie was rapidly making notes. "That's all I need from you. You made a perfectly clear and reasonable statement, sir. Not," hastily, "that I mean to imply it's a formal statement, but it's clear."

The General was appeased. "Colleen, tell the man where you were."

"Well, I left right after lunch, around one-fifteen, to pick up this other kid" — Colleen indicated Persis — "in Somesville. I went straight over and got there around one-forty-five, as her grandmother's caretaker can tell you, if you know who he is, which I sure don't. Just some hick. Then I had to drive the old lady to Bangor, and then I got back with the kid around four, or so."

"You left me and drove off to the village, Miss O'Cassidy," Persis was firm. "And you didn't get back for a while." She smiled proudly at Buzzie.

"I went to the store for something I needed," Colleen glared, "and was back darned soon, tickety-boo! And that's all I know, officer."

Buzzie noticed the look Elizabeth Lamb, the General, and Persis gave Colleen. He made some notes and turned to Mrs. Faven.

"You, mam? Mrs. Faven, is it? I think my uncle worked for you some years ago, when you had a cottage over on the Sound."

"Possibly." Mrs. Faven was gracious. "If your uncle is Shad Higgins, you have a very intelligent and capable relative. My statement: name, Elise Shattuck Faven; resident of Canton, Massachusetts. Staying this summer at the Asticou Inn, as I have for many summers, since my husband died. And during all those summers, I have never killed anyone; I have lived for almost eighty years without doing so, although often tempted. I walked here this afternoon from the Asticou, arriving about five-thirty. I hope you are as intelligent as your uncle.

"Now, young man, please question Mrs. Hackley, my friend for more than twenty years, who has probably not murdered anyone today, either, and let us old ladies go to our beds." Mrs. Faven took up her coffee cup with a steady hand and smiled at everyone.

"Yes, mam, I've got all that. Mrs. Hackley? You're the General's neighbour to the left and share the beach with him?" Buzzie refused the coffee offered him by Ludwig, who sat down heavily in a chair by the fireplace and closed his eyes. Elizabeth Lamb thought that Ludwig must be suffering greatly from his cold to so breach *Iwo Jima*'s military discipline.

"Oh, that beach!" said Mrs. Hackley. "I wish it had disappeared in that hurricane last fall! Maybe it will in the next one. Oh, dear, what is it you want to know?"

"Where you were this afternoon," Buzzie said patiently.

"This afternoon? But I was here."

Buzzie was still patient. "Before you came here."

"I was in my brewery. My cook can tell you. I was talking to this little girl and then I went to Mr. Shinowara to ask him to bring me some lunch there while I did a few things. I couldn't do much because I needed some yeast, which I had sent my grandson to Bangor to get — oh, dear, *what* did I do with it?"

"It's under your chair, Mother," said Cynthia, yawning widely.

"Oh, yes. Where *is* Philip, Cynthia?"

Elizabeth Lamb looked toward the stairway. Mrs. Hackley's glance followed hers. Philip stood almost at the top, rocking from side to side. He lurched down a few steps, to collapse on the stair from which his mother had earlier made her dramatic ploy. He put his hands to his eyes, his body still swaying.

Before anyone else could move, Mrs. Hackley had sprung from her chair and was beside Philip. Murmuring distraught endearments, she pulled him to his feet and held him strongly to her as she assisted him down to the floor. The others rushed over, following Bix and Buzzie.

"Oh, my dear," Mrs. Hackley said weakly, "so dangerous! You might have fallen, and broken your neck like that poor young man." She half-carried Philip to a chair.

"Look!" Bix shouted. "The fire! Don't you smell it, Ludwig?"

Ludwig had remained seated by the fireplace, apparently asleep. At Bix' cry, he leapt instantly to his feet, knocked aside the fireplace screen, and pulled on the handle of the damper. Most of the smoke that was eddying into the room disappeared up the chimney. The General opened windows.

"It'll clear in a trice," he said. "Must have been sneaking out just a little ever since Ludwig lit the fire. Sometimes does that, and then a downdraft makes it billow. I must say I often forget to open the flue, but Ludwig's never been off the mark before. Heh-heh. Good thing he laid a small fire.

"God's sake, man, didn't you smell the smoke, sitting right beside it?"

"I'm sorry, sir," Ludwig said thickly. "I'm unable to smell or taste anything when I get a cold like this. My apologies, ladies."

Mrs. Hackley was expressing little moans of commiseration as she patted Philip's hand and offered him her smelling salts. He pushed them aside impatiently. "Cat, I'm fine. I just drank too much beer, on top of all that damned traveling today and with not much food, either. Just got a little dizzy. If you want to help, get me a sandwich, would you?"

Bix quickly fetched the platter and poured coffee for Philip. "Now," said Buzzie, when everyone was again seated, "you were saying, Mrs. Hackley?"

Mrs. Hackley's small face was screwed up in concentration. "But there isn't anything else I can remember. I certainly did not see anyone loitering about, on my walk."

Buzzie sighed. "On your walk. You took a walk. Where and when did you take a walk?"

"Why, merely through the woods, for a brief time. The *sansui* — the landscape I have created in my little forest is calming. I was upset because I did not have what I needed for my brewery's next order" — she looked reproachfully at her oblivious grandson, who was eating hungrily — "and *shibumi* — the quality of restraint, of beauty concealed, you know — is everywhere in my creations. *Shibumi* rests the spirit. Then," she ended, switching easily from the soulful to the pragmatic, "I went home to lie down, before dear Lem's party."

"There was another damned — another poem on the desk in my study, Catherine," the General asserted. "Saw it when I was phoning, and it wasn't there this morning. You must have come over this far."

"Goodness, did I?" Mrs. Hackley pondered. "Why, yes, so I did! But I wasn't near your desk, Lem, dear. I would never invade a gentleman's *shoin*. Not knowingly. Oh, dear, am I beginning to forget where I go?"

"No, you put the poem under the door by the pool, Mrs. Hackley," Elizabeth Lamb assured her. "I took it to the study."

Mrs. Hackley beamed. "Well, then! That's all, isn't it, officer? I'd like to go home. My grandson will run over and get his car, and perhaps we could drop Mrs. Faven, off, too? It wouldn't hurt your poor arm to drive such a short distance, Philip, dear."

"In just a minute, mam," said Buzzie. "Your grandson, now; where were you this afternoon, Mr. Dickcyn?"

Mrs. Hackley beamed even more happily. "He was gone from our cottage from just a little after half-past twelve until he and the man I sent with him to Bangor returned. Philip came straight to the party, and I remember he didn't come here till after six-thirty. Wasn't that when you and Philo got back, dear?

"Oh," she turned back to Buzzie, "this man Philo doesn't like pigs, so he'll tell you the truth about how long they were gone." She smiled proudly at the display of her knowledge of modern slang. Buzzie again looked surprised at the way Mrs. Hackley's mind made irrational assumptions that bolstered whatever opinion she was currently holding.

"Cat, I *can* speak for myself; it was my arm that was broken, not my larynx," Philip answered his grandmother testily. "Yes, Lieutenant, the man who drove me, Philo Gaynor, lives in that house right beside the General's driveway; you passed it coming in. He can verify how long we were gone. He'll remember we got back at six-thirty, because his wife screamed the time at him — among other things.

"Now, may I leave to get the car for my grandmother? She has not been very well, and this was a tiring day for her." At Buzzie's nod he left, carrying a sandwich with him.

"Perhaps I may leave when my mother does?" Cynthia was not too exhausted to use the throaty tone in which she addressed all males. She smiled enchantingly. "You have my name, Lieutenant. I was in the woods discussing — music with Mr. Baxter, here, from noon until about four. I'm afraid I missed lunch. Then I went back to my mother's cottage and changed for the General's party. I got here shortly after five and did not leave at all, except to walk to the terrace once or twice."

"In the woods, too, you were," Buzzie said gloomily. "Did you happen to see your mother or the General walking around? Or anyone else? Mr. Cooke, here, maybe?"

"You heard before where I was," Mr. Cooke announced, before Cynthia could answer. "Was around my place all day, from noon on, till I came here. And I don't go through any woods to get here; there's a path along the top of the rocks between my cottage and this one. There was plenty of fog over the harbour, and I couldn't see far to my right, as I came, but I certainly didn't meet anybody on land. And I viewed the body, remember, and it was no one I'd ever seen.

"Here's Philip. Now, may I leave with the ladies?"

Buzzie nodded, but continued to regard Cynthia. "No, I didn't see anyone," she answered, "or I would have told you. Mr. Baxter and I were very involved in our — discussion, though, and anyone might have walked by. And I did not go near the beach, either. That's all I have to say, Lieutenant, except to add" — she again smiled charmingly — "that I am *so* very pleased that someone so delightfully personable was sent on this unhappy case. Now, may we go?" She opened her eyes wide and leaned slightly towards him. Bix turned away and winked at Dusty, who was resting his chin on his chest and looking as if he were about to doze off.

"Yes, mam; don't see why not. I will," Buzzie said firmly, "be back tomorrow morning. In daylight, I may be able to catch something I missed tonight — some evidence, maybe, of what the deceased was doing here."

He looked in turn at Mrs. Hackley and Lem. "I'll want to go over the grounds and perhaps glance through your cottages, if that's all right with you. There could be something the boy was up to that might've escaped your notice. Perhaps you'll look over your places tomorrow before I get here to see, like, if anything's missing? I'll bring a technician from the Crime Lab with me, not that I expect he'll be able to turn up anything on the beach, after several tides."

"You'd better bring a search warrant, too," Philip said unpleasantly.

Buzzie ignored him. "Would I have both your permissions to conduct a sort of informal look-through?"

"Certainly," the General rumbled. "I've got nothing to hide. Just don't mess around with the papers on my desk, though. I'm having enough trouble with this damned indexing." He turned quickly to Colleen, "Despite your expert help, my dear.

"What time will you be here?"

"Mid-morning," Buzzie said vaguely. "You, mam? All right with you?"

"Oh — oh!" Mrs. Hackley looked about to faint. "I — suppose so. Oh, Lieutenant, my — cook uses marijuana for — his glaucoma. You won't be upset if you find some?"

"It's illegal, mam," Buzzie said stolidly. "If he told you he got it from a doctor, he's not telling the truth. Nowhere in the country, far's I know, is an eye-doctor allowed to prescribe marijuana — not yet, anyway."

"Oh, dear. Nowhere in the country, you say? I'll — tell him. Ah, when will you be coming over tomorrow? I mean, how much time will we have — to get a good breakfast ready for you, I mean. Mr. Shinowara is especially good at American breakfasts."

"Can't say, mam, but I'll want to be here for a time when the tide is out — for all the good it'll do. I'll see you tomorrow morning."

"Yes," said Mrs. Hackley, trying to smile as she nodded her farewells. "All right. Cynthia, let me take your arm. This has been a great strain. Now, Cynthia, I want you —"

Mrs. Hackley could be heard giving faint exhortations to her daughter as the *Nihon* party headed for their car. Mrs. Faven, looking as fresh as she had when she arrived hours before, followed them, after giving her host a firm handshake and nodding pleasantly at those who remained at *Iwo Jima*. Philip was heard to slam the car doors and depart hastily, the driveway gravel scattering under his tires. Tate Cooke made a quick exit, murmuring amongst his "good-nights" that he had better go check his rose garden — to see if there were any bodies there, he added, looking at Buzzie.

Colleen slumped in her chair and loudly yawned. "This is as slow as a stunned mullet. How much longer?"

"I just want to hear from these gentlemen, mam, but you could go. I've got your statement."

"Naow, guess I'd like to hear what everyone's got to say. What about the General's houseman, here? We don't seem to know much about him, or, at least, that's the idea I get from the General."

The General was angered. Ludwig was not. "I, too, saw the dead person, Lieutenant," he said calmly, "and did not recognize him. I was here in the cottage all day, after a trip to the market in the village in the early morning, and saw nothing of a suspicious nature."

"That caterer said you went out once or twice," Colleen corrected him.

Ludwig raised his brows and regarded her thoughtfully. "Only to pick some mint from the bed below the terrace, for the drinks. And to bring in the bags of ice from where I had stored them in the shed." He rubbed his chin, even more thoughtfully, and looked a little anxious.

"Anything more?" Buzzie asked him.

"No more," Ludwig answered, beginning to collect glasses and cups. "If I remember anything else, I'll tell you tomorrow. Privately," he added, glancing at Miss O'Cassidy.

Dusty had seemed to be asleep on the sofa, Persis cuddled up beside him. He opened one eye, as Ludwig spoke, and looked at him. Bix

112

also looked at Ludwig, as thoughtfully as Ludwig had scrutinized Miss O'Cassidy. Then he addressed Buzzie.

"I did not see the boy, Lieutenant," he said, "until I went down to the beach with Mr. Cooke and Ludwig, and I did not recognize him, either. I have quite a remarkable memory for faces."

"You were with Mrs. Dickcyn all afternoon?" Buzzie asked.

"As she said, around four she went back to the cottage, and I returned to Mrs. Hackley's teahouse, which Dusty and I share — it's just a few yards in that direction." Bix gesticulated towards the northeast corner of the living room. "And then I took a nap."

"You're a musician with the jazz band that plays over to the Harbor?" Buzzie consulted his notes. "What do you play?" Colleen sighed impatiently.

"The saxophone."

"And you don't do anything else?" Buzzie asked slowly.

Bix looked surprised. He smiled. "I play the trumpet, too, sometimes."

"And loudly," put in the General.

"Wouldn't have thought there was much of a living, nowadays, in being a full-time jazz musician?" Buzzie said, on a note of interrogation.

"Oh, there is if you're good, as Dusty and I are," Bix answered pleasantly. "And we travel around; get to see a lot of the world."

Buzzie looked at his notes. "This feller's real name is Dusty?"

Dusty opened both eyes. "It's really — Cecil," he said. "I'm kind of a — descendant." No one except Elizabeth Lamb and Bix seemed to know what he was talking about. He shut his eyes again.

"Go on," said Buzzie. "Just you now, and we're almost through. For tonight."

"Well," said Dusty, standing up and stretching, "Cecil isn't a great name for a trombone player, so I use my nickname." He ambled toward the door.

"Go on," said Buzzie, "and I guess I've had enough of your name. Where were you this afternoon?"

"I was down on the rocks between the General's place and Mr. Cooke's, just reading or lying there, from about one o'clock on. I dozed off, and when I woke up, the fog was pretty heavy, so I went back to the teahouse where Bix was asleep. Around four, this was. He didn't wake up when I came in; seemed pretty exhausted." Colleen sniggered.

"Do you have to walk through those woods to get to the rocks where you were?" Buzzie asked. "Did you see anybody at all, all afternoon? The part of it you were awake for, that is," he added with some sarcasm, as Dusty yawned ponderously.

"Not a soul. Through with us? I'd like to hit the sack. Had a tiring day."

"No doubt," said Buzzie, nodding them away. Bix paused to express his thanks to Lem. Dusty, eyes half-closed, merely nodded polite acquiescence to Bix's well-mannered farewells.

"Why don't you go to bed, my dear?" the General asked Colleen.

Colleen smiled sweetly. Elizabeth Lamb was amazed at how pleasant she could look when she chose. "I'll just stick it out with you, Lem, dearie," she answered. Ludwig gave her a caustic look from the kitchen door.

"Buzzie," Elizabeth Lamb asked, "can Persis go to bed? She was awfully sleepy even before we found the boy dead." Persis sat up indignantly and informed her that she was not at all tired, that she was only a week younger and did not need to be supervised, and that Elizabeth Lamb need not always be such a Know-It-All. She then fell back into slumber.

Elizabeth Lamb smiled. "Buzzie, we found the boy around six-forty-five—maybe a little later. High tide was at six-thirty, and he was lying in the edge of the water. His neck was all to one side. We turned him over, and he was dead. We ran back up here.

"You said there was nothing in his bag but shreds of marijuana, but I thought I saw him holding those papers they roll it in. You know?"

Buzzie shook his head. "Yes, I do, but I'm surprised you do. Well, no, I'm not; you know a heck of a lot. The papers could have blown away, or fallen into the water. Still" — he made a note.

"Now," he said, "you and Persis turned the body over. I wondered about that. The sand showed he'd been moved, but they'd told me two little girls found the body, and I figured most kids wouldn't have touched it. Anything else?"

"Well, I told you what he said when I saw him around twelve-thirty." The General gritted his teeth but held his tongue. "The tide was low then, as you know. So, why don't I take Persis to bed and we'll see you tomorrow? I'd like to see you alone. Maybe I'll think of something else."

Buzzie agreed, pocketing his notebook. "Yep, I think that's best. After some sleep, somebody might remember something more." He removed his hand from his pocket and opened the palm. "Maybe somebody might remember how come we found this red stone right there by the body. Looks like it might've come from a necklace, don't it, now?

"Well, I thank you all for your time. See you tomorrow."

Colleen and the General stared at each other, their faces showing puzzled apprehension. Ludwig carried Persis up to her room, where she roused herself long enough to undress and fall into her bed. Elizabeth Lamb took off her clothes quietly and put on her robe. As she left for the bathroom, Persis raised her head.

"I'm sorry I was rude, Elizabeth Lamb," she said. "And I know you feel bad about that boy, too. But don't you worry, because you and I and Buzzie will Solve The Case."

Elizabeth Lamb gently pulled the covers up to Persis' chin: "Russell, that nice boy I told you about, is coming over tomorrow to spend the day again. Cousin Lem likes him. And he's got a very good mind. You go to sleep, Persis. Remember how we used to say, 'Eleven o'clock and all is well —' "

" 'And those who ain't can go to hell.' " Persis finished. "Is it really that late? I'm glad you're not mad at me, Elizabeth Lamb. Good-night."

Elizabeth Lamb was still smiling as she lay in a soothing hot bath, heavily fragrant with the "4711" bath salts the General provided, declaring often that ladies had no need to smell of anything more feminine, dammit. The doorknob was impatiently shaken.

"I'll be out in a few minutes, Colleen," she called. "There's still plenty of hot water."

"You always say that." Colleen was irritable. "My mum used to say

115

kids have to find themselves; wal, all I say is, you must have lost yourself in a bathroom someplace, the hours you spend in them looking!" She stamped back down the gallery.

Elizabeth Lamb smiled again, but finished hastily and donned her pajamas. As she lay in the darkness, there was no sound in the house except Persis' deep breathing. She relaxed every muscle in her body, but sleep evaded her. "Some hot milk with nutmeg will do it," she decided. "Ludwig mixes it just right, but maybe he's gone to bed."

The night was warm. She put on only her slippers, and crept along the gallery. As she rounded the corner to the stairway, Colleen was half-way up the stairs. Colleen wore a remarkable purple chiffon robe and her customary petulant expression. "Goodnight," Elizabeth Lamb said affably. Colleen glared.

Elizabeth Lamb waited a minute, and then, with her usual curiosity, put her head around the corner. The purple robe passed the bathroom and continued on to the General's bedroom door. It disappeared through it and the door was shut soundlessly. Elizabeth Lamb raised her brows and sighed, and continued downstairs.

One dim light was burning in the living room. As she approached the kitchen, Ludwig was speaking quietly into the telephone, leaning against the refrigerator, his back to her.

"— for me," Ludwig said. "Absolutely nothing, I tell you." He turned and saw Elizabeth Lamb. He spoke again into the phone, his voice soft and slow: "Now, *liebchen,* I didn't mean it that way. It's just that it's much too late to see you tonight. I'll call tomorrow, as usual.

"What?" His voice became caressing. "No, dearest, there's no one at all with me. The little girl who lives here just came in; that's all. Till tomorrow, then."

He hung up the receiver and opened the refrigerator door, beckoning Elizabeth Lamb to him. With his head far inside the door, he hissed quietly at her: *"Don't* look at the window. Ho's still in the woodshed. Go through the pool doors and let her out and tell her: 'Ho; PACK.' Get it? Quick now: 'Ho; PACK.' "

As Elizabeth Lamb left, he called loudly after her: "Yes, I saw your mug on a table by the pool, dear. I'll start heating your milk."

She slipped quietly through the pool doors and the bushes that separated the pool area from the driveway. She pushed frantically at the door of the woodshed on its farther side. Hohenzollern whimpered and leaped against the door, thwarting her efforts. "Down, girl," Elizabeth Lamb whispered, and as she managed to open the door, said urgently, "Ho; PACK. PACK, Ho." The dog hesitated a moment, sniffing, with pricked ears, and then raced ahead of her toward the terrace. As they reached it, Ludwig opened the doors; the dog passed him and led the way through the cottage and out to the pool.

"He went around the house and towards the driveway," Ludwig gasped as they ran after her. "Smart; those skins on Gaynor's fences will confuse the scent. He knew I'd get Ho —"

A gunshot exploded nearby, then another. Ludwig gave a low cry and ran faster. When they reached Philo's house, a huddled furry body lay beside one of the fences. The yard light came on, and Philo was with them, carrying his rifle. Ludwig sprang from where he had knelt beside his dog and seized him by the throat.

"No, no! It wasn't me!" Philo choked out. "Stop it! Honest!"

Ludwig loosed his grip and knelt again beside the dead animal. "Then who?" he asked expressionlessly.

"It was some feller all in black. Had somethin' over his face, far's I could see. I heard runnin', and looked out, and this black thing was aimin' a gun at the dog. One shot and she fell. I grabbed my gun and fired, but he run off, down the road.

"God, Ludwig, why fer would I shoot your dog?"

"You threatened to, once." Ludwig was calm, but Elizabeth Lamb could see his hands clenching and unclenching in the dog's fur.

"Hell, but I didn't! Can't you tell by the bullet if 'twas from my Winchester?"

"It went right through her head. God knows where it is. By tomorrow," Ludwig said tiredly, "you'll find it and get rid of it. Let me see that gun."

He cocked open the rifle. One spent shell flew out and fell a few feet away. He rapidly worked the mechanism again and again, until four whole cartridges had emerged.

"See!" Philo said. "I only shot once."

"You could have ejected the shell before you fired the second time. It could be anywhere." He moved toward Philo, who backed away.

"For pity Minerva's sake!" came a shrill voice. "What the hell is all this shootin' and talkin'? A woman with kids to raise needs her rest."

"Gloria," said Philo, still retreating, "tell him that gun wasn't loaded full. I only had five cartridges left, after I shot at that deer this mornin'. You know a Winchester takes seven shells and that's all, Ludwig."

"How'd I know if it was loaded full or not?" Gloria asked reasonably. "I got more to do than watch over that damned gun." She had been tightening one of the pink plastic curlers in which her hair was encased; as Philo turned to her she moved her hands protectively in front of her face.

"Well," she said, peeking through her fingers, "I know he took a couple of shots earlier at that cussed deer that's always after the corn in our gaadin. Ain't loaded the gun since, to my notice. That help, Philo?"

"Ludwig," Philo stopped backing and tried to look pitiful, "I only shot once, at whoever 'twas in my dooryard. No way could've hit the dog, because I shot high. By then, she was jest layin' there. No need fer you to hurt me, now." Elizabeth Lamb noticed that his Adam's-apple was moving up and down, and not sideways.

"Ludwig," she said, as with an exclamation of disgust he knelt again by the dog, "I don't think Philo did it. It must have been whoever was outside our window. I feel awfully bad about Ho, Ludwig."

She put her hand on his bent head. Gloria muttered her way toward her house. "Kin I help you with the dog?" Philo asked. "I got a shovel here, somewheres. And you had ought to tend that cold, Ludwig. Hot clam broth's the best thing they is fer a cold like that. You got to take care of yourself; can't do nuthin' fer that critter. She warn't very agreeable but — I'm sorry."

Without looking at him, Ludwig picked up the body and walked quickly back up the driveway. Elizabeth Lamb ran after him. "Ludwig —" she began softly.

Ludwig's voice was remote, but gentle. "I know. Don't say any more. There's an old sail in the shed. It's clean. Bring that, and the spade with the long handle. Oh, and the flashlight from the kitchen."

When she returned, he was still holding the dog, his face bent. He seemed to be murmuring into the fur. Bix Baxter, barefoot and wearing only pajama bottoms, stood beside him. Ludwig did not respond to his muted questions. Bix shook his head in bewilderment and turned towards the teahouse.

Elizabeth Lamb and Ludwig went silently a short distance into the land between Mr. Cooke's cottage and *Iwo Jima*. They stopped at a mossy place below a single tall pine, where she had once seen Ludwig reading, with Hohenzollern lying close beside him. She lightly patted the stiffening body while Ludwig worked grimly with the spade. He wrapped the dog in the sail and quickly filled in the grave. He lifted a large flat pink granite rock and placed it at its head.

He had not spoken as he worked, nor did he as they walked back to the house. When they reached it, he asked her in an almost normal tone if she wanted her hot milk. She refused, thanking him and putting her hand briefly on his sleeve.

As she left the kitchen, he said: "She was a good dog, you know. A good dog." Staring at the blackness outside the window he added, "She saved my life three times. A good dog —" His voice broke, and he went into his room, quietly shutting the door.

Elizabeth Lamb lay stiffly, with her arm over her eyes, too tired and confused to sleep. The day seemed to have lasted a month. Over and over, she pondered what it all meant — the dead boy on the beach, the intruder outside the kitchen, the killing of the dog. And Ludwig himself — how was it that the life of a houseman was so dangerous that Hohenzollern had saved his life three times?

"I don't know any answers, but, then, I don't even know the right questions," she thought. "I feel like Gertrude Stein when she was dying, and asked, 'What is the answer?' And when no one spoke, she said, 'Then what is the question?' And then she died — like Ho." She turned her tear-wet face into the pillow and sobbed soundlessly.

On the clear night air, a trumpet sounded softly. Very, very beautifully, *Taps* was played, just once. As the last mournful note faded away, Elizabeth Lamb said quietly aloud: "It's like Bix to do that. He always does the right thing. But is he playing for the boy on the beach, or for Ho? Or for both? Which answer; which question?" She sighed, and slept.

• CHAPTER 6 •

September, Remember

PERSIS AWOKE at about eight-thirty the next morning. Her cousin was deeply asleep in the other bed, with her Marine Corps blankets, the only kind used at *Iwo Jima*, pulled protectively up into a wad about her shoulders. Where her head should have been there was a pillow, from under which issued the sound of heavy, even breathing. "She's sleeping in a pillow sandwich again," Persis murmured. "She only does that when she's worried."

Persis gently removed the top pillow and smoothed out the blankets. "Elizabeth Lamb? Are you asleep? It's bad for you to sleep with a pillow over your face, you know. Mummy says it causes bad dreams. Are you awake now?"

"Of course I am. How could I not be? Persis, I *wish* you would stop saying or asking what is always perfectly obvious. Why don't you go have breakfast? I'll be down soon." Elizabeth Lamb replaced the pillow atop her head, curled herself up and was instantly asleep again.

"Well," Persis answered indignantly, "I'd go down to breakfast if I could find any proper clothes. My suitcase must be in the

121

car. I'll just have to put on something of yours."

There was no response as Persis urged her round little body into shorts and a shirt. "It's a good thing we wear the same size sneakers," she murmured, "and she doesn't have to be so mean to me, either." She went to the window. Despite her cousin's prediction of good weather, the day was sunless. The sky was a strange sullen yellow and a few dark, threatening clouds hung directly over the cottage. She secured a sweater and slipped along the quiet gallery and down the stairway.

Ludwig was in the kitchen, preparing breakfast with his usual quick and exact movements, but his face was flushed and his eyes swollen. His voice, as he bade her "Good-morning", was hoarse and thick. "I'd like a four-minute egg," Persis requested, "and all the toast and orange juice I can have. Do you know how to make a four-minute egg, Ludwig? It's not easy, because it takes only three minutes if you do it properly, you know. I'll just walk around outside till it's ready. Is that all right?"

Ludwig nodded glumly and Persis wandered out to the pool and then, after a pause to call to Ludwig that there were a great many leaves in it, down the driveway. She cheerfully addressed the man who was crawling around on his hands and knees, pawing over the gravel. "Hello, what are you doing? Do you live in that house? It needs painting. And I think all those animal skins are unsightly. Don't you?"

"Another cussed kid," Philo muttered to the driveway. He rose and surveyed her. He sneezed.

"I'm lookin' for a shell what might prove I didn't kill that dog," he answered, with another sneeze. "And I'll paint my house ifn and when I please. Would seem you must be related to that Lizzie? She's great on givin' orders. Come to stay with the General, hev you? Place is becomin' a danged kindeygarden." He loudly blew his nose into a rag with which he had cleaned something very dirty.

"What dog? You're getting a bad cold, just like Ludwig."

"Ludwig's dog, that's what dog. I didn't shoot her. And ifn he'd took some good hot clam broth like I told him to, he'd be better. *And* I was up all night; no wonder I'm gettin' sick-like. A man

122

what's got to pertect his property don't git his rest."

"I didn't know Ludwig had a dog. Where is it? Who shot it?"

"Don't know who shot it — wish I did. He burreyed her over in the woods — beyond that laidge, there. Saw the grave this mornin' when I was havin' a look-round. Planted a little wild rose bush on it, I did. Least I could do, though I never liked the crittur. He feels right bad about her."

"I think you must be a *very* nice man," Persis assured him. "What's your name? I'm Persis Halstead, Elizabeth Lamb's cousin. I'm awfully glad to meet you."

Philo glowed. His Adam's-apple bobbed up and down with emotion. "I'm Philo. Please to make your acquaintance. Like your looks, I do, better'n that skinny cousin of yours. Bet your mumma gave you plenty of cod-liver-oil; that's what makes kids handsome. All my five git it."

There was a series of crashes from his abode, accompanied by children's screams. Philo's name was called shrilly. He hastily headed for his truck. Turning, he said, "Got to meet a feller over to the Harbor. I like you, Miss Persis, I do. You take care today. That's a lowry sky and means a bad windstorm. Not to mention we got crazy people wanderin' around with guns, and bodies washed up on the beach. You mind now, you hear?

"When I git back, mebbe you'd like to go along of me down to the shore, to a place I know, and we'll git us a mess of clams before the storm sets in?"

Persis nodded happily, also glowing with the knowledge of being appreciated. Ludwig served her a proper four-minute egg at the kitchen counter, and provided a large quantity of buttered dark rye bread and freshly squeezed grapefruit juice. "The General's secretary says grapefruit juice burns calories," he explained, "so we never have orange juice, now."

"That nice man Philo says he didn't shoot your dog," Persis told him, perched on her stool and eating hungrily. "And I believe him. He says *you* should drink clam juice. Where's Cousin Lem and that lady? Should I wake them up for you? Is the lady still asleep? She must hear us talking."

Ludwig raised a brow. "Better not bother them. Why don't you take another walk, till Elizabeth Lamb comes down? You could take Mrs. Hackley the package of yeast she left here last night. I'll show you the path to her place. It isn't far, and if you see anyone at all in the woods, just come straight back here, but I don't think you will."

"I'm not ever afraid in Maine, though I wish your dog could go with me. I'm awfully sorry about her."

"Yes," Ludwig said remotely. "Well, I'll get a new dog, but there won't ever be another like Ho."

When Persis emerged from the woods into *Nihon*'s courtyard, Mrs. Hackley was just coming out of her brewery. She greeted her yeast with delight and said she had been about to go over to dear Lem's to retrieve it. "My poor daughter and grandson are *so* exhausted, after that *dreadful* evening, that they are still asleep. Now, if you will excuse me, dear, I must finish off a small order of ginger beer."

"I'll help," said Persis, neatly side-stepping Mrs. Hackley, who was making a feeble attempt to shut the heavy door.

"Oh, no, darling, sweet little girls' dirty hands mustn't touch my *Sakana*. Don't they want you at *Iwo Jima*?" faltered Mrs. Hackley, unsuccessfully grasping at Persis' sleeve as she dashed to the sink for a thorough washing.

"No, they don't. What are you doing? What is that you're putting into the bottles? I can mix it."

"Oh, it's just for the ginger beer," Mrs. Hackley answered, giving up on ousting Persis, who had competently tucked a large apron around herself and was standing ready for orders. "I found when I served it to paying guests — did you know that all of *Sakana* started from a very modest operation in my teahouse, where we offered ginger beer and rice cakes as well as tea and cinnamon toast? Oh, dear, what was I saying — oh, that some patrons found the ginger beer too bitter; Americans have such *sugary* natures, and it comes out in their palates. So we served little lacquered cups of powdered sugar with each order. And stirrers with fish tails for handles — wasn't that clever!

"Now where in the world did I store the stirrers that were left when we closed the teahouse and went into wholesale production of

Sakana beverages?" She gazed earnestly at the ceiling, as if the answer to her question might appear there. "Oh, why am I so forgetful! If I could find them, I could give you some to take home to your cousin so that you could play tea party," she ended hopefully.

"No," said Persis, "nobody wants me home just now. Elizabeth Lamb would stay and help and I can do anything she can. Do you measure the sugar with these kitchen measuring spoons? I'll do that. But where are the lacquer cups?"

Mrs. Hackley laughed weakly. "But, dear, as I told you, we haven't the teahouse any more! Now, I wonder where I *did* put the cups, too — oh, well. We now place the sugar in these little plastic bags, and the customer who buys the beer can use it or not, as he pleases. I like everyone to be happy, and my concern is what has made *Sakana* so very successful. Oh, my; I need more sugar. Would you run over to the kitchen and ask Mr. Shinowara for another box of it? The kitchen is just inside that door across the courtyard."

"There's enough right here, in this little jar," Persis answered, but Mrs. Hackley had had enough of Persis' independence. "No, there isn't," she said strongly. "Go get some more, as I asked you to. And this is too coarse to use alone; we need Superfine. I have three dozen bottles to go out in this order, and it must go to Ellsworth today, with everything *just* right. Oh, I *do* wish Philip would get up, the poor boy."

When Persis returned with the sugar, Mrs. Hackley was still mumbling her desire for Philip to rise and assist her. "Who will deliver the order?" she asked Persis, who was reminded of the Little Red Hen. She could not answer, but cheerfully put plastic ties tightly around the tiny bags as Mrs. Hackley filled them and handed them to her. "I don't see why you have to use a looking-glass," she criticized. Mrs. Hackley sighed and explained that her diabetes had made her eyes much weaker than even would be natural at her age, and that everything that went into *Sakana* must be perfectly, perfectly exact. "There," she said, "what was in the jar was *just* enough, with some of what you brought added to it. We are a good pair!" She permitted Persis to replace the porcelain stoppers in the bottles, murmuring that little hands were *so* strong and clever!

Then they packed the ginger beer in a heavy cardboard box.

"Mother!" came from the courtyard, accompanied by a pounding at the door, which Mrs. Hackley had locked behind Persis. At a nod from Mrs. Hackley, Persis went to it and turned the large brass key.

Cynthia was devoid of makeup, and fully dressed in a genteel shirt and skirt. "Good God, Mother! What are you doing over in this damned place, with detectives on the way to grill us? That Lieutenant Higgins just called. Come back to the house and help me cope. I can't get Philip out of bed. And your eyes are watering again; Mother, really, you must not over-do. You are not well."

"Now, dear," Mrs. Hackley quavered, "it's all perfectly fine. I'll put my eye-drops in presently. And I've taken care of everything! Mr. Shinowara is in the kitchen right now making the batter for his rice pancakes and frying up quantities of bacon. And there is a cold ham, and he'll give them eggs, and I squeezed four dozen oranges myself!"

"Are you planning to get rid of them by drowning them in orange juice? Really, Mother, it is unnecessary to give them breakfast. It will be after ten when they get here and you know Natives eat breakfast at dawn."

"Then they will appreciate my mid-morning sustenance. Were you not raised to show honourable hospitality, Cynthia? I, myself, taught you the rules of *kantai*.

"Now, there is something that must be done and you will do it better than poor, tired Philip. It will also remove you from the proximity of Lieutenant Higgins. I think that might be best."

"I am *not* going to help you mix up these damned mucks! I hate this cold, depressing place and you know it. You could certainly afford a few more lights in here, especially now that your eyes are so bad."

"*Sakana*," Mrs. Hackley replied, her delicate chin quivering, "must *not* be called a damned muck. What would we do without my income from it? You would have to go to work, my dear."

"Well," Cynthia's tone softened, "what do you want done?"

126

"Merely for you to drive these three dozen ginger beer to Ellsworth. They go to that little specialty shop where you went with me once. They want the beer for a customer who summers in Blue Hill for him to take back to New York tomorrow. We are getting double the usual price! But it must be delivered this morning, as he wants to pick it up this afternoon.

"The carton is all packed and sealed. This little girl can help you get it into your car. The store owner is elderly and punctilious and always pays in cash; he will give you an envelope."

Protesting, but with an air of some relief, Cynthia departed on her errand, pausing only to apply lipstick. Smiling happily and murmuring to herself, Mrs. Hackley began to put a number of articles into a large handled basket which she covered with a red-and-white checquered napkin. "She's switched from the Little Red Hen to Little Red Riding Hood," Persis thought, and said aloud, "I hope you don't meet a wolf."

"Why should I, dear? Now, come, I'm going over to *Iwo Jima*, and you may carry the basket." As they left, she paused thoughtfully, and announced that they would leave the door unlocked, for the policemen's convenience. Persis was requested to fetch a trowel from the garage, and this was placed on top of the napkin.

They proceeded slowly through the woods, Mrs. Hackley stopping often to gaze about her and to beam at her little "prospects." She led the way off the path to one of her Buddhas that sat on a shelf-like protrusion of a huge rock that was twice as tall as Persis. She had Persis assist her in moving the figure forward a little on its perch. She tucked behind it a sizeable package wrapped in a grey cloth through the folds of which a shiny material gleamed. The cloth was arranged so that the package was almost invisible against the grey granite, and then they pushed the Buddha firmly back against it.

"Are you planning a scavenger hunt?" Persis asked politely, trying to see what else was in the basket.

Mrs. Hackley was amused. "No, dear, I'm planning to thwart one. That is something of my daughter's that I do not think the police should come across, and you must never, never tell anyone I put it

127

there. It *may* be lawful for her to have it, as she says, but I don't think so. Do you promise?"

Persis promised, ardently crossing her heart, and happy with the thought that she knew something Elizabeth Lamb did not. Mrs. Hackley put the trowel down beside the path. "I'll get it on my way back," she said. "I don't need it, now that I remembered the Buddha in the cleft of that rock. Besides," she smiled, "one doesn't need a trowel to plant grass!" She laughed a little, as did Persis, who wondered why there was cause for merriment. They walked on, with many more pauses by Mrs. Hackley, who was now beginning to remind Persis of the Cheshire Cat, so often did she smile at, apparently, nothing.

During one of their pauses Mrs. Hackley stopped smiling and frowned worriedly. "Oh, dear," she said. "Perhaps I should have just thrown it in the ocean?" At Persis' look of bewilderment, she explained, "That package of my daughter's, I mean. But she would only buy more, and everything is *so* expensive nowadays.

"Really," she went on angrily, "that dreadful President of ours said four years ago he would cut inflation — or was it that he would get us out of that stupid war in Asia? Oh, dear; I forget."

"Probably both," Persis observed. "Politicians are very good at promising. My daddy says if Mr. Nixon would stop being so smarmy, and not run again this fall, but maybe try for the Senate so he could concentrate on world affairs, about which my daddy says he understands a thing or two, we'd be better off. He says Mr. Nixon made a sickening speech about a dog once that made him go straight out and register as a Democrat."

"Well, he won't stop being President. He'll stay so he can drive the price of beef up further; I blame him completely for the outrageous amount it costs. I eat little meat because of my upbringing, but Philip is delicate and requires steaks, although Mr. Shinowara detests cooking them. And they cost so much!"

"But *Life* said last June that real wages are up for the first time in seven years. Elizabeth Lamb read it. What do you suppose 'real' wages are? *And* that 56% of Americans approve of President Nixon,

128

according to the Gallup Poll."

"Americans!" rejoined Mrs. Hackley. "After what they did to my beautiful Japan, I don't want to hear what 56% of them think. All their sugar and meat is affecting their brains."

"But didn't Japan bomb us first, in Hawaii, and kill people and sink ships? We learned that in school."

"You can learn anything in American schools," Mrs. Hackley said bitterly, "except how to be civilized."

Persis practised civility and said no more. The slow journey to the General's cottage continued.

At *Iwo Jima,* Elizabeth Lamb was greeting her Cousin Lem, who was at Ludwig's counter enjoying his usual breakfast of two boiled eggs and one bran muffin, interspersed with quantities of prune and carrot juice with which Vitamin E capsules were downed. He was also smiling, his expression as feline as his neighbour's recent one.

He tendered her a jovial "Good-morning," apparently forgetting his description of her, the night before, as a serpent's tooth. Ludwig had obviously told him about Hohenzollern's death, since the General was declaiming the ordinary platitudes of commiseration, but it did not seem to affect him greatly. "Some crazy teen-ager, all doped up, probably out for a little cat-burglary," was his version of the intruder outside the window, which he was expressing when Elizabeth Lamb arrived downstairs. "I'll pay for a new dog, Ludwig, since the feller was here trying to rob me. We'll get you a Doberman, hey? They're tougher than German Shepherds. And isn't it a *beautiful* morning! Heh-heh."

"It's a terrible morning, Cousin Lem, in every way, not just the weather. And there was a deep red sky last night, too." Elizabeth Lamb spoke coldly, deploring the General's bland disregard of Ludwig's feelings at his loss. "Where's Miss O'Cassidy? She's never late for meals."

"Heh-heh. She'll be along. Bit tired, I suppose. Works awfully hard, that dear girl." Both Elizabeth Lamb and Ludwig regarded him caustically.

"Often is a red sky before a hurricane, you know; saw many of 'em in the Pacific," he continued. "One's due to hit us, tonight or early tomorrow. Might blow out to sea, of course. Expected one this fall, because we had such unusually hot weather in May and June. There's an old saw about it:

> June too soon; July stand by.
> August, you must.
> September, remember. October, all over.

Heh-heh. Never seen it to fail."

Elizabeth Lamb had been favoured by Ludwig with a little herb omelet. "This is *so* good, Ludwig. You must what, in August, Cousin Lem?"

"You must prepare for the hurricane in September, of course. Still, we must take what comes, and sometimes it can be delightful. Heh-heh."

"Could I have some more bread, Ludwig? I never thought a hurricane could be delightful, Cousin Lem. You are certainly in good spirits this morning."

"Wouldn't call the king my cousin. Oh, there you are, my dear. Have a good bath?"

"There's not enough hot water, *as* per usual," Miss O'Cassidy answered, going to her room and slamming the door, which caught on her purple ensemble. She was heard to tear the robe loose, with the noise of something dropping, and a loud expletive.

"I didn't hear any bath water running, did you, Ludwig?" Elizabeth Lamb murmured. "Doesn't Miss O'Cassidy usually wash in the downstairs powder room in the morning?" She and Ludwig smiled at each other, as he poured her *café au lait.*

"Indeed a day to be marked with the whitest of stones!" declared the General, hastily explaining the day was memorable because he had, earlier, checked his manuscript and ascertained that the end of the tiresome indexing was in view.

Miss O'Cassidy re-appeared, wearing a rumpled cotton dress that seemed to have been thrown on rather than donned, sandals that gave too generous a view of her splayed feet, and her customary unpleasant expression. She ran her fingers through uncombed hair and demanded "a quart or so" of grapefruit juice and a "couple of rashers" of bacon. "Exercise makes me good and hungry," she stated, glaring at General Alison. "*And* stiff; my bottle-and-glass is right sore, not to mention my Joe Hunt." Ludwig looked at her with distaste, the General with disbelief, and Elizabeth Lamb, who had been acquainted with a Cockney cleaning-woman during one of her and her mother's sojourns in London, with slow comprehension. Miss O'Cassidy grinned. Elizabeth Lamb spoke quickly.

"That's good, Cousin Lem: 'the whitest of stones.' It's from Roman history, isn't it? Did you know — or so, at least, the classics mistress at school told us — that the ancients believed you lost your memory if you read epitaphs?"

Colleen snorted through the two small pieces of bacon which were all that Ludwig had issued her. "There's some ancients I know that're about to get their memories refreshed right soon," she said, looking nastily smug.

"Hello, everybody," came from the open terrace doors. "Am I too early? Had real good luck hitch-hikin' today."

"Russell!" Elizabeth Lamb cried. "Hi! You'll never believe it when I tell you the terrible thing that happened on Cousin Lem's beach.

"Here's Russell, Cousin Lem. Ludwig, is there a doughnut or something for him?"

Colleen departed for her room, ignoring the newcomer. He entered shyly, but with a composure far beyond that displayed by most fifteen-year-old Native boys, the General thought. He was fairly tall, and very thin. His brown hair was cut short — "in the last non-military crew-cut in the Western world," the General had often remarked — and his hazel eyes, behind thick spectacles, were candid and alert. His face was tanned, with a strong chin and an inquiring expression, and prepossessing, despite that his very white teeth were large and crooked and his nose snub.

"You're looking better every time I see you, my boy," the General said pleasantly. "Just about over that — accident you had, aren't you? Keeping you busy at the lab? You haven't had a day

131

off to come over here for almost two weeks.

"Well, I don't know that we'll swim today, but I'll take you and your friend here for the sail I promised you, before the wind makes up too much. And my little cousin Persis is with us — Elizabeth Lamb, where is she? You're supposed to look after her. Is she still in bed?"

Ludwig explained the absence of Persis as he produced doughnuts and scrambled eggs for Russell and made him and Elizabeth Lamb some fresh *café au lait*. "And, General," he said, "you know that jade bowl in the form of a duck that you got in China? Well, I saw Mrs. Dickcyn using it as an ashtray, last night, and I couldn't find it when I straightened up this morning. I should have told Persis to ask Mrs. Hackley if she's seen it; Mrs. Dickcyn must have taken it — ah, by mistake — but her mother would return it."

"Cynnie nabbed that, too, did she?" the General asked glumly. "My God, every time she comes in here she takes something she fancies! A damned kleptomaniac, that's what she is."

"No, Cousin Lem, she isn't a kleptomaniac, because things she takes are always left in plain sight at *Nihon*. And I always bring them back. I'll go over and get the ashtray later," Elizabeth Lamb assured him.

"Leaving things you steal around doesn't mean you're not a klepto," began Russell, who had a scientific nature, but he was interrupted by a chuckle from the General, still in unusually high spirits.

"Know what she did at the Somerset Club?" he asked. "She was in Boston last winter — probably on a shop-lifting expedition — and convinced Chub Cooke to put her up there overnight as his guest. After she'd gone, and the maid went to her room to remove the breakfast tray, there wasn't a damned dish on it! The woman had pinched the china and carted it off! And they suspected she'd lifted a couple of dessert spoons at dinner the night before, as well as some crystal pendants from a wall sconce.

"Chub got a good dressing-down from the Club about it. And I wrote a Rhyme. You'll want to hear it, of course?"

132

"Yes, please, sir," said Russell, who quietly admired everything about his uninhibited host, even his verses.

Lem put down his coffee cup with a clatter and declaimed:

"The china's gone; we eat on tin.
The staff is in the looney-bin.
A brace of Cabots has resigned;
The Ladies' Entrance door is mined.
Now no one speaks to Chub, who let
The Cyn into the Somerset.
Though Brahmins, in tones clear and drear
Moan; 'How'd she cop our chandelier?'

Heh-heh. Now, I've got to get Miss O'Cassidy started on some typing, and then I'll give you a short sail. Maybe Persis will be back for it."

"Ludwig, did you throw away those old sneakers I left out on the terrace? I can't find them, and Persis must have taken my good ones," said Elizabeth Lamb. Ludwig explained that he had thought there was still some wear left in the sneakers, and, following the General's oft-repeated dictum of: "Use it up; wear it out; make it do, or do without," had put them in the shed.

Elizabeth Lamb resignedly left to search the shed and Russell wandered about the grounds. Just as he passed beside the open study window, he saw a cardinal perched in a tall pine and, as the bird was fairly rare on Mount Desert Island, stood immobile to observe it.

"Incest!" loudly came through the window. "Are you joking, my dear girl? Not very funny, though. Heh-heh."

"Too right I'm not joking," said Miss O'Cassidy, in a low, hard voice. "I'm in dead earnest. General Stanley and the rest of the muckety-mucks would love to hear the tape I made in your room last night, wouldn't they, naow? You may be my dear old long-lost dad, but I haven't got much sentiment for you, all things considered. Doing a bunk on me and Mum wasn't quite the article, let alone seducing your own flesh and blood. Took you all summer though, till

133

I gave in last night, didn't it?

"It'll take a bit of payment — which I'll send home to Mum, a'course — to make up for what you did to us."

Russell, mouth agape, sidled closer to the house. His widowed mother had often expressed to her beer-drinking cronies the wish that "Russ wouldn't always be so nosy. Up and down street he goes, all the time, findin' out ever'thin' that's goin' on. Knowin' too much's a sight more risky than not knowin' much of anythin' atall, like I do." Mrs. Stark's friends agreed with her, but neither they nor she had ever told Russell that it was both unmannerly and, on occasion, dangerous to eavesdrop, so he had continued his early-childhood tendency to listen avidly to any interesting conversation. This one promised to be most interesting.

"But I'm *not* your father, Colleen. How could I be?"

"Mum's got letters, dinkum ones. You were in Sydney just nine months before I was born in June of '50, and for quite a bit before that. *And* she's got pictures; she's a photographer, you remember. She'll be pleased to send me copies of the letters, and the pictures are right interesting. When I give the straight gen to your superiors, General, *sir*, it'll cause a proper blow-up. 'Course, payment from you, which poor old Mum sure could use, 'll prevent any unpleasantness."

"Remember your mother's a photographer! I don't even know her name! And I'm certain I never even met her. You're upset, my dear. This isn't the sweet girl I *know* you are."

"Come off it. Virginia was her name, and you have reason to remember it. Don't try coming the raw prawn on me, 'cause I'm just as tricky as my dad."

"I knew a Virginia," the General said slowly, "but not very well. She went around with a fellow-officer. And she had a lot of friends, but I don't remember any photographer."

"You'll remember. Mum is very talented; had to be, to support herself and raise me, but she's a real drongo — believes anything a slick talker tells her. Wal, it's time you paid up, for the fun you had."

"But, Colleen, if you think I am your father — which I certainly am not, my dear — how *could* you — well —"

"That's rich, that is. How could I? I've had to do a lot harder things than put on an act all summer and pretend to be crazy about you last night. All in the line of work, General; in the line of duty, as you'd put it. My duty's to my mum. I'll talk to you after dinner and tell you what I figure you owe us. Hope you'll decide by then to take the easy way out and pay up. And don't try looking for the tape; it isn't under your bed any more. It's in a real safe place.

"Speaking of work, I'll get on with typing up as far as we've got on the indexing. It'll give you a bit of time to think."

Russell quickly and quietly left for the terrace, where Elizabeth Lamb was gloomily regarding her feet, whose toes were protruding through holes in the old sneakers. The General came out, face red and eyes blazing, but his manner was calm and his mouth set in a firm, military line. "Oh, *God*," he said fiercely as Mrs. Hackley appeared on the terrace, Persis behind her.

Mrs. Hackley took a startled backward step, bumping into Persis, who dropped the basket. The General regarded its spilled contents with displeasure, since they all exuded an Oriental aura. He headed towards the path to the *Nihon* float, shouting tersely over his shoulder: "Good morning, Catherine. Sorry you can't stay. Hope there's no more damned poems in that stuff.

"Hurry up, you two, so we can sail before the storm starts. Persis, come along if you want."

The two paused to assist in re-packing the basket. Mrs. Hackley anguishedly attempted to smoothe a bent scroll as she admonished Russell to carefully put back the lid of a large round red tin, decorated with gold chrysanthemums and emblazoned with bold black Japanese characters and under them, in English, "Finest Rice Powder for the Lades." Instead, Russell dropped the tin, which caused Mrs. Hackley to shriek and drop the scroll, which Persis instantly trod upon as a porcelain vase slipped from her hands and fell, luckily, into the earth of a potted terrace plant. "Lades?" murmured Elizabeth Lamb as she retrieved the vase from the shrub, ignoring Mrs. Hackley's profusion of little moans.

"The Japanese do not always spell English correctly," Mrs. Hackley said defensively, "nor do Americans, you know. And Japanese are *never* clumsy. These things are some of my treasures, and that is the

135

finest, purest powder one can buy. It is so lucky I cut plastic for an inside cover, or it would have all been spilled and wasted, and it is *very* expensive. Look, a bit *has* leaked out!" She looked accusingly at Russell, who blushed, dropped the tin again, and managed to step on a spray of silk cherry blossoms as he picked it up. He nervously gnawed a fingernail while Mrs. Hackley smoothed out the flowers, sighing and shaking her head.

He and Elizabeth Lamb quickly followed the General, without Persis, who, pursuing her streak of independence, announced that Mrs. Hackley wanted her to help fix up the powder room and that then a nice man wanted her to go clamming. She put out her tongue at Elizabeth Lamb, who paused to request that her new sneakers not be returned muddy.

Colleen observed the passage of Persis and Mrs. Hackley from her desk facing the open study door. She stopped her work to inform them that there was no use their attempting to tart up that dismal place for her benefit, since she would probably be leaving for Boston soon. "After I get all that's coming to me," she said with a hard look at both of them, and continued typing noisily.

The decorators were somewhat cheered by the thought of Miss O'Cassidy's imminent departure, although a frown had appeared on Mrs. Hackley's face at the sight and sound of Miss O'Cassidy. The frown was replaced by her usual smile as they decided happily where their artifacts should be placed. "She's thinking that now Cousin Lem will be nicer to her, maybe," thought Persis, who though not as observant nor worldly as her young cousin, was not a fool.

The blue and white vase, with the pink silk blossoms placed in it, was finally lodged on the wide window sill (although Persis had advocated the top of the toilet tank) because "the beautiful flowers will help hide that dilapidated screen, dear." Since there was a small mirror on the inside of the door, but none over the washbasin, both agreed that the paper scroll, which, unrolled, depicted small yellow birds frolicking amongst lavender leaves and buds, should be hung over the basin. There was no argument as to where a framed orange and gold wood-cut depicting "ladies," said Persis — "courtesans," Mrs. Hackley corrected, "but *very* accomplished ones!" — should be hung, since the only remaining clear wall space was above the water-closet.

Persis now insisted that a little brass incense burner should be put on the tank, and Mrs. Hackley was equally firm that it should go on a small hanging shelf, beside the red powder tin. Persis won, and a white porcelain bowl with green and yellow figures was placed on the shelf — "safer there," Mrs. Hackley agreed. The last ornament was a blue-green bowl shaped like a duck, which was also placed on the shelf. Mrs. Hackley frowned at it and said that her memory was *certainly* failing, since although she had found it in her kitchen that very morning, she had absolutely no recollection of ever having seen it before that. "I really don't like it, because ducks eat fish, don't they, dear? And it has, to me, a Chinese look."

As a final touch, Mrs. Hackley unfolded a straw mat dyed a brilliant cerise from the bottom of the basket, and laid it in the center of the floor. "There!" she said. "Now ladies can come in here without being depressed. We have done our best."

"My goodness," Persis said. "What a difference in this room! It's certainly gay now."

Mrs. Hackley chuckled. "Since the woodcut is titled 'The Gay Quarters of Shinga — Shinta — ' — oh, dear, *what* is the rest of it? I cannot even remember Japanese names!

"Do you think," she dubiously regarded the floor mat, "that the *tatami* is perhaps a bit *too* gay?"

Persis reassured her and went to the ringing telephone, which Miss O'Cassidy was ignoring. "It was your grandson," she informed Mrs. Hackley. "He says, if you're here, to tell you that Gloria called and said Philo has been arrested in Northeast Harbor, and that your cottage is overrun with cops, and would you come home?

"Oh, why has that nice man been arrested? Now I can't go clamming with him."

"Oh, my," said Mrs. Hackley. "I suppose I'll have to bail him out again. Thank you for all your help, dear. You are welcome at *Nihon* at any time." She faltered her way down the driveway to the Gaynor house.

Persis lay disconsolately beside the pool, breathing the heavy air and wishing she had been one of the sailing party. She hoped that Ludwig, who had disappeared into the woods, would return soon, in case Miss O'Cassidy decided to come out and join her. "I can always get away from her by helping him, as I did Mrs. Hackley," she planned.

The sailing party had marched in single file through the woods, the General, in the lead, casting alert glances into the dimness of the pine and spruce as if looking for a skulking "damned Nip," as he was accustomed to term anyone of any race whatever whom he disliked. "Or a blackmailer," thought Russell, following close behind, and speculating as to what Miss O'Cassidy might set in motion. He worriedly chewed on a pine needle to alleviate the numbness in his tongue, which he had not felt since his recuperation from a fractured skull earlier in the summer. "Put back my recovery, she has," he murmured, wryly.

Russell greatly admired the General, who had taught him the rudiments of sailing and gently tried, ever since Elizabeth Lamb had first invited him to *Iwo Jima*, two months before, to correct his more outlandish Native terms and pronunciations. The General had used his association with one of the scientists at a genetic research laboratory near Bar Harbor to secure Russell a job as a summer assistant. Russell, still loyal to the movie theatre where Alison-Worthington relatives had employed him for several years, handled both jobs with aplomb. They did, though, restrict the time he had for some of his past recreations, such as robbing lobster traps and putting together dangerous chemical concoctions, and for some of his present interests, which often centered around Elizabeth Lamb, almost five years his junior "but awful smart; she understands me," as Russell said to his mother on occasion.

He sat cross-legged and silent on the float, Elizabeth Lamb beside him, while General Alison rowed out to his sloop. He looked up at the lowering sky and pondered while she informed him of the previous events and the part she and Persis had played in them. "And he seemed such a nice boy, too, Russell. I wonder who he was?" Russell wondered too, and thought perhaps he had been a confederate of Miss O'Cassidy's of whom she might have disposed, "to save giving him a cut," thought Russell. With one eye he nightly observed a great many movies with devious plots (while his employers assumed he was keeping both eyes on the customers), and they stimulated his already-active imagination.

The General brought the sloop under power up beside the float and the two clambered aboard. "Don't like anything about this whole damned day," said Lem. "Don't like the sky, don't like this flukey wind, and I don't like the air — it's stifling.

"We'll go out the Eastern Way as far as Bracey's Cove, then come back and Ludwig will give us some lunch beside the pool. I think swimming might be more pleasant today than sailing. You take the tiller, Russell. We'll keep the kicker on till we pass that nun buoy up ahead. Leave it to port, remember."

Russell beamed with pleasure as he handled the tiller. "Awful nice boat you got, General. How big is she?" he asked, as he did every time he was allowed to steer, to cover up both the pride and nervousness he felt.

"A thirty-footer, my boy; you ask that whenever we sail. Forty years old; they don't make 'em as they used to — boats *or* people. Except Marines, of course. Put in the head and the little galley myself; we three and Persis might go on an overnight cruise before the girls leave for Boston. If," he concluded morosely, "I don't have to sell her to pay — my debts."

"Why would you, Cousin Lem?" asked Elizabeth Lamb, heading below to the galley and glancing back at the tender, bobbing on *Iwo Jima*'s mooring. "I see Ludwig finally nailed the letters on the stern of *Tripoli*."

"Oh, you called the new little tender *Tripoli?*" Russell asked.

"What should I've called her — *Corregidor, Arizona?*" the General replied testily, eyes on the buoy ahead and then on a craft coming along the Western Way. He proffered Russell an overfull mug of ginger ale and opened the tin of ginger snaps Elizabeth Lamb handed him from the companionway. "*Don't* spill anything on my teak deck," he admonished, as usual, and then, as usual, "and, dammit, watch for that rock between Nun 2 and Can 1."

"When I was little," said Elizabeth Lamb, coming up on deck, "I always wondered why pointed buoys were called 'nuns.' And I was raised in Europe, too, where nuns wore all sorts of coifs, some pointed. Nun buoys should be black, though, and cans red, because nuns wear black habits.

"I don't see why they have to be different shapes, if they're different colors. Look at that big yawl coming in, Cousin Lem! Beautiful, isn't she?"

"Never liked yawls, somehow, though the old gaff-rigged ones were somewhat graceful-looking. Man who writes the Navy's history has one — named it *Amelia* or *Emily* or some damn fool thing. Told him it should have been *John Paul Jones*, or, at the very least, *James Lawrence*. Heh-heh. Told him a feller I know says a yawl is a sloop caught in the act of giving birth to a cat-boat. He didn't like it."

"Buoys are different shapes, Elizabeth Lamb," Russell advised, regarding her with astonishment, "because sometimes at twilight, or with the sun in your eyes, you can't see the color. And I suppose there're color-blind sailors, too."

"Red and black are tricky, though, my boy. Sometimes they fool me. A lot of things have fooled me," said Lem gloomily, glancing back at the shore.

"Are you color-blind, Cousin Lem?" Elizabeth Lamb hastily slid the cushion on which she had been sitting down to the deck to cover the ginger ale she had spilled. "Sometimes I've thought —"

"I saw that, Miss! Go below and get a sponge, quick!

"And how could I be color-blind?" he asked, glaring at her as she wiped. "I'd never have gotten to be a general. Do have a talent, though — never figured out why. Friends of mine used to take me along on bombing missions against Nip islands because I could always tell camouflage nets from real underbrush. We got a lot of little slants because of me."

"That's because you've got —" began Russell scientifically, observing the General, but he was interrupted by a bellow. "For God's sake, boy, keep your eyes dead ahead! We came too close to that rock.

"Now, I think I'll raise the main, but we'll keep the kicker on. Head her a bit into the wind when I go forward. Elizabeth Lamb, loose the main sheet and take out the boom crutch."

Lem moved agilely to the bow, muttering that the wind was too damned changeable. "But it's mostly west," Elizabeth Lamb called, over the noise of the engine. "You always say a west wind is the best." Her cousin, grunting as he tugged on the halyard, ignored her. Russell kept the bow pointed west and the sail was soon raised. "Ease her a bit back downwind, on an easterly course," Lem called, as he cleated the halyard. "See he keeps on the starboard tack, Elizabeth Lamb." He headed back towards the cockpit, looking up uneasily at the sky.

A sudden fierce gust of wind from the north caught the sail. The boom slammed to starboard, carrying the General overboard with a splash. Elizabeth Lamb quickly freed a life ring and tossed it into the sea near her cousin. She seized the tiller and put it hard to starboard, shouting, "Russell, don't take your eyes off Cousin Lem." The bow of *Semper Fi* was now pointed into the northern surge and the boat came about.

"Russell, be careful of the boom. Watch your head; I'm falling off now."

"You too? But why? He already done that," Russell stammered, still gazing at the small dot in the water.

"I just mean I'm heading downwind. We have to reach across the wind to get back to him. Keep looking at him, Russell."

As they neared the figure flailing in the cold Maine water Elizabeth Lamb saw that it was grasping the life ring with one hand while the other, made into a fist, was being shaken furiously at them. Now that rescue was imminent and her cousin obviously undamaged, she permitted herself a small smile at how the General's day, so triumphantly begun, was developing. The smile vanished as she realized that she and Russell would be forever blamed, world without end, amen, for the submersion. She pushed the tiller to port, coming into the wind, and *Semper Fi*, with wind blowing only on her mast, slowed almost to a stop. She reached down beside the tiller to put the craft in neutral.

The General swam to the boat. Russell hauled him aboard and then dashed down to the cabin for a blanket. "Get her in gear," the General ordered, teeth chattering. "Close-haul the sail, Russell. And, dammit, get me back to a hot bath before I *keel*-haul the two of you."

The wind had dropped, and their passage back was swift and quiet except for the "dammit to hell" 's emerging from the shuddering, black-striped olive blanket which was huddled about every part of the General's person except his eyes. Russell was helpful and subdued and Elizabeth Lamb exerted all the seamanship she knew. "Benevolent Protective Order of Elks," came from the blanket as they neared the harbour. Elizabeth Lamb smiled and assured her cousin that they knew to keep the black buoy to port on entering. As they passed Bear Island, with *Nihon*'s float in sight, she began to laugh, ignoring the mutterings from the blanket. "Cousin Lem," she said, "I've done one! I've done one of your rhymes. Listen:

> The General fell off the boat
> And wouldn't swim and couldn't float.
> When Colleen heard, she merely smiled.
> 'Naow we'll get the bathroom tiled!'

Isn't that good, Cousin Lem?"

Only two cold blue eyes flashed an answer. The General's teeth had stopped chattering and were now being ground together. *Semper Fi* came smoothly up beside the float and Elizabeth Lamb lept off with the bow line as Russell cut the engine and then jumped to secure the stern line. They dropped the sail and followed the General, who had stalked ahead of them along the lengthy bridge to the shore.

"You'll have to go out with Ludwig later, Russell, and get *Semper Fi* on to her mooring, with lots of chafing gear, too, and maybe an anchor, if there really is a hurricane," Elizabeth Lamb directed.

"Guess the General'll be able to tell us what to do by then, Elizabeth Lamb," Russell answered reprovingly. "You were real good, though, when he fell overboard. If 'twas up to me, we'd still be heading down the Eastern Way and he'd be drownded by now, or have pneumonia.

"Now, look, sit down a minute, because I want to tell you what I heard that O'Cassidy woman saying to him this morning."

Elizabeth Lamb was smiling proudly as they sat on a rock and Russell began to talk. Ten minutes later she was frowning as they rose and followed the path to *Iwo Jima*. "Maybe it's just as well he fell off," she said. "Miss O'Cassidy will have to leave him alone for a while. Maybe he'll just stay in bed in his room, with the door locked, to get away from her. And maybe we can figure out how to help him, because I think that woman is, to put it mildly, just *dreadful*."

• CHAPTER 7 •

Still Waters

E LIZABETH LAMB and Russell were, to put it mildly, surprised to find the General reclining beside his pool with a rum swizzle in his hand, talking animatedly to Mrs. Hackley. His brown hair was wet and somewhat disarranged, since he seemed not to have bothered to anoint it anew with his redolent Frances Fox Hair Tonic, but he had changed into a dry shirt and shorts and the tanned skin on his face and limbs glowed from a vigourous toweling.

"My goodness, shouldn't you be in a hot bath — or in bed, Cousin Lem?" Elizabeth Lamb asked.

"Had a bath, and The Corps doesn't take to bed because of a little sea water," her cousin answered. "Ludwig, another swizzle for Mrs. Hackley. Would you like one too, Russell?"

"I don't think I ought," said Russell, although tempted.

"Oh, Lem, dear," said Mrs. Hackley, "thank you, but I must be getting home. I had to sit down and just rest a bit, after speaking with Gloria and calling my lawyer about getting Philo out of jail. Gloria is so *very* exhausting to talk to. I mustn't intrude any further; I know you write in the mornings, and, dear

144

Philip wanted me back, with the police there."

"Nonsense, Catherine," the General replied, pushing Mrs. Hackley none too gently back to her chaise. "Enjoy your company, my dear; don't see enough of you. You must stay to lunch. Philip can handle the detectives.

"Maybe your two lodgers will be over. We might as well all sit out the afternoon here beside the pool, where it's sheltered. Who knows" — he glanced towards his cottage — "what storms the night will bring, hey?"

"But," Mrs. Hackley quavered, "I must put in my eye-drops. And did I take my insulin shot this morning? Oh, yes, thank goodness; I remember I did." She beamed proudly and began to rise again.

The General seized her shoulders and shoved her back. He firmly placed the drink Ludwig had provided in her hand. Ludwig, looking puzzled, went back to scooping leaves out of the pool. "Russell, here, can put the drops in for you," the General ordered. "He's planning to be a doctor, aren't you, my boy? Heh-heh."

Russell looked astounded, much as Elizabeth Lamb had looked before she realized her cousin's unprecedented warmth toward Mrs. Hackley and his favourable view of Bix and Dusty were designed to keep people around him and the calculating O'Cassidy at bay. "I'll do it, mam," Russell said confidently, "although I'm thinking of being a physicist, not a doctor. Where are they?"

Mrs. Hackley made a feeble attempt to get up, regarded her stern host, and desisted. She murmured weakly that perhaps the dear boy would run over to her cottage; that the bottle should be beside her bed and Mr. Shinowara or Philip would show him. She then drank a little of her rum and her face began to glow almost as brightly as the General's.

"No," said Persis, appearing suddenly with a tray of nuts and cheeses, one of Ludwig's red-and-white striped aprons wrapped just under her arms, "I saw you put the bottle in the sash of your kimono, when we were fixing the ginger beer. I guess you forgot again."

The eye-drops were produced, after some flutterings by Mrs. Hackley, and Russell operated successfully. Persis turned back to the kitchen announcing she was making sandwiches so Ludwig could clean and sterilize the pool, and that then they should all swim. "I put your sneakers in your closet, Elizabeth Lamb, because Ludwig found my clothes for me. I brushed out all the sand you got in them, and so now they're cleaner than they were. You all enjoy yourselves," she added bossily, "and lunch will be along soon, whenever I remember how to make Grandmother's mayonnaise. I bet none of you know mayonnaise was invented because Napoleon, or maybe one of his generals, ran out of olive oil during a siege —" she looked searchingly at Russell.

"Oh," she smiled, "I'm Persis Halstead, and you must be the boy Elizabeth Lamb *always* talks about. I guess she forgot to introduce me." She smiled again and disappeared, leaving an aura behind her that the annoyed Elizabeth Lamb suspected came from her own cherished bottle of *Réplique* perfume.

Elizabeth Lamb informed Russell that Persis was beginning to be insufferable and that she wished he had met the child when she was younger. Russell informed Elizabeth Lamb that at least Persis smelled good, not like that old lady, who reminded him of the lab. "I never smelled so much medicine on one person in my life; might's well have stayed at work today instead of tryin' to get some fresh air into me. Noticed it when I picked up her basket, and those eye-drops now almost made me puke. What's that she's wavin' around? Smells like ammonia. Geez!"

"That's her smelling salts. She takes a lot of medicine because she's got diabetes. The doctor said so last night, and he said she shouldn't drink, either. Goodness, I think Cousin Lem has given her a great deal too much rum."

As if to reinforce her apprehension, the General and Mrs. Hackley suddenly burst into song. "Tell me the tales that to me were so dear," he roared, beating one hand on his bare knee and grasping the back of Mrs. Hackley's neck with the other. "Long, long ago, long ago," she piped. They then laughed merrily and drank thirstily.

"My God," Colleen said loudly, from the cottage doors, "sounds — and looks — like the Lawrence Welk hour." Bix was behind her, smiling at one and all. "Good morning," he said. "Hope you don't mind some company. I just got a call that the concert tonight is being cancelled because of the hurricane, so we're taking the morning off from practising. Dusty was asleep on the shore, but there's quite a wind down there, so I woke him and brought him along."

He expressed gratitude for the drink the beaming General lavishly poured him. Dusty shambled in and gladly accepted his portion before he settled on a chaise beside the pool with closed eyes and an air of content. Lem called to Ludwig to mix up another pitcher or two of swizzles and went back to Mrs. Hackley.

Philip, hair rumpled and face red, descended upon his grandmother demanding to know why the hell she hadn't come home, where the hell his mother was, and why the hell he had been left to cope with the fuzz by himself. "They went through just about everything except the bureau drawers," he announced to Mrs. Hackley, who, for once, did not seem unduly sympathetic to his distress, "and when they didn't find any God-damned clues as to who that kid was or what he was doing here, they started to drain the pool in the inner courtyard. I guess they think we drowned him there and then dragged him to the beach and —

"Cat, for Christ's sake! Really, General, you know she's not supposed to drink! I'll go get her some cold water. If I may," he added cursorily, heading for the cottage.

Mrs. Hackley, in slightly rebellious tones, called after him that she was just fine. "Guess the police'll be over here next," the General said cheerily. "Oh, well, all in a day's work. What say we all have a swim before lunch? We've got plenty of suits in the cabana, there. Or should we skinny-dip, Catherine?" He winked raffishly.

"Oh, my," Mrs. Hackley answered, winking back. "I don't think so; not just now. We'll do it some moonlit night, perhaps, Lem."

The General beamed. "It's a date. Hey there, Chub! Come over for a free lunch? We're going to swim first, before the storm sets in."

Mr. Cooke was accompanied by Mrs. Faven. "I was walking back from the Rockefeller Gardens," she said, "and came across Chubby searching the underbrush along Peabody Drive. We thought we'd drop in to see how you all were. Has anyone discovered the identity of that unfortunate young man?"

Mr. Cooke was as red as Philip. "Somebody stole my Winchester," he announced angrily. "I forgot to bring it in last night, after all the hullabaloo here, and when I looked this morning it was gone. Might have been dropped somewhere by the thief, so I went through my grounds and was starting on yours when Elise came along. I suppose that Gaynor feller's sold it to a fence by now, though. Hear anything suspicious last night?"

Lem provided his friend with a cooling swizzle while Elizabeth Lamb recounted the story of the night intruder, with some embellishments by the General, who made a number of mis-statements she corrected, gently reminding him that he had been — asleep. When she came to the shooting of Hohenzollern she lowered her voice, but Ludwig, wearing a face mask, canvas coverall, and rubber gloves, was scattering a powder over the pool, his back to them, and did not appear to listen.

Russell wandered over to him, keeping a respectful distance upwind of the powder, and they began a learned conversation about different ways of sterilizing swimming pools, Ludwig's part of the discussion somewhat muffled by his mask and his hoarse voice. Calcium hypochlorite, they agreed, was simplest. "Especially," Ludwig said, through a fit of coughing, "since the General won't buy agitating equipment because of the high cost of electricity up here."

"I got great respect for him, but he's a mite close," Russell agreed. "I see he's keeping the old pool thermometer right there beside the new one, 'case it starts to work again, I guess!" As Ludwig gestured to him to move further away from the sterilizing process, Russell assured him, "I know how dangerous chlorine is if you breathe it in or get it on you. Specially if it gets mixed with ammonia or vinegar or other stuff. Friend of mine was baby-sittin', and the kid got under the kitchen sink and poured some bleach into a pail of toilet-bowl cleaner her dumb mother had got ready and jest left there, and the kid was 'most suffocated. She was lucky our science teacher had told us all jest what to do 'bout things like that!"

Russell's voice was loud and earnest. Mrs. Hackley, firmly refusing to drink the water Philip still urged upon her, shuddered and said plaintively that she did so dislike sad stories, amazing Russell, who had thought the ending a happy one. She and the General then began an off-key rendering of "My Darling Clementine." Persuaded by this, Philip and Bix joined the group, seating themselves by Dusty and hoping for more anecdotes from Russell. Mrs. Faven and Mr. Cooke picked up their drinks and wandered away from their melodious friends. Colleen served herself from the pitcher, with a sarcastic grin directed at the harmonizers. "Ugh!" she said to Ludwig, who had finished a careful stirring of the pool waters with the long-handled leaf scoop, "You've mixed too much of that junk in there. It stinks to high heaven."

"The mixture as before, Miss O'Cassidy," Ludwig answered politely, collecting his gear. Philip, looking at her with distaste, observed that it smelled better than the pool at Harvard.

"You go to Harvard?" Russell asked shyly. "Is it true that everybody there's got to swim a couple of lengths in that pool before they give 'em their diploma? I heard so, but it don't seem likely."

Philip replied that it was all too true, although he had known a girl whose English tutor was smitten with her and so, delegated to watch her swim her lengths, had turned his back while she struggled, and then passed her. "My friend," he explained, "though she'd had swimming lessons since she was four, was what one of the poor devils who tried to teach her termed a 'born sinker.' "

"But why the rule?" Russell persisted. "I'd like to go to Harvard, if not M.I.T., but I think I'm a sinker, too, though I never had a chance to learn to swim."

Philip regarded him with condescension and said he thought it was because some old lady's son had gone down with the *Titanic*. "And he'd gone to Harvard, but had never learned to swim, and she was convinced that if he had he'd have survived. So she told Harvard that she'd donate a pool, and money for its upkeep, if they'd make swimming a requirement for graduation."

Russell began to question Philip about his studies, and Philip began to eye Russell with growing respect. The ever-helpful Bix volunteered to help carry Ludwig's chemicals and other apparatus to the shed, and the rest of the men, aware that lunch would appear sooner if Ludwig could return to the kitchen, assisted him. Mrs. Faven civilly engaged Colleen in conversation, recounting long stories of various friends of hers in Australia, inquiring after each anecdote if Colleen happened to know those mentioned. Colleen finally answered impatiently that she had been brought up so far in the outback that she'd hardly ever met anyone, and that when she got to cities, she'd had to work for a living, "which I don't reckon any friends of yours are likely to have done," she ended nastily.

Mrs. Faven raised her brows, but politely nodded her agreement that growing up "beyond the black stump" would limit one's circle of acquaintances. "What black stump?" Colleen answered suspiciously, glaring around. Mrs. Faven concealed her smile and replied, sweetly, "Where the galah birds nest." Colleen frowned in bewilderment and Russell, who had, amongst his other activities, tried to listen to everything Miss O'Cassidy said, laughed and pointed to the large stump of a pine in the woods at the edge of the pool area, where the tray with Persis' almost-demolished supply of nuts and crackers had been placed by someone. A male cardinal and two females, ignoring the nearby company, sat on the tray, polishing off what remained. At Russell's gesture, the female birds flew off, but their lord remained, preening his bright plumage with one wary eye on the humans. "Oh, Lem," Mrs. Faven called softly, "you are so lucky! I never get any cardinals at my feeders, and that lovely red colour is so perfect against the pines. Look!"

The General looked and asked why she was getting so excited about some damned sparrow. Mr. Cooke looked and said beauty was in the eye of the beholder and he'd bet that little bugger would mess up his roses as quickly as the gulls did. Mrs. Faven sighed at the Philistines, but brightened as Persis and Ludwig, the latter now in a white jacket, appeared with a trolley of trays of food. Bix helped them arrange the provender on the long, slate-topped table that took up almost all of the small lawn at the far end of the pool, the only area of grass that the General had permitted about *Iwo Jima*. He announced often that lawns around the summer cottages of Northeast Harbor were not only an insulting disregard of the natural beauty of Maine wildsod, but also proved that "those Philadelphia people have more money — and more gardeners — than brains. Heh-heh."

Lem and his guests flocked to the table, Mrs. Faven courteously assisting Mrs. Hackley, whose gait was a trifle unsteady. As courteously she complimented her host on the verdant colour of his lawn and merely smiled at his ungracious reply that it always looked drab to him, in spite of the green of the many bills it took to buy fertilizer and pay for watering and mowing the damned thing.

"Never would have had an inch of grass on the place, but that patch was here when I paid a fortune" — he looked at Mrs. Hackley — "for the property," he explained to Russell, who was waiting for his elders to be served. Russell keenly regarded the General and nodded agreement, either to the pronouncement or to some thought of his own.

Mrs. Faven helped herself to a great deal of lobster salad, after she had served Mrs. Hackley, explaining that she had walked to Seal Harbor and back and was "absolutely famished. And are those rolls Mrs. Purvear's? How I love them!" She put a number of small chicken sandwiches on her plate, added a substantial amount of Ludwig's artistically-cut raw vegetables, and sank into a chair with an expression of content, unfolding her large napkin with a flourish and tucking a corner of it into the round collar of her starched blue linen blouse. She observed Russell's surprise and gently informed him that "all good trenchermen eat in the most sensible manner possible, as long as no one is offended, my dear young man. Having clothes washed is expensive, you know. And what is your name?"

Russell was hastily presented to her by Elizabeth Lamb, who remembered that she had not introduced him to Bix or Dusty, either. She did so, explaining their occupation in Northeast Harbor. "So you play the saxophone?" Russell asked Bix. "I'da thought you played the trumpet, from your name." Bix smiled and said yes, he did that, too; he was another 'young man with a horn.' "And Dusty, here, concentrates on the trombone, at which he excells." Russell said he didn't like a trombone as well as a sax, and then blushed uneasily.

"The evangelist Aimee Semple McPherson," Mrs. Faven observed kindly to Dusty, "once said that her idea of a perfect man was one who was good-looking, six feet tall, intelligent, a preacher and able to play the trombone. I would say you would fill all those requirements, if you could preach. Can you?"

151

Dusty, his mouth full, also blushed. He shook his head regretfully and for the rest of the lunch sat by Mrs. Faven, regarding her with as much appreciation as he did the large amount of food he consumed.

Colleen regarded with no appreciation at all the glass of iced tea Ludwig served her, after he had provided the rest of the adults with theirs, and Elizabeth Lamb and Persis with mugs of milk. "Out of beer, as usual?" she asked sulkily. "Look, you," — to Persis — "just run in and get my bottle of ginger beer out of the fridge. Was saving it" — she looked unpleasantly at Mrs. Hackley — "since it's only the second I've been able to get my hands on all summer." She gazed thoughtfully up at the lowering sky.

"You don't look at all well, Ludwig," Mrs. Faven observed, as he passed her the plate of butter Persis had painstakingly shaped into the curls her grandmother demanded at table. "Lem, Ludwig should be resting this afternoon, with such a heavy cold. You're working him too hard."

Mrs. Hackley, delicately nibbling at her salad, declaimed unsteadily, in between a hiccup or two, that there was *never* any need for Ludwig to work at cleaning dear Lem's beautiful swimming pool, because "water purifies all." The General groaned at hearing this yet again and assured Mrs. Faven that Ludwig would be able to rest until dinner, for which he wished them all to return, and "weather out the storm together, in good company, if the storm ever gets here." With an eye on Miss O'Cassidy, "And *I'm* going to shut myself up with Ludwig till then, making sure he takes aspirin and lies down perfectly flat with his eyes shut. After," he added hastily, "we all have a swim, and so on. Not meaning to speed the parting guests, by any manner of means. Heh-heh."

"We were going to swim *before* lunch, you said, Cousin Lem," Elizabeth Lamb reproved him. "It's getting a little too cold to swim now." Mr. Cooke rumbled through a mouthful of his favourite raw vegetables that if God had meant people to swim, they'd be born with fins, and the only use of water, as he saw it, was to put out fires. "Certainly not to drink; Lem, how about some of that great brandy to top off this wonderful meal?"

"Wouldn't get me in that pool even if the sun was blazing and it was filled with brandy," Miss O'Cassidy stated. "It's always freezing cold, and all for the sake of the few dollars it would cost to heat it. I haven't had a swim all summer."

"You could drive over to the swim club, Miss O'Cassidy," Elizabeth Lamb suggested hopefully. "Their pool's heated and, even though Cousin Lem isn't a member, I'm sure Mrs. Hackley would let you go as her guest."

Mrs. Hackley graciously assented, also looking hopeful, but Miss O'Cassidy confounded them. "Wouldn't catch me in that jumped-up place. Can't stand all those sailing types sitting around trying to look posh, staring at you down those dumb, big noses slathered with zinc oxide."

"Maybe they're having a tenament you could watch," Persis said earnestly, following Elizabeth Lamb's lead. She was discomforted as everyone laughed and Elizabeth Lamb gently explained that it seemed to run in her family, this combining of words. "Tenament" was declared by the tennis-haters present, Mrs. Faven and Mr. Cooke the loudest, to be the perfect word for those ordeals, and Persis was heartened enough to produce a smug smile for her helpful cousin.

"Don't know why I hate cold water so," Miss O'Cassidy mused, " 'specially since my dear old dad is so fond of it." Elizabeth Lamb immediately joined her Cousin Lem in urging everyone to return for dinner. Mrs. Faven demurred that Ludwig was "too much under the weather" to cook for so many people, after having produced such a *divine* lunch. Ludwig said thickly that he was "quite well, mam; but thank you for your concern."

As an end to the dispute, the bushes along the driveway parted to reveal Philo Gaynor edging through them bearing a huge, deep iron pan at least three feet wide that displayed a topping of fluffy mashed potatoes dotted with large slabs of butter. "Gloria made this pie up for your supper, mam," he announced to Mrs. Hackley. "Figured you might be up here, all the commotion I heard, so I brung it along 'stid of over to your place. It was real good of you to git me outta jail, and Gloria's grateful." He then sneezed explosively upon his offering. Bix quickly secured it for Ludwig to carry to the kitchen.

"Why, Philo, thank you," Mrs. Hackley said. "I'll leave it over here for Lem's dinner party and we'll all enjoy it, I know. Gloria makes such a delicious shepherd's pie. I hope she added garlic to the lamb this time? It gives a wonderful flavour — one almost Japanese!"

"Wouldn't 'zactly say 'twas lamb she used," Philo said easily, sitting down beside the almost-empty pitcher of swizzles, "but you'll find it tasty, mam. Mind if I heve just a taste of this, for my cold?" he asked the General.

"Native beef, I suppose, that is," Mr. Cooke snorted. "Whose gun did you shoot it with?" Philo grinned amiably and involved himself with the glass into which the General had, not so amiably, dumped the contents of the pitcher. "Hope a game warden doesn't come along with the other police," he told his uninvited guest. "Where *are* they, anyway?"

"Police comin' here agin?" Philo asked, swallowing his drink in one gulp. "Guess I'll be goin'. Seen enough of them today, persecutin' a honest man jest for a little tunk on the head of some jeezly son of a hoore what said some things in a way I didn't rightly care for."

"Oh, dear, Philo," Mrs. Hackley quavered, "who *was* it you hit? Not a friend of ours, I hope."

Philo was edging toward the bushes. "Don't know him, but I seen him onct afore, over to the village. Askin' too many questions of a hard-workin' man tryin' to hev a peaceful beer. Questions about jest everybody — maybe even you, General. Sounded like some constipated college perfesser, with a funny turn of speech. Had a fancy white coop car and talked jest as stuck-up as people from Boston, but funnier."

He disappeared, leaving the Bostonians present with mixed feelings of annoyance and amusement, except for the General, who felt rage mixed with apprehension. Mrs. Faven laughed merrily. "By 'funnier than people from Boston,' " she said, "he probably means the man was British. Oh, I do hope he wasn't a visiting English bishop trying to save that reprobate's soul. Catherine, you had better instruct your protegé in how to decipher the nuances of various accents."

A car was heard speeding into the driveway. Its door slammed shut, and Cynthia Dickcyn was with them, disheveled and angry. "Mother!" she said. "Here you are!" She fell into a chair and glared at

Mrs. Hackley. "Mr. Shinowara has left! Simply packed his things and called for a lift to Bar Harbor. He said he cannot bear upset and will not endure large, hairy policemen in his kitchen.

"Oh, God, what next? Mother it is *all* your fault for not being there to ease things. You *knew* how sensitive he was. And those detectives are *thieves*; there was a jar of — oregano — in the kitchen, well out of Mr. Shinowara's way, that is now completely empty. *What* do you intend to do about all this? *Why* can't someone make me a drink?"

Bix had disappeared into the cottage as soon as he heard the car. He produced a large gin-and-tonic for Cynthia, and sat beside her, soothingly rubbing the back of her neck. "He may think twice about leaving the scene of a suspicious death, Cyn," he said quietly, "although legally he can, I think. And he liked his job. I bet you'll get a call, probably tomorrow, that he wants to come back.

"Where have you been? You look awfully tired. Just relax and have your drink. What are the police doing now, at *Nihon?*"

Cynthia drained her glass and Bix signalled Ludwig to make her another. "I was delivering some damned ginger beer to Ellsworth, and the traffic was *unspeakable*. And then I get back to find a detective dusting my room for fingerprints and another waddling around the atrium with a tiny jar of water that had all the goldfish crammed into it. He was trying to fill the pool the stupid fools had drained, and unable to figure how to turn a tap!"

"Oh, no!" Mrs. Hackley put her hands to her heart. "My precious little carp!"

"It's all *right*," her daughter answered. "I got the water on and the fish are *fine*. While you all were having a great time, *I* had to do everything! Philip, they've left to trample up the beach but you should go home and see that they haven't stolen anything else!" She shoved a crumpled envelope at her mother. Colleen eyed her with interest as she announced that she didn't dare leave so much money at *Nihon* with uniformed crooks about.

Philip made no move to leave. He looked uneasily at his grandmother. "Cynthia," she said, unsteadily tucking the envelope into the sash of her *obi*, "we do *not* have an atrium. That is a Roman term. We

155

have a courtyard. And the — oregano — got, got spilled this morning when I was helping Mr. Shinowara. I will — find — you more, since I know how you depend on it. Cynthia loves to make delicious pizza — so nutritious," she ended feebly. Everyone except Bix, Philip, Colleen, and Persis, who was a trusting child but not a stupid one, looked puzzled, since Mrs. Dickcyn had never impressed them as a lady of domestic tastes or talents.

"Good God, Mother!" said Cynthia. "Never mind my pizza just now! If nobody's going to do anything, at least I could be offered some lunch, Lem."

The mention of doing something reminded Persis that the irascible Miss O'Cassidy, who had been unnaturally quiet for some time, perhaps awed by the dramatics of Philo and Mrs. Dickcyn, had long since demanded her ginger beer. She left quickly for the kitchen, where Ludwig was cleaning up some of the luncheon debris and making a shopping list. "Are you going to send Miss O'Cassidy to the store?" she asked, with some enthusiasm. "Oh, good, we're going to have ice cream. Why do you make your capital 'C's' so funny, with a loop at the top and the bottom? Does that say 'brussel sprouts'? I certainly hope not. You'd better get some more milk, too. Elizabeth Lamb and I drink a lot. You should go look at the beautiful powder room. Oh, you have? Would you like us to decorate your room, maybe? You don't have to roll up your eyes and sigh like that, Ludwig. I'm going back now."

Bix had provided Mrs. Dickcyn with a full plate, and she was haranguing her mother, as she ate, about her many and varied faults. Mrs. Hackley sat quietly, with closed eyes, and listened, more or less attentively. Russell, Bix, Dusty, Philip and Mr. Cooke moved to sit apart, to drink their tea and speculate as to when the police would arrive at Iwo Jima and what, if anything, they had discovered so far about the death on the beach. Mr. Cooke advanced various ploys for recovering his gun from Philo, despite Bix's reasoned statements that, first, he had to be sure that Philo was the culprit. "It may have been whoever shot Ludwig's dog," he suggested, to Mr. Cooke's scorn. Colleen joined the men, listening more than she spoke, and sipping her ginger beer appreciatively.

"Don't know why pools are called so," Russell mused aloud, tiring of Mr. Cooke's plans for recovery, one of which was that "some young man" go over and engage Gaynor in conversation while "another young man" enter the Gaynor home and whip out with the Winchester. "A pool," said Russell, "is 'a deep place in the river.'"

"It's also a 'small body of still water,'" Philip answered. "That's why."

"And 'still water runs deep,'" Russell rejoined. "That don't seem to apply, to pools, though. Maybe it does to Dusty, but I sort of think, maybe, more to Bix. Wonder who said that first, about 'still water'? Never could find out, and I'd like to know."

Elizabeth Lamb took Persis aside: "Persis, last night Cousin Lem and Colleen Did It!" Persis was aghast: "Do you think he made her, Elizabeth Lamb? Maybe it was like you told me that actress said, 'Never turn a man down flat.' Maybe Miss O'Cassidy needs her job."

Elizabeth Lamb was exasperated. "No, she doesn't. And Mae West didn't mean to Do It, just to ease *gracefully* out of it. I can't tell you now, but O'Cassidy's up to something bad. I'm going to sneak up and look around her room. You stay here and talk to people and if she starts for the house, you run ahead and call me, loudly, and say you want me to do something."

"To do what?" asked Persis, bewildered at the thought of being the social focus of what was left of the luncheon party.

"Oh, anything! You can think of something. Now, start circulating."

Persis circulated apprehensively, aware that she could seldom do or say the right thing when she was required to conceal guile. She took a deep breath and assured Mrs. Hackley that the shepherd's pie looked very good and that there was nothing she liked better except, maybe, barbecued spare ribs. "I love outdoor barbecues," she added, her voice rising nervously. "I have a friend whose family has a great big barbecue pit, but my daddy says only proles cook outdoors and someday they'll burn each other up." Mrs. Hackley turned white, although Cynthia continued to eat and drink and regarded Persis cynically.

Mr. Cooke looked coldly at her as she approached his group. "If you're inviting people to a barbecue," he said, "I'm going home.

Thought you were a sensible young lady — uneducated, but sensible."
Persis assured him both that there was to be no barbecue and that she
would never, never tell her friend Buzzie or anyone else that he shot
seagulls. "Nor that you hide your silver in the beds when you go
away. Cousin Lem told my mother how you hid a teapot once, and
forgot to empty it, and a guest came to visit and got cold tea all over
his feet. Or was it her feet?" Mr. Cooke frowned. Persis said she was
glad Russell was all better and since he had got hurt robbing lobster
traps — "or something like that" — maybe it was all for the best, as
trap robbing was dangerous and Elizabeth Lamb would *so* hate to lose
her only boyfriend, to date. Russell ducked his head in embarrass-
ment, with a quick glance up to see if Philip had heard, and Persis was
also a little embarrassed, because she realized "to date" might have
been too graphic a way to end her observation.

She quickly turned to Dusty and announced that although she had
read people of very low mentality *did* sleep a lot, maybe he just had
something glandular? Miss O'Cassidy snickered and Persis assured her
that just because Mrs. Hackley hadn't got around to putting the little
bag of special sugar in the ginger beer she'd given her didn't mean she
didn't *like* her. "It's only done just before shipping and I'm *sure* she
likes you, even though maybe no one else does." Philip was first
amused and then annoyed, with reason, since Persis considered him
thoughtfully and decided that he would probably become *much* more
masculine-looking as he aged, and she had heard premature babies
were usually *much* handsomer than timely ones. "Or is nine months
after a wedding premature?" she wondered. Ludwig had appeared
with brandy during her remarks to Dusty, and Persis, racking her
brains for further interesting conversation, told him that *no* one
believed he had *ever* been a Nazi, because he was probably too young,
even though "dyed hair makes people look older, not younger, my
grandmother says." Ludwig received this calmly and, encouraged, she
informed Bix that, even with dyed hair, older women often were *very*
attractive, and she didn't blame him a *bit*.

She left the thoughtful group and, passing the General, seated
peacefully beside Mrs. Faven and answering her sprightly remarks
while casting calculating looks at the sky, hissed in a loud whisper that

she and Elizabeth Lamb would *swear* they hadn't heard a thing last night *and* that he had locked his door and slept alone. Her cousin, puzzled and horrified, dropped his glowing cigar ash on his knee and cursed loudly. Mrs. Faven reached into her glass of tea for a cube of ice, placed it on the burn and advised Persis to run along. Persis ran along back to Mrs. Dickcyn, whom Ludwig had supplied with a double brandy, and announced she still had one of the beads picked up "after you stood on the stairs and broke them to make all the men look at you" and would fetch it from the pocket of the dress she'd worn last night.

Exhausted with her success in making interesting and pleasant conversation, she left for the cottage to tell Elizabeth Lamb how ably she had performed and to give a prediction that the group might not linger beside the pool for long. "Somebody will have to go to the bathroom," she advised, from the doorway of Colleen's room. "Go out and stand by the pool doors for a minute or two," she was ordered. "I'm almost done, Just watch to see she doesn't come up."

"It's practically three o'clock," Mrs. Faven said, eyeing the small look-out on the steps, "and that little girl seems to be standing there wishing us all to go home." She smoothed back her glossy, neat hair and prepared to rise, expressing gracious thanks to the General.

"No, no, Elise!" The General glanced at Miss O'Cassidy and pushed Mrs. Faven down as ungently as he had earlier handled Mrs. Hackley. "Tell us about your walk. Where did you go?"

"Well, Lem, I really should go back to the Inn and lie down after that superb and enormous luncheon, and with the prospect of a delightful dinner here, too! I'll say only that the Rockefeller Gardens were, as always, enchanting. And now, goodbye, till this evening."

"No, tell us more," the General implored. "Who was there? Lots of mangy tourists, I suppose."

"No one was there. The Gardens are open to the public only on Wednesdays, as surely you know. And," she reproved him, "I've heard your little cousin tell you that we are all tourists somewhere."

Russell joined them. "Do they let you in special?" he asked shyly. "I never been there. Mean to go, sometime."

Mrs. Faven laughed pleasantly. "An old hand like me doesn't wait till they're open," she said gaily. "I merely walk along the road beside Long Pond, cut up into the woods on the hill, and when I see the lovely, huge gilt Buddha through the trees, make my way down — and there I am!"

"A Buddha?" Mrs. Hackley quavered. "Oh, Elise, I've never seen him. And don't the gardeners ask you to leave? How brave you are!"

"The Buddha is up in the woods, as I said. You probably just poke along on the garden paths. Really, Catherine, if you would exercise more vigourously! And, of course, I wait until I think the men are off on their morning break and then just nip in! One gate in the wall is usually open.

"You know the story — possibly apocryphal — about some Rockefeller who visited China after President Nixon's visit? Well, he was shown the Great Wall and it is said he looked at it for a time and then decided: 'Very handsome. It reminds me of the wall around my mother's garden in Maine.'"

"China!" Mrs. Hackley sniffed. "There was no reason at all for that dreadful man to go there. Why doesn't he stay home and do something about the price of beef? Furthermore —"

"Never mind Mr. Nixon, Mother," Cynthia interrupted, eyeing Bix and Dusty, the latter again asleep. "Why are you two lounging around here? You're always practising the day of a concert." She gave Bix a hard look and added, "Or so you tell me."

"Now, Cynthia," said her mother. "They got a call telling them the concert was cancelled. Let's all go home now. I'm really very tired."

"A call to where? Don't tell me those interfering police answered the phone at our place?"

Dusty opened an eye. "Bix insisted we have a phone in the teahouse. Didn't you know? It's always out of sight — he pushes it under his bed, for some reason. Still, you might have heard it ring when you were —" He closed his eye and subsided.

Cynthia laughed. "I'm always too involved — in conversation — when I'm there. Funny, though, Mother hasn't permitted a phone in the teahouse since Bill What's-his-name was lodged there four years ago. She said Lem complained he could hear it ringing all night."

"Could, too," the General affirmed. "My bedroom window's too

160

damned close to that damned — to the teahouse. That feller got calls from midnight till three a.m., often. Whatever happened to him, anyway?"

"We heard he was killed in an accident in California, a few months after he left here," Bix said quietly.

"See! I always said telephones were dangerous," Mrs. Hackley, with her usual peculiar logic, informed him. "I hope nothing happens to you, Bix, dear. I like you so *very* much. You're so polite, unlike most young people." She looked at Colleen.

Bix smiled at her. "Nothing will; I always keep the phone under the bed, Mrs. Hackley." Mrs. Hackley nodded in relief, quite satisfied. Colleen sighed impatiently, rose and headed for the cottage. Persis left her stance shouting: "Elizabeth Lamb, there's somebody — something we have to do. We have to get Mrs. Dickcyn her bead I picked up. I promised."

Mrs. Faven waved farewell and moved gracefully towards the driveway, the General quick-marching in pursuit. All the men except Bix took the opportunity to rise and stretch. Mr. Cooke walked to the house, prudently carrying his brandy glass. Russell, realizing the bathroom facilities might be much in demand, disappeared into the woods.

Elizabeth Lamb and Persis passed Mr. Cooke in the doorway. They grasped hands and walked toward Cynthia, whose mother was still concerned with her lodger. "Are you comfortable in the *chaseki?*" Mrs. Hackley pursued. "I mean —" "*Wakana masu,*" Bix answered. "*Hai.*" Mrs. Hackley looked vaguely pleased, patted Bix's hand and, as Cynthia rose with an obvious powder room purpose, boldly took a sip of brandy from her daughter's glass. "I wonder if I should have brought another scroll for dear Lem's powder room?" she inquired of Bix. "Just a *pretty* scroll, of course, not a scroll of honour, a *tokon — toka* — oh, dear, I can't remember —"

"*Tokonoma.*" Bix and Philip supplied the word in unison, Philip with exasperation. The General led Mrs. Faven back, having successfully persuaded her to stay until her friend went home. "Needs you to look after her, Elise," he was saying. "May be younger than you but not so fat and sassy. Heh-heh."

161

Mrs. Faven murmured to him that perhaps he *was* beginning to appreciate that more than wine improved with age? She smiled as he reddened and, with her usual sense of *noblesse oblige*, seated herself again and took the brandy glass from Mrs. Hackley. Colleen flounced back and announced that the powder room certainly looked brighter—something like a Chinese whorehouse. Mrs. Hackley caught the adjective but not the noun and took genteel offense. She urged the General to inspect it for himself. Cynthia arrived from it with a dazed expression, and agreed that it was a masterpiece. Elizabeth Lamb explained that the garnet Persis had picked up had obviously been lost on the beach, as it was no longer in her pocket. She then uncrossed her fingers.

"Well, well, there goes my only clue," proclaimed a cheerful, quiet voice. Buzzie had arrived unheralded within a few feet of them.

"Ha, our gumshoe!" the General exclaimed, looking proudly about him for recognition of his modern slang. "Who're those fellers?"

"Couple of men from the Crime Lab," said Buzzie, waving them toward the house. "I'd like them just to look over the cottage, as you said we could, for a few minutes. They might print some surfaces, maybe, just to see if there's any evidence of a stranger having been in. Not in the living room, of course, with all those people here yesterday, but in your private rooms."

Elizabeth Lamb looked thoughtfully at him. She forebore to ask how, if he did not have their fingerprints, he would know which were a stranger's.

"It won't take long, General." Buzzie was smilingly reassuring. "This place's not as big as Mrs. Hackley's cottage, and with one fewer resident, so we'll be quick."

"Only one fewer?" The General was counting on his fingers.

"Well, we counted the lodgers in the teahouse as belonging to *Nihon*," Buzzie explained. "We had a quick look-see there," he added, to Bix. "Hope we didn't disturb anything."

The General muttered to Mrs. Faven that he'd have hoped they'd impound that damned saxophone and that God-damned trombone. "Live in hope and die in disappointment, as my grandmother was fond of saying," she told him equably. "Officer, we don't know any more than we did last night; at least, I don't. You're not going to question us again, are you? Have you identified the dead boy yet?"

"Going to drain the swimming pool?" Philip put in sarcastically. "Might be a clue there."

"No," Buzzie answered gravely. "I can see by looking that nothing — no weapon, for instance — could have been — accidentally, of course — dropped in it. Your little pool had lots of plants and rocks, so we checked it.

"And, yes, mam," to Mrs. Faven, "we've learned the identity of the deceased. As to what he was doing — and it does appear that he might have been waiting for someone, since he didn't leave right away when Elizabeth Lamb, here, saw him — we're at a loss. I'm glad to find you all here together. Thought I might ask you a few questions about the party guests. Didn't go over them too thoroughly, last night."

He nodded politely to Mrs. Hackley. "Your fish are okay, mam. Sorry about your cook. We told him he could go, since he was set on it, but we advised him to stay on the island for a few days, and he said he would. My guess is that he'll come back."

Mrs. Hackley was appeased, but Cynthia was not. "My mother is tired and needs to rest. For God's sake, tell us who the man was *and* what you want to know and don't take all day about it!"

"His name was David Jones." The General snorted. "He was a paid hand on that party boat, the *Sea Rover*, that came in yesterday. He was twenty-two and a student at a little college outside Philadelphia. Had joined the schooner in her home port, Jonesport, in June, and had never been to Northeast Harbor before: the other two times the *Sea Rover* put in this summer, he'd been sick or on leave."

"Was he a native of Maine?" Elizabeth Lamb asked. "He said he was."

"We don't know any more about him than the captain of the boat knew, which I've told you. We're checking with some people at the college and — at a couple of other places."

"Philadelphia, hey?" The General was triumphant. "Might have known it. Known to have a bad rep."

"It seems unlikely," Buzzie said, "from what we know that he

163

would have had any connection with any of you — I mean, with this place and t'other — so maybe he was known to somebody at the party. I'd just like to ask you what the guests were like and if any of 'em said or did anything you remember as being out-of-line, sort of."

"First tell us when and how he died, why don't you? Or aren't we supposed to know?" asked Philip.

"Death was caused by a severe fracture of the skull. Looked as though he'd been hit very hard with something, but we've been over the beach and the land around it and there's not a sign of a weapon. 'Course, by the time we got here it could've been carried out by the tide, or disposed of 'most anywhere. I think, myself, from the looks of his head and grains of sand in the hair, that he fell, hard, off that iron ladder and smashed his skull on a rock. Naturally the water's washed all the rocks on the beach clean, 'cept the tops of the biggest ones, and they don't show anything."

Mrs. Hackley shuddered. "I've told you, Lem, how dangerous that ladder is. There's *no* need for it. I don't see how anyone could *bear* to go down it; why, I can't even bring myself to look over the top of that dreadful cliff!"

"It was there when I came along," the General rumbled. "Don't go trying to blame me for it, Catherine. Go on, Lieutenant."

"And the feller's neck was broken, but that doesn't always cause death, as you may know. That, and the bruises on his throat and face, could have come from landing on the rock and sort of bouncing over on it, you see, from the force of the fall."

"He could certainly have fallen accidentally," Chub Cooke said. "Probably nobody was anywhere near him."

"It's certainly possible," Buzzie agreed. "But, we've still got to try to be sure he was here by accident and died accidentally, and if nobody on the premises at the time had ever known him, then that's what must've happened.

"As to when he died, with the body partly in the water from the moment of death till he was found, they can only put it from two to six in the afternoon. That's pretty general, I know. You get almost complete rigor in five to six hours, but rigor wasn't nearly complete — his broken neck hadn't even finished stiffening

164

— but, you see, the cold water would inhibit the onset."

He sighed. "About all we can say for certain is that he was alive sometime before one when Elizabeth Lamb talked to him, and dead sometime before seven, when she and Persis found him." He looked at Russell. "Were you one of the guests here last night?"

"No," the General answered for Russell, "but he's a guest now."

"My name's Russell Stark. I'm from Bar Harbor," Russell said politely to Buzzie, who seemed to recognize the name. He half-turned to Elizabeth Lamb, who nodded. "And, General," Russell went on timidly. "I was wonderin' if 'twould be all right if I stayed till about ten? I know it's a long time, but there's a friend of my mother's what works at the Asticou and she gets finished work then. I could call to see if she'd pick me up. I know it's an imposition." He blushed.

"No, no! Delighted to have you!" The General was ecstatic. "Maybe if the storm gets bad — and they say it won't hit till eight if it hits at all — she'll spend the night at the Inn and you can share my quarters. Got an Army cot somewhere; we'll look it out, my boy."

He addressed Buzzie. "Now, Lieutenant, what can we tell you? You have the invitation list Miss O'Cassidy gave you, but I can tell you right now that there were people here I never saw before and certainly did not invite."

"Too right!" Colleen agreed. "What you might call a motley crew, they were. Wish my mum had been here to take their pictures and then you'd see what I mean. She's a professional photographer, and a good one, as the General here can tell you. She's what you might call big name in Sydney; isn't that right, General?"

The General reddened. "If you say so, Colleen. Don't ever remember meeting her, as I told you this morning."

"Sounds as if the guests might have been pretty colorful, Miss O'Cassidy," Russell offered shyly. "Does your mother specialize in color photos?"

"Black-and-white only. She's done real well with her portraits," Colleen spoke with ostentatious pride. "If she hadn't been born color-blind, she wouldn't have made it so big, she always said. My dad should've stuck around to get his picture taken, him with all his medals."

"There's the cardinal again," Russell interrupted. "Look!"

The company looked. "Mighty pretty. We don't have them in Australia; nothing so bright red, anyways. Do we, General?" said Colleen, smiling unpleasantly.

"No red cockatoos?" Mrs. Faven asked. "Only pink galahs?"

"For God's sake!" Cynthia was disgusted. "Let's cut out the ornithology and get on with it!" Her voice softened. "Lieutenant, what do you want to know?"

"Let me say," Mr. Cooke announced firmly, "That there may have been some I didn't know, but they didn't have time to go down to Lem's beach. Drank steadily, they all did; and smoked steadily, some of 'em. *Very* dangerous."

"Not *my* beach, dammit!" said the General. "And what's wrong with a good cigar?"

Bix disagreed with Mr. Cooke. "No, I'd say there was a *lot* of coming and going. If any of them had a plan to rendezvous with the boy, he'd have had time to slip out and slide in again without being noticed. The point is, since none of us, myself included, seem to have known everyone at the party, how can we say who might have known the boy? Or even tell you who to ask?"

"We can't," Mrs. Faven said briskly. "I assume you have called everyone on the list and asked if they brought their houseguests, or anyone else?"

"Yes, mam. Only a few admitted to it, and they say they introduced them to the General and that their guests stayed close beside them all through the party. And we've asked the bartender . . ." To Mrs. Faven's look of respectful surprise, he explained: "First person we called gave us his number. He said there were people he didn't recognize, and he knows a lot of people, and, furthermore, he said some of 'em didn't really seem to know too many, if any, of the other guests. He gave it as his opinion that you had six or seven crashers, General."

"Only six or seven? Must have been more. Used twice as much liquor as I'd figured on." He groaned. "Oh, God. Now I've got the reputation of being an easy mark for gate-crashers as well as of having people dying free and easy on my beach. *Our* beach, should say, Catherine."

"What would you say the people you didn't know were like, mam?" Buzzie addressed Mrs. Faven. "Generally speaking, that is. Any that didn't seem to fit in atall?"

"No," Mrs. Faven answered promptly. "But some were snarky, as we put it. You know — the sort of person who is rude and ungracious without having the wit or the breeding to carry it off. And there were several of the young people who seemed the type who would promise fertility at a wedding ceremony instead of fidelity."

Buzzie smiled. "Everyone dressed right? I don't know what would be proper for a cocktail party here, but you would."

"Oh, they were dressed properly, if you overlook those chiffon pajamas women are wearing to parties now, even here. They just seemed a bit — brash. And there was a couple who had got lost sailing, or so they said, and arrived here in pants, still, evidently, lost. I *have* seen rude people come to cocktails without bothering to change — they think it makes some sort of statement, I suppose. But no one seemed to know these two."

"They were okay, though, mam. One lady mentioned them, and told us they're visiting a cousin of hers, the girl's mother. The lady didn't bring them, though, and thinks they crashed."

"*I* can put the women guests in a nutshell, Lieutenant," Cynthia volunteered. "They were all, except for the few of us who showed some style," — she smiled at her mother and Mrs. Faven and pointedly not at Colleen — "that dismal Bostonian plain-living type; you know, no make-up, long, lank grey hair in a knot and Grandma's emeralds in dirty settings. Or the dead-Palm-Beach-type, as I call them. Palm Beach's full of them in the winter: white skin, bleached blonde hair, too much lipstick, and large garden hats with wreaths of flowers, to shade their face-lifts. And *none* of them looked capable of murdering anybody."

"I guess you didn't see the young girls, Mrs. Dickcyn," said Miss O'Cassidy. "There were quite a lot of them, pretty, too." She rose and yawned. "Wonder why you don't notice younger women?" She grinned, and told Buzzie: "I figure I can't be any help. Didn't know all the names on the invitations I sent out, so I couldn't say if they were here or not."

She smiled with unwonted sweetness at Mrs. Faven and Mrs. Hackley and told the latter she was meeting someone in the village and almost had tried the powder she'd noticed in that *very* colourful powder room, but thought she'd save it for a more notable occasion, adding it was *certainly* generous of Mrs. Hackley to share her things. This attempt at civility having exhausted her, she told the General tersely that she would *certainly* be back for dinner. "We have some work to finish after that, you know?" She took herself off to the General's car, which quickly left the premises.

The General was happier at her departure. Buzzie went to check on his men. "I think, Russell," Lem said good-humoredly, "you might just sneak in and dial 599 and then hang up. When the phone rings, answer it and tell the police they're wanted urgently in Australia, or somewhere —" He grimaced, "No, never mind Australia; make it believable, like Bangor. I'd like to get rid of them and take a walk. Don't think we're going to get much of a wind, but we're certainly going to have a heavy rain tonight."

"You can make your own phone ring that way?" Persis asked wonderingly. "Elizabeth Lamb, couldn't we have fun at school!"

Mrs. Faven got up spryly. "I'm getting away while the getting's good," she announced. "There's absolutely nothing more I can tell that nice young man. Do you want us back at eight, Lem?" The General and Mr. Cooke rose, which they had not done at Miss O'Cassidy's departure.

"I'll come along with you, Elise," Mr. Cooke said. "I'm absolutely fagged out. Think I'll sack out for a bit before we come back. How about seven, though, Lem? Have to have a stinger or two first, don't we?"

Bix helped Mrs. Hackley rise, and she leaned heavily on his arm as they followed Cynthia to her car. Philip quickly made for the path to *Nihon* and Dusty followed him, yawning. "Don't forget, be on time!" the General shouted. "We all need company tonight."

There were murmurs of assent, and from the languid Dusty, one fainter reply: "But on the whole, I'd rather be in Philadelphia."

• CHAPTER 8 •

Caviare to the General

PLEASE. WON'T YOU wait?" Elizabeth Lamb implored quietly as Russell, obedient to the brisk command of, "Come along, my boy; we'll tend to *Semper Fi* and then look out that cot," followed the General as he strode towards the woods. "Russell, hadn't we better tell Buzzie what you heard Miss O'Cassidy say to Cousin Lem? Blackmail's a crime, isn't it? Maybe he could do something."

"Ab-so-lute-ly *not*; the General wouldn't thank us for it. He'd be real embarrassed and there's no need atall," Russell answered firmly, then ran to catch up with the loudly-echoing "Russell!" 's. He stopped and called to her. "Not a word!"

"Not a word about what?" Buzzie appeared from the cottage. "Something I should know?"

Elizabeth Lamb considered. "Well, there is, actually." She told him about Hohenzollern's death and about the disappearance of Tate Cooke's Winchester. "Do you think any of this is connected with the boy on the beach?"

"Couldn't say. Probably 'twas just what the General thought: some kid trying a little breaking-and-entering to see what he could pick up. Maybe he'd noticed a party going on here and figured the household would all be tuckered out and sound asleep.

"Funny he had a gun, though, but maybe he knew there was a dog." He pondered. "Yes, does seem funny, because these kids usually don't try anything *if* they know of a dog. Hmmm. I'll have a word with that Gaynor on my way by and see if he can give me a better description. Might get in a question about the missing rifle, too; don't expect I'll get any satisfaction for Mr. Cooke, but we'll have a go at it, delicate-like.

"Anything else go on here that you noticed — or remembered?"

"I guess not," Elizabeth Lamb answered slowly. "That garnet you found on the beach last night, though, really must have dropped out of Persis' pocket when we turned — when we were down there. Could you bring it back for Mrs. Dickcyn when you come over again — do you think you'll have to come?"

"If we don't uncover anything out-of-the-way about this Jones feller and we can't get any leads on why he was here, probably not — not on business, anyways. Guess we won't be working on this case together, you and me, since there doesn't seem to be a case." He smiled at her and turned towards Persis, who was efficiently loading the trolley with the despoiled luncheon trays.

"Goodbye for now," he called. "Maybe I'll be able to visit with you girls when I bring the garnet over; if not, there's always next year." He rounded up his men and left.

"I'm going to help Ludwig get things ready for dinner, Elizabeth Lamb. Why don't you take a nap?" Persis spoke kindly. "I heard you telling Buzzie how late you were up. Ludwig says after they deliver the grocery order he's going to lie down, too. I think I'll go see if that nice Mr. Gaynor will take me clamming. I hope the tide isn't still too high, or it isn't too windy."

Elizabeth Lamb went disconsolately up to her room. She sat staring out the window at the wind-tossed branches while a slight rain spattered against the glass. She felt vaguely discontented; about what, she could not decide. "I'll try to go to sleep awhile," she thought. "I still wish we had told Buzzie about Colleen."

When she woke, the beat of the rain on the windows was heavy. Someone, probably Persis, had drawn the curtains and switched on a small lamp. Elizabeth Lamb still felt tired and confused. She was cold. She put on a sweater and skirt and brushed her hair. "It's too dark for early evening," she said aloud. "Did I oversleep?"

As she went along the gallery she met Persis at the bathroom door. With one hand she was rubbing a towel over her wet, curly hair, and another towel was tucked around her chubby body. "Oh, good; you're awake," she said cheerfully. Elizabeth Lamb sighed. "Well, obviously, Persis. Why are you taking a bath so late? What time is it, anyway? My watch's stopped. And don't *ever* use two towels or Cousin Lem will have a fit. He checks our bathroom and says Marines can get dry with one."

"Goodness, Elizabeth Lamb, it's not nearly seven o'clock yet. I got soaking wet and cold coming back from Gloria's. She's not so bad, but I'm beginning to think Mr. Gaynor is. He just sat and drank beer all afternoon and talked about hating cops while she tried to clean up the house.

"I played with the children. Elizabeth Lamb, they don't have *one* book! I told Gloria she could go over to the library in the village and get out some books for them but she said Philo wouldn't take her and she can't drive the truck and it's too far for the children to walk. She made me instant coffee and I showed her how to make cinnamon toast but I had to run back here for the cinnamon. And the butter she had was margarine. I'm going to go down and take off the margarine on that pie and put butter on it because you know how grandmother always says nothing gives flavour like butter.

"I brought them some of your shampoo, too. We washed the children's hair. One of them had a big lump on his head and I think Mr. Gaynor did it to him. Oh, Elizabeth Lamb, Native women, some of them, have a hard life!"

"Yes," sighed Elizabeth Lamb. "So do lots of people — and some of them don't live to have one. And dogs, too. You never knew Ho, but I'm beginning to feel awfully bad about her. I feel bad about that boy, too, and I didn't even know him.

"Why is it so dark and quiet downstairs?"

"Ludwig's still lying down and I guess Miss O'Cassidy isn't back yet. Russell's in Cousin Lem's room. I heard them laughing and talking when I came up. Philip got here when I did; he said his mother told him to walk over first because she would be late driving his grandmother over. He was wet and mad. I put an onion in the oven to roast."

"For heaven's sake, Persis, why? You are getting as bad about food as your brother. You're always fixing it or talking about it."

"I am not, either. Rachel at school says her mother always roasts an onion when she's late with dinner. The nice smell makes Rachel's father think something good is cooking. She says her grandmother did it, and her great-grandmother, and all the way back to a great-great-great —"

Elizabeth Lamb, smiling and nodding agreeably, gently shut the door on the matriarchy of Rachel's family and went slowly down the stairs. Philip was lighting a small fire. "Don't put any more logs on it," she advised him. "Maybe it will burn down by the time Mr. Cooke comes. You know how he is. Don't you think it's dark in here?"

Philip replied sulkily that the dark was restful and he didn't care *how* the old fool was but that *he* was cold and wet and tired and sick to death of having to think of everything and perform every damned unpleasant job that came along.

"What do you want to be —" Elizabeth Lamb had almost said, "when you grow up?" She rose to turn on a second lamp and amended her question to, "when you get out of college?"

"Rich," Philip answered promptly. "So rich I can do whatever *I* want."

"Nobody can do just what he wants," Elizabeth Lamb stated with authority. "Everybody knows that. Not even the President or the Queen of England. Them least of all, I guess."

"I don't intend to be President," said Philip. "That's a sucker's job. All I'm going to be is rich. That's one thing I'm determined on."

"My grandmother says, 'Be very careful what you make your heart's desire, for you may attain it,'" Elizabeth Lamb directed him. Philip directed her to shut up, for once, and slumped down in his chair, closing his eyes. Elizabeth Lamb went to the dark kitchen and turned off the smoking oven, which Persis had set on Broil. Ludwig had already prepared a tray of cocktail biscuits and relishes, put out glasses and bottles and filled an ice bucket. There was no sound from his room, so she knocked on the door and called softly that the guests would be arriving soon.

As if on cue, a bulky yellow form tugged open the terrace doors. Mr. Cooke doffed his hooded sailing jacket and waved it around, scattering drops of water indiscriminately, before he tossed it on the brass coatrack. "What's that smell?" he demanded. "Is something burning? Where's everybody? Dark in here; Lem saving on his electric bill again? Is there a screen in front of that fire?" He switched on all the kitchen lights, peered to see that the oven was off and muttered at the cinders inside, then poured himself a goodly amount of bourbon.

"Good to see you, Chub," the General said jovially, descending the stairs, a smiling Russell close behind him. Persis, wearing her Liberty frock and Mary Janes, followed them. "Have a drink, why don't you? Heh-heh.

"See you brought a flashlight. Good thing, because Russell's is the only one in the place; guess Gaynor's been in since the last blackout. They think the lights may go out if the storm gets worse. Friend of mine called from Bar Harbor to see if we had electricity; it's gone off twice over there. Find your Winchester yet?"

"No, I did not. Fat chance." Mr. Cooke replenished his drink. "Saw somebody leaving here when I came out of the woods. He was carrying a flashlight, I thought, but I was a good distance away and the rain slowed me down. Slippery path."

"That was Bix," Philip yawned. "He came in a little while ago. Thought Dusty was right behind him, but when he didn't show, Bix went back — to light his way, I guess. Looks after him like a mother hen." He closed his eyes again.

Persis ran to open the doors for Mrs. Hackley, who was huddled under a large black umbrella her daughter carried. Elizabeth Lamb noticed that both ladies had forgotten they were entering by the "devil gate." Bix and Dusty appeared behind them and helped them out of their raincoats. Mrs. Hackley wore a round peaked straw Japanese hat which drew a grimace from the General as he hung it on the rack and gallantly conducted her to the fire, now almost out. "Cold, Catherine?" he asked solicitously, reaching for another birch log.

"You don't need that, Lem!" Mr. Cooke seized the log and tossed it back into the basket. "Let me just turn up this baseboard heater a bit. There!"

"Oh, dear; we should conserve electricity, Tate." Mrs. Hackley fluttered her hand at him. "We'll need it all if the lights go out. Philip heard on the radio that they may." Mr. Cooke raised his eyes to heaven and turned the baseboard dial to high.

Mrs. Hackley's frown disappeared as Cynthia handed her a sherry glass filled to about a half-inch. She smiled agreeably at everyone, as did her daughter, who was demolishing the Bloody Mary which Bix had made for her: "Guess what, troops? Mr. Shinowara called just before we left and said he'd changed his mind! He dislikes Bar Harbor intensely and will be back day after tomorrow. Till then, he's promised to help out a friend who runs a restaurant and just lost her cook. He says the help in public restaurants shows absolutely no gratitude and leaves whenever they like, and *always* around Labor Day. He was very disapproving."

"Oh, thank you, Bix, dear; another is just what I need."

Philip muttered audibly that the damned ingrate his grandmother paid so lavishly should have been told to come back tonight, and *not* day after tomorrow, and then they could have all stayed home and been comfortable. Bix immediately asked Ludwig, now moving about the kitchen, if there were any of that good Australian beer? Philip opened his eyes, sat up, and looked more amiable.

"Well, isn't this lovely! Here we all are together, warm and dry!" His grandmother was beaming, both at her quota of sherry and the promised return of her cook. "Everybody is here except Elise."

"And Miss O'Cassidy." Bix was handing the General the large Scotch-and-water Ludwig had issued him. "Could she have had an accident, do you think? The wind seems to be dropping, and the rain had slackened when I came back, just now, but it has been very heavy. The roads must be slick."

"Don't anybody look too worried, naow." Colleen's voice was sarcastic. She grinned from the doorway of her room. She cast calculating glances at Bix and Philip, smiled again, and asked them which *gentleman* would hand her over a mug of her favourite brew. Philip regarded her with a frown and shut his eyes. Bix hastened to the kitchen.

"Well, my dear!" The General was extremely pleasant, to the astonishment of Elizabeth Lamb and Persis, who were sitting quietly in a corner till their cousin should become flushed and jovial and not notice their slipping to the kitchen for sustenance. Russell, beside them, looked stolidly at Miss O'Cassidy. "Here you are," said Lem amiably, "safe and sound! I'm very relieved; didn't hear the car."

"I drove in long over an hour ago. Just quietly sitting in my room where I've been — thinking — planning — relaxing — looking — listening." She grinned around again.

"Well then, my dear, since you've been resting, perhaps you'd fetch Mrs. Faven from the Asticou for me?" The General spoke courteously, but more as a command than a request. "I don't think she'll walk in this rain, and perhaps she can't get a car."

Colleen looked steadily at him over the rim of her mug. She raised her brows. Her employer looked steadily back, curtly nodding once.

The apparent impasse was resolved by Mrs. Faven's appearance at the pool doors. She came in gaily, shedding her ancient Burberry and whisking off the printed kerchief that had been tied under her chin.

"A lovely storm!" she announced. "I do so love a variation in the weather! The rain is slackening, though, and they say at the Inn that the hurricane turned east just below Portland. We'll miss all but a little of the winds," she said with regret, as Lem pulled forward a chair by the defunct fire and Ludwig produced a large vodka with ice and lime.

He returned to the kitchen for his tray. Mr. Cooke quickly appropriated the largest stalk of raw broccoli before the tray was proffered to Mrs. Faven and Mrs. Hackley, both of whom declined with pleasant smiles, before they began to talk together animatedly.

"Oh, Lem," Cynthia Hackley said, selecting a biscuit and then hastily replacing it, "I thought these all had caviare, but Ludwig's slipped in that Provencal stuff again. Really, I've never known anyone except you and your secretary who could stand it."

"Love it; love black olives and anchovies and olive oil and capers and they grind 'em all together for Tapenade. 'Poor man's caviare', they call it." The General was licking his lips in anticipation while Bix and Dusty carefully chose biscuits that held real caviare. "Those Frogs know a bit about food; nothing much else, though."

"You certainly have exotic — not to say, contrary — tastes, Lem," Cynthia pursued, glancing at Miss O'Cassidy. "Some play my husband's dismal family performed put it just right — 'pleased not the millions; 'twas caviare to the general,' it went. Can't remember the name of it, some obscure thing, I guess. I found it rather dull, but I always remembered that line."

Tate Cooke looked incredulously at Cynthia, but the General chuckled at her wit. "Very fitting: 'caviare to the General,' " he said. "After you, my dear," he addressed Miss O'Cassidy, whom Ludwig, as usual, had left till the last. With deliberation, she picked up the half dozen crackers spread with the General's favourite, sniffed them loudly, and tossed them into the fireplace. "They smell just like the swimming pool; you've added Clorox or some other bleach to that stuff, I'd say. Not trying to burn out the General's gut — or mine — are you, fella?" She glanced around.

The General gathered up the discarded biscuits and held them to his nose. Ludwig was icy. "The jar was an unopened one, Madam, and I put nothing else on the crackers. The remainder of the Tapenade is in the refrigerator. I noticed nothing amiss — nor is there any bleach of any kind in the house."

"But, as you told us yesterday, Ludwig, you can't smell anything," Lem reminded him. "These do reek of something awfully strong — sour — ammonia, is it? Can't place it. Perahps you should put them in the trash. They'd smell up the house when we start another fire. And better throw out the jar; hate to waste a gift from — who was it, Ludwig? — oh, that feller who came to stay in June. Better safe than sorry, though."

"I'll put them down the w.c., General," Colleen offered. "You don't want to knock off a raccoon or one of those Gaynor kids that's always in the garbage cans. Pretty strange, this." She looked deliberately and appraisingly at everyone in turn, her gaze lingering on Cynthia. "Maybe we should have the stuff analyzed. I'd like to know what's in it."

The General impatiently waved her towards the powder room and turned to his silent guests, rubbing his hands together briskly. He jovially urged everyone to get his drink replenished and "then let's have a good round of skittles before dinner. Russell, build up the fire, would you?"

As Russell rose to obey, all the lights in the cottage went out. There was a loud, disgusted cry from the powder room, a louder oath from Mr. Cooke and a moan of distress from Mrs. Hackley before the lights came on again. Colleen kicked open the powder room door and joined the group, declaring that, even in the dark, that place "fair blinded" one. "And, speaking of gifts, not to say Greeks bearing 'em, it's a beaut case in point!" She grinned and carried her pink gin to the fire to watch Russell's efforts. Mrs. Faven left Mrs. Hackley to her and went to assure Ludwig how very delicious, always, everything was, and to ask if she could help with dinner.

"Never mind dinner just now, Ludwig," the General dissented. "You'd better fetch more wood from the shed. If the damned electricity quits again, for a time, we'll need it. There should be a couple of boxes of candles you might look out, too."

He switched on the lamp beside the skittles table. "Turn off all the others, Ludwig, would you? The surge when the damned things come on, after a failure, 'sbad for 'em. Can burn the bulbs out faster, too, and you know what they cost." The men joined him, Bix smiling at his host's economy, but Philip remained to listen to his grandmother's and Miss O'Cassidy's conversation, and Mr. Cooke went to the kitchen. He opened the refrigerator door for light by which to pour his bourbon. "Colleen, where's the box of dimes?" Lem called. "Find it, would you? Come on, now; let's get some exercise." He bumbled about in the semi-darkness, muttering that things always seemed to be missing, lately, just when he needed 'em. Persis called to him that she had been reading that people of genius always lost things, which did not appease him. Colleen, smiling and gesturing widely, began a quiet conversation with Mrs. Hackley which Elizabeth Lamb, curious as ever, could not overhear. With a final grin, she left the older woman leaning back in her chair, close to tears. Philip, also upset, took her hand and spoke quietly. On the other side of the large fireplace, Elizabeth Lamb moved close to Russell, on his knees blowing on the kindling under the logs: "Russell, I found out something! You-know-whose passport says she was born in England. She's not Australian at all! So how could Cousin Lem be her father? And what was she saying to poor Mrs. Hackley just now? She's so mean! I bet she was tormenting her about trying to snag Cousin Lem by fixing up the place."

"Couldn't quite hear, but you're probably right; more of her cultch about that powder room and what to spend money on in her garden, more grass and fewer something. I already figgered out she wasn't an Aussie, or, at least, not from where she says. I think that other lady did, too — the tough old one.

"As for your cousin not being her father, just her being born in England doesn't prove it. There's planes, you know. But I *told* you not to worry." He blew forcefully and Elizabeth Lamb sighed in exasperation.

Mr. Cooke took his drink to the television at the pool end of the long room, announcing that he, for one, had enough exercise for the day, and news was what he was interested in. Somebody ought to know whether we were going to blow away or not, he informed his host. "At least I can see to get my glass to my mouth by the light from the screen; it's free, too, with the picture! And will somebody keep an eye on that fire!"

Mrs. Faven produced two small plastic flashlights from her handbag, thoughtfully handed one to Mrs. Hackley, and made her way to the powder room. Mrs. Hackley faltered toward the kitchen, murmuring that no one ever gave her enough ice in her water, although Elizabeth Lamb noticed she carried her sherry glass. She and Persis sat by the fire, strategically near the table that held the tray of *hors d'oeuvres*, waiting for the game to engage the attention of the General, who was loudly commanding that he and Bix would first take on

178

Cynthia and Colleen and that Dusty could tend the scoreboard, a handsome appendage of mahogany, brass and gilt-numbers-on-leather that was affixed to the head of the table. It was directly under the framed motto on the wall: "Playing well is the best revenge."

Dusty yawned and asked to be excused from his post, pleading exhaustion and sinking determinedly into a chair in the corner, under the single lighted lamp. He patted the telephone on the table and said he might have to make a call, then leaned back and closed his eyes. "I'll keep score," Russell volunteered. "I know how."

"First, does anybody have any dimes? I've only got one. Colleen, *can't* you find that brass box with the dimes? I've looked everywhere," said the General.

Bix reminded his host that he and Dusty had got out of the habit of carrying change in their pockets — "distracts us when we're playing, you know." Russell groped through his, and produced a dollar bill and a quarter. Tate Cooke gruffly replied, to the General's peremptory shout, that his money was home. "Didn't think a dinner invitation called for cash, Lem."

"Come on! Let's start," Cynthia demanded. The General was obdurate. "Money talks, my dear. If you haven't any, don't give orders. Heh-heh. Won't get but a few minutes of play with one solitary dime. Colleen, you're the best at nipping into the coin drawer inside. I'll lift up the table top and you empty out the dimes."

Miss O'Cassidy moved slowly to comply. The General grunted as with both arms he began to lift the mahogany-rimmed end of the heavy, felt-covered slate table. "For God's sake, General," Philip said. "That thing weighs a ton. Hold on; I'll put up the supports."

The phone beside Dusty rang loudly, the lamp went out, and the end of the long room was completely dark. There was a howl of pain from the General, a crash, and then the thud of something heavy falling to the floor.

"God in heaven!" yelled Mr. Cooke. "What are you doing up there?"

Mrs. Faven had paused beside him to watch the television. She quickly used her flashlight to find her way to the lamps near her, directing Mr. Cooke to the others. Mrs. Hackley came in from the kitchen, crying out at the sight of the General's body face down on the floor, half under the skittles table. She dropped her light and knelt beside him.

The others had stood frozen for but a few seconds. Ludwig came in and threw down his bag of logs before he went quickly to the table. "Don't anyone touch him," Bix commanded. "Stand back and let me look. Dusty, try to fix that lamp."

"Look all you like, dammit," came from under the table, "and then turn me over — damned gently — and help me up. I think my Christless right shoulder's broken. Will somebody answer that phone!"

"Elizabeth Lamb," said Bix, "hold this flashlight. You, Russell, help me turn him." He folded back the General's tweed jacket and passed knowledgeable hands over his shoulder and arm. "There's nothing broken, I'm sure. You might have torn the rotator cuff, though. I think a doctor should look at it tomorrow. Stand up, General, and tell me how it feels when you lift the arm."

"It feels like hell," he was answered. "My God, if I hadn't dodged, that table could have cracked my skull open. Somebody shoved me as it came down and it just got the shoulder, and knocked me flat. Why the devil didn't you stop it, boy?"

"I couldn't see," Philip stammered. His grandmother looked at him reproachfully. "Dear Lem might have been killed," she faltered. "Damn it!" Philip was angry. "I was raising the support on the right side when the lamp went out and the next thing, I heard you shout and the table fell."

"Why didn't you keep holding it up, Lem, till Philip had the support in place?" Mrs. Faven asked reasonably.

"Dammit, I was pushed, I told you! Where's Colleen? My God, reaching for the coin box puts your head right inside the damned thing."

Colleen, as white and shaking as Philip, was standing by the kitchen doorway, just out of the circle of light. Ludwig went to turn on the kitchen lights, looking at her sharply as he passed. "Something made me duck," she answered sullenly. "Instinct, I guess. Then I nipped over here, in case something else happened. Why'd you let go of it, General?"

The General's face was apoplectic. "I — was — shoved — backwards — and — to — one — side. I've *said* so, for Christ's sake! Ludwig, I need a drink. Who the hell was on the phone?"

"Nobody," Dusty said quietly. "When I picked it up, nobody said anything."

"General," Russell spoke timidly. "I was standing right by the scoreboard at the other end of the table, where the top is hinged on to the frame. I guess my hand was on the rim, because, jest when the light went out, I could feel the end you held was going down. So I jest real fast jumped, and pushed out in the dark, to get anybody out of the way who might've got caught. Thought Miss O'Cassidy would be the one; she was reaching in jest before. But I guess I pushed you."

Colleen's face completely drained of colour. "If it hadn't been raised so high, I wouldn't've had time to pull out. Nice goings-on, I must say. First the biscuits are poisoned, and now this!"

"Miss O'Cassidy," said Ludwig, his voice loud and uneven and his face red, "you can inspect the jar of spread and I assure you that I added nothing to it. You could have had the biscuits inspected, except that *you* disposed of them."

"Now! Now!" the General spoke quickly. "No more, please. Accidents do happen. We're all safe and sound, so let's have another drink! You fellers can play; think I'll just sit down with these lovely ladies while Ludwig gets dinner ready. Did you bring the candles in, hey?"

Dusty, still reclining, held up a brass box and a small white object. "The box of dimes was under the chair where I'm sitting. Found it when I checked the lamp cord. The lamp was plugged into this" — he indicated the white rubber plug — "and it was in the outlet. It's one of those automatic things the lady gave you yesterday at the party, General. The ringing of the phone right beside the lamp turned the light off. Funny, I thought I had left it attached to the TV, but, then, there were two, weren't there?"

"I took the other up to the General's bedroom this morning," Ludwig said, with raised brows.

"Well, well, someone moved this one; that's all." The General was

181

hearty. "Doesn't matter. *I'm* happy, since I can lift a glass with my right hand now. Heh-heh.

"Catherine, for God's sake stop sobbing. There are no casualties, my dear. Here, come over to the fire. Chub, go on back to your boob tube."

The lights went out. People moved to retrieve the packets of candles from wherever Ludwig had dropped them, get them lighted and placed in some sort of holders. As soon as a dozen tapers were shedding a glow on the proceedings, the electricity came on again. "Damn!" said the General. "Nobody turned the lamps off."

"Really, Lem," Cynthia answered, "we were having enough trouble getting some light in here without worrying about the price of your bulbs. Bix, let's have a game. Dusty and I will take you on."

Ludwig announced that dinner would be ready in about half an hour. He added that he would take the precaution of heating Mrs. Gaynor's pie in the oven of the small gas stove the general had prudently installed in a cupboard in his study after the nine-hour blackout he and some winter guests had endured at his cottage one Christmas Eve.

"Always thinking of chow, Lem, aren't you?" Tate Cooke observed. "Still, it's a good idea not to rely solely on electricity on this island; I've hardly seen one summer that an idiot or two didn't drive their cars into a pole, and then it seems to take hours to find the break and repair it."

"The electric power company does seem a bit inefficient," Mrs. Faven remarked judiciously. "I've lived in a good many places and neither paid so much for electricity nor had it fail so often. Why, tonight there's hardly a wind, much less a hurricane."

"Maybe there's more than it seems," Dusty said. "I just tried to make a call, and the phone's out. The one in the kitchen's dead too, so it must be the line."

"Well," the General was determinedly cheerful, "when the phones don't work, it's impossible to call up to complain, hey?"

"Do you think," Mrs. Faven frowned thoughtfully, "that it is the independent Yankee spirit that makes them resistant to criticism as well as to new ideas?"

The General snorted. "Do you know, a feller from up Aroostock way — what they call 'The County' — was complaining on the radio the other day that many of the potato growers there simply refuse to wash the potatoes before they're bagged. California, Idaho, and Canadian growers do it, and their potatoes look more appealing and sell well, but the majority of Mainers won't — too new-fangled an idea."

Miss O'Cassidy had been sitting apart, pale and thoughtful, drinking more than usual. "The County?" she roused herself to ask. "That's a pretty primitive place, so I've heard. They say that on some Maine islands a virgin is a girl who can run faster than her brothers, but up in The County she has to run faster than her father, too." She laughed unpleasantly. "Did you ever hear that one, General?"

"Really, Miss O'Cassidy!" Mrs. Faven frowned and indicated Persis and Elizabeth Lamb, to their discomfiture, since their mouths were, at the moment, full of contraband canapes. Russell rose and stood in front of the fire. He spoke loudly.

"Father-daughter relationships're a fascinating subject," he said with authority. "At the research lab where I work, you hear all sorts of int'resting things. For instance, did you know that a lady who isn't color-blind, but has a mother who is, has to've had a father who wasn't color-blind? The General and I were talking about that jest this afternoon, because he's color-blind, though he was able to cover it up enough to get into the Marines, years ago."

His audience looked slightly confused and more than slightly disinterested, except for the General, who beamed and nodded, and Miss O'Cassidy, whose face turned an angry red. "So," Russell went on, "we were thinkin' how, if he'd ever had a daughter — or wants to have one," he hastily added, "he'd have to marry a woman who wasn't color-blind, else his daughter would be, for sure. It's an absolute law of genetics, and people like lawyers and judges know it now, as well as scientists."

"Well said, my boy." The General had fetched a half-mug of beer and now raised it in a salutory gesture as he handed it to Russell, who blushed, sat down next to Elizabeth Lamb, and sipped delicately. "Told you," he muttered to her. "Weren't you

183

noticin' all the things that showed *he* is and she *isn't*?"

"Aren't you a little young to drink?" Miss O'Cassidy asked, in her most abrasive tone. "I heard you had a bad accident this summer; you might just have another one — if you don't keep your wits about you, that is."

Russell smiled. "I'm very careful now, mam. And my friends all look out for me." He returned her look steadily.

Colleen drained her glass. "Guess I won't be here for dinner after all," she called to Ludwig. "I'm going to take a last run to the village to see about my ride to Boston tomorrow, and I'll find something to eat there. Hate to miss this lively party, General, but working girls have to do what they must, as I reckon you realize.

"Probably," she gave him a brief nod, "I won't see you before I go, but all the typing's done, up to where you stopped indexing. Maybe you'll just put my check on your desk tonight? It's been beaut here; no hard feelings, I hope — about my leaving before Labor Day, I mean." She waved a hand, picked up her raincoat from the rack, and was gone. The sound of the General's car starting could be heard clearly through the light rain.

Mrs. Hackley's face might have been a calendar illustration entitled *The Season of Joy*. "Oh, your secretary has resigned, Lem? Cynthia," she interrupted her daughter's loud self-congratulation on her skittles' prowess, "Lem's secretary is leaving. Imagine!" Cynthia called that she couldn't care less about that b —, about that beautiful young lady except that one fewer for dinner assured larger portions for everyone, and she was starving. "And Ludwig is either too hoarse or too polite to announce that he's ready, but let's go!"

Ludwig was standing by the large tureen on the sideboard, a copper ladle poised above a tier of heated soup plates. Mrs. Faven briskly made for him, secured the first filled plate for herself and took the seat at the foot of the long table. "Or am I at the head, Lem, since I can look out at the pool — or I could if it weren't such a dark evening. You all must excuse my rushing to be the first, but 'age before beauty,' you know!" Mr. Cooke, seating himself beside her, gallantly added: "And pearls before swine; here I am, Elise, hungry as a hog." Mrs. Faven nodded her appreciation and tasted with gusto the sherry the General poured her. "Besides quick-witted gentlemen, we have delicious sherry. And this turtle soup, Ludwig! You are too good to us. What a delightful hurricane!"

"Only tinned soup, madam, I am afraid. I promise you better the next time you dine with the General." Ludwig's voice was so thick as to be almost unrecognizable.

Cynthia was across the table from Mr. Cooke. He ogled her decolletage with exaggeratedly pursed mouth and raised brows and informed her, "Madam, your dumplings are boiling over. Ha!"

"There are no dumplings in this divine soup, Tate," Mrs. Hackley called from her seat at the General's left. Cynthia laughed raucously, bewildering her mother. "Cat," Philip explained gently, "Mr. Cooke is being funny again." He sat down beside her. His grandmother turned away from him with an over-the-shoulder reproof that at least Mr. Cooke was not killing anyone with his wit and if dear Lem had been hurt by Philip's reckless, heedless — oh, dear, if he had — well, she would never, never forgive —

"Catherine," Mrs. Faven interrupted loudly, "that long vista of the shore and mountains of Mount Desert you painted above the pool doors is perfectly charming. When was it done? I forget."

Mrs. Hackley was pleased to abandon her lecture. Philip was more pleased. "Oh," she fluttered, "it was years and years ago. I don't think, at the time, Lem liked my using such a Japanese treatment, but, really, now I think he *loves* the little mural." The General muttered into his soup. "And," Mrs. Hackley went on, "dear Sargent is so ethereal, *just* like dear Fuji-san."

Persis looked up from her plate. She and Elizabeth Lamb were placed at a low round table in front of the television set, since the long dining table, that occupied almost all of that end of the living room, seated only ten. "Ethereal?" she asked incredulously, craning her neck around the back of Russell's chair to view Mrs. Hackley. "Sargent Mountain ethereal? Have you ever climbed it? It's hard. My daddy says it's a real bugger." Mrs. Faven raised her brows, but smiled. Elizabeth Lamb kicked Persis gently. "Didn't they put people out to die on Mount Fujiyama when they got too old, Mrs. Hackley?" she asked, suppressing an "Ow!" as Persis kicked her back.

185

Mrs. Hackley shuddered. "Oh, not just because they became old, I am sure," she replied, her voice trembling. "Look, Elizabeth Lamb," said her grandson, "suppose you either keep quiet or think of some more pleasant dinner conversation. No one could be so cruel as to do that," he assured his grandmother, who looked gratefully at him. "You know the Japanese respect and love the elders, as we all love you, Cat."

"I can certainly respect the time it must have taken Philo's wife to make this enormous pie," said the General, who had been portioning out large amounts of it on plates for Ludwig to hand around. "If anyone ever sets up a statue to that woman — and it'd have to be a big one, heh-heh — they can with perfect truth inscribe it, 'Somehow, she made good deermeat pies.'

"Try some of that Portuguese red Ludwig's got there, Chub. It's that Ferreirinha the feller at the Club told us about. Pretty rare."

"Ahhh!" Mr. Cooke loudly smacked his lips together. "It's excellent. Where'd you ever find it, Lem? They can put on your statue, 'Somehow, he found good wines.' " He drank some more and chuckled. "Though, considering how long it's taking you to finish that Marine history, they might put: 'He was only a half-fast writer.' Ha!"

"Very funny, Chub. Almost as good as what they originally put on that statue of Phillips Brooks in front of Trinity Church, that says 'Lover of mankind.' The day before it was to be unveiled, or whatever, somebody intelligent looked at it."

"And?" asked Cynthia, who was doing such justice to the Ferreirinha that the General had reluctantly signalled Ludwig to produce another bottle.

"They'd first inscribed, 'Lover of men.' Heh-heh. And he was a bishop, too!"

"Is that really true?" Persis asked. "But was he —"

"Eat your dinner, little girl," Mrs. Faven admonished gently. "You should watch your tendency to become verbose. You may grow up to be one of those people who writes inscriptions for statues and public buildings — anything where they can use six or seven words where one would do. My husband always said that when 'Equal Justice

Under Law' was put on the Supreme Court Building, in Washington, they could have saved money and said the same thing with only one of the words."

"Which?" asked Elizabeth Lamb, who had begun to feel better after the routing of Miss Cassidy and was trying to catch Ludwig's eye for a second helping. "Think about it. Quietly," Philip answered her.

"I wonder why she put corn in this?" Bix asked. "I've never known anyone to do that, in a meat and mashed potato dish."

"Following an old Maine custom," his host answered. "And so no one is ever going to leave out the corn, though it adds nothing much to a good shepherd's pie — or hunter's pie, as you might call this one. Ha! I tell you, Mainers are just too set in their ways to try anything new or different."

"Then I suppose it would follow that the marijuana smuggling they say is going on along the coast is done by non-Mainers?" Dusty questioned, happily accepting the last of the pie and supplementing it with a final helping of sliced tomatoes and avocado dressed with olive oil and vinegar. "Since marijuana is a fairly new commodity in Maine?"

"How do you know about that, Dusty?" Bix asked. "I thought you hardly ever read the papers up here."

"Goodness, young man, one doesn't have to read local papers — it's been widely mentioned, even on television. And people talk about it; I believe I heard Lem's secretary speaking of it only last night," Mrs. Faven observed. "There are so many uninhabited little coves on thousands of miles of coastline that Maine is a haven for smugglers. Remember how boats from Canada brought in liquor during the Prohibition, Chubby? My husband had a regular supplier, when we were here."

"Not just from Canada, Elise," Tate Cooke corrected. "My God, half the Natives who could beg, borrow, or steal a boat were in on it, I swear. But booze was, and is, a traditional thing; I bet the only Mary Jane smugglers are summer people or, as I've read, people from out of state who pay hefty prices for pieces of isolated coastal property. The Coast Guard is getting smarter about watching places like that, though."

187

"Why would anyone smuggle in Mary Janes?" asked Persis. "You can get them in Boston almost anywhere, and nobody I know really likes them."

Even Ludwig, clearing away the plates, laughed. Persis looked tearful. "Let's help and we'll get dessert sooner," Elizabeth Lamb whispered to her. "And don't feel bad, because hardly anyone calls pot that, anymore. Mr. Cooke is a bit old-fashioned, you know."

They helped Ludwig fill a large, heavy pottery bowl with yellow vanilla ice cream. He sprinkled warm brown sugar on top, poured over it the contents of a pan that had been heating on the stove and held a match to it. Persis and Elizabeth Lamb ran behind him as he whisked it to the table. Mrs. Faven applauded the creation. "How in the world did you do that?" she asked. Mr. Cooke had risen in alarm. "However you did it, I'm certainly glad it's burned itself out. My God, Lem!"

"Heh-heh. Ludwig's own special creation. Perfectly safe. *And* delicious, Chub, because it's made with Hancock County ice cream. Live all winter on the thought of that ice cream. It's the best in the world, except for what they could make before some damned Democratic busy-bodies reduced the required percentage of butterfat! Ludwig said there was another kind on sale this week for 65¢ a half-gallon; tempted me, but I'd rather pay a little more for this.

"Russell, let me give you a large helping. You deserve it, my boy. And the alcohol has all burned out of the rum," he added, with some regret.

Russell had been quiet during dinner. Mrs. Faven courteously tried to include him in her conversation. "Is your mother's friend at the Inn a chambermaid?" Russell, his mouth engaged with ice cream and the plain saltines the General insisted were the only proper thing to serve with it, nodded. "They all must have fascinating stories to tell at home," she went on. "The maid who does my room told me about an old Philadelphia gentleman, said to be very rich, who comes here every year. When straightening up his room the other day she threw away a tube of toothpaste that seemed to be completely empty, but the old party was very upset. He rang for her and admonished, 'Why, there were at least two brushings left in that. I have a little sterling silver key that forces the last bit of paste out of the tube.' Can you imagine!"

"People from Philadelphia will do anything," Cynthia said, "and always the same way. A bunch of boring old copy-cats. And I have never understood why practically all of them who summer here are blonde. Is it inbreeding, or required in William Penn's charter, or something?"

"My dear," Mrs. Faven explained, "it was all those blonde German immigrants who came to Philadelphia. Years and years of that is bound to have an effect. No," — as Bix and Dusty smiled — "I'm quite serious." She looked at Philip, who had made an exaggerated face expressing disgust, and was muttering under his breath to his grandmother. "Don't they teach you genetics at Harvard?" It was quite obvious to all that only her good breeding had prevented her from adding, "And manners?"

"Philip is more interested in literature," Catherine Hackley said defensively. "When he finishes college, he is going to write a novel. He has told me the plot, and I know it will become an instant classic!"

"All her geese are swans — or else dead ducks," Mr. Cooke muttered to Bix, on his left. Aloud, he informed Mrs. Hackley: "Writing classics, my dear Catherine, takes some time, or so I've heard. I hope Philip is prepared to spend some. And 'instant classics,' I would say, is what they call a contradiction in terms. Am I right, young man?"

Philip abruptly rose, ignoring Mr. Cooke, and more or less politely expressed his thanks for dinner. "Cat," — he turned to his grand-mother — "if I'm going to start a novel, there's no time like the present. Why don't we go home before the rain gets heavy again?" His mother raised her brows and slightly shook her head at him, but his grandmother instantly made ready to depart.

"Oh, well." Cynthia Dickcyn yawned widely. "I must say I'm rather tired. Philip, you can take your grandmother in my car and Bix will walk me back through the woods. A little fresh air and landscape is what I need before — bed." She grinned at Bix.

Everyone got up, smiled, and pronounced civilities. Dusty asked to accompany Philip and Mrs. Hackley, "to try your phone, if I may. If it's out too, I've still got a chance that ours in the teahouse is working — whenever I can get in there," he finished, glancing at Bix and Cynthia.

General Alison also looked at Cynthia. "My dear," he said, "I believe you put your coffee spoon in your bag, instead of your cigarette holder." Cynthia merrily produced the spoon and the General was not really surprised to see that the holder was beside it. Bix smiled, raised both his brows and her umbrella, and walked away with her.

Mrs. Faven announced that she had ordered a car to call for her at ten. It arrived promptly and Mr. Cooke gladly accepted her offer of a lift. Russell and the General, the latter thankfully and prayerfully intoning the Marine Hymn, went in search of blankets and pillows for the Army cot they had earlier retrieved from storage. Persis and Elizabeth Lamb helped with straightening up the living room and stacking the dishwasher. Ludwig, looking very sick, sat down in the chair by the skittles table when they were almost finished. He leaned his head back wearily.

"Ludwig, why don't you go straight to bed?" Elizabeth Lamb asked. Persis disagreed. "He hasn't eaten anything all day, and Grandmother always says, 'Feed a cold and starve a fever.' I'll heat you up some canned chicken broth, or would you like a milkshake?"

"Oh, Persis," Elizabeth Lamb said impatiently, "what she says is, 'Feed a cold: starve a fever.' It means if you eat much when you have a cold, you'll get worse, feverish, and then you mustn't eat anything.

"Would you like some hot lemon-and-water with honey and whiskey, Ludwig? That's awfully good for a heavy cold."

Ludwig nodded gratefully. "Thank you, Elizabeth Lamb. But just a touch of whiskey. I don't drink when I'm on duty. I shouldn't," he ended ruefully, "get as sick as this, either."

"I should think your work is over for the day." Elizabeth Lamb finished cleaning the pans while she heated water and then generously poured whiskey and bottled lemon juice into a large mug. While she searched in the cupboard for the honey, Persis added at least two fingers more of whiskey. They turned out the lights in the kitchen, but Elizabeth Lamb thoughtfully went into Ludwig's room and switched on the one beside his bed. Persis invitingly folded down a corner of the neatly-tucked sheet and blankets and then patted the bedding back into its military tightness.

They said goodnight. "I think Cousin Lem and Russell are already asleep," Elizabeth Lamb said, "and you should go to bed when you finish, Ludwig." He smiled at her and assured her he would. The little girls left the large living room in darkness except for the lamp behind his chair, and went wearily up the stairs.

Ludwig picked up the telephone beside him. There was still no dial tone. He swallowed half his drink slowly, appreciating the warm feeling it gave him but unable to taste its strength. He went to the kitchen and poured more whiskey into the mug. He glanced at his watch and sat down again. He drained the mug, turned off the lamp, and, as he settled back in the chair and closed his eyes, willed himself to awake in exactly one hour.

It was eleven forty-five when he woke, exactly an hour later. The phone was still dead. He passed a hand over his eyes, rose unsteadily and got his poplin jacket from the rack. "Fifteen minutes to get to a phone in the village," he thought, feeling for the set of keys for the General's car he always carried in a pocket. He went out into the rain, now heavy again.

He had been gone for only a minute or two when a figure appeared at the pool doors, peering into the dark cottage. It entered noiselessly, carefully deposited what it carried, took what it had come for, then as quietly emerged and moved around the corner of the house to the washroom window. The window was slowly and cautiously shut and wedged with a thick piece of bark and then the wooden shutters were fastened tightly across it. This done, the figure stood gazing up at General Alison's bedroom window, directly above. At the sound of a car turning into the driveway it stiffened; under the concealing mask there was a smile.

Ludwig, wet and cold, his useless keys in hand, also heard the car as he entered from the terrace door. He stood waiting in the dark for Miss O'Cassidy to appear, furious with himself for not ascertaining that she had returned before he went out into the rain, and furious with her. "Damned slut," he muttered, swaying as he stood. "Bitch." He spoke unclearly, but loudly enough to advise the waiting figure at the other end of the house that someone had gone in.

There was a noise, as though someone were trying to open the washroom window. Ludwig's rubber-soled shoes made no sound as he went unevenly but rapidly through the cottage and entered the washroom, stumbling through the darkened doorway. He stood a second, orienting himself, and then crept cautiously to the window. He fumbled at it, but it was tightly fastened; he wondered vaguely why the glass was so dark, with no raindrops visible. He felt dizzy and leaned against the wall, knocking ajar the little hanging shelf. His inborn neatness sent his hand out in the dark, to clumsily straighten it and the two objects on it. He stood there for a number of minutes, inhaling deeply. He felt very sick, confused, and his breathing became difficult. He fumbled for the light switch; the light did not go on. He turned and pushed weakly at the door, but it would not open. He pushed again, hard; it would not open.

He had never panicked in his life, which was why he had lived so long. He was not frightened now, but as he kicked heavily at the door waves of nausea passed over him. "The latch — is — stuck again," he thought disjointedly, "but something may be — holding it." He slumped to the floor. "More air here," he thought; "What is it. What did I miss?" And then he realized. He knew what was gone. He knew why, and where, and who. Lying flat, he pushed against the door, with all his diminished strength. There was a faint sound from the other side; a nervous little laugh, quickly stifled.

Ludwig gritted his teeth and pressed one fist hard against his labouring chest. He put out the other to push at the door one last, exhausted time. His hand, in the dark, wavered; he was losing his sense of direction. It went past the bucket in the corner that contained what was killing him, that he could not smell, but it encountered the can of scouring powder that he kept under the toilet. With his last remnant of will, with all that remained of his years of training and discipline, he knocked it over and scrawled erratically in the spilled powder on the wooden floor. And then he lost consciousness, forever.

• CHAPTER 9 •

The Kind Old Sun
Sets . . .

COLLEEN O'CASSIDY had been talking quietly just outside the General's shed, leaning well into the open window of the white convertible that had driven behind her as she came from the village. She finished with an emphatic nod, turned abruptly and ran through the rain to the cottage. She entered soundlessly, leaving the terrace doors open and tossing the car keys carelessly towards the skittles table. In the dark, she did not observe the black figure quickly leave the house by the doors at the other end, nor that it remained just outside. Nor did she hear, as she switched on lamps, the muffled exclamation of surprise that came from the watcher.

She noticed the light shining through the door of Ludwig's room, and went softly to inspect. Almost immediately, she came out and entered her room. The watcher retreated a few yards into the night and stood motionless for ten or fifteen minutes before she emerged with two suitcases. She set them down and went towards the powder room, the door of which, still unnoticeably wedged, did not respond to her tug at the latch. She kicked it slightly several times, desisting at a slight noise from the second floor. She gave up with a shrug of her shoulders and went into the study. There was a murmured "Damn skinflint" as she emerged and stood irresolute, glancing toward the stairway, shivering a little as she considered. A car horn sounded briefly. She quickly picked up her luggage and left the premises as quietly as she had entered.

The watcher moved closer to the house, halting as a light went on in the window above. General Alison came slowly down the stairs, carrying a slip of paper in one hand and holding his right shoulder with the other. He went into the study, head and neck rigid, and then into the kitchen. He came out, looking puzzled, turned off all the lamps except the one by the terrace doors, and went stiffly back upstairs, grimacing and extending his free right hand for balance.

The watcher outside, heedless of the rain that now beat down harder, waited until the light above went out. Then the figure reentered the cottage and removed the wedge from the washroom door. A light flashed briefly on the body on the floor. The door remained open, as did the pool doors as the figure came through them carrying a bucket which it set down carefully while opening the washroom shutters and window, after removing the wedge. The figure left as it had come, disappearing into the dark carrying the bucket and what had been previously taken from the cottage, and leaving the wind and rain blowing through *Iwo Jima*.

The rain had stopped by dawn when Russell came down, but there was still a stiff breeze. He closed the terrace doors before he called his mother and assured her he'd be home soon. He went to the pool doors, and as he shut them he glanced into the powder room. Moving to the body, Russell put his hand to Ludwig's cheek, but touched nothing else.

He ran upstairs quickly and unceremoniously into the girls' room. He took several deep breaths before he gently shook Elizabeth Lamb awake and spoke with studied calm: "Don't be frightened, but tell me quick where we can reach that police lieutenant. Ludwig is downstairs, on the floor. He's dead. I guess, maybe, you'd better call while I tell the General. Don't go into the washroom and don't touch a thing, more'n you can help; you know that."

194

Two policemen were already by the body when Buzzie arrived, accompanied by a doctor. The General, both angry and frightened, was sitting by the fireplace clad in pajamas under a remarkably colourful paisley dressing gown into which only his left arm was fully inserted. Persis, barefoot and also wearing pajamas, was attempting to persuade him to drink the coffee she had made them while she arranged his robe around his injured shoulder. Elizabeth Lamb and Russell, fully dressed, stood stiffly beside him, their faces impassive but their minds in turmoil.

"Persis," Elizabeth Lamb said haltingly, "you — you go get some — some clothes on or else you'll get a bad cold, too —" her voice broke, and she stopped, looking toward the powder room, where the officials were talking quietly. Persis left docilely. Elizabeth Lamb went into Ludwig's room, sat on the bed that had been turned down for him, and tried to think. She heard more people come into the cottage and went out to see an ambulance in the driveway and two men with a stretcher.

Buzzie met them and motioned toward the doctor, rising to his feet in the powder room doorway, where he had been kneeling beside Ludwig's body. "Elizabeth Lamb," Buzzie said gently, "I'll want to talk to you all in a minute. But suppose you and I go back into the kitchen now and you make us some cereal or something while they take the — him away. I got the feeling you liked him and there's no need for you to remember him 'cept like he was."

The four of them sat at the kitchen counter, glumly forcing down the rather lumpy oatmeal Elizabeth Lamb had produced. Persis, solemn in one of Ludwig's aprons, had made more coffee and squeezed grapefruits. The General cleared his throat and dropped his spoon into his bowl with a clatter. "Well," he demanded of Buzzie, "what happened to Ludwig? Don't you fellers know?"

Buzzie hesitated. Before he answered, Bix and Cynthia knocked lightly on the terrace doors. Elizabeth Lamb noticed Cynthia was wearing the low-cut gown of the night before. "We heard cars and a lot of talking here, from the teahouse," Bix explained. "Has something happened? Is everyone okay?"

"Ludwig's dead; that's what happened," the General answered

loudly, "and they've taken him to Bangor. Russell, here, found him this morning, on the powder room floor. All the doors wide open, too. Some bastard of a burglar, I guess, and I want him found and damned quick, so I can break his neck myself. The police don't seem to want to tell us what they know — which is probably damned little."

"General," Buzzie said quietly, "the M.E. can't tell how Ludwig died; that's why we have to have an autopsy. I wanted to ask you if he had any disability that you knew of — a bad heart, for instance? Was he taking any medication, or prescription drugs? I took a quick look in his room and bathroom and there's nothing in his medicine cabinet 'cept toothpaste and aspirin. No papers or letters in his room, and nothing at all of what you might call a personal nature, except a pipe and a tobacco pouch. No address book, no snapshots; sort of Spartan-like, the whole thing, I'd say. Strange."

"Dammit, the man was a Marine! He didn't take drugs or medicines. He was in top physical condition and he was neat and orderly. Somebody killed him, God knows why, and I want the murderer found and hanged. And quickly!"

"We don't hang in Maine, General. I'd like to ask you about last night. Who was here and what went on? The more you cooperate, the quicker we'll figure out what could've happened."

"I'll cooperate," the General said grimly. "Just find the killer. Who the hell is this?"

A tall, pale, nondescript grey-haired man stood outside the doors Bix and Cynthia had left open. He wore a grey suit and tie and a lighter grey shirt. He regarded them all, nodded politely, and addressed Buzzie.

"They told me I'd find you here, Lieutenant. Could you come outside a minute?"

Russell and Elizabeth Lamb answered Bix's and Cynthia's questions as best they could while Buzzie and the stranger conferred. Persis left them. The General drank cold coffee and smouldered. Buzzie, looking puzzled but somehow satisfied, led the caller in.

"This is Merrill Sargent, from Boston, General Alison," he said. "He flew up this morning to check on Ludwig Vonn. I'd like him to listen in while I ask you about last night. He's sort of an assistant — policeman."

"From Boston? Why the hell is he here about Ludwig? What's going on?" The General's face was dangerously purple.

"He was supposed to report to me — on a regular basis," Mr. Sargent said. His voice was as colourless as his appearance. Elizabeth Lamb was reminded of Ludwig's voice. "When he didn't call in, I came up."

"Report to you? Why to you? Are you a probation officer? Are you saying that Ludwig was a criminal? My God, what next!"

"You could put it that way, if you wanted to," Mr. Sargent said noncommitally. "Believe me, General, I am as anxious as you to find out how Ludwig Vonn died. Could we just proceed with Lieutenant Higgins' questions, and then I'll get out of your way."

"Was anyone but members of your household here last night, General?" Buzzie asked quickly. "That's about all I need to know now, unless there was anything sort of unusual you might remember about the evening."

"We six were here," the General answered, somewhat pacified. "Suppose we get to some comfortable chairs." He led the way, moving stiffly. Persis joined them, complaining that the powder room light was not working. With a glance at the General, Buzzie explained that the light bulb had been loosened in the ceiling fixture, and that it had been sent to the Crime Lab for fingerprinting. The General opened his mouth. Buzzie quickly forestalled him.

"How did you hurt yourself, sir?" he asked. He placed himself in front of the fireplace and opened his notebook.

"Thought all you wanted to know was who were here and if anything out-of-the-way went on? I'd say finding a light bulb unscrewed in a room where a man died was pretty unusual but *I* didn't know anything about that. *You* did, and what are you going to do about it, hey?"

Buzzie ignored the question and put one of his own. "Well, your arm and shoulder appear to be injured, and you were all right yesterday afternoon. How did it happen?"

"The top of the skittles table fell on me during a game we were having before dinner. Could happen to anyone. Confounded thing is heavy, and I was raising it to get the dimes out of the coin box inside, without supporting it properly. Why don't you forget me and concentrate on the damned light bulb? Were there fingerprints on it?"

"No," Buzzie said quietly, "there weren't. We just sent it to the lab to make sure."

"Well, then, sir, why don't —"

"Cousin Lem," Elizabeth Lamb interrupted, "before the table fell on you, the light went out. And more than six people were here. You didn't say —"

"Lights were going off and on all evening," her cousin replied testily. "And didn't anyone ever teach you not to interrupt, miss? Dammit" — he raised his voice as Persis and Russell, as well as Elizabeth Lamb, began to speak — "I want to get out of this hubbub. I need to go to Bar Harbor and find some sawbones who'll X-ray me. *I* didn't get killed; Ludwig did, so stop questioning me, because I can't remember anything unusual about him last night except that he had a bad cold. Poor feller." He brushed his hand quickly across his eyes.

Elizabeth Lamb sighed. "Buzzie, couldn't Cousin Lem go over to the hospital? Russell or Bix could help him get his clothes on. We could tell you who else was here and what happened before we went to bed; Ludwig was still up then."

Buzzie frowned thoughtfully at her. "I'll drive you, General," Bix offered, "if we can leave." Buzzie transferred the frown to him. "You might let this young man drive the General, Lieutenant," Mr. Sargent suggested diffidently. "I think it would be all right, don't you? He really should see a doctor." He nodded firmly.

The General's preparations for his trip were brief but loud. Several shouts of "Damn it, you; be careful!" alternating with cries of, "Watch it, boy, I said!" came from above before he appeared, an exasperated Russell behind him, followed by Bix, calm and smiling as usual. With a final, "And be *sure* you're out of here when I get back *and* that you've found out who did it!", he and Bix departed, after a furious search for car keys, found eventually on the floor where Miss O'Cassidy had tossed them.

The two were barely outside before Elizabeth Lamb, Persis, and Russell all began to talk excitedly. "Whoa, there," said Buzzie. "Just let me ask Mrs. Dickcyn if she can think of anything that might shed some light. And would you list for me all the people here last night, mam?" The children shrugged and subsided, Elizabeth Lamb raising her brows at her friend and shaking her head sadly.

Cynthia wrote, yawning prettily and announcing that a warm shower and a few hours sleep might do wonders for her memory, since she really could recall nothing extraordinary about the previous evening. "And the sooner, the more effective," she hinted.

"But didn't you just get up?" Persis asked. "And why did you put on your dinner gown again this morning? Or didn't you go home last night? Were you talking to Bix?" Cynthia informed her that personal questions were in very bad taste as Elizabeth Lamb kicked her ankle. Mr. Sargent smiled slightly and leaned back in his chair, although he continued to regard Cynthia through half-closed eyes.

"I really did not notice the houseman, Lieutenant," Cynthia said, handing Buzzie her list. "He was merely as competent and as self-effacing as usual. Except for the slight altercation with the unpleasant secretary — oh, dear, I forgot to mention her; has she left yet, Elizabeth Lamb? — about poisoning the spread on the cocktail biscuits —"

"What?" Buzzie exclaimed. "Poisoning what?" Mr. Sargent opened his eyes fully. "That's what I was going to tell you about, Buzzie," said Persis. "But you wouldn't let me."

"And I was trying to say I looked in Miss O'Cassidy's room and all her clothes are gone," said Elizabeth Lamb. "But the check she asked Cousin Lem to leave for her is still in the study. Isn't that strange?"

"And I wanted to let you know it was kinda funny how the phone rang and made the light go out by the skittles table and then it fell down on the General — or it would have, or maybe on the secretary, if I hadn't pushed him and brushed by her and she jumped back," said Russell, all in one confusing breath.

"It looks, Lieutenant," Mr. Sargent said quietly, "as if a good deal went on here last night that might be called unusual. What it has to do with Vonn's death I'm not sure, but while these kids tell you about it, I think we might let this lady go, for the moment, don't you?" He nodded at Buzzie again.

"Now," said Buzzie, when Mrs. Dickcyn had glided her way homeward, after sweet smiles and firm hand-pressings for both policemen, "I'm going to listen to you fellers one at a time. You first, Persis."

He took notes as they talked in turn, asked perceptive questions of each of them, and went back and forth, over and over, from the time when Persis arrived from the Gaynors', and found the first guests, to when she and Elizabeth Lamb said goodnight to Ludwig. They sank back in their chairs and looked expectantly at him. He and Mr. Sargent regarded each other thoughtfully. Persis went to the kitchen to make more coffee.

Buzzie addressed Elizabeth Lamb: "So Miss O'Cassidy wasn't back when you went to bed, but she's gone now, and we won't know till we find her if she saw Ludwig when she came back to get her things."

"I still wonder why she didn't take her paycheck," Elizabeth Lamb said. Buzzie wondered too. "Have you any idea where she might have gone?" he asked her.

"No," she replied sweetly, "nor what name she's using. I looked at her passport yesterday, and it's British. It said she was Caroline O'Connor, born in England in 1940. She went by 'Colleen O'Cassidy' and claimed she was born in Australia in 1950 — or so Russell heard her say when she was trying to blackmail Cousin Lem."

"What did you say?" Buzzie jumped up. "Blackmail?"

"I *said* we should have told him, Russell." Elizabeth Lamb's tone was even sweeter. "Suppose you tell what you heard yesterday morning."

"Suppose you do, Russell," Buzzie said grimly, sitting down again.

Russell did. Then he and Elizabeth Lamb related, with excitement and pride, how Miss O'Cassidy had been informed that the General was having none of her scheme. "So the missing lady was trying a little theft by extortion," Buzzie reflected. "You've explained how you cut off her try at General Alison, but I wonder if she had a go at anyone else? They may have paid up, and so she didn't bother to collect her paycheck from the General."

"She may have been frightened off — perhaps by finding Vonn," Mr. Sargent suggested. "Or just given up and gone on to a more promising set-up. We need to locate her, I would say, and ask a question or two. I'd like to know if the mug you found with traces of liquor in it was hers, for one thing."

"You don't think this woman might've had something to do with Vonn's death?" asked Buzzie.

"I've known him for a long time," Mr. Sargent answered. "No offense to the ladies present" — he half-smiled at Elizabeth Lamb and Persis — "but it would have had to be not only a remarkably strong woman, but a very acute one, to have got the better of him."

"A lot of women are clever," Persis said reprovingly. "I'm clever enough to be able to tell you that it was Ludwig who used the mug, when Miss O'Cassidy wasn't even here. Elizabeth Lamb made hot lemonade for him and I put whiskey in it."

"You *did*?" Elizabeth Lamb was surprised. "Persis, you are just too officious. I had mixed it properly, with a good deal of whiskey. You must have made Ludwig drunk, almost."

"I doubt, then, if it was Vonn who drank what was in the mug," Mr. Sargent observed. "He was a most temperate man when he was — working."

"He had such a bad cold he couldn't smell, and prob'bly couldn't taste," Russell informed him. "He even said so, I remember." Mr. Sargent frowned. "That's not so good, then," he admitted. "Well, I've got some things to do. I'll look you up later, Higgins. I'll want some copies of photos of Vonn's body and the room, among other things. Hope the car I rented in Ellsworth makes it back there."

Buzzie sat quietly, chin in hand, looking at Russell for a few minutes after Mr. Sargent had left. "Russell," he said finally, "I'm taking you at Elizabeth Lamb's valuation, you know. I'm assuming that you hadn't met or heard of Ludwig Vonn before she invited you over to sail, this summer. Am I right? And that you didn't know a thing about the young feller found on the beach night 'fore last? Suppose you just assure me that both my assumptions are correct, solemn-like."

"Buzzie, for goodness' sake!" Elizabeth Lamb was exasperated. "Of course he didn't —" Buzzie held up a firm hand. "I'd like to hear it from him direct, dear."

Russell sat up as erect as if he were on the witness stand in court. He looked Buzzie straight in the eye: "I swear I didn't know nothing about the dead man, nothing atall, and I didn't know Ludwig 'fore I first come over here, in late July, nor have any reason to harm him. He barely said a thing, times I was here, but he was always real good to me — made me breakfast, and all, and sometimes he give — gave — me a sandwich to take along hitch-hikin' back to Bar Harbor. I'd like to help find out why he's dead, Mr. Higgins."

"Buzzie," Persis put in, "Russell wasn't over here when we found the boy, and he wouldn't have been here last night except for the storm. Why are you being so mean to him?"

Buzzie sighed. "Persis, it's not being mean. I'm about to tell you that we found something Vonn had tried to write on the floor, and ask you and Elizabeth Lamb what you think it might mean. I just had to convince myself Russell's an innocent bystander, like." He held up a hand as Persis opened her mouth. "Yes, I know there's nothing on the floor: I photographed it and then we cleaned it up."

"What did he write?" Russell and Elizabeth Lamb spoke simultaneously.

"That's the trouble. He only started to write something." Buzzie drew on his pad. "He scrawled this in some spilled cleaning powder." He tore off the page and held it up. All that was on it was $\mathcal{P}$.

"That's all? That's the way I start to write my name," said Persis. "Was he trying to write a capital P?"

"Not a P for Persis," said Russell. "But maybe a P for Philip. Or Philo? Or what else? Philadelphia?"

Persis had taken the paper from Buzzie. She wrote with his pen. "Look," she said. "He made the beginning of his C's like that, too. I watched him writing a grocery order, and he capitalized everything. He wrote C's like this." She held up the page, on which was $\mathcal{C}$.

"C for Colleen?" Elizabeth Lamb asked. "Or Catherine? Or Cynthia?"

"That feller Rhodes real name is Cecil," Buzzie observed.

"The boat the dead man was from is called *Sea Rover*, you said.

Could he have been tryin' to write its name and jest written C for sea, to save time?" Russell was somber. "I figger he knew he was dying."

Elizabeth Lamb got up and stood looking out the terrace door. "Russell, please, please don't go on like that about Ludwig," she said. "Oh, hello, Mrs. Hackley."

Catherine Hackley came in slowly, stumbling a little over the sill. She carried a small sheaf of white chrysanthemums. "Good morning," she said faintly. "My daughter told me there has been another accident. Where is Lem?"

"He's in Bar Harbor getting his arm looked at, Mrs. Hackley," Elizabeth Lamb explained. "Are those flowers for him?"

"What is the matter with his arm? Oh, dear, so many bad things are happening!"

"The top of the skittles table fell on him last night. You remember. It hurts awfully, he said. Do you want me to put those in a vase?" Persis asked.

Mrs. Hackley sat down suddenly. She seemed about to faint. "Oh, no, *nothing* must happen to Lem. Oh, Philip is so careless — so heedless. How *could* he have let Lem get hurt!" The chrysanthemums fell to the floor as she put her hands to her face and wept. Buzzie at first was embarrassed, and then became thoughtful and interested.

Persis went to gently pat Mrs. Hackley's frail, shaking shoulder. Elizabeth Lamb picked up the flowers. "Shall I get a vase and put them in Cousin Lem's room?" Mrs. Hackley shook her head and continued to weep. Buzzie cleared his throat. "What did your grandson have to do with the General's injury, mam?" he asked quietly.

Mrs. Hackley wiped her eyes with a small lace-trimmed handkerchief she took from the sleeve of her kimono. She opened her mouth and breathed in deeply. "No, dear," she answered Elizabeth Lamb. "These flowers are to comfort the spirit of the dead man, and to show respect and sorrow. I will put them where he died, as his spirit may still be near. Cynthia said he was found in the powder room." She retrieved the sheaf and went slowly to the other end of the cottage.

On her way back to them, looking somewhat relieved, she slipped into the study. "I have put a poem in dear Lem's *shoin*. It may cheer him, and I hope he will forgive the intrusion into his room. When do you expect him back?"

Buzzie cleared his throat again. Mrs. Hackley turned to him. "Lieutenant," she said strongly, "my grandson was remiss, that is all. He was attempting to put up the table supports when the power failed, and in the confusion that followed the General dropped the table top on his shoulder. Philip possibly could have prevented the injury, were he quick-witted, but he would not have tried to *hurt* Lem. I am *so* glad that I have never permitted him to have a firearm, despite all his pleas, because even a crack shot needs to have his wits about him and Philip is a *most* inattentive boy. I suppose all sensitive and artistic people are, somewhat — oh, Philip, dear, I thought you were still asleep."

Philip stood frowning outside the open door, looking angrily at his grandmother. "Cat, you shouldn't be here. It's dangerous. I mean — my God, you walked through the woods alone! And I can't find Chin-Chin. I think he's run away." He was near tears.

"Won't you come in and have some coffee?" Persis said, maintaining her role as lady of the house.

Philip ignored her. "Cat, I'll walk you back. Please come home now and rest. You wear yourself out talking so much." He slumped into a terrace chair, hands jammed into his trouser pockets and legs outstretched.

"Mam," said Buzzie, "before you go, would you please list for me all the people who were here last night?"

"But Cynthia said that she had done that. Don't you believe her?"

"I have to ask everybody who was here, mam." Buzzie was stolid. "It's a rule. Sometimes one or more people are forgetful." He raised his voice: "And you too, Mr. Dickcyn, please?"

"I'll do it when I get home," Philip answered rudely. "Hurry up, Cat." He worked his chair around so that his back was toward the people inside the cottage and began to whistle a monotonous tune. Russell slid the glass door half-way shut.

Mrs. Hackley wrote delicately, with many little pursings of her lips and "Oh, my's." Russell sat down and abstractedly traced a series of

C's on the notepad by the telephone. Elizabeth and Persis watched him. Buzzie watched Mrs. Hackley.

"Well, hello," came a cheerful voice. "It's a bit windy, but I thought Lem might like a walk. Why, Catherine, were you and Philip here for breakfast, dear? And Lieutenant, you, too?"

Buzzie rose politely as Mrs. Faven came in, with her customary buoyant step. Under the visored white linen cap she wore, her black hair was wind-ruffled and her tanned face alert and composed. Her still-pretty mouth was smiling as usual and complemented by a dash of bright scarlet lipstick.

"I was going to call you, Catherine," she said. Mrs. Hackley looked up, smiled vaguely and continued writing, her sensitive forehead furrowed in thought. "Because," Mrs. Faven went on, "the Inn is having a buffet dinner tonight and I'd like you and Lem to come as my guests." She laughed deprecatingly. "It's only seven-fifty a person, so I can afford to ask Chub, too. He's probably marketing in the village and I'll see him there. Where is Lem?"

Again Elizabeth Lamb explained the General's absence, and was relieved to hear just as she finished, a car coming up the driveway and then a series of martial, "Dammit!"s. Her cousin entered, his arm in a sling, and glared at everyone, most especially Buzzie, before he gingerly lowered himself into a chair. Bix came in quietly and sat near him.

"Do we have an ice bag, Ludwig?" the General called. "And I could use a shot of whiskey." His face paled. "Dear God, I forgot," he muttered, putting his hand over his eyes.

"Forgot what, Lem?" Mrs. Faven was brisk. "Don't you think a little stroll in the fresh air would do your arm good? Better for you than spirits."

"Dammit, Elise, Ludwig was found dead this morning! Why the devil do you think this detective is here again? And I've got a dislocated shoulder all strapped up that nothing but cold compresses and rest will help. No damned exercising!"

Buzzie made a brief explanation to Mrs. Faven and set her to writing her list of those present at *Iwo Jima* the night before. Bix was asked to do the same. Persis went to the kitchen for Scotch. Elizabeth

205

Lamb followed, taking the tumbler Persis had filled and pouring most of it back into the bottle.

"Well," said Mrs. Faven, handing her list to Buzzie and standing up energetically, "you must stay quiet and rest today, Lem, but you'll need a nourishing meal tonight. I'm going to the village to shop for dinner, and I'll be back at six to cook. You come over too, Catherine, and bring Cynthia and Philip, since your man is not due back yet from Bar Harbor." She turned civilly to Bix. "And you and your friend, of course."

"No," Mrs. Hackley demurred, rising slowly, as if she were twenty years older than her friend instead of the reverse, "I don't feel very well, Elise. I'm going to just go to bed and stay there, after I call Philo and — oh, it will be a long, sad day for you, Lem! The days pass so slowly, anyway, don't they, as we get old? But the years, oh, the years go so fast. And then there are no more, no more." She faltered toward the door, her eyes brimming with tears.

Bix quickly rose. Before he put a steadying hand under Mrs. Hackley's arm, he thanked Mrs. Faven for the invitation, explaining that he must refuse it for himself and Dusty because they were playing at the concert postponed from the night before. He nodded at everyone with his usual grace and handed Mrs. Hackley over to her grandson, saying he would walk back to *Nihon* with them.

"So," said the General, "who killed Ludwig, hey?"

"We don't know." Buzzie shut his notebook and rose. "I'd like for you to write down who was here last night, General, sometime today when you feel better."

He went on: "Vonn may have suffered a natural death, you know. We'll be a little more sure in a few hours. The M.E. thinks he died sometime between midnight and two or two-thirty."

"My God! I came downstairs to leave a check for my secretary around twelve-thirty. I saw nothing of him — looked into his room, even. D'you suppose he was dead then?"

"Could be." Buzzie took out his notes again. "Thank you, General. That might help. But would you just jot down whoever 'twas recommended your secretary and where I might contact him — or her?"

Elizabeth Lamb was about to remonstrate that "contact" was not a verb, but the General overrode her. "Anything more about the man on the beach? You realize, don't you, he died while the tide was in, or he would've been washed out? And when do we hear about Ludwig?" He wrote down a name and telephone number and handed it to Buzzie.

Buzzie edged out, nodding and smiling evasively. Persis returned from the attic with an ice pack and helped her cousin to the leather sofa in his study. Elizabeth Lamb went with Russell to the main road.

They walked silently down the driveway. Philo's house was quiet, the door and windows shut and his truck gone. To avoid thinking of Ludwig, Elizabeth Lamb asked, "How come you were so sure Colleen wasn't colour-blind and Cousin Lem was?"

Russell was energetically gesticulating at the east-bound traffic on Peabody Drive, fist clenched and thumb extended. "She saw the cardinal — knew it was red. He called it a damned sparrow. And he has trouble with red buoys, and says that bright green grass by the pool looks brown. He's got the type that can't recognize red and green; he was useful in bombers because he didn't see the green of jungle camouflage: he just saw the *shape* of it and could distinguish it from foliage.

"I finally got him to tell how he fooled them when he was taking his service physical, almost forty years ago. He's never admitted he's colour-blind and he covered it up darned well. He's a smart old coot and, with that temper of his, anytime he messed up, he hollered and bellered and people forgot what started it. I guess his men in the Marines covered for him, too. But when I told him how we could stymie O'Cassidy, he fell right into line."

A small open truck with two men in the cab slowed to a stop and Russell jumped into the back. He grinned and waved goodbye, shouting, "You be careful. Tomorrow's Saturday; I'll be over if I can get a lift. Watch out for Persis, too!"

The day passed. The high wind persisted, and there were occasional showers. Persis and Elizabeth Lamb built a fire and sat staring into it or at the poetry they had been assigned for summer reading. At regular intervals, or when summoned by a shout, Persis put

207

fresh ice in the General's pack, or heated him soup or coffee. Several times there were louder shouts, when the wind carried the sounds of trombone and saxophone from the teahouse, to be sure the "God-damned windows and doors" were shut.

Around five Persis, who had been half-asleep, roused herself to make tea and spread toast with anchovy paste. While they were, more or less enjoyably, consuming it with their cousin, he directed them to tear up that God-damned woman's check, still on his desk. "And what the hell is that scrawl beside it? Not my writing."

"It's another of Mrs. Hackley's *haikus* she left to cheer you up, Cousin Lem," said Elizabeth Lamb. "It's not so bad. Listen:

> " 'The kind old sun sets
> But the stars hold its wise glow
> To warm their long night.' "

The General roared with rage as Bix and Dusty were joined by percussionist and piano-player. "Go upstairs and be damned sure all the windows are shut, Persis, please," he requested. "My God, there's no end to my torment! What does that damned thing mean, anyway?"

"*A String of Pearls?*" asked Elizabeth Lamb. "I really don't think it means —"

"What pearls? No, no, that damned setting sun thing. Is she talking about Ludwig? That woman has more damned nerve!"

"I don't think she is. *Haikus* are supposed to express a mood, set a feeling, something like that. I wasn't paying an awful lot of attention when we learned about them. I probably could write one, though; in fact, I had to, for class. Even if people don't understand them, they say they show great sensitivity . . ."

"Never mind, never mind," the General said hastily. "I understand; I'm not stupid, you know. And I've had enough damned tea. Get me the bottle of Scotch, and a glass. Excellent tea, Persis," he added, nodding ingratiatingly, as she returned. "Don't know what I'd do without you two girls. Ludwig gone, bodies on the shore, snakes in the grass, the indexing not done, my shoulder stove up — oh, God, I'd give anything to have Ludwig alive!" His eyes glistened and his voice broke, rather effectively, Elizabeth Lamb thought.

"The easy tears of the old," she murmured, absently, thinking more of Mrs. Hackley than the General. "Where did we read that, Persis?"

"GODAMMIT!" he roared. "Here I am, on a lee shore, stranded with two ingrates! I tell you, you little —"

"That's enough, Lem." Mrs. Faven stood in the doorway. She regarded him coolly. "Suppose you come out here and be pleasant, or at least civil company while I cook your dinner. I should think you could build up the fire with one arm. The children can help Mr. Cooke bring in the groceries.

"There's no profit in self-pity, I've found, Lem, and little pleasure. You would be the better for a *small* amount of Scotch, and some aspirin, though."

The General and his young cousins meekly did her bidding. Persis and Elizabeth Lamb set the table while the gentlemen sat with calming drinks before the meager fire that was all Mr. Cooke would permit. "Turn on the radio, Chub. Might get some nice soft music to drown out that damned caterwauling."

"They've stopped, Cousin Lem," Elizabeth Lamb called from her place beside Mrs. Faven, who was pressing cracked pepper into an enormous thick beefsteak. "You often think you hear them when they're not playing." Persis nodded agreement. "Oh, my, that looks good," she said. "I'm starving. We've barely had a thing to eat today, you know."

The General entered to inspect. "Certainly does. Though how you can think of your stomach with that dear feller dead and gone, I do not know. I can hardly face the thought of eating. Hmm — Chub, how about opening the last bottle of Ferreirinha to go with this? We have to try to keep our strength up."

"And she's making cauliflower with buttered crumb sauce, and there's a loaf of homemade bread, still warm, and she brought a raspberry pie from the village; oh, my," said Persis, "there's so much, we really ought to ask the musicians over. They always look hungry, poor things."

The General, Mrs. Faven and Elizabeth Lamb spoke in unison, but diminishing volume. "No, we ought not! You be quiet, miss," yelled the first. "Really, Persis, you must learn to refer to people by their names, not by pronouns," the second said rather sharply. Elizabeth Lamb was by the window: "Hush, Cousin Lem. They're coming around the corner of the house."

"We thought we'd drop in to see if we could do anything," Bix said affably, as he entered. "You must miss Ludwig. And here's Dusty's list of guests for Lieutenant Higgins. He stopped over to the teahouse but Dusty was in the village."

"Thought he was playing the trombone all afternoon; sounded like it," the General snarled.

"Have a drink?" Mr. Cooke amiably invited. Mrs. Faven looked severely at General Alison and said, "If you have time, we're just about to have dinner, as soon as I finish frying the steak. Won't you stay?"

The newcomers gladly accepted liquid sustenance. "But we never eat before a concert, and we've got to leave in about half an hour," Bix said regretfully. Dusty, admiring Mrs. Faven, as usual, took his bourbon and went to stand beside her. "You don't broil steaks?" he asked shyly.

"Certainly not, young man. The French simply fry their *biftecks* in copious amounts of butter, and so do I — simpler and more delicious. Fattening, I suppose, but I have never believed in the existence of cholesterol any more than I believe that there are more than twenty-seven Christmas fruitcakes in the whole country, which merely circulate but are never eaten. Have you ever seen anyone eat a piece of fruitcake?"

Dusty laughed and carried the huge platter to the table for her. He and Bix pulled chairs up close and drank, watching wistfully. Mrs. Faven promised to cook a steak for them sometime before she left for her winter home in Massachusetts, "if Lem will permit the use of his kitchen?" She assured them that she loved cooking and, especially in Northeast Harbor, the process of marketing for culinary staples: "These Philadelphia people are so very *outré*; why, do you know what I heard one of them tell another, while I was waiting in the Pine Tree for this steak to be cut? 'There are a number of Bostonians here this year,' she said, 'but not enough to spoil things'!"

There was little attempt at conversation, even by the socially-adept Bix. He and Dusty were serious and thoughtful, and the members of the *Iwo Jima* household kept glancing at the telephone, hoping that Buzzie Higgins would call to say that Ludwig's death was misfortune rather than murder. "I feel," Mrs. Faven decided, "that we should copy long-married couples in restaurants, who try to appear to be having conversations." She paused. Only Persis asked, "What do they do?"

"They recite the alphabet, with smiles and gestures."

"Good God, Elise!" said Lem. "Can I serve anyone another piece of this absolutely delicious steak?" The General was mellowing under the influence of sustaining food and wine. Everyone accepted. Mrs. Faven persisted: "You know: the wife says, 'A, B, C,' with nods and arch looks and the husband leans toward her and murmurs, 'D, E, F!' She looks coy and asks, 'I, J?' And so on."

"God, Elise," the General said again. "You know some strange people. I don't feel like making entertaining conversation, but we could turn on the telly, except some damned mountain is always in the way whenever I want to see a certain program, and bollixes up the reception. I like old movies, but I can never get 'em up here."

"Looking at movies on television is like being kissed through the telephone," Mr. Cooke pronounced. "You get the intention, but not much of the flavour comes through. Ha!"

Everyone laughed except Persis, who began a long story of a television program that originated in 1953 in Houston, Texas, and was received in England three years after it had gone off the air. "Is there any point to this, miss?" Lem finally asked. "Well, I always hope I'll see something like that, Cousin Lem. I'll turn the set on, if I may."

The small magazine listing the programs was missing and although the General loudly blamed Mrs. Dickcyn, Elizabeth Lamb recalled seeing Philip put it in his back trouser pocket the night before. "And that's not the first thing, either!" said the General. "Dammit, she's raising that boy to be a klepto, too. He's walked off with stuff before; both of 'em have the lordly idea they can take what they please. I've a good mind to go over to *Nihon* some day with the wheelbarrow and retrieve all my belongings."

"Mr. Gaynor borrowed the wheelbarrow a while ago, Cousin Lem," Persis informed him. "I heard his truck and saw him take it out of the shed."

The General was finally soothed with a large piece of pie and a cup of strong black coffee. Persis tuned in a station airing a knowledge quiz. The question asked was what artifact of the Western world introduced into Japan after the Second World War had liberated Japanese women to the greatest extent? "The Pill, of course," Elizabeth Lamb said knowledgeably. Persis nodded agreement. The General and Mrs. Faven and Mr. Cooke looked at each other and gravely shook their heads, sighing sadly.

"No," said Bix, followed by Dusty as he took his glass to the kitchen sink, "it was the Yale lock." The General and Mr. Cooke laughed loudly and disparagingly. When all the contestants failed with their answers, the m.c. announced the correct item was — "the Yale lock."

"How in the world did you know that? And why did it liberate them?" Elizabeth Lamb was amazed. Bix paused behind Dusty in the doorway to raise a hand in graceful farewell. "They didn't have to stay home all the time to watch over the house when they were able to lock shut the *shoji* — the sliding outer doors. And I knew it because I lived in Japan for a time, as a kid; one of my grandmothers was half-Japanese." He smiled and was gone.

"Hm," said Lem. "Strange. Never would have thought that young feller was a Nip." He turned to the set, where the question was what the name of Japan meant. "I know that. Nippon — or Nihon, as poor benighted Catherine calls it — means 'source of the sun.' Heh-heh."

"Really?" Elizabeth Lamb asked. "A lot of her poems refer to the sun, don't they? She didn't feel well this morning; I hope they're all right, over there. Maybe they'll go to the jazz concert."

Her cousin announced that they were as all right as a bunch of Jap-loving kleptos could ever hope to be and begged her not to remind him of jazz.

After dinner, Mrs. Faven and Mr. Cooke played several spirited games of skittles while the General watched television, emitting well-timed moans so that he was frequently provided with more ice for his shoulder compress and more brandy for his peace of mind. Elizabeth Lamb and Persis washed the dishes and waited for Buzzie to phone. "Ludwig did dye his hair, Elizabeth Lamb," Persis said. "I could tell. It was much darker near his scalp. But I wish now I hadn't mentioned it yesterday. It wasn't very kind. I should try to be nicer. I'll start right now being nice to the mother raccoon with two kits you've seen." She opened the window above the sink and tossed out the enormous T-bone from the steak. "There!"

The guests left before ten, Mr. Cooke warning his friend to be alert and to call the police instantly if there were any sign of intruders. General Alison told his young cousins that he, for some reason, felt much better — "it's probably all that brandy," Persis gravely informed him, "but liquor is a depressant and you'll soon be very sleepy" — and, with a glare at Persis, that although he wasn't a *bit* tired, he'd be able to get himself to bed now, as they should. "And lock all the doors, will you, and then I'll check 'em. Be sure to lock the door of your room, you two, and holler if you hear anything. My pistol's loaded and I can shoot with my left hand as well as my right, thank God."

"I don't think anybody will try to get in, do you, Elizabeth Lamb?" Persis said when, washed and brushed, she turned out the light by her bed. "I mean, why should anyone want to hurt us? Or Cousin Lem? He's nice to everyone — or means to be, I should say."

Elizabeth Lamb was leaning out the window, listening to the wind still wildly playing among the tops of the tall pines. Little clouds were being blown across the moon. She smiled, at both the whimsical appearance of the moon and Persis' question. She could think of a number of people to whom General Alison, in the course of his six decades, might not have been very nice, but then considered that he had probably not offended any to the extent of their wanting to do him bodily harm. "Although, why would anyone want to kill Ludwig?" she thought.

Aloud she answered, "No one wants to hurt us. And probably Ludwig just had a heart attack, or something. He didn't feel very well, you know. Go to sleep. I'm so tired I'll sleep till morning. Remember what we say at The Bungalow:

213

Ten o'clock and all is well and those who ain't —"

"Can go to hell," Persis responded drowsily.

But Elizabeth Lamb did wake, after sleeping for only about fifteen minutes. Her watch, on the bedside table under the lamp, read ten-thirty. She crept to a nearby window and gently raised it further. Faintly she heard soft footsteps, and rustlings, in the bushes by the pool.

She pulled a heavy dark sweater on over her navy-blue flannel pajamas and quietly went to her cousin's door. It was locked. She rattled the knob and called his name, softly at first, and then louder. A staccato of military snores, rather like rifle shots, were her only answer. She hit the door several times with the palm of her hand. "I'll frighten Persis," she thought, "and it's probably only the wind."

Nevertheless, before she stole down the stairs she took an old cavalry sword from its scabbard above an antique Chinese chest at the end of the hall. Bright moonlight filled the lower floor of *Iwo Jima*. She could hear a delicate padding sound outside the pool doors. She crept toward them, clutching the sword across her chest. Softly, she said aloud: "This is probably the stupidest thing I've ever done. I'm behaving just like those dumb heroines in books who bravely go to investigate and end up thrown down a well or, at least, getting a terrible surprise."

She, indeed, received a surprise, but a distinctly pleasant one. Brilliantly revealed by the moonlight, two small, furry, black-and-white forms scuttled back and forth on the flagstones that rimmed the pool, pushing the steak bone Persis had tossed out the window. The larger one, the old cat belonging to the Gaynor children, which Elizabeth Lamb had occasionally rescued from their too-ardent caresses, waved her tail gaily as she cavorted, sometimes crouching to chew on the bone and sometimes rolling about on her back as her playmate, a small skunk, seized the trophy and trundled it along.

Elizabeth Lamb, laughing in relief, pressed the lock and slid the doors apart. The two animals looked up, and then began a dignified withdrawal. The cat secured the bone and walked without haste to the bushes along the driveway. The skunk followed, his uneven gait like that of "an old gentleman in tight boots," as Elizabeth Lamb had once read. He paused every so often to regard her calmly and then hopped on. Elizabeth Lamb was wise enough not to follow too closely. She sat in one of the metal chairs, hoping they would come back, and enjoying the temperate wind, still strong but surprisingly warm and pleasant. She leaned back, relaxed and unafraid, and half-dozed.

Startled, she opened her eyes and sat up alertly. The wind had shifted and brought the sound of voices to her from the direction of the teahouse, only a little more than a hundred feet away. She picked up the sword and quietly followed the wooded path that led to the *chaseki*.

The rustic building, clay-walled, with the traditional thatched roof that had cost Mrs. Hackley a good deal in repairs after each of the many Maine winters it had survived, was situated in a little clearing in the woods. Elizabeth Lamb could hear, as she approached from the rear, that the tiny, low-walled portico on the front was occupied by two people. An old iron lantern shed only a dim glow over the little porch but its light extended far enough into the clearing so that she did not dare venture around the corner of the house. She crept to one of the small holes in the wall that served as windows, and listened. "I should be ashamed of myself," she thought. "The concert must be over and Bix and Mrs. Dickcyn are just discussing jazz, or Essee-ex, or something."

The wind had picked up, and now carried the voices away from her. "Plus I'm trying to hear through the whole depth of the house, and those darned bells under the eaves are making such a racket. I'd better give up and sneak home," she thought. "I'd hate for Bix to know I'm so stupid and nosy."

As she turned quietly away, very clearly some words were blown to her: " — only meant to frighten — damned slut — tell you! — said she knew what you put — " Elizabeth Lamb jumped back to the window so fast that she slid on the slippery pine needles underfoot and fell to the ground. She struggled to her feet, her hip painfully bruised, and leaned into the deep window again, thankful that the austere Mrs. Hackley had insisted on authentic little screen-less apertures, even if she had also insisted on the authentic bells.

215

There was more conversation, obscured by the tinkling din. Then — "why here? — she can't hear everything — or the boyfriend — too nervous — cracking — frighten me." The wind shifted again. Elizabeth Lamb considered the danger of moving around nearer the front of the *chaseki*. The answering voice stopped her: "— didn't need to kill him —" Fear held her where she was. The voice went on: "how do you know he — police Wednesday night?" She felt dizzy and opened her mouth to breathe deeply. An answer: "— told you I was after *her* — didn't mean — why don't you believe me? Anyway, served purpose — scared her off —"

There was a sudden calm in the wind. Elizabeth Lamb held her breath and listened as hard as she could. One of the voices seemed to have moved away: "— might have been dear Lem — or anyone — so dangerous — need him." Elizabeth Lamb gasped. "That's Mrs. Hackley!" she thought. "But who is she talking to?" The other voice was also fainter, as if it was moving after the first: "no need — mention gun — foolish — get a grip on — just as well he's gone — told you what I heard —"

It seemed that Mrs. Hackley was sobbing. The other voice came stronger: "where it won't be found ever — never mind — stuff safe, too — don't worry — you were fine at first — smart to use — the empty hand — maybe we should —" Very sharply, Mrs. Hackley cried, *"Iie!"* Then followed several sentences in rapid Japanese. Elizabeth Lamb caught the word *"bushido."*

" 'Code of honour,' " she thought. "And she said 'no' as if she were frightened. No to what? And who is she talking to? Bix knows Japanese. Maybe Dusty does?"

Mrs. Hackley was speaking again. "— necessary then — packet lost — what could I do? — you are safe — you must never —"

The person with Mrs. Hackley laughed. It was a cruel, mocking laugh. Elizabeth Lamb was suddenly overcome with terror. Leaving the sword below the window where she had dropped it, she ran hard towards *Iwo Jima*. She thought she heard someone behind her, and turned. As she did, she stumbled and fell, hitting her head on one of the low stumps of pine in which it was her cousin's fancy to plant new little spruces. She lost consciousness.

216

Mrs. Hackley walked slowly along the path to her cottage. She went a little way into the forest to kneel before one of her statues of Buddha. She heard someone moving some distance off, on one of the many paths she had created, perhaps more than one person; perhaps an animal. Still she knelt in contemplation. She was no longer frightened or anxious. When she arose, she was determined as well as unafraid. What she had planned, she knew she must really do. Then she would live, if poorer, at peace.

When she reached *Nihon*, she went cautiously into the garage, glancing over toward her cottage at the lighted window of Philip's room. She made several trips from the garage to the brewery, her arms, strong as in her youth, heedless of the weight they carried. In the brewery, she carefully arranged what she had bid Philo Gaynor place there that afternoon, undid the tops of the containers she had just brought in, and used the long sash hook to open the windows, high up above her head in the thick concrete walls. She reached into her *obi*, but her hand encountered only the heavy key she had replaced there after locking the door behind herself. "Dropped in the woods," she thought. "Like Richard the Third, for the want of a nail —" She retightened the tops of the containers and left the brewery.

Cynthia drove her Mercedes into the courtyard as her mother crossed it. "You've been a long time," she told her daughter, fretfully.

"I went back to the teahouse to have a quick drink with Bix and Dusty," Cynthia replied, yawning. "Mother, you must have the piano tuned again, and, really, it should not be left in that damp place over the winter. Dusty was trying to play and it sounded dreadful."

"That's because he's a competent trombonist but a rotten piano player." Philip, holding a book, stood in the open *shoji*. "Cat, for God's sake, where have you been? It's after midnight! Muz, we didn't know you had gone to the concert; we thought you were sleeping. Cat, what do you want in the kitchen? Are you hungry?"

Mrs. Hackley stopped on her way to the kitchen door. She regarded her grandson with her usual affection, mixed this time with a touch of sadness. "Why don't you go to bed, Philip? I'm going to. I'm very tired; I've been walking — and thinking. Cynthia, I'll call the piano tuner tomorrow." She faltered her way across the little entry foyer and to the hall along the glass wall of the inner courtyard that led to her room. Cynthia went along the wall opposite to hers, announcing that the concert had been better than usual but that she absolutely hated those leeches who hung around musical groups on the pretense that they were ushers.

Philip followed his grandmother. She sat at her little writing desk and fumbled through the drawers, looking surreptitiously at him. He sat on a floor cushion and regarded her with a frown. "Do you feel all right, Cat? You're not — worried about anything?"

"No, my dear. Not worried. Just a little — regretful."

"What about?" Philip asked uneasily. His grandmother merely looked at him without speaking. "Would you get me a glass of milk, Philip? It might help me sleep."

"Why do you need help to sleep? And you haven't had your insulin shot today, have you?" He shook his head but left willingly. During the fairly long time he was gone, Mrs. Hackley finally found what she needed and secreted them in her *obi*. Philip returned with a glass of milk in one hand and a hypodermic needle in the other. Holding the needle, he went to her bathroom for alcohol and cotton. His grandmother held her milk with one hand and extended her other arm toward him, murmuring that she had not used that arm for her shot for several days.

Usually, she fixed her eyes on the far distance when an injection was being administered by someone else because, despite her brave words to Persis, it always hurt her. This time, as she sipped her milk, she turned her head and looked at her arm. She instinctively jerked it away from the needle, so that almost all of the clear liquid was sprayed uselessly over her arm and wrist and into the straw *tatami* under her chair. "You were putting it into the vein," she said faintly. "A little, a very little, did get in, though not into the vein, thank God. You *know* — insulin — is not put in the vein."

Tears ran down Philip's cheeks. "I'm sorry," he said pitifully. "I'd — I'd better get more, Cat."

"No," she answered firmly, looking steadily at him. "This will be quite enough. I love you, Philip. I want you to go to bed now. *Massu gu!*"

He bent to kiss her and stumbled away. His grandmother rose unsteadily. Cynthia knocked briefly, slid aside the *fusuma* and came into the room. Her red hair hung down her back, over a deep green silk dressing gown. "I can't sleep," she said. "Why does Philip look so strange? Like the time his puppy drowned and he couldn't save him, though we knew the poor child tried, no matter what his nurse said.

"Mother, you were going to get me more pot. I can see why you got rid of my stash in the oregano jar, with the police coming, but you did promise."

"I hid it behind the Buddha that sits on the big rock on the Third Path," her mother answered. "You can get it in the morning; perhaps you would call the tuner, too? Suppose you go to sleep now, dear."

She went to her daughter and embraced her. Cynthia was surprised at the show of affection. "Are you all right, Mother? You seem strange, as though you are not really here! I wanted to tell you I noticed that the windows in the brewery are open. There is still quite a wind."

"I opened them. Cynthia, you must love Philip and take care of him. I have tried. If something should ever happen to me, there will be plenty of money for him. It is all left to you, because he is so — young."

Cynthia was embarrassed, as her mother clung to her hand. "Well, of course, Mother," she said uneasily. "*Wakari-masu*. I understand." She patted her mother's shoulder and turned to leave. "Well, *oyasumina sai*."

"*Sayonara*," her mother answered. She paused a minute, to let Cynthia get to her room, and then she walked as quickly and as quietly as she could out to the courtyard and across to the brewery. She was breathing rapidly and her heart was beginning to pound irregularly. She felt alert, though, and noticed the beauty of the stars far above through the clear Maine air, and the scent of the flowering bushes on the perimeter of the courtyard. "I will have left a glow to warm their long night — *my* little stars," she thought, half-humourously. She was relaxed and, almost, happy. "It is for the best," she murmured. "The Gods have decided. Probably I would never have had the courage. This will end everything."

Unlocking the door and going into her brewery, she moved fast, beginning to sweat. She again uncapped the gasoline containers and poured them over the segments of thatching she had spread around the interior just a short time before. She removed the packets of matches from her *obi* and held them in her hand. It was cold and shaking. Her head ached and her vision was suddenly blurred. She was nauseated and yet hungry.

She could think less coherently now, but she realized there would not be enough time to carry out the plan she had made when she first realized, in her bedroom, what had happened. The lowest pool in the forest, the deep one which no one would ever think she would violate, was too far away. It would have hidden her safely forever, and made Philip safe, and its water purified all the evil she had done in her life, but she knew she did not have time to reach it before she would fall. She must die here, by the means she most feared.

"I thought not much went in, but it was enough to cause a diabetic coma," she thought painfully. "I wonder if he read it can have that effect? But it is good, because I may collapse any moment. I may — not — feel much." The terror she now knew made her small hand tremble violently as she lit the first match and threw it on a pile of the rice straw thatching. She staggered quickly through the building, until all the thatch was crackling with flames. Heavy smoke rose from it. She choked, and, weakened by fright and the effect on her frail body of the drug, her heart, the heart that had so dearly loved her grandson, stopped its painful beating. She never had any knowledge of the dreaded fire that consumed her.

• CHAPTER 10 •

What Is The Answer?

ELIZABETH LAMB had lain unnoticed beside the path when her follower came rapidly along it, peering straight ahead and so intent on moving softly that the small recumbent form in its dark blue clothing went unseen. Had she not fallen, she would have been overtaken, but the follower, satisfied that what had been heard running was, most probably, an animal, passed along and did not return that way.

When she opened her eyes, she did not know where she was. Then realization came, and with it not panic but anger, anger at whoever had killed Ludwig and laughed so cynically about it. Her head hurt as much as her hip, and she felt strangely light and unreal as she rose and limped home.

She paused cautiously outside the pool doors of *Iwo Jima*, listening intently. She entered and drew the seldom-used heavy red curtains across both sets of doors and pulled down the shades at every downstairs window. Her head throbbed unbearably. "Though I'd be sick to my stomach if I had a concussion," she thought reassuringly, "and I'm not."

221

She avoided the powder room and went to dash cold water over her forehead at the kitchen sink. She sat at the General's desk. "If I don't write down everything before I fall asleep, I may forget a lot," she said to herself. When she finished, she concealed the paper under the desk blotter. She left the lamp on — "if somebody's prowling around, he'll think we're awake," she thought — and locked her bedroom door before she climbed, exhausted, into bed.

She heard the same loud snoring from the General's room when she came upstairs as she had earlier — how much earlier? She looked at her watch. Only an hour had passed since she had heard the cat and skunk. Although she was determined to stay awake as long as possible, frightened as she was by the conversation at the teahouse and because she knew that people with head injuries should not sleep, or must be wakened frequently, almost instantly she fell into deep slumber.

Persis and the General slept soundly all night, unaware of Elizabeth Lamb's cries as spectres stalked her dreams. They were still asleep when she woke with full sunlight shining in her eyes. She was dazed and disoriented. "Could I have dreamed the cat and skunk and people in the woods?" she said aloud. From the other bed, Persis murmured, "Elizabeth Lamb, don't talk. It can't be time to get up," before she turned her face into her pillow and slept again.

"My head is just plain pounding," Elizabeth Lamb thought. "I guess I didn't dream it." She got stiffly out of bed. She was not dizzy, but she felt weak and hot. She took off her sweater. There was a hammering noise coming from the lower floor. The General's door was still shut as she slowly descended the stairs.

Someone was banging with ill-considered force on the glass of the terrace doors. She pulled the curtains aside to see Philo Gaynor's face peering into hers. He stepped back with an expression of relief. It changed to one of astonishment as she opened the door. Putting a hand up to shade her eyes from the light, she said quietly, "Hello, Philo. Is something the matter?"

He opened his mouth and then shut it again. "For pity Minerva's sake!" he exclaimed. "What in tarnation happened to you, Lizzie? You look turrible — like you was rode hard and put away wet! Plus you got a black eye, child."

"I fell down. Did — did you hear anything — anybody last night? Walking around, I mean? Is that why you came over?"

"Did I hear anything last night?" Philo repeated wonderingly. "Didn't you? All them sireens, and the fire engines? You must've been deafer'n a haddock not to! Don't you know?"

"Philo, come in. I've got to sit down. Know what?"

"Mrs. Hackley's bottlin' plant burned down last night, that's what. Wal, the walls are standin', but that's all. And she was in it. The General wasn't over there, and I usually hear him hollerin' every mornin' not long after sun-up, so when I didn't, I come over to see if you people wuz all right here."

"My God," the General said mildly. He was coming down the stairs dressed in shirt and shorts, moving stiffly but showing some of his customary vigour. "There might as well be a continual pineapple set on my gatepost, the way everybody feels free to come in and enjoy my hospitality, day or night. What d'you want, Gaynor?"

Elizabeth Lamb sat down heavily. "Mrs. Hackley is dead, Philo says. Her brewery burned up with her in it. Philo came to tell us. He was worried because you weren't there and he didn't hear us this morning.

"Cousin Lem, I can't believe it. Mrs. Hackley —" She began to cry, her aching head in her hands.

"And Lizzie's all bunged up. What you bin doin' to the pore little kid?" The General looked at her. She shook her head reassuringly. "I'm all right. I just can't believe —"

Philo went to the kitchen — with which he seemed to be familiar, the General noted with annoyance — and began to open cabinets. He inspected the contents of the refrigerator. "I'll make some good strong coffee. Maybe a chadge of my flannel cakes, too. I heard about Ludwig. Didn't rightly know what to do, though Gloria wuz after me to come over, so I didn't do nawthin', but I kin make you breakfast now.

"Did they find out what killed the pore feller?"

"No," the General answered grimly. "But this about Catherine Hackley — are you sure?"

223

"Certain sure. I wuz there. Follered the engines. The brewery was blazin' away, door locked and so thick, by the time they stove it in the place was what I heerd 'em call an infernaldo. Couldn't git her out. Winders too high and too little to go through; all they done was cause a draft that made the fire wuss."

Elizabeth Lamb had stopped crying and was drinking a cup of very strong black coffee. "But are they sure she was in there? What started it?"

"She was in there, all right. The door was locked. She had the only key and they found it, all melted like, in amongst the — bones."

He hastily presented grapefruit juice he had squeezed, looking as if he regretted the explicit explanation. "Now, don't take on, Lizzie. She meant to do it. Yestiddy afternoon she had me move in all that rice straw she gits up every year from down South, fer the teahouse roof. It's always kept off in a little storage bin outside the garage, so fer why did she want it in the brewery if not to help start burn the place up?"

"Why did you take it in then, man? And not tell Mrs. Dickcyn?" The General was appreciating a plate of Philo's delicately browned pancakes and spoke with restraint.

Philo was aggrieved. "How fer did I know what she was plannin'? Whenever she tole me to do somethin', I done it. Who'da thought she was goin' to commit harrycarry? Gorry, I ain't a mind reader."

"She *did?*" The General was amazed before he realized Philo was speaking from television or movies and not from fact. Elizabeth Lamb was eating hungrily. She summoned her manners and, pushing Mrs. Hackley out of her mind, told Philo he was a very good cook.

"Learnt from my old man, I did. He cooked fer lumber camps." Philo was very pleased. "Better'n Gloria, I am. It don't do to let her know, though, else she'd jest set on her behind and let me do everthin'. Where's that little Persis? I'll start another batch fer her. Starvin' yourselves won't help Mrs. Hackley now, nor Ludwig neither."

Persis responded quickly to the General's yells. Fully dressed, she was doing justice to Philo's cuisine when Buzzie Higgins and Mr. Sargent, Russell behind them, knocked. They accepted coffee before

Philo made his exit, declaring audibly as he shambled away that, 'stid of lookin' sideways at a hard-workin' man, them cops would do better to see that nothing more happened to Lizzie. He raised his voice and announced that kids might be the better fer a little tunk here and there, now and agin, but as fer a black eye — well!

Elizabeth Lamb, a good deal less shaky physically but more emotionally upset than ever, had gone to dress while Persis ate. When she appeared, the callers put down their cups and stared. "Elizabeth Lamb!" said Russell. "What happened to you, dear?" Buzzie asked gently.

"I'll tell you later. There's more to it than what happened to me. Have you come about Ludwig?"

"And why've you brought Russell? Best suspect you've got?" The General was irritably attempting, with one hand, to straighten up the debris Philo had left in the kitchen.

"Merrill and I drove from Ellsworth with Mrs. Dickcyn's garnet," Buzzie said. "He wanted to get a look at the set-up at *Nihon* and we thought it'd be a good excuse. Russell was on his way over here and we picked him up at Raggedy Ass Corner, and went over to Mrs. Hackley's first." He paused. "Quite a surprise we got."

"And what do you think?" Elizabeth Lamb asked.

"I think it's time we had a little confab, all among friends. There's no way, as I figure it, that the General here could've had anything to do with the fire or Mrs. Hackley's death, not bunged up the way he is. And I guess most of the events around here are tied in with the suicide. I call it suicide because that's what it sure seems to be."

"*What?*" came from the General. "You thought *I* could have — that — Ludwig — the boy on the beach — My God!"

"Well, sir, some funny things have been going on. I don't claim to know everything about 'em; thought that we all might talk it over, put our heads together. You've been right on the spot, and Merrill has another slant on things, so if we could —"

"Buzzie, did you find Colleen?" Elizabeth Lamb interrupted. "Did she have anything to do with Ludwig's dying?"

"Well, I guess," Buzzie responded, "starting with that lady might be good. Get her out of the way, like, once and for all.

225

She doesn't appear to have been a major —"

"Except she might have been the reason Ludwig died," Elizabeth Lamb had retrieved her notes from the study. Her cousin turned his head and glared at her. "She killed him?" he asked. "How do you know that? Dammit, speak up!"

Elizabeth Lamb rubbed the bruise on her forehead and did not answer. "Killing's not her line," Buzzie said. "Not from what I've heard about Miss O'Cassidy."

"What *did* you hear? And from whom?" the General asked irritably. "Since you've graciously decided I'm not a criminal, suppose you talk."

"Well, I called this Alice Roth in Boston you said recommended her. She sounded like she was about to faint and would hardly say a thing so I gave up on her and checked with the Massachusetts police. Nothing at all on Colleen O'Cassidy, or on the name Elizabeth Lamb gave me, Caroline O'Connor, either." He raised a hand as the General opened his mouth and said quietly, "She happened to see a passport. But I figured Miss Roth was nervous about her friend for some good reason, so I checked with the F.B.I."

"And?" the General asked.

"She's got a record a mile long, from California to Illinois. A couple of convictions for theft by extortion; a number of cases that never came to trial. Her partner's an Australian she met in England — where she was born, General, not in Australia, like she claimed. He passes as an interior decorator, does inside painting and stuff like that. Good way to get to know useful things about the client as well as to pick up a little honest cash —"

"She said she talked to a 'bloke' about tiling our powder room!" Elizabeth Lamb put in. "Was he up here with her?"

"— and *she* specialized in being a temporary office helper. Another good way to get useful information."

"But how did Alice know her? And why recommend her? And — My God! — you said she wasn't born in Australia —"

"I'll get to Australia in a minute, General. I was talking to Sydney this morning. As to how Miss Roth knew her, they met when O'Cassidy filled in at one of the Harvard offices where Miss Roth works after classes — or before; I don't know much about big colleges. By the way, Miss O'Cassidy never got nearer to Radcliffe than the work she did in that office. Miss Roth did say that much.

"So," he went on, "I called a feller who's a detective in Boston now, knew him at the Academy. I'd met his mother, and she's one of those big, warm-hearted women everybody confides in — they're black, by the way, if that matters. Don't to me, but, anyway.

"I knew the mother was a nurse connected with one of the Harvard health services, and I got her number, sort of on a long shot, on the chance that she might have known this Alice Roth, or even Miss O'Cassidy. And it paid off. She'd met Alice after an operation she'd had, and though she wasn't awful talkative about her, I got an idea."

"That she'd had an abortion," said Elizabeth Lamb, "and Miss O'Cassidy found out and was blackmailing her. Probably she found out everything about anyone she worked with. Is that it, Buzzie?"

"Well, yes." Buzzie was somewhat dashed. "I called Miss Roth back, and told her O'Cassidy had tried something on the General but that she'd probably stay out of Massachusetts as well as Maine for a while, and she spilled. O'Cassidy got her to give up her job with you this season, General, and send her up instead. Figured the rich summer crowd up here would be easy pickings."

"Ha!" said the General. "Guess she'd never tried to blackmail a true Bostonian before, or one of those tight-fisted Philadelphians, either!"

"Well, but, Lieutenant Higgins," Russell asked, "how do you know this O'Cassidy woman didn't have anything to do with Ludwig's death or the boy on the beach, either?"

"I don't, not for sure," Buzzie admitted. "But the Bureau's got what you might call a profile on her — mentions her abrasive manner, for instance, which is a helpful trait in a blackmailer, you know; no one expects one to be anything but smarmy. And it says she and her confederate — Percy Donnely, his name is — have never been remotely connected with any physical violence. They run at the smell of it, which is just what she did, it would seem."

"Maybe this Percy was the one Philo said talked funny and was asking about you, Cousin Lem," Persis suggested.

"I'll bet he was." The General beamed. He looked so relieved that

Elizabeth Lamb deduced that he had been more worried by Philo's report than he had let on. "And Gaynor said he had a car, so God knows where the two of 'em are by now. You'll never find them, Higgins. They probably have a dozen names."

He looked worried. "You said she wasn't born in Australia. Then how did she know I'd been there, and if her mother isn't a color-blind Australian photographer, then who the devil was she?"

"Well, General, I knew you'd get to worrying about that, so I used a little of your tax money to call Sydney this morning. I wanted to set your mind at ease, if I could, because I want your cooperation in figuring out what might've happened here, and at *Nihon*. Sort of a return favour's what I'm after."

"She referred once to Adelaide as 'Adeline'," said Elizabeth Lamb.

"And she didn't know 'beyond the black stump' means way out in the boonies, where she claimed to've been raised," said Russell.

"So had she ever even been there?" asked Persis, regarding Buzzie with reproach. "I think you wasted Cousin Lem's tax money."

Buzzie spoke loudly and firmly. "I asked the Sydney police — Miss O'Cassidy had mentioned Sydney at the pool, you remember — if they knew of a famous woman portrait photographer who worked in black-and-white. They right off gave me a name, and I got her and she was real helpful. She said Miss O'Connor, as she called her, had visited Sydney with this lady's nephew — who just happens to be Percy Donnely, by the way — and she didn't think much of her. Had been very nosy about all the well-known people the lady, a Miss Virginia Ryerson, had photographed, and was real unpleasant when she didn't get any answers. I gathered she and Donnely left Australia in a hurry for some reason connected with police trouble. Miss Ryerson didn't exactly say, and I figured there was no need to check that out further."

"So how did Colleen know about me?" asked the General.

"Well, since they visited a couple of weeks and O'Cassidy was in and out of the studio, she might have seen old snapshots, photographs, and recognized you when she got up here. *Or* she may never have heard of you till she finagled the job out of Miss Roth, and just been lying about everything, not just *part* of it."

"But if this woman isn't her mother —"

Buzzie was smug. "I asked Miss Ryerson what she knew about O'Cassidy's parents, and O'Cassidy'd just happened to mention that her mother was color-blind, like Miss Ryerson! So, General, since this girl wasn't born in Australia nine months after you were there, since she was born in England ten years earlier, and since whoever her color-blind English mother was, you probably never even heard of her, I think you can stop worrying about Miss O'Cassidy-O'Connor. Really, sir."

"Well, I thank you, Higgins." There was a silence. "What's going on at *Nihon?*"

"When we left, they were calling for inspectors from the State Fire Marshal's Office in Augusta to go over the place. Mrs. Dickcyn is right broken up, they said. The Baxter feller's with her. The boy ran off crazy-like into the woods during the fire, I heard, and didn't come back till dawn. His mother made him go to bed and called a doctor."

Mr. Sargent cleared his throat. "Higgins, we were going to put together what all of us know about this whole thing. If this young lady and her friends are as observant as you say, maybe we can wrap it up, though I see no way of getting a conviction for — anything."

"Well," said Buzzie, "let's start by explaining who you really are, and why you came up here." Buzzie turned to address the cousins. "Mr. Sargent is with the Boston office of the B.N.D.D. and he was Ludwig Vonn's contact. Vonn was supposed to call in every twenty-four hours at a specific time, as all their agents do, and when he didn't call night 'fore last, Merrill knew something had happened. They give 'em a few minutes leeway before they push the panic button but —"

"Agent?" roared the General. "Contact? Is this some kind of income tax check? I don't like things called by initials, dammit!"

"B.N.D.D. stands for the Bureau of Narcotics and Dangerous Drugs," Mr. Sargent informed him quietly. "Among other activities, the B.N.D.D. deals with drug smuggling and distribution."

The General's jaw dropped. Persis was very frightened. Her voice shook: "I helped Mrs. Hackley hide the other lady's marijuana before you went over to *Nihon* on Thursday," she said, "but honest, Buzzie, I didn't realize what it was. I guess I should have, because she made a joke about planting grass, but it was only when the other lady, her daughter, said she couldn't find her 'oregano' and — oh, Buzzie, I was afraid to tell you. I didn't even tell Elizabeth Lamb. Am I a necessity to the crime? Do you have to tell Grandmother?"

"It isn't marijuana we're worrying about today, young lady," Mr. Sargent reassured her.

"Then what? Aspirin? Good God, man, the papers are full of how they're bringing marijuana into Maine harbours," said the General. "Isn't your bunch planning to do anything about it?"

"We're doing something about it. All the time. And in the course of doing something about it, last winter one of the Maine dealers we nabbed turned informant. They often do that to get their sentences reduced, but this fellow was special: he'd had a very, very big cartel going.

"He was so big that he was scared of continuing to use his own identity, because he'd given us a lot of leads and we'd pulled some of them in. And they had friends, of course — anyway, we set him up with a new name, job, were re-locating him — all the rest of it. He was in a little diner in New York with one of our men who was undercover, of course, and certain that neither of them had been spotted or followed. Our man handed over the fellow's papers, and cash, and as he stood up to go, he thanked our agent and said he'd make him a present of a tip, because he thought he'd been pretty decent.

" 'It'll give your career a boost,' he said, 'if you can collect all the snow that's falling on that little beach up in Northeast Harbor every summer. There's stuff going on that makes what I ran look fairly small-time.' And then he grinned — sort of cocky he'd been, all through — and left to catch his plane."

"And the agent jest let him go?" cried Russell. "Snow means cocaine; I know that. You never questioned him about it?"

"By the time our man paid the check and got out to the street, the informant was in no condition to be questioned. He'd been smashed into a wall a few doors down, by a van that witnesses said suddenly started up and leapt the curb. It got clean away, too, leaving him very dead."

"Gorry!" said Russell. "That makes my blood run cold, that does. How old do you have to be to join up with the Bureau?"

"No, Russell!" said Elizabeth Lamb. "You should go to college and get educated before you start looking for excitement. And so, Mr. Sargent, you sent Ludwig up here to Northeast Harbor?"

"Well, I didn't personally. I'm just a small cog in the works, and mostly an office one, at that. Getting a bit too old to be out in the field. But we learned that there was only one beach in Northeast Harbor, and so we made inquiries and pulled strings to get someone into one of the two households that used the beach. We got a kind of volunteer in, too, who helps out sometimes, and I'm kicking myself that we thought it better not to tell Vonn. If we had, he might be alive, but that's all I'm going to say right now about that."

"My God!" said the General. "If there's another spy around, you certainly ought to tell us, sir!" Mr. Sargent firmly shook his head. "And I was told," the General pursued his sense of grievance, "that Ludwig was an ex-Marine down on his luck; by a man I trusted, too!"

"Well, General, prevarication is the soul of detection, as someone might have said," Buzzie pronounced.

"But who was the boy we found dead?" Elizabeth Lamb cried. "Another agent?"

"We figure he was a mule," Buzzie answered. "He'd come to that college as an orphan kid on a scholarship, with very little spending money and shabby clothes. His first summer vacation, he worked in Florida, and suddenly he was flush. Last summer, the same. He had several bank accounts and drove a sporty car and a girl who knew him at school says he was knowledgeable about drugs and got coke and pot for a couple of rich kids. She was brought up strict and she dropped him after that. This summer, he moved to Maine to work — as a lot of cocaine is moving north now; not as much as pot, but enough."

"Gorry!" Russell said again. "You sure work fast." Buzzie deprecatingly indicated Mr. Sargent. "Not me; them. They have a bigger organization than we do here in Hancock County," he smiled. "But," Russell asked, "what's a mule?"

"They deliver the drugs. Couriers. Don't ask me why they're called that. I'm just a country boy."

"Whatever they're called," said Mr. Sargent, "they're usually not killed — except for the consignment they're carrying. It's unlikely this boy died naturally, so, who might have known he had it and killed him for it?"

"Elizabeth Lamb," Buzzie asked. "when you saw this boy, who'd you tell about him?"

"I told Cousin Lem, after lunch. Ludwig heard, too. And before —"

"I did *not* go down to the beach, Higgins. I did not see the feller," her cousin interposed. "*And* I did not kill him, on the beach or off it."

"— and before that, I went to *Nihon*. I told Mrs. Hackley, and Philip and Philo were there."

"And what did they say, at *Nihon?*"

"Mrs. Hackley looked like she was going to cry and said it wasn't time yet for people to be bothering them, on the beach. She was upset because Philip had lost a package of yeast. She made Philo take him to Bangor to get more. She said to go straight to 'dear Lem's party' when he got back. He was mad because they had just got back from Augusta, from a delivery, and he was hot and tired. She's — she was — always so considerate of him, I was surprised she didn't let him just go lie down, or something."

"Can't you get yeast nearer than Bangor?" Buzzie asked. "There's a couple of little plants that make their own soda pop and birch beer around Ellsworth, and a feller who makes beer from spring water; I've read about them. And stores must sell it. They always did. My sister used to make home-brew."

"She said not. Philo said they could. But they went off, and they took hours and hours. Philip got to the party very late."

"That's right," Persis affirmed. "I remember his grandmother said it was six-thirty and asked how it could have taken them so long. And right after that Elizabeth Lamb and I found the dead boy."

"She made a point of it, then," Buzzie said, "so everybody noticed he'd been away all afternoon. And he was tired but she'd sent him off on a long drive, and with somebody who could be a witness, to get something this Gaynor probably could have got by himself without going on a hundred-mile-round-trip, either. So then, who killed the boy? And how? Her daughter?"

"Not the daughter," said Mr. Sargent. "We can leave her out of this. She's clean. I guarantee it."

Buzzie was surprised, but nodded agreement. Elizabeth Lamb looked thoughtfully at Mr. Sargent. "You'd better both read these notes of what I heard Mrs. Hackley and somebody else saying at the teahouse last night. I couldn't tell who the other one was because I couldn't get near enough and they talked quietly. And the wind was blowing and those bells on the roof were crashing around. They spoke some Japanese, and I thought the other person could be Mrs. Dickcyn, but if you say she doesn't know anything, then I'm wrong."

The General stared angrily at her while the two men read. "What do you mean by this, miss? Hey? You went out last night, did you! By God —"

Buzzie looked up. He was also angry. "Is that why your face is all bunged up? Did they catch you? Elizabeth Lamb, I thought you had more sense. What happened?"

Elizabeth Lamb stood up and spoke rapidly. "There were noises so I went out and listened and I heard people over by the *chaseki* and I sneaked through the woods and then I got scared and ran away and I fell down and hit my head and when I woke up I came straight home and wrote down what I could remember." She took in a breath. "And no, they didn't catch me, and if it helps find out who killed Ludwig, I should think you'd be glad, Cousin Lem."

"So there!" said Persis, awed. "Elizabeth Lamb is so brave! You should be proud, not mad at her."

"Another definition of 'brave' is sometimes 'stupid,' " grumbled the General. "If your grandmother ever finds out you were ambling around the woods at night with murderers on the loose, she'll have my head on a platter."

Russell was looking over Buzzie's shoulder. "You didn't write which one was speaking, every time," he pointed out. "Was it Mrs. Hackley talking about an empty hand?"

"No, the other person. And he — or it could have been 'she', you know — said something about 'smart' first. I wrote that, didn't I, Russell? I was so scared and sort of dizzy when I got back that maybe I didn't remember everything."

The General muttered angrily. "You wrote it," said Russell. "You kept your head real good, I'd say. But do any of you know what they mean by that? Bet you don't."

" 'Empty hand' — not getting paid, maybe?" Elizabeth Lamb guessed. "For what, though? For the cocaine?"

" 'Karate' means 'empty hand'," Russell said triumphantly. "We played a movie over to the theayter about karate, and that was its title. So the other person was telling Mrs. Hackley she was smart to use karate. But on who? Not Ludwig, or it would've showed up, wouldn't it?"

"It wasn't Ludwig," Buzzie answered. "We know now what killed Ludwig." He ignored General Alison's exclamation. "Go on, Russell."

"Well, was it Mrs. Hackley who said this about 'didn't need to kill him' jest 'fore 'police Wednesday night'? Geez, I'm all mixed up. Who heard or saw police Wednesday night? Geez, we all did. They were at the beach and here!"

"I know!" Elizabeth Lamb shouted. "It was Wednesday night after everybody'd left I came downstairs around midnight and Ludwig was on the kitchen phone and somebody was outside the window. I told you, Buzzie. And then the dog was shot. I thought Ludwig was talking to a girl, but maybe the person outside thought it was police."

"Vonn was talking to me," Mr. Sargent said. "When you came in, he pretended. He had reported the death of the boy we think was a mule and that he could not yet connect it with the cocaine supposed to be arriving on that beach. If the listener heard all of that, why wasn't he killed that night? Hmm. Maybe he just caught a little."

He looked around. "It seems obvious the old lady used karate to kill the mule. A blow to the throat of an unsuspecting person at the top of that ladder would have knocked him right off, for a very pretty fall. He wouldn't have been afraid of a frail old woman. Higgins said she was steeped in Japanese customs and tradition; her place certainly evidences it."

"That's nonsense. Catherine Hackley was plain terrified of heights," the General flatly declared. "She'd never get near that ladder. Why, she would never even go up that stairway over there."

"But she did, Cousin Lem," Elizabeth Lamb reminded him. "The other night, when Philip had a dizzy spell on it, she ran right up and practically carried him down. She'd do anything for Philip, and she'd just keep saying how awful that ladder is to cover up, if she'd killed the boy."

"Yes, she'd even kill for Philip, it looks like," Buzzie said. "But *why* kill the boy? You don't kill off your suppliers, not if you want to stay alive and in business."

"Young lady," Mr. Sargent said, "you said she was very disturbed because the grandson had lost a package of yeast on the way back from Augusta. That so?"

"Yes, awfully upset. She was crying and wringing her hands."

"Drugs usually go for cash. If her grandson had transported the stuff to Augusta, got cash for it and lost it, she had reason to be upset. There was probably more in the package he lost than yeast — like maybe fifty or sixty thousand dollars. Maybe more. And there was a mule on her beach with another shipment she had to pay for in cash — which she didn't have."

"So she sent the grandson she doted on well out of harm's way and went down to deal with the situation. But why kill him?" asked Buzzie. "That was mighty foolish."

"She may not have definitely planned to, at that point. She may have tried to argue the kid out of the shipment, got angry and just hit out. As I said, he wouldn't have been on his guard against a delicate old lady. After he fell, she'd just go down and get the stuff out of the pouch. Tough, if you don't like heights, but I guess she was desperate.

"And, of course, she *may* have planned to kill him, figuring she couldn't possibly be blamed; that his bosses would believe someone else had robbed and killed him. She would have been wrong, as she certainly would have found out, had she lived. These Colombian families are nobody to fool with."

"So there's fifty thousand dollars worth or more of cocaine around here someplace, if you're right," Russell said. "You say he could've carried it in a pouch, so it couldn't be a very big package, but how big?"

"I figure it was a key, by the size of the pouch. It's up at Higgins' headquarters. That's a kilo — a little over two pounds. Think of a two pound box of sugar." Persis stirred as Sargent went on: "What I don't understand is why or how this old lady got into it. I mean, just receiving cocaine and then driving it to Augusta, there's not much profit. She'd have had to cut it and distribute it more widely, to make any real money. A key's worth fifty, sixty thousand, but she should've sold it for more, to make a profit.

"And she *did* make a lot of money in the past four years. She's got a number of bank accounts in Florida and New York and Boston. No deposit more than ninety-five hundred each time, of course, so there were no reports made. Oh, yes, General, we've been checking up on you in the past few days, too. I'd sort of like to know" — Mr. Sargent raised his voice to cover the General's angry rumbling — "how it was swung. Now she's dead, and we're pretty sure she was receiving cocaine, there's an end of the snow falling on this beach, as the fellow put it, but how she made money —"

Russell interrupted. "Were the owners of the party boat in on what you figure the boy was doing?"

"No, we're sure they're in the clear. A lot of stuff comes into Jonesport, we've had indications, and some wise guy must have got the idea of putting kids with it on some of the boats that go out of there, up and down the coast. We have our eye on the other young fellow who came in here on the *Sea Rover* when Jones was off, and now we'll keep looking at the other party boats as well as the ordinary pleasure craft that cruise the coast in the summer. The ports in Florida, we've been watching all year round for some time; not too successfully," he ended wryly. "But enough so that drugs are finding their way in by other than Southern seaports. Cocaine's only a trickle, so far; not a lot of users yet. But in a few years, we figure it'll be a flood."

"About Ludwig," the General began belligerently just as Russell asked, "And what would this kilo of cocaine smell like, or taste like? Or look like?"

236

Mr. Sargent, always temperate, chose to answer Russell. "It wouldn't have any smell, I figure, since it probably wouldn't have come in cut with anything. That *would* give it a smell. No taste, either, but it would numb your mouth if you tasted it. And it would look like coarse sugar, with some bigger chunks. It's not a uniform substance."

"Numb your mouth?" Russell repeated slowly. "That tin of ladies' rice face powder Mrs. Hackley brought over — remember, Elizabeth Lamb, how she dropped it? I picked it up for her, and then *I* dropped it, and a few grains leaked out of the paper and she carried on so and made me so nervous I was chewing on my finger, like, remember?"

"No, I don't," Elizabeth Lamb answered. "So what are you saying?"

"That my mouth went numb right after, that's what!"

Persis raced to the powder room. "It's not here," she called. "We put it right on that little shelf, between two bowls. Only the bowls are here. Now I can't get a reward!"

"It wasn't there when I photographed the room yesterday," Buzzie said.

"It was, the night before! I noticed it when I went in there before dinner. Do you think someone killed Ludwig to get it? If there was cocaine in it, and Mrs. Hackley hid it there and I helped her, I'm more a necessity to the crime than ever! Oh, my! I carried something worth sixty thousand dollars!" Persis was shaking with excitement.

"Did Vonn see you put it in there?" Mr. Sargent asked.

"No, but he saw the room after, because I told him he should look at how pretty it was and he said he had. But there was a plastic cover she'd cut to fit over the powder and he was awfully sick, so even if he'd opened the tin and looked, since it doesn't smell, he wouldn't have thought anything of it, I'll bet."

"He should have. He would have if he'd been feeling like himself, and I certainly wish he had. Maybe it came to him later what it could have been. He had the kind of mind that retains and analyses, sort of subconsciously." Mr. Sargent sighed. "He was a good man."

"I wonder if the C he scrawled on the floor stood for 'Cocaine',"

237

Elizabeth Lamb speculated. "He could have realized and been trying to tell you."

"*Will* you tell me what killed him?" her cousin demanded. "Instead of trying to pin cocaine smuggling on poor deluded Catherine Hackley, I wish you'd remember a man — a good man, as you say — is dead, and find out who did it."

"The post mortum didn't indicate anything," Buzzie said. "But then I got to thinking. I started figuring how a trained agent could die in a small room with not a mark on him and all I could think of was he'd been suffocated. So I had the Crime Lab people go over him. And to make a long story short, the excess content of carbon dioxide and nitrogen in the blood showed I was right.

"And they found more. Those fellers are a lot more thorough than the ordinary coroner. The lungs and other membranes, the tissue in his throat and nose and the burned cilia there, showed it was a gas. He'd been suffocated by a gas. Now, you have to think hard: any of you see or hear anything of a gas around here?"

"There's a propane gas stove in my study," the General said slowly. "We used it Thursday night to cook dinner because the electricity kept going off."

"I know. I saw the stove when I looked through the place yesterday morning. But we can rule that out. There's no way."

"Chlorine gas!" said Russell. "We were even talking about it at the pool day 'fore yesterday, Thursday, about how when chlorite is mixed with even jest common household stuff it makes a gas that kills quick. And there's a big canister of calcium hypochlorite in the shed, for sterilizing General Alison's pool."

"Who was talking about it?" Buzzie asked.

"Well, jest about everybody heard. Except Mrs. Dickcyn. She didn't get here from Ellsworth till lunch was 'most over. And when Ludwig finished with the pool, we all put the sterilizing stuff back in the shed for him — me and Dusty and Bix, and Philip and Mr. Cooke, too. So people knew where it was."

"Should we go see if it's still there?" Persis asked.

"No," said Russell. "It was in a big, heavy cardboard thing, 'most full. It wouldn't show if a little had been taken out, and jest a mite, mixed in a pail with ammonia, or vinegar, even, is all you'd need. I can't see how someone could've got Ludwig into that little powder room with that stuff, though, and keep him there till he died."

"The light bulb was unscrewed; he mightn't have seen it," Buzzie reminded him.

"And he'd had an awful lot to drink." Elizabeth Lamb looked reproachfully at Persis, who became tearful. "And, also, remember, he was awfully sick," she added quickly.

Persis rallied a little. "Miss O'Cassidy said the stuff on the cocktail biscuits smelled like what Ludwig put in the pool."

"I don't understand that one," Buzzie said slowly. "Why would anyone doctor up crackers with stuff that smelled so strong no one would eat them?"

"Only Miss O'Cassidy and Cousin Lem ever ate that spread," Elizabeth Lamb announced. "We've had it before when people were here, and everybody knew that. Remember how I wrote down that the person at the teahouse said he — or she — was 'only trying to frighten the damned slut.' Maybe it was just like a warning to her and nobody was expected to eat it. She was in her room, I remember, and when she came out, she said, in a nasty way, she'd been 'looking and listening'. Maybe she *knew* it had been done!"

"Could be," Buzzie answered. "We'll probably never know. But why? Why go after O'Cassidy?"

Mr. Sargent was impatient. "Good God, Higgins, the woman is an extortionist. Here's an old lady who's receiving shipments of cocaine. She would have been threatening her. What else!"

"Mrs. Faven said yesterday she heard 'Lem's secretary' talking about marijuana Thursday night, and she was sitting near Colleen and Mrs. Hackley. You heard Colleen talking, Russell. What was she saying?" Elizabeth Lamb asked.

"I was building the fire. Wasn't paying much attention. Something about gardens — and grass, that's so! — and money and how much things cost —"

"And Mrs. Hackley was almost crying! I noticed that." She stopped and looked thoughtful. "But that was *after* the biscuit thing. But wait a minute! On Wednesday night, while we were waiting for you,

Buzzie, she was talking to Mrs. Hackley, too, and Mrs. Hackley looked the same way. But on Wednesday night, the only thing that had happened was that a boy had been found dead. Oh, dear!"

The General was interested. "Anything is grist to a blackmailer's mill. I found that out. Heh-heh. She just may have been hinting to Catherine how strange it was that someone was dead on her beach — sounding her out. And with all the talk of marijuana smuggling, Colleen may have put two and two together and come up with twenty-two; right idea, wrong drug!"

"Could be," Buzzie said. "She certainly could have been trying her game on others. But if she had the wrong drug, why were they worried?"

"Oh, Buzzie!" Now Elizabeth Lamb was impatient. "Because they didn't want to be suspected of *anything*, of course!"

Persis had been quietly thinking. She spoke timidly, chin in hand, her little rounded brow furrowed. "Mr. Sargent, you said how cocaine looks like sugar. Well, I helped Mrs. Hackley put tiny little bags of sugar in her bottles of ginger beer before her daughter took it to a store in Ellsworth Thursday. Maybe what you think is cocaine is only sugar."

"Persis," Lem began, "that makes no sense. He knows what he's talking about."

"Why would she have done that, Persis?" Elizabeth Lamb asked. "She's given us ginger beer and there were no bags of sugar in it."

"I know, but there are when she sells it. Just like she used to serve it with glasses of ginger beer when she ran the teahouse. There wasn't any in the bottle she gave Miss O'Cassidy, either."

"You did *what*, little girl?" Mr. Sargent had been writing. He looked up at her. "Let's go over that again, what you were saying about sugar."

Persis obligingly related her activities in the brewery on Thursday morning. "And she had some sugar there," she concluded, "and when she sent me over to the kitchen because she needed more, the cook gave me a box that said Domino on it and it was still sealed shut. So all she was putting in the little bags was sugar. And she was very careful to get just the right amount in, so she mixed it on a big piece of looking glass so she could see better. Her eyes were weak, she said."

Mr. Sargent groaned. "Young lady, she was cutting cocaine with the sugar you fetched. And they often use mirrors so as to be sure not to waste a speck." He brightened. "*Now* I see how she made her money. Very cute: she was both wholesaler and distributor. Probably she cut the stuff so much the stores she sold the beer to merely handed it over to the buyer and got a slight commission. No, for the risk, it would have to be pretty substantial, but nothing like — hmmm. Maybe there was one more link, too.

"And you say she put it only in the ginger beer?"

Persis was red and angry. "But it *was* sugar. She said she gave it to customers in the teahouse and they mixed it into ginger beer with little fish-tailed stirrers, because a lot of them thought the ginger beer wasn't sweet enough."

Lem grunted. "Been in that damned place many a time and never saw that. Every secretary I ever had wanted to go over there and sit cross-legged on the damned floor and drink that God-awful green tea, or ginger beer served with half-raw rice cakes, and there was *no* sugar presented with the ginger beer, Persis. *Never.* I was glad when she closed that place four years ago and started selling her stuff wholesale. My digestion improved."

"Four years ago. That's when her bank accounts took a jump," said Mr. Sargent.

"And that was when she started renting out the teahouse to people from that damned jazz group," Lem informed him. "Went to hell on a handcart, poor Catherine did. Consorted with those loud jazz fellers and, if what you say is so, became a damned drug dealer."

"I wonder how she got started in it," Mr. Sargent mused. "A great many musicians get mixed up with drugs. Wonder if one of the first men she rented to saw an opportunity here?"

"I dunno," Russell said. "But she was saying the other day at the pool that one of them who came four years ago got killed in California — or was it Bix or her daughter who said that? Anyway, it was the one the General said got phone calls in the teahouse at all hours of the night."

"Looks more and more firm," Mr. Sargent said. "Elizabeth Lamb, did they say anything Wednesday about where in Augusta they took the shipment?"

"It was to some man, or maybe store, that began with an A. I could probably remember, but Philo Gaynor could tell you where it is. And Mrs. Dickcyn took some to Ellsworth on Thursday — and I remember she brought an envelope of money back for her mother! But," she questioned, "you think *she* wasn't in on any of this?"

"Right," Mr. Sargent affirmed briefly. "I'll get the addresses. And the daughter may know other places they supplied with ginger beer. Some of them could have been getting it without coke in it, of course.

"Now, you — Persis, is it? — you told the secretary about the bags of sugar in the ginger beer bottles, you say?"

Persis nodded resignedly. "She may have got smart enough to figure something was fishy, and possibly just what," Buzzie suggested.

"Yes, maybe," Elizabeth Lamb said, "because before she left the pool to go to the village, she went to the powder room and then came out and told Mrs. Hackley, in that sort of spiteful way she had, that she'd almost tried the powder but thought she'd save it for a special time — something like that, anyway.

"And, Buzzie, when I said a while ago that maybe Colleen was the reason Ludwig got killed, well, you see what I wrote down. When Mrs. Hackley said something about 'didn't need to kill him,' the other person said he had *told* her he 'was after *her*' and that it 'served purpose, scared her off.' "

Buzzie looked at her notes again. "Maybe so. You also wrote 'you said the damned slut knew what you put —'. Maybe she did and maybe she *didn't* know what Mrs. Hackley had in that tin, but it seems the feller who said that first tried to frighten O'Cassidy and then tried to kill her and got Ludwig; I still can't figure *how*. Who would you all say this confederate might be, from what we know and what we're guessin'?"

"Somebody who tried to scare her, maybe, by letting the top of the skittles table fall on her, too. Or maybe it *was* meant to hurt her." Russell said. "Somebody who heard the General say how you can make your own phone ring by dialing 599, and who got another somebody to do that, after he'd put one of the remote-control plugs in

242

the lamp by the skittles table. Somebody who hid the box of dimes under the chair. Every time I've played skittles here, it was Miss O'Cassidy who reached in and got them out of the table, when there weren't any in the box."

"Dammit, how would he have known I'd be trying to save the bulbs by turning all of them off except the one by the table?" the General asked.

"There was a hurricane going on, Cousin Lem," Elizabeth Lamb said. "The lights could have gone out at any time, and everybody knows how you try to save money — I mean, how you would try to save the bulbs and appliances by turning them off, if there was a blackout," she ended feebly.

"Where were these people when the light by the table went out, Lieutenant?" Mr. Sargent asked. "It seems to me, from reading the girl's notes, that this skittles thing upset Mrs. Hackley greatly, maybe enough to persuade her to call the game off — and I don't mean the skittles game. She seemed more disturbed by it than by a man's death, though that may have compounded the way she felt."

"She was upset because Cousin Lem could have got hurt," Elizabeth Lamb informed him. "She thought a lot of him and maybe she realized how dangerous this other person was becoming." Her cousin, blushing, informed her that she could be quiet about Catherine Hackley's feelings, such as they were.

Buzzie was abashed to admit that he had no idea where people had been standing. He looked appealingly at Elizabeth Lamb. She closed her eyes and pondered. "Mrs. Hackley had gone to the kitchen, where the other phone is. She said something about wanting ice, but she was drinking sherry. Mr. Cooke was way at the other end of the room, watching television, and Mrs. Faven was down in the powder room. Dusty was in the chair under the lamp. Mrs. Dickcyn and Bix were standing together by the table, on the side away from Dusty, and Russell was standing at the head of it. Persis and I were over by the fire. Cousin Lem raised the table to get dimes and called Colleen to reach in and Philip said he'd hold the support. The phone rang and the light went out and Cousin Lem yelled — but I told you all the rest of it."

"This Dusty," Buzzie said thoughtfully, "was right by the lamp."
He looked at Mr. Sargent, who shrugged. "We've speculated about
that young man, Higgins," he said. "I just don't know. Neither Vonn
nor — anyone else had figured him out."

"And Mrs. Hackley was talking to someone in front of the
teahouse, where he lives," Buzzie said slowly. "Did anyone here ever
hear him speak any Japanese?"

"No," said Elizabeth Lamb, "but in my notes it says the person
asked 'why here?' and said 'she can't hear everything, or the
boyfriend, either.' "

"That doesn't signify much," Russell commented, "except that they
didn't want Mrs. Dickcyn to overhear, or Bix, either, it seems to me."

"So who was it?" Buzzie asked. "I can't see that it would be
anyone but Philip Dickcyn or Dusty. Gaynor doesn't speak any
Japanese, does he? That Dusty's been sort of an unknown quantity.
And a mighty sleepy, quiet one. What about Dusty?"

"Dusty?" It was Cynthia Dickcyn's voice. She came in by the pool
doors, face pale and hair carelessly tied back. She carried the sword
Elizabeth Lamb had dropped the night before. "Did you want
Dusty?"

She walked slowly to them, motioning gently for the men to stay
seated. She sank, exhausted but still graceful, into a chair by the fire
after she had laid the sword on the pine mantel above it. "Isn't this
yours, Lem? I've been walking in the woods, trying to be calm, the
way Mother would have wanted. This was lying behind the *chaseki*."

The General looked threateningly at Elizabeth Lamb. Cynthia lay
back in her chair and closed her eyes, then gave herself an admonitory
shake and sat erect. "I'm afraid Dusty's taken Philip to Bangor to
catch the Boston plane. They left several hours ago, so he should be
back soon. Philip begged to go back to Cambridge. He says he cannot
bear it here, where —"

Her voice broke, but she went on. "I thought it best for the poor
boy. He was desperately fond of Mother. He took just a small bag. I'll
have to send the rest of his clothes to his housemaster. He was so
upset he packed the strangest things — his woolen ski-mask, for
instance, and it must be eighty degrees in Boston!"

"Where is —" Mr. Sargent began. He whispered to Elizabeth Lamb: "Ask her where Bix is."

Cynthia had risen to wander restlessly about the room. She was evidently too upset to think the question strange. "Oh," she answered, "he's gone to Bar Harbor to get some things I needed. I suppose he'll scold because I let Philip go, but, really, there was no reason for him to stay. He and I have never been close, and I can do what I must alone, with Bix's help."

She smiled apologetically at the General. "Oh, dear, I'm forgetting why I came over. They're permitting me to bury Mother's — ashes in the garden. Dr. Phillips arranged it. He's so kind. Now, please come over tomorrow. There will be a brief ceremony at two. I'm going back to call the rest of her friends."

The General rose and embraced Cynthia. "Of course, my dear. I want you to sit down quietly for just a minute before you go, though. I'll drive you back — dammit, I forgot I can't drive! But you must have a drink first."

"I'd really like a cup of tea, Lem. Persis made such good tea the other night." She smiled at Persis, who went proudly to the kitchen, not mentioning that the absent Miss O'Cassidy had made the tea.

"Is there anything at all we could do, Cynthia?" the General asked.

"No, and please let's not talk about it. About Mother — anything. Oh, Mr. Shinowara came back a little while ago. He is scrubbing the whole house furiously. He insists he must get all the germs and bad spirits left by the police" — she looked apologetically at Buzzie — "out of his kitchen. He wanted Clorox, and I forgot to tell Bix to get some. Do you have any? Mother always kept some in the brewery —" she choked and rubbed her hand across her mouth.

"We don't have any at all, Mrs. Dickcyn," Elizabeth Lamb said. "I heard — Ludwig say so the other night. Maybe you could suggest Mr. Shinowara burn incense?"

"Why of course, Elizabeth Lamb. How clever you are!"

Elizabeth Lamb went on: "Ah, would you have a gun Cousin Lem could borrow? We heard there's a, a big bear loose, and we'd feel better if we had one."

Cynthia looked amazed, as well she might. "A bear? In Northeast

Harbor? I hadn't heard that. But, no: Mother would never permit a gun. Philip begged desperately for a gun, many times, and since Mother had him trained to be a crack shot, I felt it could do no harm. But she was always so fearful for him —" She buried her face in her teacup.

"Did she have him taught karate, too?" Elizabeth Lamb persisted, despite the General's frown.

"Why, no. Like me, he never could learn. She was greatly disappointed in both of us. She was an expert, you know. She had a brown belt at twelve."

She walked aimlessly about again. "Lem," she asked, "forgive me for what I am about to say. It puts you on the spot, but — could you think of anything, anything at all that would convince me it was an accident? I know I said let's not talk of it, but I feel so helpless, so remorseful, to think she meant to do it. They say she must have."

General Alison went to her. "Cynthia, dear," he said, "on my honor, I tell you that your mother once told me she had taken a strict vow in her youth — ah, a Shinto vow, it must have been — that she would never take a life, her own or anyone else's. You must just remember that."

"Oh, Lem, thank you. You see, when I left her last night, I said 'good night,' — 'Oyasumina sai.' And she — and she answered, 'Sayonara.' That's 'good-bye,' you know. And she had said a little before that she would call a piano tuner today, but later she asked me to do it. I've thought of those things all day."

"Nonsense, my dear. Just slips of the tongue, or forgetfulness. She often," the General continued to lie steadfastly, "said 'sayonara' to me, at the end of an evening. Means nothing."

"I'm so relieved. And here's Bix! He can drive me back. I'll see you tomorrow, dear Lem." She rose as gracefully as ever, slipping into a pocket the silver-cased box of matches she had been nervously fingering.

Bix had come to the door. He was preparing to enter, but Cynthia took his arm and led him to her car. "My God!" said the General. "Did you see that! She's stricken with grief, and yet she's a klepto. Wouldn't have put it past that boy of hers to have nabbed Chub's gun, too. She said how he always wanted one of his own."

Mr. Sargent came from the kitchen telephone. "The last morning Bangor-Boston flight got there over an hour ago," he informed Buzzie. "I would imagine there's an extra key of cocaine in Boston or Cambridge by now. And too late for me to get anyone on him. He'll have it pretty well hid or disposed of by now."

"To get somebody on who?" Buzzie asked. "Rhodes or Dickcyn?"

"It has to be Philip," Elizabeth Lamb said. Russell agreed. "My money's on him, too. Jest a sort of gut feelin'."

"I've got more than that," Elizabeth Lamb replied. "We all do. Persis said he was here by himself when she came in Thursday night. Ludwig had got the cocktail tray ready, and he was in his room, with the door shut. Philip could have put some of the swimming pool stuff on the biscuits; he must have gone and got it by then. And he knew what those plugs Cousin Isabella brought would do, and he could have plugged one into the lamp while he was alone. His grandmother went to the kitchen, where there's a phone, while he was holding up the table — the other phone rings, the light by it goes out, and Colleen could have been hurt. Naturally they'd planned it, or planned to take advantage of anything that might happen, and who else was as close? It took two."

"I'm with you Elizabeth Lamb," Mr. Sargent said. "If I'd known in time Dickcyn was on his way to Boston, I'd have arranged a reception of some sort at Logan."

"But look, Merrill," Buzzie said, "the point is that we don't know how close any other two people were, to have done what Elizabeth Lamb says. If Rhodes, say, and Mrs. Hackley were in cahoots, they wouldn't be advertising it."

"Buzzie," Elizabeth Lamb said patiently, "Dusty wasn't going around delivering ginger beer with packets of cocaine in it! I know we probably can't prove Philip was, but it's likely. Philip knows Japanese. He is a good shot, and Ludwig's dog was shot just after *someone* heard Ludwig talking, someone who could have deduced he wasn't just a houseman. And getting rid of his dog would make it easier to get rid of him, if they decided to. The gun is probably gone, 'where it won't be found, ever,' as I heard him say.

"He heard Mr. Cooke say he'd left his gun in his garden, and Philip had always wanted a gun, and both he and his mother just pick up things they want. And remember that the person at the teahouse said something about 'foolish to mention gun'? Mrs. Hackley talked yesterday about his wanting a gun, and he came in and heard her. I think it was just accidental that he was at the window Wednesday night after he stole the gun, but what he heard made him determined to kill Ludwig, no matter what he told his grandmother. I think he wanted to kill Colleen, too; I think he's a born killer."

"Elizabeth Lamb," Buzzie answered slowly, "you're doing a lot of thinking, but *I'm* thinking that two could have got on that plane, and not just one. We'll never prove any of this, but I've never liked that Rhodes feller and it would give me a lot of satisfaction if he chooses to get out while the getting's good."

"Philip heard me tell Miss O'Cassidy about the sugar his grandmother put in the other ginger beers," Persis volunteered diffidently. "He looked sort of mad, but I thought it was because it was his turn next to have me talk interestingly. I don't think Dusty heard. Goodness, I'm glad Philip's gone back to school. I don't like having him around."

Merrill Sargent rose, stretching his shoulders. "I'll be going back to Boston, too. Did you get that about the Clorox Mrs. Hackley kept in the brewery?"

"What about it?" the General asked.

"Clorox, or any laundry bleach, is used by drug wholesalers to test the purity of the cocaine they receive. The stuff is dropped into a clear glass filled with bleach. Pure coke dissolves in a few seconds, and any residue left shows the proportion of anything used to dilute it. The way the residue, if there is any, behaves even indicates what substance has been used to cut the purity. I'd say this lady had been well taught. She was no fool."

The company digested this information. "I just can't see Catherine Hackley burning herself up, though," the General said thoughtfully. "She was terrified of fire. I was lying to Cynthia, of course, but I still think the gist of what I said was true."

"If she wanted out of the whole thing, as well as destroying the means for the grandson to keep on with it, she could have killed herself just as she started the fire," Mr. Sargent said. "Dealers know about cocaine. If she injected enough pure coke into a vein, she'd die almost at once. Even getting some just under the skin would kill her, though not as quickly. I don't think she was a user, though, from what I've heard of her, so she wouldn't have had the equipment — the needles. And only a very small number of users 'shoot' it, anyway. Too dangerous."

"She would have had the equipment, though," Elizabeth Lamb said slowly. "She was a diabetic."

"Then I doubt even more she was a user. Cocaine can cause fatal comas in diabetics. Well, she probably figured death by fire was less painful than living to see her grandson convicted as a murderer. She may even have had some remorse about the boy she killed."

"Before you go," Persis asked, "couldn't you tell us who was helping you here, besides Ludwig? It's like a spy story."

"I'm afraid that's confidential information. We'll use the person again, somewhere. He — or, remember, it could be 'she,' you know — feels very strongly about drugs. Let's say 'he.' He and a sister were alone in the world, and the sister was a beautiful girl, a singer; made a lot of money and was putting our fellow through medical school. She got hung up on drugs, career ruined, tried suicide, missed and ended up brain damaged. She's in a special home; doesn't even know who she is. Or was. Sad case.

"Well, you all have my sincere thanks. I hope to see you again, but it won't be professionally, I imagine."

"It won't," Persis said sincerely. "It certainly won't. We're too smart."

"Then stay that way. The young lady I just spoke about was awfully smart, and had a lot of talent, I'm told. At the beginning. That's the only reason I told you the story; to show it can happen.

"And I'd be very careful, if you ever run into this Dickcyn fellow again. Keep your distance."

"We're going home to Boston soon," Elizabeth Lamb said, "and we certainly will. But can't you possibly prove anything? It's terrible if he killed Ludwig, and his dog, and gets away with it."

"If he did everything we think, something will catch up with him. He's the only one his suppliers have to blame for the death of their courier and the loss of the consignment. As I said, you don't fool around with those people. I wouldn't like to be in that young man's shoes.

"Let's go, Higgins. I've got miles to go before I sleep."

After they left, Buzzie promising to call when he got back to Ellsworth, to see if Dusty had returned, Russell and the General looked glumly at each other.

"I suppose," said the General, "Catherine did do what they said." He brooded briefly and then burst out, "I never would have thought that fool of a woman could pull off such a stunt! Both wholesaler and distributor! A killer, too. And, dammit, she might've been selling that poison to people right here in town. Talk about fouling your own nest! My God, old Bishop Doane and and all those tight-lipped Eliots must be turning over in their graves."

His frown changed to a grin. "Elizabeth Lamb, didn't I always say there was something *fishy* about that whole damned Nip set-up over at *Nihon*? *Sakana*, hey? Heh-heh."

Russell was also brooding. "But I wonder if this whole thing's a hoorah's nest, speaking of nests. Geez, I mean, we all put our heads together, like they said, but we really don't know a thing, for sure. In books, there's one smart guy who's seen most of it and deduces the rest, and gets everybody into the liberry and proves who did it, and how. We can't. I feel dumb."

"You're not dumb," Elizabeth Lamb consoled him. "Real life is different from books: you can't count on somebody leaving a clue on page fourteen that some genius remembers on page two hundred and fifty two. Detecting is mostly noticing; people *see* but they don't *notice*. We couldn't see everything, but we noticed what we saw. What we all figured happened, and how, is probable, even if it would be impossible to convince a jury of it."

"Always liked what old Aristotle said," the General pronounced. " 'Better impossible and probable than unconvincing and possible.' Heh-heh.

"Well, as we say in the Marines, 'we've lived another day, you

250

bastards, so let's have a drink!' Sun's well over the yard-arm." He became solemn again. "Wish Ludwig had lived another day. Wonder what his real name was and where he came from? Maybe he *had* been a Marine; if he hadn't, on my honour, he could have been! I don't say that about many men. I'll get some sherry for you three and you, Russell, might just look around in Miss O'Cassidy's room and see if there's any sign of a — tape; you know what I mean."

"I did already, sir. There isn't."

The General unhappily and awkwardly made himself a gin-and-tonic. "Well, well, no matter. Maybe it didn't exist."

"Did you say anything on her tape, Cousin Lem?" asked Persis, who was adroitly substituting white wine for the very dry sherry the General had poured for them. "Was it a tape you made at a party? My daddy's a lawyer, you know, and he says people should be very careful what they say when they're having a good time, even more so than when they're unhappy. Now you'll worry as to what you said for weeks and weeks. Were you *very* happy when you —"

"NEVER MIND!" her cousin roared. "Wouldn't you and Elizabeth Lamb like to leave for Boston a little earlier than planned? I'll certainly hate to lose your company, but I'm only thinking of you, you know. The swan boats are still out in the Gardens, and your grandmother surely would like to see you — though God knows why your parents would," he ended to himself. "You, Miss!" to Elizabeth Lamb. "Keep out of that gin!"

"I was only getting a drink for Bix," she said. "He's been sitting out there by the pool for a few minutes. He looks awfully tired."

Bix thankfully accepted her offering. "I was feeling lonely," he said, as they sat down around him. "Dr. Phillips came over again and gave Cynnie a shot and put her to bed. I got tired of sitting in the *chaseki* talking to myself. Wanted to hear some agreeable conversation."

"Guess you've been up all night," said the General.

"Most of it. Dusty and I heard the commotion and went right over there."

"And now Philip's left for Boston with Dusty," Elizabeth Lamb said in a tentative manner.

Bix frowned. "Cynnie never should have let — oh, well. We were

251

talking before the doctor came. She's going to sell *Nihon*. She's always wanted to open a little night club in Palm Beach, and she wants me to be her partner. It will give her something to do, and I'd like to settle down and just play in my own club. I'm getting tired of traveling."

"You're awfully good on the sax. And Dusty is a really good trombone player, isn't he?" Elizabeth Lamb's manner was still hesitant.

Bix laughed. "Wasn't it a character in one of Shaw's plays who said 'many a bloke has got to Heaven by playing the trombone'? Something like that." He looked thoughtful. "I used to worry about Dusty, couldn't quite figure him out, but I guess he'll be all right. Maybe he'll get to Heaven someday.

"Cynnie said Mer — that Sargent fellow and Higgins were here?"

"They've gone," the General answered briefly. "Nothing more for them to do, they decided." There was a silence. "Do you really think," the General asked, "Cynthia has a cool enough head to run a night club?"

"She's got her wits about her. She sees through most people — unless they're awfully close to her, of course, but then, all of us have that failing."

Elizabeth Lamb remembered Cynthia Dickcyn in *Nihon*'s forest pool, shouting at Bix that he was using her. "The other day, when she was in the pool, she seemed to think you were — you were something you weren't, maybe?" she ended lamely.

"Very perceptive, she is," Bix answered calmly.

"And so are you," said Elizabeth Lamb. "It's a shame you didn't finish medical school. Doctors need a lot of insight."

Bix observed her over the rim of his glass. "Oh, well, another life; another try," he said smoothly. "I try, wherever I am. Florida's as good a place as any, to try."

"Maybe a very good place," she answered. "Nowadays."

Bix rose, politely concealing a yawn. "Well, I'm going back to try for a nap, too. Thanks for the drink, General. I'll see you tomorrow. Keep cool, Elizabeth Lamb. Don't think too much and don't take any wooden nickels, as my — as my grandmother used to say."

"I never do, Bix," she said. "You could take a nap right here, on

252

one of the chaises. It must be lonely at the teahouse without Dusty."

"Dusty?" Bix was moving slowly towards the path to the teahouse, in his usual relaxed manner. He grinned at her. "Dusty will be good company, as always, when he wakes up. He's back from Bangor and sound asleep. Long drives tire him, poor guy. Well, *konichi-wa.*"

"There, now," Russell said. "General, when that Higgins calls, let me tell him? I'd like the satisfaction. I think you got the idea that he's smarter than he is, Elizabeth Lamb."

"Now, now, my boy. Never thought you had green eyes. What say we all walk to the village and find ourselves a hamburger? Might stop for Elise along the way. *If* those damned tourists doing eighty miles an hour along Peabody Drive don't put an end to us before we get to the Inn."

As they walked in single file, the General in the lead, Elizabeth Lamb looked over her shoulder at Russell. "What makes me so mad about the whole thing, besides that we can't *prove* anything, is that Philip Dickcyn is just sitting down there in Cambridge laughing."

Persis crouched by the roadside to remove a pebble from her sneaker. "You know what they say, Elizabeth Lamb. It goes —"

"Don't quote it, Persis, please! I've always hated the alliteration in it. And who's laughing last? Not us."

Persis tied her laces and got up. "I was only going to tell you what grandmother says. She's not illiterate, Elizabeth Lamb." She spoke with a dignity that made it hard for Russell and the General to keep their countenance. She says, 'Better the last smile than the first laughter.' "

Elizabeth Lamb pondered this as they again marched along. "I don't know that either laughing or smiling is always the sensible thing to do. If Cousin Lem had paid serious attention to Mrs. Hackley's *haikus* over the last four years instead of making fun of them, he might have got some indication as to her state of mind. Do you realize —"

"Why're you talking about Boston, hey?" Lem had protectively moved further ahead of the column and was shaking his good fist at every car approaching them at more than twenty miles an hour. "All these speed demons have *Pennsylvania* licenses, Miss!"

"Or Maine or Massachusetts. I wasn't talking about Boston,

Cousin Lem. Why do you think I was? I was trying to say —"

"Heard you say 'state of mind.' They always say Boston isn't a place, but a state of mind. True, too. Dammit, you moron, SLOW DOWN!"

"I was trying to say that those poems, the last two, anyway, sort of indicated her subconscious thoughts."

"What?" Russell was scornful.

"Well, that last one: it talked about the kind old sun setting but leaving a wise glow for the stars. I think she meant she was the sun, and she was quitting what she was doing but had made enough money to last Cynthia and Philip. She could have meant dying, instead of just quitting, because Philo said she'd had him carry in that rice straw that morning, remember? Though I still can't believe she'd ever want to die in a fire."

"Kind of far-fetched," Russell observed. "Those *haikus* can mean jest about anything."

"Yes, I know. But the first one, about the fog coming in, and the light disappearing, and the sea waiting. That was after she had killed the boy, I guess, and his light had been covered by the fog of death and the sea was waiting to take him out."

"Oh, geez, Elizabeth Lamb! You read too much poetry."

"We have to," said Persis. "We have a monster who teaches us English who loves poetry. I'm thinking about one of the poems we had to read this summer, about the fog coming in 'on little Cat feet.' Get it, Elizabeth Lamb? It certainly fits. Don't you think I'm clever? She had awfully little feet." She regretfully looked down at her own size nine sneakers.

"Ha!" the General called. "Pity she had a brain to match."

And that, Elizabeth Lamb reflected sadly, no matter what eulogies would follow tomorrow, was probably the most fitting epitaph for the late Catherine Hackley.

• CHAPTER 11 •

The Last Smile

HELLO: I HAVE a person-to-person call for Miss Elizabeth Lamb Worthington."

"This is Elizabeth Lamb. Who's calling?"

"Go ahead, sir."

"Hello there. It's Buzzie Higgins here. How's everything? School okay? Was Christmas good to you?"

"Everything's fine. Christmas was fine. Did you call just to ask that? Are you in Boston, Buzzie?"

"I'm still up here in Bangor. Freezing to death, today. I sort of wondered if you'd seen yesterday's *Boston Globe*?"

"No, I haven't read a newspaper for a week. I've got a terrible term paper on Keats that our monster of an English mistress is making us do — but what was in the *Globe*?"

"Well, it has a report of the death of Philip Dickcyn. Our friend from last summer. He was killed by a hit-and-run driver Saturday night. Foggy in Cambridge, they say. He'd just left a bar near Harvard Square, but his friends what was with him in the bar say he hadn't had much to drink. Just a beer or two. No witnesses as to what the car looked like, either.

"Elizabeth Lamb, are you there? Kind of poetic, isn't it?"

"That's not what I'd call it. Poetic sort of means spontaneous; that's what the monster is always calling Keats' stuff, anyway. This was certainly premeditated. It was bound to happen; you know what Mr. Sargent said. I think you mean 'poetic justice.' And whatever we call it, I'm awfully glad about it. And so are you, I'll bet."

"You could say that. Funny thing, too. This bar had one of those skittles tables just like your cousin does. Dickcyn'd been having a game or two; his last act on earth, you might say. His friends mentioned it, to show he was sober. But it kind of makes you smile, the coincidence, doesn't it?"

"It does, Buzzie. That's for sure. Here was that nasty little murderer thinking he'd got away with it, that his life after all *was* going to be 'all beer and skittles,' and then they get him!"

"And Dusty. Got a postcard from him the other day. He's down with the Baxter feller, in his club. Well, Elizabeth Lamb, I hope to see you when you come up to the island. Keep your chin up, now, and keep smiling."

"That's just what I'm doing. I'm smiling the last smile. It'll make Keats a whole lot easier to take, tonight. Goodbye till next summer, Buzzie."